Storm Clouds Over Byland Crescent

ALSO BY BILL KITSON
FROM CLIPPER LARGE PRINT

Brothers and Sisters of Byland Crescent

Storm Clouds Over Byland Crescent

An absolutely heartbreaking and unputdownable historical family saga

Bill Kitson

The Cowgill Family Saga Book II

Originally published as *Renaissance*

W F HOWES LTD

This large print edition published in 2023 by
W F Howes Ltd
Unit 5, St George's House, Rearsby Business Park,
Gaddesby Lane, Rearsby, Leicester LE7 4YH

1 3 5 7 9 10 8 6 4 2

First published as *Renaissance* in the United Kingdom in 2018

Revised edition first published in the United Kingdom in 2022 by Joffe Books

A CIP catalogue record for this book is available from the British Library

ISBN 978 1 00410 673 8

Typeset by Palimpsest Book Production Limited, Falkirk, Stirlingshire

Printed and bound by
T J Books in the UK

FSC www.fsc.org
MIX
Paper from responsible sources
FSC® C013056

For Val
My wife, lover and best friend.
Also my copyeditor, continuity girl,
proofreader and agent.
So many reasons to admire her talents.
So many more reasons to love her.

PART ONE

1923–1929

'Into my heart on air that kills
From yon far country blows:
What are those blue remembered hills?
What spires, what farms are those?

That is the land of lost content,
I see it shining plain,
The happy highways where I went
And cannot come again.'

A.E. Houseman (1859–1936)
A Shropshire Lad

CHAPTER ONE

When Rachael Cowgill reflected on all that happened during the autumn of 1922 it seemed to her that the reappearance of her husband Mark, known to one and all as Sonny, was merely the prelude to a series of further shocks – some pleasant, some not. Sonny's return, when all had thought him dead, killed in the war, was dramatic enough in itself.

His condition, diagnosed by their family doctor, was a severe case of shellshock causing amnesia. He advised rest, time for him to adjust and become accustomed to his surroundings, continuing to be nursed at home by his wife.

There had been many changes at the Byland Crescent house in Scarborough, now bereft of the servants of previous years with only a butler, a cook and a housemaid to tend the depleted family. The Cowgill family had taken up residence in 1897 when Albert Cowgill, a partner in the biggest wool merchants in Bradford, had moved to Scarborough along with his wife and family of five children.

When Sonny had returned, only his mother

Hannah, his wife Rachael and young son Mark, of whose existence he was unaware, were living in the large rambling house. Visiting at the time from their home in Baildon had been his sister Connie, her husband Michael Haigh, convalescing from illness, and their three children. All had been anxious to know the circumstances of Sonny's missing years but allowed him the opportunity to talk when he felt more able.

Over time, Hannah, now aged sixty-five, had sat patiently with her youngest child and told him most of all that had happened during the war and the four years since his disappearance. From her, he learned of the two strokes his father had suffered. The second of these proving fatal after the telegram, believing Sonny to be killed in action, had arrived. He learned of the loss of his sister, Ada, killed while nursing casualties in France, and of the loss of several young men from Byland Crescent, sons of neighbours, most of them Sonny's playmates as children. Equally distressing were other losses his mother listed from within their family rank, his nephew Saul was chief amongst these. 'The only one to survive unscathed,' Hannah remarked with unaccustomed bitterness, 'was your father's nephew, Clarence Barker, and no one would have missed him.'

Sonny was puzzled by one of the casualties mentioned. 'Saul?' he asked, 'who is Saul? Saul, my grandfather, died before the war.'

It was his sister Connie who answered him. 'No,

not grandfather. Saul is, or rather was, James and Alice's son. You do remember your brother James who went abroad so long ago?'

Sonny smiled. 'Yes, I remember James. He left with Alice the housemaid when father threw them out.' From almost out of nowhere he added, 'They went to Australia.'

Connie and Hannah stared at him in amazement. 'What makes you say that?' Connie asked. 'James has never told us where he and Alice went, they could be anywhere. Even though we have written to each other via his London solicitor for years, he maintains his privacy.'

Sonny was adamant. 'Saul was Australian. I know that. Don't ask me how, but I do.' Then he added, 'He was a lot like James.'

Hannah looked at her son, her expression a mixture of surprise and dismay. 'How could you know that, Sonny? You never met Saul.'

Sonny furrowed his brow in concentration. 'I'm not sure. Maybe I did meet him. Perhaps it is part of my memory that's still not clear, but I'm sure I can recollect a face, a voice.'

Connie found her voice. 'I think Sonny may be right, Mother. James wrote to tell us of Saul's death.' She turned to her brother. 'He was convinced that you were with Saul when he was killed and that you died together, but I suppose at the time, it was just after father's death, we were too upset for it to register. So maybe James is in Australia.'

* * *

Although Sonny's memory was returning quickly, he could not recall anything immediately prior to his incarceration in a French mental institution. When the horrors that replayed over and over in his head had begun to fade, he had walked out of the hospital and found his way to England. His account of his epic journey, one lasting over two years, with only a vague idea of his destination was one of determination and endurance.

One evening after dinner the family was seated in the sitting room. Rachael and the others were held spellbound, when Sonny had begun to relate his story of events prior to, when thought to be an injured tramp, being found by Rachael on her ward in Scarborough hospital where she was Sister.

'I'd been painting all the time I was in *The Place*,' he told them. 'I never knew its name, just *The Place*. I always painted the same scene, a ruined abbey amongst fields, close to a village. Each time I finished it I destroyed it. At first I didn't know why but gradually I realized there was something wrong with the painting. It was incomplete, but I wasn't sure why. Then by chance I worked out there should have been a group of people in the painting. That was when I knew I had to find the abbey. Not for itself, but for the people. When I got there I was terribly disappointed, the people in the painting were not there. My befuddled brain hadn't worked out that time had moved on. I stood outside Byland Abbey and still failed to recognize the significance of the name. What still puzzles me is how I connected Byland Abbey with Byland Crescent, or what the significance of the people in the painting was.'

'I can answer that,' his mother said. 'Come with me, all of you.'

She led Sonny, Rachael, and little Mark, up the wide staircase of the Byland Crescent house. Connie followed with Michael, all of them wondering what Hannah had in mind.

She paused at her bedroom door and then eased it open. The family crowded into the room. On the wall above the dressing table was a large landscape in oils. Sonny gasped aloud.

'That's it,' he exclaimed excitedly. 'Just as I painted it. How come I remember this painting? Where did it come from?'

Hannah beckoned them closer.

'I remember now,' Connie said. 'It was the picnic.'

'That's right,' her mother agreed. 'Surely you remember, Sonny. Your father and Grandfather Ackroyd took us all to stay for a weekend in the Yorkshire Dales during the school holidays. We stopped for a picnic on the way back. We wanted to see Byland Abbey because of the name. You would have been about fourteen years old.'

Hannah indicated the group of figures in the painting. 'That's your grandfather and grandmother talking to Albert and me, with Connie and Michael alongside. There you are with your sister Ada and Connie's little daughter.'

'Who painted it? Whoever it was, they have far more talent than I.'

Rachael, who had been holding Sonny's hand throughout, squeezed it gently.

A cloud passed over Hannah's face. 'Ada's friend, Eleanor Rhodes. She was staying with us at the time and wanted us to have it. It was her way of saying thank you. After your father discovered the true nature of Ada and Eleanor's relationship, that painting was banished to the attic. But eventually, he brought it down again. It was only a few weeks later that we heard that Ada had been killed. I think your father was comforted a little by what he had done. He told me he thought Ada would know that he had forgiven her. Eleanor also painted that portrait of you in cricket flannels, the one with the abbey in the background. She gave it to Rachael when we all thought you were dead.'

'I remember Eleanor,' Sonny said. 'She was pale and fair, slim built. A very gentle girl, a lot like . . .' the sentence tailed off into silence.

Hannah finished it for him. 'That's right. Eleanor reminded us all of poor Cissie.'

Saddened by the memory of the sisters, first Cissie, lost to tuberculosis when he was only a small boy, and now Ada, Sonny felt tears pricking at his eyes. A small hand slipped into his free one. Sonny looked down into the eyes of his small son. Mark smiled.

'Daddy,' he began hesitantly, 'ask Grandmamma to show you the other painting, the one of you playing cricket. Then perhaps we can go down to the beach and you can teach me all about leg breaks.' The ensuing laughter puzzled the small boy but lightened the hearts of the rest of his family.

Later, after Sonny had helped Rachael put Mark to bed, and Connie had supervised her children retiring, the adults gathered again in the sitting room. The talk turned to more mundane matters. It was Michael who prompted it. 'Have you any idea what you are going to do?'

'I haven't given it a thought,' Sonny replied. 'Technically speaking, I suppose I'm still an army officer. I've written to the War Office and no doubt they will have a few awkward questions to ask before they will release me. After that I shall have to consider returning to work. I presume I am now the Cowgill of Haigh, Ackroyd and Cowgill?'

Michael nodded. 'You do remember I don't work for the company now, don't you?' As son of the late Edward Haigh, one of the founders of HAC, Michael had relinquished his seat on the board following many disagreements with his father-in-law, Albert Cowgill, over his employment of his nephew, Clarence Barker. Michael was now managing director of WPF&D, their biggest rival.

'It could prove problematic, though,' Michael continued, 'you've picked a bad time. Trade is shocking at present. HAC is no longer a market leader in the wool industry. Things are bad enough for all of us, but heaven knows the extent of the damage Clarence Barker has done while he has been in control of the company over the past years.'

A few days later, they were to find out.

When they retired for the night, Rachael questioned Sonny further about his memory of Saul.

'I'm sure I remember Saul. I can picture his face, hear his voice, but no more than that. I see the figure, hear the voice, and know that it is Saul. It must seem odd, but my memory's patchy at best. At the worst let's just say there's a lot I'd rather not remember.' He returned to the subject of his nephew. 'I can't remember his surname, but I am certain it wasn't Cowgill.' He turned towards the bed as he spoke. The sight of Rachael's naked loveliness as she slid into bed aroused him instantly. He discarded his dressing gown, climbed in alongside her and took her in his arms. Much later, as they lay wrapped together, Rachael heard his familiar chuckle.

'Well, that was worth the walk,' he murmured.

That flash of humour settled any lingering doubts in Rachael's mind. The Sonny who had returned was the Sonny she had fallen in love with all those years earlier.

The following morning, Sonny succumbed to Mark's pleadings and took his son down to the south shore, one of Scarborough's flat, sandy beaches, there to instruct him in the art of spin bowling. Everyone was wrapped warmly for protection from the cold wind blowing off the North Sea. Mark had co-opted his mother and cousins as fielders, with his grandmother acting as umpire. Eventually, hunger caused them to call close of play and the cricketers returned home.

When Sonny had seen Byland Crescent for the first time in almost eight years, he had been impressed by how little it had altered in his returning memory. Only one house, number 6, stood out from the remainder, a glaring exception to the neat, well presented frontages whose paintwork gleamed and windows sparkled with reflected sunlight. Sonny gestured to the dingy façade of the house. What little paint remained on the door and window frames was peeling. There was a thick patina of dust and grime on the windows. Rotting curtains could be seen, albeit dimly through the opaque glass.

'That house looks so dreary and neglected,' Sonny said to his mother. 'I seem to remember there was some mystery or scandal involving the people who lived there, but for the life of me I can't recall what.'

'Your memory is certainly improving,' Hannah said. 'It is rather a sad story. The couple who lived there moved in shortly after we bought number one. As I remember, he was in his mid-thirties and she was a few years younger. Nobody knew a great deal about them, they kept very much to themselves. About ten years after they moved in, she vanished. They were still as distant from the other residents as when they arrived. Rumour at the time was that she had eloped with a lover and had gone to live abroad. The husband continued to live in the house, although the rest of us saw even less of him, if that was possible, then eventually he also seemed to have disappeared. The police were called and had to break into the house. They found the husband lying dead in bed. He had been there, they estimated, somewhere in the region of six months. He had committed suicide by taking an overdose of some kind. Close to the body they found a packet of letters written to the wife by her lover. Next to them was a suicide note from the husband, saying he couldn't go on any longer without her and begging her forgiveness.'

Hannah lowered her voice and continued, 'Since then, the police have been trying to trace the woman and her lover, but without success. They searched the house several times, even took up floorboards, and dug in the garden, but to no avail. As time passed and they were getting nowhere their efforts petered out. Then the war came and the whole matter was forgotten. There has been some talk recently about a nephew of the husband trying to obtain the title deeds to the house with the object of selling it, but that's just a rumour.'

The children listened to their grandmother with awe, tinged with delight. It was the first time she had told such a wonderfully gruesome and macabre story. Mark could barely wait to relate it to his friend Jennifer, daughter of their cook. 'Was there much blood?' he asked hopefully.

Sonny grinned, but Rachael rebuked her son. 'Don't be such a gory child.'

CHAPTER TWO

On their return the party was heading for the lounge when the phone rang and was answered by the butler. The call was for Michael Haigh. He was on the phone a long time. When he eventually replaced the receiver he turned to Connie, his expression grave. 'I think you'd better get the family together – not the children. I've got some bad news.'

'That phone call was from Simon Jones.' He saw Sonny's puzzled frown and explained. 'Your cousin Simon is my deputy. I took him on after the war and he is both diligent and highly competent. Simon rang to tell me the news from Bradford. The newspapers are full of it. Clarence Barker has been arrested. He has been charged with murder. Well, to be precise, two murders.'

Michael paused to allow this shocking news to sink in, and then continued. 'That's all the newspapers have reported, but Bradford is buzzing with rumours. The most persistent of these is that Barker is to be charged with fraud and embezzlement from HAC. Apparently, the police are at the Manor Row offices examining the firm's books.

Simon says nobody knows how serious things are, but he suggests someone ought to go immediately to sort things out.' Michael paused once more then added gently, 'If you wish, I can go on your behalf and see what I can do? I am still a shareholder so I have the right, and I do have to return to Bradford soon.'

Sonny pondered the news for a moment. 'No, I'm coming with you.' He turned to Hannah. 'Mother, could you look after Mark for a few days? I'd like to take Rachael with me when Michael and I go to Bradford to see what we're faced with. Connie, will you and the children stay with Mother?'

'Of course I will, and while I'm here you must both stay at our house in Baildon. There's plenty of room and it will save you travelling.'

The following morning, the detectives were working their way patiently through invoices and delivery notes at Manor Row in Bradford. The doors to the offices of Haigh, Ackroyd & Cowgill had been locked to the outside world and HAC staff warned to stay away from the premises until the investigation had been completed. It was something of a surprise to DI Sam Clayton therefore when he saw the tall figure of a man approaching him down the long corridor between the sample room and the director's offices.

'Who the hell are you?' he demanded, his quick temper roused by the sight of not one, but three intruders.

The foremost of these eyed him for a second and then replied, 'No, who the hell are you and what the hell are you doing here?'

Clayton withdrew his warrant card from his pocket. 'Detective Inspector Clayton, Bradford CID.' To his consternation the stranger took the card and read it through before returning it.

'Well,' Clayton repeated, 'who are you?'

'I am Captain Mark Cowgill and I am the majority shareholder in this group of companies. Now perhaps you could explain exactly what is going on here?'

'But you can't be, you're dead,' Clayton exclaimed.

'Yes, a lot of people were of that impression, not least my own family. However, *missing in action, believed killed* is not always the same as *killed in action* as the War Office were wise enough to realize, and as you can see I am very much alive.'

'Can you prove your identity?' Clayton persisted.

'Not exactly, not yet anyway,' Sonny told him. 'But perhaps you will accept my wife's word on the matter' – he indicated Rachael. 'And this is Michael Haigh, not only my brother-in-law but son of the founder, and a shareholder. I am sure they will vouch for me.'

Once Sam Clayton recovered from the shock of Sonny's return he was most cooperative.

After two days poring over the books, ledgers and bank statements of all HAC companies, Sonny and Michael had some idea of the gravity of the group's financial position. Although Michael Haigh now headed HAC's largest competitor, he still owed great allegiance to the company he and his father had helped to develop. It was Michael, who, staring at the draft figures Sonny had placed before him, remarked, 'I'm going to ask Clayton if I can have quarter of an hour alone with Clarence Barker. I'll save the expense of a trial and relieve the hangman of a job.'

Sonny nodded. 'Join the queue.'

It was a subdued trio that returned to Scarborough four days later. 'Things are about as bad as they could be,' Sonny told Hannah and Connie. 'We have some serious and painful decisions to make. If trading conditions had been better we could have traded our way out of the difficulties given time, but as things are I cannot see that as a possibility. The only alternatives are a massive capital investment, but that might be good money thrown after bad. Leaving that aside, we could simply allow HAC to go into liquidation, but pride makes me reluctant to go down that road. Grandfather Ackroyd founded the business along with Michael's father and made it one of the biggest names in the industry.

'HAC is no longer what it was twenty years ago. The wool merchant's business is losing money, the scouring plant is in a mess, and the blending company has been the subject of massive fraud.' He directed his gaze at his mother as he continued, 'The dyeing and finishing operation is now only a shell company since my cousin Charlie and his son Robert Binks left, taking the dye patents with them. That leaves the last, and as I see it, the only viable alternative, to close the wool merchant operation and the dyeing company, then sell the scourers and the blending plant. That would mean the end of HAC but at least it would be a closure with honour. That decision is not entirely mine however, I must write to James's solicitor. James owns as many shares as I do. No decision can be acted on without his agreement.'

Although Rachael was concerned about the parlous state of the company finances she was secretly delighted with the way Sonny had handled the crisis. 'He has been so calm throughout, even when faced with the outrageous behaviour of Clarence Barker,' she told Hannah. She repeated the interchange between Sonny and Michael on the subject of Barker. 'I asked him afterwards if he would have been tempted to do Barker an injury, given the chance. Sonny just shook his head and replied, "I've seen too much meaningless violence to consider adding to it." Then he listed the options you heard earlier. He thought it through so clearly, I'm confident he is recovering well.'

James read Sonny's letter three times before he passed it to his wife. Time had been kind to Alice, for she looked much younger than her forty-three years. Although she had borne James seven children she still retained the slim figure and raven-haired good looks that had captivated James twenty-four years earlier and still entranced him.

They were sitting in the study of their house in Western Australia, a large airy room overlooking the landscaped grounds that sloped gently down to the river. Ceiling fans gently stirred the air, the temperature both inside and out, was extremely warm.

On the walls were photographs of their children. The most striking of all was the large portrait on the wall behind the desk. It was of Saul, James and Alice's eldest son, pictured in uniform before his departure for France where he had been killed in action in the closing months of the war.

Alice read the letter and looked at James. 'What are you going to do?'

He did not answer her directly. 'When we left England, I changed my name to yours, to Fisher, to avoid our being discovered. We have maintained that deception throughout the years and the family did not know of our whereabouts until Saul died. We have been hugely successful here, Fisher Springs is now one of the largest companies in Australia, and we are amongst the country's wealthiest citizens. Several times, when the question has arisen I have said that I would never return to England. That temptation has never been stronger than now.' James paused and looked at Alice's troubled expression.

He shook his head. 'No,' he continued, 'I am

not going back on my promise. I shall never return to England. Of course I am overjoyed at Sonny's return, although heaven knows what he must have suffered. I'm also glad he was with Saul when he died. From what little Saul wrote it was obvious they did not know they were related, and also obvious he liked him. It was impossible to dislike Sonny. We have so much to be grateful for, despite losing Saul.

'I haven't been much of a brother to Sonny, but I feel in some way it would please Saul if we do whatever we can to help him, Rachael and little Mark. Perhaps it was also something of this nature that Grandfather Ackroyd had in mind when he left me those shares in HAC. Besides, the family are totally unaware of our success, our business dealings or that we have already bought into the textile industry through our subsidiary.' James saw that Alice was going to say something so he continued hastily, 'Let me tell you my idea.'

It was a considerable time before he finished. Alice pondered the plan for a few moments, then rose from her chair and crossed to her husband. She put her arms around him and kissed him gently. 'You're a good man, James Fisher. I am so glad I chose to let you seduce me.'

It was mid-March 1923 when the postman delivered two letters to Byland Crescent. Both were for Sonny. The first was from his brother James, routed, as were all his letters to the family, via

Ralph French, a London solicitor and old school friend of James. Sonny grinned as he read James's congratulatory message regarding his escape from France: 'When Grandfather Ackroyd said how lucky you were I thought he was only referring to your batting.'

Sonny's face grew grave when James touched on the death of Saul, a situation of which Sonny still had no memory. James explained how they understood from the contents of Saul's letters home that his regiment was serving alongside Sonny in the trenches and how he and Alice believed them to have become friends.

Sonny was especially moved on reading the lines Alice had inserted expressing her own gratitude for Sonny's kindness to their son. He hoped that one day the pieces of this strange jigsaw that his memory had become would slot together.

James's letter went on, '*The aboriginal tribes here have an expression they use for when they go into the outback to seek spiritual guidance or solace. They call it "going walkabout" and I believe your sojourn in France and the long march home might have been something similar.*'

The last paragraph held Sonny's attention for a long time. James had basically agreed to go along with Sonny's plan for the business, but only as a last resort. Could they first, James suggested, try to sell HAC as a whole. He ended by advising Sonny not to rush into any decision making for the time being.

The second letter, by comparison, was terse to the point of abruptness. It was from the War Office, advising Captain Mark Cowgill that his presence was required at a court of inquiry to investigate his conduct. Sonny grimaced at the official tone then laid it aside to return to his brother's communication.

CHAPTER THREE

When the founders of HAC's rival company WPF&D retired and had appointed Michael Haigh to run the business, the company was bought anonymously by James and Alice Fisher. Using their company name Fisher Springs allowed them to maintain their anonymity.

Although WPF&D was named from the initials of the company founders it had long been known throughout the wool trade by its nickname. Someone, when asked what WPF&D stood for had answered, 'War, pestilence, famine and death.' From that time on the company was known as, the Four Horsemen. Now, ably assisted by Simon Jones, Michael Haigh had turned the Four Horsemen into the largest textile conglomerate in Bradford.

Michael received a letter from WPF&D's parent company. When he had digested the contents he went to the door leading to the adjoining office, opened it, and looked in.

Simon Jones was totting up columns of figures

in a large ledger. He looked up as Michael entered. 'We're still making a profit,' he announced. 'Not a big one, but at least we're not losing money as most of our competitors are.'

'Good,' Haigh replied, 'because we'll need it. Come through to my office. I have something I want you to read.'

The instructions contained in the letter from Australia were concise and unambiguous. It originated from the Managing Director of Fisher Springs Exports Pty. Michael and Simon Jones studied each detail closely. Simon was the first to comment. 'Knowing what we do about the financial position of HAC, it seems a little odd that we are being asked to make this offer.'

'I agree entirely,' Michael replied. 'This bid values HAC at somewhere close to its worth before Barker got his thieving hands on it. I think we should cable Australia and make them aware of the current position.'

Together they drafted the telegram, explaining in detail how much money HAC was losing, adding that with Outlane Chemicals being a non-trading company and both A & C Scouring and HAC Blending the subjects of massive fraud the suggested terms were far too generous.

The reply was almost instantaneous. It consisted of only four words. 'You have your instructions.' It was, as Michael remarked to Simon, the curtest communication he had ever received from their parent company.

‘How do you intend to approach making the bid?’ Simon wanted to know.

‘I think I’ll telephone Sonny, without giving him details. I’ll arrange for us to meet up at Scarborough. I’ll suggest taking Connie and the family. Perhaps you’d like to come along and bring Naomi and your children.’

The explanation Michael Haigh gave Sonny must have been convincing, for the reply was in essence an invitation to a family party. As the guiding lights behind it, Hannah and Rachael consulted with their cook Joyce Holgate over the catering arrangements. The relationships between employers and servants had become less formal following the war. Joyce was regarded now more as part of the family. This atmosphere was aided by young Mark Cowgill and Jennifer, Joyce’s daughter. The two children were inseparable, enjoying a bond that had been sealed in the days following Jennifer’s arrival at Byland Crescent. Joyce’s husband had been killed in the latter stages of the war and the two fatherless infants soon built a firm friendship from this basis. Even Sonny’s return did nothing to disturb it, rather it enhanced it. Soon after his reappearance Sonny remarked to Rachael, ‘It’s as if I’ve gained a son and daughter all in one go.’

With Mark’s cousins Marguerite, Edward, and George, plus Simon and Naomi’s son Joshua and daughter Daisy in addition to the seven adults, it was the biggest social gathering at Byland Crescent since before the war. The big house was roomy enough for such numbers, so Hannah and Rachael had extended the invitation to include a weekend stay.

As the weekend approached the excitement of the forthcoming event communicated itself even to the domestic staff whose numbers had been swelled temporarily by two extra pairs of hands from a local employment agency. Only George, the butler, strove to distance himself from the gossip and chatter.

When the Cowgill family moved into Byland Crescent shortly after its completion, visitors had arrived by hansom cab, the only sound being the ringing of horse's hooves and the whirring of the wheels on the cobbles. These had long since been replaced however, and it was a pair of bone-shaking and asthmatic taxis that chugged and wheezed their way up Falsgrave Road from the railway station before turning into Byland Crescent to drop their passengers outside number one.

It was a bright, clear spring day, so, after a light lunch Connie and Naomi took charge of their own children, plus Mark and Jennifer, and set off for a walk through the town to the south shore. Hannah had retired to her room for a rest. During their absence the rest of the party met in the study.

'OK, Michael,' Sonny began proceedings. 'You were very mysterious on the phone but you said you had important news for us, so let's hear it.'

'Right-oh.' Michael pulled some notes from his

jacket pocket. 'In my capacity as managing director of WPF&D I have been instructed by the parent company to make an offer for the whole of the issued share capital of all HAC Group companies.' He paused to glance at his audience. With the exception of Simon, Sonny and Rachael were registering bemusement amounting to incredulity.

'The offer values the shares at three pounds each,' he told them. 'This is, I feel a very generous sum, but it is conditional, and without agreement to each and every condition the bid will be withdrawn.'

Sonny found his voice. 'What are the conditions?'

'The first is that the offer must be accepted by all the shareholders. In fact there are only three, you, your brother James, and me, so I don't see that as much of a problem. From what you told me, James has already indicated that he will go along with your decision so I think we can safely say that the first of the conditions can be fulfilled.'

Sonny nodded his agreement. 'What are the others?'

'The second involves the restructuring of the enlarged group to incorporate the new companies. Much of that will devolve upon Simon. The result will be a group with three distinct components. The first of these' – Michael turned to the second page of his notes – 'will comprise all raw materials processing. That means scouring, blending, wool-combing and spinning will all be run as one operation.

'The second part will be the trading arm. It will combine brokerage, merchanting, import, and export. There is an instruction that particular emphasis must be made to expand the export market. Thus the trading division will have access to all products from within the group to give it a rounded portfolio.

'The third part of the set-up will be the manufacturing division. That will consist of woollen and worsted, hosiery, dyeing and finishing, and chemicals. The strategy seems aimed at making the group self-sufficient within each compartment, giving the parent chance to divest itself of redundant or under-performing units. But the overall emphasis is on expansion.' Haigh paused once more and turned to the last sheet of paper he was holding.

'Now, I had better explain the final condition. Under the new set-up, each division will report to a UK parent company. This will have three directors based here, plus a non-executive director from Australia. The directors of the UK holding company have already been chosen. I have been appointed chairman and managing director, in charge of the overall administration of the group. Simon will be group finance director and company secretary for all group companies. His responsibilities will also include acquisitions, by which I am led to believe that the intention is for the group to expand beyond the bounds of textiles and associated industries.' Haigh paused once more before delivering the bombshell.

'Finally, the group will need a sales and marketing director. Our parent has selected Mark Albert Cowgill to fill that office. They want you, Sonny, and if they don't get you, the whole offer fails.'

The takeover bid for HAC was a welcome relief for the Cowgill family. The euphoria following Michael Haigh's announcement lasted much longer than the weekend party. The family was spared the embarrassing and potentially costly outcome of Clarence Barker's misdeeds. A career had been created for Sonny into the bargain.

Once the excitement abated, Hannah, who knew more of family events than the others, pondered the opportune timing of the bid. She realized this wasn't the first time good fortune had befallen a family member when they had needed it most. On each occasion the solution to the problem seemed to have followed James learning of the crisis. Was James pulling the strings from the other side of the world?

Hannah made enquiries of Simon Jones who was seated next to her at dinner. 'Tell me about your parent company, Simon. Who runs it and what other businesses do they own?'

Simon found the question easy to answer. 'To be honest, Aunt Hannah, it would be simpler to tell you what they don't do. Although they don't advertise the fact, Fisher Springs Pty. is one of the biggest concerns in Australia. They own banks and newspapers, they are involved in food distribution, construction, transport, mineral extraction, and who knows what else besides. They own substantial sheep stations, but I think wool is incidental to the rest of their operations. From what I hear they run the stations more for the meat than the fibre.'

'Tell me more,' Hannah persisted. 'Who owns all this, is it a public company?'

'No, it's a private concern, but who the owners are I have no idea, neither does Michael. Someone called Fisher perhaps, or Springs. I'm led to believe they value their privacy. Even their executives in Australia know little more than I've told you.'

Hannah, hearing the name for the first time, felt a vague memory stirring. Her sleep that night was disturbed by vivid dreams centred round her son James and his wife Alice.

Strangely Hannah did not feel jaded when she awoke the following morning. Over breakfast she heard the family making plans for the day. As she listened she made her own. Every Sunday the Cowgill household went to morning service. Today, after returning to Byland Crescent for lunch Michael and Connie Haigh intended to catch the afternoon train to the West Riding, while Sonny and Rachael were to take Simon, Naomi and the children to visit the picturesque old fishing port of Whitby before their return to Bradford. Naomi was avid to see as much of her adopted county as opportunity allowed. Having escaped Vienna at the onset of the war, she had fled to England to find her English lover, without success. She had settled in Bradford where she met Simon. Now she felt she was putting the Cowgill family to too much trouble.

'Don't worry about that, Naomi dear,' Rachael corrected her. 'What Sonny really means is that he's desperate to show off his latest toy.'

Sonny had recently acquired a motor car, a huge, sleek Bentley, well capable of seating four adults and three children. When Rachael saw the powerful monster for the first time she exclaimed, 'What on earth made you buy something so big? It's far too large for us.'

Sonny leered at her in response. 'It will be useful for carrying the family.'

'But we only have one son,'

The leer turned into a wicked grin. 'So far,' Sonny retorted. 'But now you've mentioned the subject I think we ought to alter that without delay. We can't afford to waste time if we've got a Bentley to fill.'

CHAPTER FOUR

For some years Hannah had been in the habit of taking an afternoon nap. The excitement of the weekend and her duties as hostess should have increased the need, but once the family had gone their separate ways, Hannah hurried upstairs. She passed her own bedroom without a sideways glance and continued up to the attic. Hannah kept meticulous household records in a small room on the top storey alongside the old servants' quarters. She stored accounts for every year since the Cowgill family first entered the house.

The search was prolonged, but eventually Hannah found what she was looking for. The large brown paper parcel was inscribed, Household Accounts 1897'. Contained within the parcel was every tradesman's invoice and detail of all other expenditure for that year. Amongst these Hannah found detail of the wages paid to their staff neatly listed by the butler. These were of no help, as each member was referred to by their Christian name. Thwarted by this, she was about to give up when she noticed a sheaf of folded papers with her handwriting, partially hidden at the back. She pulled it out, opened it, and discovered that it comprised details of interviews conducted before employing their servants. She flicked through page after page until she reached the one she was seeking. The name at the head of the page confirmed her suspicions, nevertheless she gasped with surprise as she read 'Alice Fisher, housemaid'. The full significance of the name dawned. Fisher, of course. But Springs? From Alice Springs, a small town in Australia? If Hannah entertained any doubt, that resolved it.

She carefully replaced the page and secured the package with the string. As she returned from the attic she pondered what to do with her knowledge. After considerable thought she decided to do nothing for the time being, but to keep the discovery secret, at least until the takeover had gone through.

A week later Hannah received further evidence of James's intention to help and protect his younger brother. It came in the form of a letter from the solicitor Ralph French, addressed to Sonny who opened it as the family was seated at the breakfast table. He puzzled over the contents for a moment before sharing it with Rachael and his mother. 'Listen to this.'

Dear Mr Cowgill,

I understand that the War Office intends to conduct a Court of Enquiry into your conduct and absence from duty following events in France. I have been instructed to offer our services and those of counsel should you not have legal representation.

If you wish us to act on your behalf I would be willing to seek out and obtain witnesses prepared to testify for you. Please advise me if you wish to proceed, giving the hearing date and names of any parties whose evidence would be beneficial to your cause. In the case of witnesses unable to attend the hearing in person I will obtain sworn depositions acceptable to the Court.

Costs incurred in respect of any actions on your behalf have already been underwritten.

I remain, yours sincerely,

Ralph French LLB.
Senior Partner. French, Wise and Costello.

Sonny placed the letter on the table and looked across at his mother. 'James?' he asked.

'Undoubtedly,' Hannah agreed. 'He would not want you to suffer any more than you already have.' She checked the impulse to reveal what she knew, continuing instead, 'Perhaps he feels it to be a duty, having been absent while you were growing up. I'm sure he never ceased to care for his family.'

Sonny pondered. 'It would be churlish of me not to accept his help. I'll write back to French today.'

Sonny had barely had time to send off his reply when he received another communication, again regarding a court appearance. It was a summons from the Public Prosecutor's Office, requiring Captain Mark Albert Cowgill MC, to give evidence at the trial of Clarence Barker on charges of murder, fraud, theft and obtaining money or goods by false pretences. Sonny smiled wryly at this letter. It seemed he would be spending most of the year in courtrooms.

By the beginning of July, Sonny's diary, if not overflowing, was almost full. The takeover had encountered no obstacles and he was busy in meetings with Michael Haigh and Simon Jones planning the fine details of the merger. With the Court of Enquiry set for the end of the month and the Clarence Barker trial due to commence in September, Sonny was anxious to progress the integration of the groups beforehand. In addition, Rachael had announced that she was pregnant, the baby due in December. Sonny, barely able to contain his delight said, 'Good, we're starting to fill the Bentley.'

* * *

Although their happiness would not be complete until the findings of the Court of Enquiry were known, much of their stress was relieved once the merger documents were signed.

They had gone to the beach and were talking as they played cricket. On one question Sonny was adamant when Rachael asked, 'What do you intend to do with the money you get for your HAC shares?'

'I'm going to invest it for Mark. Well, not just for Mark, for a whole Bentley full of children. Let's face it we have more than enough for ourselves. There's the money my father and grandfather left me for a start. I've hardly touched that. Your father left you enough to remain a lady of leisure all your life. Instead of which,' he added with a salacious grin, 'you're my lady of pleasure.'

'Not at the moment,' Rachael retorted, patting her extending waistline.

'Ah well, that won't last much longer.' Sonny was unabashed. 'I'll soon be able to get my hands on you again.'

'Seriously,' Rachael wanted to know, 'how do you intend investing the money?'

'Not in the Stock Market, that's certain.' Sonny held the cricket ball in his hand. 'Watch this.' He tossed himself a little catch, then threw the ball high into the air. Rachael and several passers-by watched as the ball soared, appeared to hover for a split second, before it plummeted back to land on the beach. It bounced a few times, losing zest with each bounce, then came to rest on the sand. Sonny turned to Rachael. 'Could you tell precisely when it was going to stop rising, and when it was going to start falling?'

Rachael shook her head.

'Neither could I,' Sonny agreed, 'and I threw it. That's the danger of the Stock Market.'

In the event both court appearances turned out to be formalities. The counsel briefed by Ralph French to represent Sonny had all the evidence at his disposal. Sonny was interested to learn from the man of a secret agenda linked to his appointment.

'French asked me to take the case and I was glad to, even though it is not my usual line of work. You see, I owe a debt of gratitude to a member of your family that I am happy to repay.'

Sonny looked at the advocate with interest. 'How so?' he asked.

'I was at Forest Manor School with Ralph and your brother James. In fact James was Head Prefect before me. He should have left at the end of the summer but because I had examinations in the autumn, he stayed on for one extra term so that I could concentrate on them without the distraction of other duties. It was no easy thing for him either as it turned out, for almost all the school was stricken down with influenza. So this is my chance to repay James, via you.'

Once the enquiry was underway they heard the

evidence of Sonny's former commanding officer, the most memorable line of which was 'One of the most outstanding and courageous officers I ever commanded'.

Added to the written testimony from the ANZAC officer responsible for burying those killed in the trench and finding Sonny's identification tag, there was little doubt as to the outcome.

Any lingering uncertainty was removed by the last witness to testify on Sonny's behalf. Speaking via an interpreter, Jacques Renaud identified himself as superintendent of the mental institution in Lisieux, Normandy. He confirmed that Sonny had been an inmate there from 1918 to 1920. He attested to the symptoms Sonny had displayed, and that his patient had not spoken a word or given any clue as to his identity from the moment he arrived until the day he walked out.

Following the proceedings, Jacques shook hands warmly with Sonny. And, to the amusement of those in the vicinity, kissed him on both cheeks, congratulating him on his recovery.

Three weeks later, a brief communication from the War Office confirmed Sonny's release from the army. 'The court of enquiry considered that Captain Mark A Cowgill MC had acted throughout in an exemplary manner and recommended that he be placed on the retired list. Should he later be called upon to serve in the army he would enter with the rank of Major.' The letter went on, in more mundane fashion, to inform Captain Cowgill that the Paymaster General's office would be instructed to calculate and disburse his back pay from the time of his wounding until the confirmed retirement date.

Hannah phoned Connie to tell her the good news. 'That's wonderful,' Connie reacted. 'I must write to tell James.'

'No,' Hannah contradicted her, 'I want you to give me the name and address of that solicitor in London. This time I shall write to James.'

'But, Mother,' Connie protested, 'you know James has always insisted that only I should contact him on family matters.'

'Connie,' Hannah told her severely, 'when you were children, both you and James did as you were told. Neither of you disobeyed me, what makes you think matters have changed just because you are older?'

'Yes, Mother,' Connie capitulated.

Ralph French opened the large envelope to find another inside. Attached to the latter was a short note. He read this, glanced at the inscription on the smaller envelope and whistled in surprise. He read the covering note once more and grinned. He penned a short note of his own to replace the existing one, addressed an envelope, and placed the whole in his post tray.

James Fisher collected the post as he and Alice reached the reception desk in the foyer of the large building that housed the head office of Fisher

Springs Pty. When they reached the office they shared on the top floor of the building with its fine views over the expanding, bustling city to the river estuary and the sea beyond, he glanced at the envelopes. All but one appeared to be connected with business. Together they opened and dealt with each item until only the private letter remained. It was from England. James slit open the envelope, finding, as he expected, a smaller one inside with a covering note attached which read, '*Dear James and Alice, it looks as if you've been rumbled at last! Kindest Regards, Ralph.*'

Curious, they inspected the inscription on the inner envelope. They read it and glanced at one another in consternation. The handwriting was not that of Connie, nor was it addressed to James and Alice Cowgill. The inscription read, '*James and Alice Fisher*'.

James opened the envelope and extracted the letter, turning immediately to the signature.

'Mother,' he said, as he shook his head and smiled at Alice. 'If anyone was to guess I suppose it would have to be her. Let's see what she has to say.'

Hannah had taken great pains over the wording of the letter. She knew she had but this one chance to say all that was in her heart. There must be, Hannah thought, no word of recrimination or repining over the lost years. Rather she wanted the letter to be a joyful expression of her love and gratitude.

Dear James and Alice, or should I write, Dear Mr and Mrs Fisher?

I have thought long and hard before writing this letter. Before I go any further I want to emphasize that I am the only person who knows your secret, apart from Mr French of course. Not even dear Sonny or Rachael, who has become like a daughter to me. Even Connie has failed to realize the truth. That is the way it will remain unless you choose otherwise, but that decision is yours alone to make.

Perhaps I should have guessed long ago, for neither of you are the sort to cast your family adrift. Once I realized the truth, so many hitherto unexplained coincidences began to make sense. Such as the timely purchase of WPF&D by an Australian company whose executives immediately sought out Michael Haigh to head the operation? Or the mysterious manner in which a firm of London solicitors discovered many years ago that Albert had failed to call a shareholders' meeting at HAC. I could write so much more, but I would be wasting my ink and trying your patience, for you know the facts better than I.

I wrote that your secret is safe with me. What I have to say next is more than a little painful for me, so please bear with me. In my more selfish moments I wish that the subterfuges could be cast aside and a reunion achieved. However, I realize that it could be harmful to others. Michael for one is so proud of all he has achieved since leaving HAC, proud too of the high esteem in which he is held by his parent company. To learn that he had been helped would, I fear, be most detrimental. Sonny too, whose confidence is high at present, but I feel that is only a fragile veneer. He has launched himself wholeheartedly at this new challenge and I believe it will prove pivotal in his long-term recovery. To find out that this career is your gift might have serious adverse consequences. Sonny will no doubt be writing to tell you of his discharge from the army which I am sure without the help you supplied would have been far harder for him to cope with.

So, is the situation an impasse? I think not, for now I know this wonderful secret, that of realizing how deeply you feel, how actively you care for us. I am beginning to think that my days are running short now, after all I am sixty-six years old and, despite little Mark, who keeps me young at heart, there is a great weariness upon me sometimes, such as I believe my mother must have experienced in her later years.

I have been determined throughout not to repine, but that weariness afflicts me most when I think of those I have lost, of Cissie and Ada in particular and of course your father. I am secure in writing this, for I know you will understand me, your own loss ensures that.

So, my dearest son and daughter, dear James and sweet Alice, I send you all my love and gratitude. I will be guided in all my future actions by your wishes and advice.

I remain, one who is proud to inscribe herself as,
Your Mother.

PS. I am enclosing a photograph. If you remember, it was taken before the Jubilee Garden Party.

Together, arms around each other, James and Alice looked at the photograph, their vision blurred by tears. The photo showed the household gathered on the steps in front of the house. The inscription on the back merely stated, '1, Byland Crescent. June 1897'.

CHAPTER FIVE

The trial of Clarence Barker was, as prosecuting counsel later remarked, 'The closest to a foregone conclusion as possible.' This, despite most of the evidence being circumstantial.

In his opening remarks he referred to the blackmailer. 'While the actions of Arthur Bilton were reprehensible, I am in no doubt that at the beginning he was motivated by fear. He had seen the accused cowering in the trench and murder an English officer, Major Hugh Ogilvy, who ordered Barker to leave the trench and join his comrades. Bilton knew that if Barker discovered him, he would suffer the same fate. The wisdom of this course of action was later justified by Barker's violent reaction to extortion demands. The court will hear that the accused tried on more than one occasion to discover the blackmailer's identity. Having failed, he determined to rid himself of the man who was tormenting him. The court will hear evidence from the ex-soldier who sold the murder weapon to the accused, a weapon later discovered in Barker's flat. You will also hear from ballistics experts that the shots that killed James Watson could have been fired from that weapon and no other. It was an unhappy misfortune for Watson that the accused was unaware that he was not the blackmailer, merely someone charged with collecting the extortion money.

'The court will also hear of the embezzlement of many thousands of pounds from the Haigh Ackroyd and Cowgill group of companies, in which the accused held the position of managing director. The prosecution is indebted to one of the witnesses for their diligence in tracing the trail of embezzled money to the bank account of the defendant, via a complicated string of nefarious transactions. Sums of money closely matching those stolen from HAC were deposited in Arthur Bilton's bank account shortly afterwards.

'On hearing the evidence the court will, I am sure, come to the conclusion that the accused murdered Major Hugh Ogilvie to avoid the inevitable consequences of his own cowardice. It will further conclude, I am certain, that upon realizing that his crime had been witnessed, he stole huge sums of money in order to buy his blackmailer's silence.

'Finally, the court will also be convinced that when the opportunity eventually arose, the accused slaughtered James Watson in cold blood, leaving his bullet riddled corpse in an isolated and desolate piece of moorland, believing the body to be that of the blackmailer.'

To the hardened crime reporters covering the case, much of what had been said was purely routine. There seemed to be little enough on which to hang a headline. Only one question exercised their minds on the first day of the trial. What was the identity of the mysterious witness alluded to by prosecuting counsel in his opening remarks? Before they learned this however, the eager newsmen first heard from the pathologist who had conducted the post-mortems on both Major Ogilvie and James Watson. His evidence, routine for the most part, confirmed the identification of bullets removed from both corpses. His statement that James Watson had died as a result of the first bullet to strike him was particularly damaging.

Ballistics experts followed the pathologist. They confirmed that the bullet fired into Major Ogilvie could only have come from a British rifle. They also verified the weapon found in Barker's flat as being the source of the bullets removed from James Watson.

The next witness to take the stand was Detective Inspector Clayton. The reporters, by now bored by technical and scientific evidence, listened with increasing interest as Clayton detailed his involvement in the case.

'I was approached by a Bradford solicitor, Mr William Sutton. He brought me an envelope containing a letter from the late Arthur Bilton. There was also a statement, sworn before a Commissioner of Oaths. The letter instructed Mr

Sutton to deliver the affidavit to the police in the event of Bilton's sudden or violent death.'

'Is that in fact what happened?' counsel asked.

'Yes indeed,' Clayton replied, 'although perhaps not in the way Bilton had intended. He was killed in a motoring accident, while under the influence of alcohol.'

'Are there any suspicious circumstances surrounding his death?' counsel wanted to know.

'To the best of my belief, absolutely none. We examined the vehicle thoroughly but found no mechanical defects. We also interviewed the landlord of the public house where Bilton had been drinking before his death. The landlord said he was surprised Bilton could stand up, let alone drive a motor car, after the amount he had drunk.'

'Very well, please continue,' the prosecutor instructed.

'Having received the statement from Bilton, we began our investigation. We concentrated on the Watson killing and the fraud and embezzlement to start with. This led us to make enquiries regarding HAC Group where Barker was managing director.'

Counsel held up a warning hand before Clayton could go any further. Turning with a small bow to the defence bench he addressed the judge. 'My lord, with your indulgence and that of learned counsel for the defence, I shall now ask the witness to read from the statements taken by the police from various employees and former employees of

HAC Group. These have already been entered as prosecution exhibits seven to eleven.' Having received this permission, counsel waited for the usher to hand the documents to Clayton. 'Please give the court the gist of these statements and tell us your actions as a result of them.'

'The first two were taken from former employees at A and C Scouring,' Clayton told the court. 'They describe how they became suspicious regarding the poor yields achieved from the scouring process and traced these back to wool supposedly delivered from a new supplier, a company trading under the name of Phoenix Wools Ltd. Acting on these suspicions they checked deliveries from Phoenix but could find absolutely no trace of such wool having arrived on the scouring premises. They reported their findings to their foreman. The next statement comes from that foreman. In it he describes how he reported the suspicious activity. A week later both he and the two workers were summarily dismissed.'

'To whom did he report these events?' counsel asked.

'To the accused, Clarence Barker,' Clayton told him. 'Next we interviewed a former employee of HAC Blending. He had been employed as a book-keeper by the previous owners of the company. Within one week of the takeover he was told that his services were no longer required as he, Barker, would assume responsibility for the books. Finally we interviewed the blending foreman. He told us that blending yields had worsened suddenly after Barker took over the book-keeping. Just as the men at the scouring plant, he also had suspicions about Phoenix Wools, but he had the foresight to keep them to himself.'

Clayton handed the statements back to the usher. 'In view of this we decided there were sufficient grounds for further investigation. We applied for and got a search warrant for Barker's flat. We found the revolver that killed James Watson hidden in a shoe box. We also found papers, invoices, statements, bank books, and other documents. These did not make sense at first. It was only after we pieced everything together that it became clear.'

'Tell me,' counsel prompted him, 'about HAC Group. How did the accused get to become managing director?'

'HAC is a family concern. It was founded in the last century by Philip Ackroyd and Edward Haigh. They were later joined by Albert Cowgill, Ackroyd's son-in-law. Both senior partners died before the war, leaving Albert Cowgill as the only director. His son, Mark Cowgill, entered the business too before the war. Barker was Albert Cowgill's nephew and originally employed at A and C Scouring, but when Cowgill senior retired, Barker was promoted to managing director. I believe this caused something of a rift in the Cowgill household. Albert Cowgill died in 1918 and there is little doubt that Mark Cowgill would have replaced Barker, but he was listed as missing in action in 1918. After the war, following his release from military service, Barker resumed his old position, shedding any members of staff who might ask embarrassing questions.'

Defence counsel objected to this surmise and the judge directed the jury to disregard Clayton's last statement. The reporters were taking notice now, for this testimony was far more newsworthy than pathology and ballistics. They waited eagerly for the cross-examination.

The rest of Clayton's evidence consisted of confirmation of the journey to France with information supplied by Bilton in his letter as to the location of Major Ogilvie's corpse, the exhumation, and the post-mortem results on the two bodies.

Defence counsel concentrated his efforts on an attempt to discredit the testimony of ex-employees, suggesting bitterness over their dismissal had coloured their statements and stressing the circumstantial nature of much of the evidence. These efforts were not conspicuously successful, however. The *Yorkshire Post* crime reporter passed a note to his colleague from the *Bradford Argus*. It read, 'He knows he's backed a loser'. The *Argus* newsman nodded his agreement. Defence counsel sat down, an air of defeat about him and all eyes turned to the prosecution bench, awaiting the next witness.

The judge nodded to the prosecutor. There was a moment's pause before counsel instructed the usher, 'Call, Captain Mark Cowgill.'

There was an audible gasp from the public gallery. In the dock, Clarence Barker, his face the colour of putty, clutched at the handrail for support with fingers that trembled with a combination of shock and terror.

In the press gallery, reporters scribbled furiously as Sonny took the oath, determined to miss none of what was to follow, for here at last was true headline material. They were not alone in the assumption. The evidence given by Sonny could equally well have been delivered by Clayton or one of his officers. However, the prosecutor knew the value of an appearance by Sonny, the returning war hero. He led Sonny gently through his own story, asking him to explain his long absence. Sonny gave his evidence calmly, his voice level and unemotional. Counsel then prompted Sonny to describe conditions at HAC on his return. 'The group was in ruins,' Sonny told him. 'It had been trading while insolvent and was on the point of liquidation.'

Counsel continued by asking Sonny to describe the process of discovery of the cause of HAC's collapse.

'The police found documents in Barker's flat,' Sonny told him. 'Using these, by checking invoices against delivery notes we were able to tally up the amount of each fraudulent transaction instigated by Phoenix Wools for wool that never existed. Then we examined Phoenix Wools' bank statements. With the passbooks in our possession we were able to follow the money trail until it landed in Barker's own account. From there we saw the subsequent withdrawal, followed soon after by a similar deposit in Arthur Bilton's account.'

When Sonny's evidence was complete the prosecution thanked him, adding a word of congratulation on his safe return. Ominously for Barker, despite an encouraging glance from his opponent inviting cross-examination, defence counsel remained seated. Neither did he have any questions for the final prosecution witness, the solicitor who had organized the setting up of Phoenix Wools. He, damningly, identified the defendant as the person on whose behalf he had acted. Once more defence counsel remained motionless.

Not so the reporters. As the judge rose to signal the end of the day's proceedings they scrambled from the press gallery to file their reports for the morning editions.

'Back From the Dead, Return of the Hero, Damned from the Grave'. The headlines said it all. With remarkable symmetry the reports below these banners opened, 'Returning from the dead, war hero Captain Mark (Sonny) Cowgill gave damning evidence yesterday in the trial of his cousin, Clarence Barker . . .'

The following day, the jury took less than an hour to reach a conclusion. Barker was adjudged guilty on each and every charge. The death sentence was inevitable.

'Prisoner at the bar, the jury is unanimous that

you committed both murders for which you stand accused. In wartime your first crime would have been an act of treason punishable by death. In time of war or peace both murders are capital crimes. You have been found guilty of these murders. I have failed to detect in you the slightest sign of remorse for the fate of either of your victims, or evidence of penitence for those from whom you stole to avoid exposure. The victims of these heartless frauds were members of your own family. You brought them to the point of bankruptcy to save your own skin. I have sought to find some extenuating circumstance that might compel the court to exercise mercy. In light of the pitiless lack of remorse you have demonstrated, I have failed to find any.'

The judge paused and picked up a small square of black silk which he placed on top of his wig. There was absolute silence in the crowded courtroom as he continued.

'Clarence Barker, you have been found guilty of the murders of Major Hugh Ogilvie and James Watson. You will be taken from this court to a place of execution and there you shall be hanged by the neck until you are dead. May The Lord have mercy on your soul.'

Late one evening in early October 1923, a warder in Armley prison heard a choking sound coming from the condemned cell as he made his nightly inspection. Investigating, he found the prisoner

Barker had attempted to commit suicide using the sheet from his bed to hang himself. The warder, a tough Aberdonian, who had served in the war as a sergeant in the Black Watch showed little sympathy after he cut the prisoner down and revived him.

'Dinnae make such a fuss,' he told the gasping Barker. 'Tryin' tae do yer sen in. That's a coward's way oot. It'll nae be lang afore ye meet Thomas and he'll dae the job properly.'

'Who's Thomas?' Barker croaked, when he could get his breath.

'The last man ye'll be meetin', the man naebody wants tae meet,' the warder told him cheerfully. 'Thomas Pierrepoint, the public executioner. He'll come along wi' his scales and tape measure any dae noo.' The warder was clearly enjoying himself. 'He'll weigh and measure ye, then he'll work out how much counter-weight he needs under the trap. He'll tak' his chalk and draw a T on the trapdoor fer your heels tae stand on so when he pulls the lever ye'll be sent straight down tae hell, where ye belong. Dinnae worry, though, you'll probably no' feel a thing. Of course,' he added conversationally, 'that's only guesswork, fer there's naebody left tae tell the tale.' He eyed the sobbing figure curled on the bed, contemptuously. 'Ye're such a worthless lump o' shite, the world will be well rid o' ye,' he told Barker before slamming the cell door.

Two weeks later, on a cold, grey, and windy morning at fifteen minutes after eight o'clock a warder posted an announcement on the wooden door of the prison. Clarence Barker had met Thomas Pierrepoint. The execution had taken place.

In the Cowgill household the short paragraph in the newspaper was greeted with relief. For Sonny it was relief that a grim chapter in their lives had been brought to a close. For Hannah, it was relief that Barker's parents, particularly her sister-in-law, Bessie, had not lived to endure the humiliation brought about by their son.

CHAPTER SIX

In Australia, James and Alice pondered the contents of Hannah's letter for some time before deciding their course of action. 'I think your mother's right,' Alice said. 'It's a shame we can't have the reconciliation but that would mean revealing our identity and that would be harmful to Sonny and Michael.'

'Yes, I take the point. It is a comfort though that Mother knows the truth and that she accepts you.'

Alice smiled. 'I've known that all along. From the day we went to visit poor little Cissie before we left England. I talked to your mother while you were chatting with Sonny and saying farewell to Cissie. She told me then that it was obvious I made you happy. She said, "Just carry on making him happy. As long as you do that you will make me happy also."'

James grinned. 'In that case she should be ecstatic. So, now things are in the open I see no reason not to keep it so. It means a lot to me to be able to write openly and freely to the family. As Cowgill of course,' he added. 'All these years we have written to Connie we have had to watch every word to avoid giving ourselves away.'

Hannah experienced a moment of apprehension before opening the reply to her letter. Her fears were allayed by the opening lines.

Dear Mother,

We were delighted to get your letter. Of course you are perfectly right, as usual. Your mixed feelings agree entirely with ours. Although it would be marvellous to be free of the subterfuge, if that were at the expense of the content and well-being of Michael or Sonny that is too high a price to pay. So, we will have to remain in hiding, shadowy figures from the past. Not from you however, which makes us both happy.

We recently got a bunch of press cuttings about the Barker trial (one of the advantages of owning a string of newspapers). Fancy my little brother being called a war hero. No more than Sonny deserves though. We are both immensely proud of him so can imagine how you must feel. It is comforting also to know that Barker got what was coming to him after all the misery and suffering he caused. If needed be I would have willingly supplied the rope, tied it, oiled the trapdoor and pulled the lever.

By stark contrast Simon Jones seems a very sound chap. All the reports we get speak of him in glowing terms. Between them I am sure Michael, Simon and Sonny will repair the damage caused by Barker.

Touching on graver matters, although both Alice and I still feel the loss of Saul, it was a great comfort to us that he and Sonny became friends before the end. We have both wondered, if things had turned out different, how long it would have been until they discovered they were related. Not long I suppose, for Saul, in the letter he was writing immediately before he was killed, was already voicing vague suspicions. Well, that was not to be, so there is no point in dwelling on the past.

As to the rest of our tribe, sorry, your grand-children, Cissie is a happily married woman, her husband is a reporter. That way we keep up to date with all the local news and gossip. Ellen has become a librarian. She was always a bookworm, so I tease her that she only took the job so she could read her way through the shelves. I don't think she will ever marry, for she seems oblivious to the existence of young men, but who knows, she may surprise us one day. Speaking of boys, our two seem to grow at a frightening rate, or perhaps I'm getting old. Philip is rising fifteen and taking a healthy (unhealthy?) interest in girls. Local matrons with young daughters are already eying him suspiciously. Alice asked me to talk to him, but I told her with my past that would be hypocritical. As for Mary, she too is studious like her sister Ellen. Luke will be seven next week. He and his younger sister Dorothy are the comedians of the family. So much so, that we have nicknamed Dorothy, Dottie. When they get together nobody can remain out of humour for long. Luke reminds me so much of Sonny when he was little.

One more item then I'm passing the letter over to Alice who also wishes to write to you. It is to express my thanks, for I have only recently learned from Alice of your extreme kindness to her all those years ago before we left England. It meant more to her than you will ever know, for the knowledge of your approval sustained her through the difficult times during the early years.

God bless and keep you,

Your loving son,
James.

Below this, Alice had written,

Dear Mother,

James has written most of what I wanted to say, but I felt it important for you to know that I share all those sentiments and more besides. We are of one mind regarding the continued deception, equally sad about the resultant separation. Remembering, as James has mentioned, your kindness to me before we left England, I promised then that I would strive to make him happy and if I have fallen short at any time it is not from want of effort.

Our thanks for the photograph you sent us. It has pride of place in our office, between our desks where we can both see it. It will remain a constant reminder of when we fell in love.

All that remains is for all of us here to wish you and all the family a very Merry Christmas.

With deepest love,
Alice.

The tears that ran freely down Hannah's cheeks as she finished reading were of happiness mixed with relief. Now that she was free to write to her son and daughter-in-law she would be able to start with some wonderful news. Hannah hastened to the bureau for writing paper. She had to inform them of their nephew's arrival. William Albert Cowgill, a lustily bawling 7lb 4oz brother for Mark, had made his world debut only the previous day.

During the next two years, life for the Cowgill's resumed some semblance of their past. Hannah was reminded of the early days in Byland Crescent when she would remain at home with responsibilities for the running of the household, while Albert travelled daily to the office in Bradford, as Sonny now did. She was happy now to let Rachael take the reins and to spend her time entertaining her grandchildren or walking Mark to school, often accompanied by Mark's constant friend, Jennifer.

Letters from Australia arrived more frequently and as Christmas 1925 approached, Hannah was delighted to receive what she hoped had now become a regular greeting. She smiled as she read the contents.

'*We are sending our second in command to England for a few months in the New Year. Ostensibly this is as non-executive director of the new group but in fact it is to give him a long overdue holiday. His name is Patrick Finnegan and he will be accompanied by his wife Louise and baby daughter Isabella. Before they leave, we will tell them our story so they are on their guard when talking to other family members. They will come to Scarborough to visit, so I am collecting photographs for them to bring you. We will write nearer the time giving exact details of their itinerary.*'

Hannah put the letter carefully in her bureau, wondering how the visitors would fare travelling such a long distance to a foreign country.

Rachael had organized a birthday party for William. Although too young to understand, it gave the family a reason for a get together – not that they really needed any excuse. The birthday party was followed by Christmas and the New Year celebrations for 1926.

It was a few days after the guests had departed for home and the household had returned to normal. The children had retired for the night and the adults were gathered in the sitting room where Rachael sat down wearily and commented, 'Well, that was an exhausting day. It will be even harder next Christmas with another little one.'

Sonny lowered his whisky glass and stared at his wife. 'You mean?'

'Yes, dear. Another one for the Bentley.'

James and Alice had conducted their annual review of the Fisher Springs empire. Although the exercise had originated purely to check the development of each sector of the growing organization it had long since developed beyond those narrow guidelines.

The process now lasted three days and encompassed examination of reports on the previous year's economic activity both in Australia and worldwide. This analysis was followed by an assessment of short, medium, and long-term industrial prospects. It was during the latter part of the review that James Fisher demonstrated an uncanny vision, one of the qualities that had contributed to the group's outstanding success. Patrick Finnegan commented on the accuracy of his predictions to Alice.

'I know exactly what you mean,' Alice replied. 'It is quite scary how he gets it right so often, sometimes totally against perceived expectations. It isn't down to luck or guesswork though. Only James knows exactly how much work goes into preparing those predictions. He spends hours reading reports and journals, newspapers and magazines. He researches statistics from every source he can find to build up a complete picture of industrial trends. He goes into his study after the children have gone to bed and shuts himself away to absorb all this material. He reads things other people would consider irrelevant and recognizes the significance of them. Quite often I wake up in the early hours and he still hasn't come to bed.'

'Do you know what he is focussing on at present?' Finnegan was curious to discover.

'I glanced at some notes he'd made yesterday morning. The headings were about European countries and their economies. He seemed to be concentrating on unemployment, industrial unrest, and inflation. Then there was a section on America, something to do with speculation fever. I've no idea what that means.'

'No doubt he had his reasons,' Patrick surmised.

CHAPTER SEVEN

It was early spring and Patrick and Louise Finnegan, with their two-year-old daughter, Isabella, were onboard a liner being prepared to dock. A week before they were due to leave, they had been to the Fisher mansion for lunch. The two couples were the best of friends, the relationship far closer than that of an employer and employee. After the meal, while the Fisher's children were playing a highly competitive game of cricket on the lawn and Isabella was asleep, the four adults sat in the comfortable study. There, for the first time since reaching Australia, James and Alice related the story of their early life in England, the rupture between James and his father and their departure to seek a new life.

Patrick and Louise sat, enthralled by the tale. Finnegan was intrigued by the way James had manipulated events to assist his family, while maintaining his own anonymity. He congratulated James on the continued subterfuge.

James grimaced and said, 'Yes, it worked very well until this last time. I overplayed my hand with the HAC takeover and my mother guessed the truth.' He glanced at Alice, who smiled.

'Not that we mind Mother knowing,' James continued, 'in fact we're very happy about it, for it means we have at least got one channel of direct contact. The problem is that we must ensure no hint of the identity of the owners of Fisher Springs gets to the rest of the family.'

'Why is that so important?' Louise enquired.

Alice explained. 'When James and I bought WPF&D we did it partly as a sound investment but also to help Michael and James's sister, Connie. Michael was having a lot of trouble with James's father at HAC. If word got out that we were in part responsible for that stratagem it would spoil everything for Michael.'

James continued to explain. 'Alice is right. Michael and latterly Simon Jones have done a terrific job at WPF&D. It is purely down to their efforts that the group is so strong. All we did was give the initial impetus. Once the ball was rolling they ran with it, to some tune.'

'That's right,' Finnegan confirmed. 'I was looking over the files on Friday to familiarize myself with the set-up. Their profits have come along in leaps and bounds every year since Michael took over and recently they have rocketed.'

'True enough,' James agreed, 'that's why we can't allow anything to put that achievement at risk. Likewise with the HAC merger. Mother summed it up perfectly in her letter. My brother Sonny has suffered terribly over the past few years, more than any of us will ever know. Now he is recovering well, but his confidence is fragile. Nothing would be more harmful than to think that he is being cared for. That is not the case. HAC is a sound investment. All we have done is paid a little over the odds for it. The success of the new group will be down to the efforts of Sonny, Michael, and Simon.'

'How did your mother come to guess the truth?' Finnegan asked.

James grinned. 'My mother's very astute and has an excellent memory. When the HAC merger was discussed she heard the name Fisher Springs for the first time. When my family moved into Byland Crescent in 1897 Mother interviewed all the staff. To the rest of the family Alice was just that, Alice the housemaid, but Mother dug back in her papers and found the record of the interview. It confirmed the accuracy of her memory when she read that Alice the housemaid was Alice Fisher.'

'So your real name is James Cowgill?' Louise asked him.

'It was,' James corrected her. 'I changed it a long time ago and am now legally James Fisher.'

'How do we throw them off the scent if they ask awkward questions?' Finnegan wanted to know.

'We've come up with an idea.' Alice told him. 'We want to try it out on you.'

'Here's how it works.' James took up the tale. 'If they ask, you tell them that we are an elderly couple, in our sixties, born and bred in Australia. Simon and Michael have received cheques and correspondence bearing the signature A Fisher. Fortunately, Alice never signs her full name. So, while you are in England, you must think of her as Agnes Fisher, not Alice.'

'What about you?' Louise enquired.

'That's easier still,' James told her. 'I was christened James Philip Cowgill, but nobody has ever used the name Philip, so I doubt whether anyone apart from Mother would remember it, especially if you shorten it to Phil. So here we are,' James spread his arms dramatically. 'Meet Phil and Agnes Fisher, an Aussie couple through and through.'

Louise stared at the youthful, energetic looking pair. 'That's the easy bit,' she told them, 'but pretending you're elderly. That'll be real hard work.'

In England, the news that the combined group, to be titled, Fisher Springs UK Ltd. was to have as its non-executive director no less a person than the Vice Chairman of their Australian parent company, and that he was to pay them a visit, was seen by the other board members as a positive indication of their importance to that parent. Plans to ensure the success were discussed in detail at one of their daily briefings. This was a practice instigated by Michael Haigh. There was always much to talk over and the three directors found that they were of such similar temperament and way of thinking that they sparked ideas from each other.

They learned that Finnegan would be accompanied by his wife and baby daughter, lending a more relaxed atmosphere to the visit.

'I like the thought that they are coming as a family,' Sonny remarked. 'From the itinerary cabled from Australia I see the trip is going to last four months, all told. That's an awfully long time for a man to be away from home.'

'We shall have to do everything in our power to make them feel at home while they are here,' Michael replied. 'They will be in London at first but it's up to us to organize such details as choice of hotel, location and so forth when they come here. I think it would be a good idea not to leave them in one place for the whole of their stay, but give them a little variety. It would give them opportunity to see more of Yorkshire than soot begrimed buildings and smoking mill chimneys.'

'How about Harrogate as a venue to start with,' Simon suggested.

'That's a great idea,' Sonny agreed. 'First impressions are so important and Harrogate would strike the right note. The question is, with so many good hotels to choose from, which one should we go for?'

'I believe the Old Swan has an extremely good reputation,' Simon proposed. 'It is very close to the Valley Gardens and is within walking distance of the shops.'

'I agree about the Old Swan,' Michael murmured.

'He's only saying that because he used to take Connie there when they were courting,' Sonny told Simon in a stage whisper. 'He even took my sister Ada along to play gooseberry.'

Michael blushed and grinned ruefully at the accuracy of Sonny's comment. 'Well, if we're all agreed on that, how long should we book them in for?'

'Let's make a reservation for three weeks, then if they want to we can extend the booking once they arrive,' Sonny said.

'Good. Simon, will you attend to that?' Michael asked.

Simon was in the middle of confirming his agreement when the door to Michael's office opened suddenly. The company cashier stood in the doorway. 'Excuse me for the interruption, but I have an urgent telephone call for Captain Cowgill from Scarborough.'

Sonny leapt to his feet and hastened to the cashier's office. He returned a few minutes later, ashen faced. 'That call was from Mother. Mark was complaining of feeling unwell this morning so Rachael took him for a walk to see if a little fresh air would do him good. When they returned Mark began to feel worse, he was being sick and complaining that his head ached. They decided to call in Dr Culleton. By the time he arrived Rachael had taken Mark's temperature and it was way above normal. The doctor decided he should be taken to hospital so Rachael went with him. Mother stayed at Byland Crescent to ring me then she's going too. She says Mark is a very poorly little boy. I'm catching the next train home.'

Patrick and Louise Finnegan's first impression of England was far from encouraging. Major sea ports are rarely entered in lists of the world's most beautiful cities and Southampton is no exception. To emphasize its lack of charm the city was cloaked in a fine mist of drizzly rain on the day their ship docked.

As they made their way across the quayside towards the Customs sheds Patrick remarked, 'If it were not for the business and the promises we made to James and Alice I'd have stayed onboard and sailed straight home.'

It was not until they were onboard the London bound train that southern England began to relent and show a fairer face to the visitors. The journey through the Hampshire countryside revealed a rolling patchwork quilt of fields and forests. Once they were clear of the coast the weather improved and the welcome sunshine illuminated a landscape of lush and vivid colours, so much in contrast to the more arid scenery back home. Commenting on the striking depth of the colours, Finnegan remarked, 'Perhaps all that bloody rain does some good after all.'

Nor were they disappointed by London. Dropped by a taxi driver, whose accent was so broad they understood little of his conversation, in front of the world-famous hotel at which James, courtesy of Ralph French, had secured them reservations, they were immediately enveloped in luxury. It was touching to see a splendid bouquet of flowers awaiting them in their suite, compliments of Michael Haigh. The message, written on behalf of Simon Jones and Sonny, welcomed them and promised a telephone call the following day when they had recovered from their travels.

The promised call came at 10 a.m., neatly timed after they had finished breakfast and before they set out to explore the capital. Michael informed them, once their sojourn in London was complete, one of the directors would meet them from the train in Leeds to take them on to Harrogate. Haigh did not explain the reason for such vague arrangements, which was due to the uncertainty over Sonny's involvement. Haigh did not wish to risk worrying the parents of a young daughter for one thing, for another the outcome was still in the balance. It was purely coincidental that the resolution of Sonny's dilemma came only hours after Haigh's phone call.

For nearly a month Mark Cowgill had been severely ill. The diagnosis, the doctors agreed, was that he had contracted scarlet fever.

Immediately they received this news, Hannah took William on an extended visit to Michael and Connie in Baildon. Bringing back memories for mother and daughter of a similar situation in 1908 when Connie's five-year-old daughter Nancy had contracted and died from whooping cough. As a baby, Connie's second daughter Marguerite had been cared for in Scarborough.

Mark's illness placed a severe strain on Rachael, a former nursing sister, now coping with pregnancy, who insisted on caring for her son at home. Her argument being that, with her, Mark would have individual attention. Relieved of the burden of caring for baby William, Rachael was now free to concentrate her skill and energy on her elder son and found great help and support, not only from Sonny, but everyone at Byland Crescent.

She had one particular assistant nurse, who, despite being in a high-risk category, refused to be kept away from the invalid.

'Mark is my friend,' Jennifer told Rachael and her own mother. Jennifer was so vehemently insistent that neither parent could deny the child, despite their better judgement.

After three weeks, during which Mark seemed to care little for anything, his condition gradually started to improve. As each symptom abated, his parents, equally slowly, indulged in a little hope. After a few more weeks he became noticeably brighter and for the first time since he was struck down, began to pay a little attention to his surroundings. It was some time later that Sonny and Rachael actually dared to voice their opinion that perhaps the worst was over.

On the same morning that Michael Haigh spoke to Finnegan, Doctor Steven Culleton paid his final visit to his young patient. After an exhaustive examination he told Mark's relieved parents that the illness appeared to have run its course and that in his view Mark would in time make a complete recovery. Much relieved by this news Sonny rang the Bradford office to report the good news to his brother-in-law. Aware that his absence had imposed an extra strain on his fellow directors, Sonny was anxious to shoulder as large a part of the burden for the forthcoming visit as possible. When the three men met the following morning, he started proceedings. 'If I bring the Bentley through tomorrow I can collect Mr and Mrs Finnegan from Leeds and take them through to Harrogate. After that I can drive across to Baildon, collect Mother and William and drive them back to Scarborough.'

Given that neither Michael nor Simon possessed a car with anywhere near the carrying capacity of the huge Bentley, there was little they could do to argue.

CHAPTER EIGHT

As a helpful porter stacked their luggage onto a handcart on the platform of Leeds City Station, Patrick Finnegan felt a tap on his shoulder. He turned, to find a younger edition of James Fisher standing before him. Although he had been forewarned about the family likeness, he found considerable difficulty suppressing an exclamation of surprise at the vision. He recovered in time to respond to Sonny's introductory words.

'Excuse me, you must be Mr and Mrs Finnegan. I'm Mark Cowgill, but everyone calls me Sonny.'

As they shook hands, Finnegan said, 'Pleased to meet you, Sonny, but I would rather you call us Patrick and Louise. Whenever somebody says Mr Finnegan, I look around for my dad.'

'I know that feeling,' Sonny responded with a laugh. He shook Louise by the hand and smiled warmly at Isabella, who responded with a shy smile of her own.

'Let's get off this draughty platform,' Sonny suggested. 'If there's anywhere less hospitable than a railway station I'd like to know, so I can avoid it.'

As the powerful Bentley conducted Patrick and Louise smoothly out of the city and northward through Wharfedale, past the grandeur of Harewood House to enter Nidderdale, the visitors began to appreciate a fragment of James Fisher's eulogies about his home county. After Finnegan had received a cable outlining their proposed itinerary, James told them, 'You'll love Yorkshire. I see they've booked you in at Harrogate, that's a good choice. It's a lovely town in itself and very handy for exploring the county. There's so much to see, so many different varieties it's difficult to explain, but all I will say is, you may be homesick for Australia when you leave here, but you'll be homesick for Yorkshire when you return home.'

With Harrogate and York it was a case of love at first sight. Harrogate boasted large open grassland, curiously named, The Stray, and a mixture of noble Georgian and Victorian buildings, well stocked and high-quality shops, and the Finnegan family's two chief delights. The first of these was the Valley Gardens where they could stroll in leisurely fashion amongst the profusion of flowers and shrubs, many of them unfamiliar to the visitors. As they walked they were entertained by the music emanating from the bandstand. Once they had worked up an appetite from their walk it was natural to take afternoon tea in Betty's Tea Rooms, where they would be serenaded once more, this time by a pianist and a string quartet.

By contrast, York's walled city presented far

more ancient charms. Australia was new, big, and impressive in its modernity. In York they wandered, entranced, through twisting, narrow, cobbled streets between buildings that were old before the land they called home was discovered.

Determined to extract every ounce of value from their stay, Patrick and Louise collected souvenirs of each notable place they visited. Most of these took the form of postcards, for as Patrick remarked, 'That way we can explain everywhere to people back home and remind ourselves at the same time.'

Not that the trip was wholly one of pleasure. Much of Patrick Finnegan's time was spent in meetings with the new Fisher Springs UK directors. He found Michael, Simon, and Sonny astute, capable, hardworking, and direct, qualities guaranteed to appeal to both a businessman and an Australian. Once again he marvelled at James Fisher's ability to gather together the most talented executives to control one of the group's assets. The directors showed Finnegan every facet of their operation. In six weeks Patrick learned as much if not more about the textile industry than many involved in the trade would know in a lifetime.

The merger of the two textile giants was hampered by the general strike of 1926. For some time the directors were concerned by the long-term damage that might result. Fortunately, the strike was short-lived.

Although the strike was more of an irritation

to the fledgling Fisher Springs UK Group, the effect on the nation went deeper and had far more serious consequences. The industrial action began as an attempt to win justice for miners threatened by lowered wages, longer working hours, and poor safety conditions. A lack of solidarity amongst strikers from other industries ensured the strike was broken within a matter of weeks. This led to bitter isolation for the miners, who felt betrayed.

The most potent result of the strike was a climate of fear. For the first time the British people had experienced a show of solidarity from the working classes, whose politics were generally held to be left wing.

Patrick and Louise were so taken with Harrogate that when they were offered the chance to move elsewhere for part of their visit they declined the offer. Not that they failed to take advantage of the opportunity to travel the length and breadth of the county, but they preferred to maintain the spa town as their base. The one exception from this was the long weekend they spent in Scarborough. When Patrick approached Sonny for a recommendation to a good hotel in the resort, Sonny grinned. 'Number one, Byland Crescent is the best I know.'

Although he knew the address, Finnegan did not reveal his familiarity with it. 'That sounds more like a house than a hotel,' he replied.

‘It is,’ Sonny said. ‘If you come to Scarborough, you stay with us.’ He held up a hand to stop Finnegan’s protestations. ‘It has already been decided,’ he said, with an air of finality. ‘If I were to go home and tell Mother and my wife Rachael you were staying elsewhere, I would finish up with my head in my hands.’

Finnegan bowed to the inevitable. ‘I can see I’m due to meet a pair of formidable women,’ he told Sonny meekly.

The weekend was a great success. If Patrick Finnegan charmed Hannah and Rachael, that was only fair, as he was overwhelmed by the warmth of their welcome to himself and Louise. It was quickly apparent that Rachael and Louise had become firm friends. Louise for her part seriously considered kidnapping William Cowgill to take home to Australia where she would call him Billy after the famous cricketer Billy Murdoch. Rachael, when told of the plan replied, ‘Only if you leave me Isabella.’

Mark, newly recovered from his illness, decided he liked the idea of calling his brother Billy and continued to do so. He was a firm favourite with the visitors, although his searching questions on Australian cricket stretched Patrick’s knowledge of the subject to the limit. The highlight of the weekend was a dinner party on the Saturday night. The large dining table was filled to capacity that evening, for Michael and Connie Haigh had travelled over with Simon and Naomi Jones. During the course of the meal Finnegan had needed to keep his wits about him, for Michael had decided it was an opportune moment to attempt to discover more about the owners of Fisher Springs. Patrick stonewalled, following the script laid down for him by James and Alice. During a break in the questioning, when Michael's attention was diverted by another topic, Patrick, who was seated next to Hannah, whispered out of the side of his mouth, 'How am I doing, Mrs C?'

Hannah laughed and replied, 'Absolutely perfect, anyone would think you've been scripted, Mr F.'

Finnegan refused to disclose the reason for his sudden outburst of laughter.

On the final day of their visit, Patrick Finnegan declined the offer to accompany Sonny to Bradford. 'I want to spend some time looking around Scarborough with Louise and Isabella. Your mother is going to show us the town. I'm sure Rachael will welcome the rest. How long is it now?'

'Only four weeks to go,' Sonny replied. 'I'll be glad when that day comes. I'm determined to fill the Bentley.'

'Good luck to it,' Finnegan responded.

Monday dawned fair and if Patrick had any illusions about a quiet day they were soon shattered. In a moment of weakness he agreed to spend the evening on the beach playing cricket with Mark and Sonny, this to follow several hours walking the resort's twin bays with Louise, Hannah, and Isabella. By the time the walkers stopped at the Pavilion Hotel for afternoon tea they were all leg weary. Tea was a long drawn out affair, as it provided the opportunity for Louise to give Hannah the set of photographs Alice had entrusted to her. In return she received recent photographs of Michael and Connie with their children and a three-generation studio portrait of Hannah, Sonny, and Rachael with Mark and William. On the back of the latter, Hannah had inscribed, 'This will be out of date by the time you get it!' The gentle quip made Louise laugh more than Hannah expected, this being unexplained until the couple were taking their leave the following morning.

Patrick shook hands with Rachael and wished her good luck with the forthcoming birth. Then he turned to Sonny and said, 'You'd better keep up the good work. Louise tells me we might have to invest in a Bentley soon.'

The Scarborough visit marked the end of their stay in England. Four days later Patrick and Louise stood on the deck of the liner as it slipped out of the Solent into the Channel. It might have been fitting for Southampton to have been bathed in sunshine for their departure, by way of an apology. Instead it was raining again.

Three days into the voyage Louise remarked to her husband, 'James was right. He said we'd be homesick for Yorkshire. My family doesn't even come from England and I already miss it.'

'What is it you miss the most? Is it the dales,

the ancient towns and cities, the quaint villages, the moorland or the coast?'

'None of them,' Louise replied. 'I miss all of them of course, but above all else I miss the people. They're honest and genuine and say what they think, but they make you so welcome.'

'Like Australians?'

'Yes, that's it, just like Australians.'

'I feel just the same,' Finnegan told her. 'Sonny and I were talking the other day and he said, "Now you've been to visit, you'll always carry a piece of Yorkshire in your heart."'

'I like that idea. And one part of us will always be a little piece of Yorkshire.' She smiled as she placed his hand gently on her thickening waistline.

CHAPTER NINE

On another liner heading west, Jessica Tunnicliffe was celebrating her birthday early. Her mother's present was an unusual one. As Jessica watched the twinkling lights of Southampton fading into the gathering gloom, she wondered how many other girls got a luxury cruise to America as a gift for their twelfth birthday. Not many would have the means, but Jessica's mother, Charlotte, was one of the wealthiest women in Bradford. Charlotte Tunnicliffe was Michael Haigh's ex-wife. An acrimonious divorce provoked by Charlotte's adulterous lifestyle had preceded his marriage to Connie Cowgill.

Jessica, worldly-wise for her age, pondered some of the conversations her mother would engage in during the voyage. She decided that Charlotte would opt for the 'war hero's fiancée' story. It was a good story, for it served several purposes. It explained the lack of a father, excused Jessica's illegitimacy, and gave Charlotte an air of glamour and mystery. The illusion was so real she could almost hear her mother's voice: 'Of course things would have been so much different if only poor Jessica's father had been alive.'

Jessica always started out as 'poor Jessica' in these stories. It puzzled her for a long time for she did not consider herself to be 'poor Jessica'. Eventually, she realized it was all part of her mother's romance. She would usually follow 'poor Jessica' with 'things are so difficult for a woman alone'. This had also puzzled Jessica. What was it that was so difficult? They had everything money could buy.

Charlotte would then wait for the encouragement of a raised eyebrow or an enquiring glance. Jessica knew from experience that the glance would almost invariably be directed at the third finger of Charlotte's left hand, which was devoid of a wedding ring. There was an engagement ring in place, but the listener would certainly not be told that Charlotte had bought it to add credence to the story. Like an expert fielder, Charlotte would intercept the glance and continue with, 'My fiancé fell in the early stages of the war.'

If the humour was on her and the audience receptive enough, Charlotte would embroider the tale to engage the listener's sympathy. It would usually go thus, 'We were to marry in spring of 1915, when he was due some leave, but he was killed (sometimes by a sniper) on Christmas Eve, only hours (or occasionally minutes) before the Christmas truce.'

None of that, as Jessica was well aware,

corresponded remotely with the truth. For one thing Jessica had been born in September of 1914, long before a spring wedding. For another, Jessica knew that her mother had no idea what had actually happened to her father. Two years earlier, on Jessica's tenth birthday, Charlotte had told her the real story. Jessica was well aware that Charlotte's husband, the man whose name Jessica bore, was not her real father. Isaac Tunnicliffe, the man Charlotte referred to disparagingly as 'the accountant', had died over a year before Jessica was conceived. Her mother told Jessica that he had died as a result of a domestic accident. She did not tell her daughter that he broke his neck falling off a ladder while spying on Charlotte disporting herself with her lover.

Instead, she told the girl as much as she knew about her real father, Jesse Barker. Jesse and his twin brother Ephraim were the younger brothers of Clarence and were both thought to have perished in the war.

'I waited for him to return, all the time I was carrying you and long afterwards. But then the war started and my hopes began to fade. He never reappeared.'

It was then that Charlotte gave Jessica the only keepsake of Jesse she possessed. It was a small studio portrait taken, as the legend on the back proclaimed, by a Viennese photographer. Jessica put the photograph in a silver frame and kept it on her bedside table. She would look at it from time to time, seeking to identify likenesses to her own appearance in the expression of the handsome young man smiling at the camera. After a time, every minute detail of his image was firmly imprinted on her brain.

What Charlotte failed to tell her daughter, for she did not know it herself, was that Jesse had been an arms dealer. It was he who supplied the weapons used by the Serbian nationalist group, the Black Hand, to assassinate the Archduke Franz Ferdinand and his wife, Duchess Sophie in Sarajevo, thus sparking off the Great War. Neither was Charlotte able to tell Jessica that Jesse Barker had spent the greater part of the war interned in a Greek prison, from which he had only been released in 1920. She was unaware of this, just as she was unaware that Jesse had spent the following three years working in Italy until he had saved enough money to afford the fare to America and provide himself with forged identity papers. During the voyage Jesse Barker, alias Jack Barlow, had made friends with several Italian men of a similar age, friends who would become useful when he landed in America.

Had the liner carrying Charlotte and Jessica Tunnicliffe docked in Chicago rather than New York, Jessica might have been given the opportunity to meet her father, although the likelihood of a twelve-year-old girl frequenting an illegal drinking establishment such as the one operated by 'Jack Barlow' was remote.

As the voyage progressed Jessica observed with quiet amusement how well her mother presented the fictitious biography. Whether those who heard it believed the tale was uncertain, but in deference to Charlotte's still glamorous looks, obvious charm and evident wealth, they did her the honour of showing a credible pretence. Her fortune was founded on the money left by 'the accountant'. During the war and afterwards, denied the company of attractive men, Charlotte had turned to investment as a hobby and an antidote to boredom. She had been lucky to begin with, then, as she learned more about the workings of the Stock Exchange and industry, she turned herself into a shrewd and skilful investor.

As the liner continued westward, the distance between Charlotte and another of Jesse Barker's former lovers increased. When Simon Jones married Naomi Fleming he was aware of her story. He knew that Joshua, Naomi's son, had been fathered by Jesse during a brief, passionate affair in Vienna during the days preceding the outbreak of war.

In those turbulent times, Naomi had been Hildegard Cabrinova-Schwarz, born half Austrian, half Serbian. As a member of the Black Hand she had been charged with liaising with the English arms dealer Jesse Barker. Taking liaison to the ultimate they had rapidly become lovers until the day Barker left for Serbia to deliver his deadly cargo. Like Charlotte, Naomi had long since decided that Jesse was dead. With the arrival of

Simon Jones in Naomi's life her interest in her former lover ceased. In the contentment of her marriage she all but forgot that Joshua was not Simon's natural son, all but forgot Jesse Barker entirely. The birth of her daughter Daisy had merely enhanced the process.

For both women the trial and conviction of Jesse's brother Clarence Barker, with the resultant publicity reawakened old memories. The difference however, was that in Naomi, it failed to awaken any sense of regret.

As the liners were in mid-ocean on their respective voyages to opposite sides of the world, two very different students were beginning to learn widely differing subjects.

In Bradford, to the pleasure of his teachers, Joshua Jones was beginning to display a remarkable flair for languages. He possessed a quick and active brain and was always anxious to learn. Joshua's headmaster authorized his teachers to further the boy's natural ability as far as the school's resources would allow. After consultation with his parents, special tutors were brought in to advance the boy's development further. Joshua could also speak, read, and write Serbo-Croat like a native. For the latter, as well as his advanced skills in German, Joshua was indebted to his mother. Naomi, relaxing her guard to aid her eldest child, allowed herself to speak both languages for the first time since before Joshua had been born.

Joshua, thirsty for knowledge, was prudent enough to forbear from asking how Naomi was familiar with these languages. He had always been dimly aware of some secret in his mother's past but had fought shy of expanding his knowledge on what he realized was a sensitive subject.

Ninety miles further east, Sonny, encouraged by Rachael, had enrolled in carpentry classes. The large stable block to the rear of the Byland Crescent house had been unused since the advent of the motor car. After investing in the Bentley, Sonny decided to have the stables converted. There was ample room for the big car and two others besides, even after which there was a considerable amount of unused space. Sonny remembered his short stint working for the cabinet maker. He converted the remainder of the stable block into a workshop. The room had several large windows and skylights in the roof, making it ideal. Once the conversion had been completed, Sonny set about acquiring the very best machinery and tools for his new hobby. The result was a workshop many a professional carpenter would have regarded with envy. Obtaining the machines was one thing, but learning to use them to the best advantage was quite another matter. That was the challenge Sonny had set himself.

CHAPTER TEN

By the time Patrick and Louise Finnegan arrived home the evidence of Louise's condition was beginning to show. Their delight at the impending happy event was able to withstand James Fisher's teasing, mostly on the beneficial effect of Yorkshire air.

Now that he knew James and Alice's story, Finnegan was even able to reply, 'Why not? After all, it worked for you two.'

'And it seems to be working for my brother as well,' James laughed. 'While you were taking a leisurely sail, we received a cable from Mother announcing the arrival of Frances Rachael.'

James and Alice were more than pleased with Finnegan's report on the progress of the merger and James in particular was delighted by Patrick's confirmation of the excellent working relationship between the three directors.

'The great thing,' Patrick told James and Alice, 'is that when I walked into the boardroom at Bradford it felt a lot like coming into your office here. The three of them haven't just built a good business understanding, it's clear they're the best of mates. The other good thing is they complement each other so well. Michael has all the skill and knowledge that comes from experience. He's a good administrator and handles people well. I tried to think up a single word to describe each of them. In Michael's case I reckon *solid* would be the right one.'

'What about my brother? James asked.

'Sonny's probably the second nicest bloke I've ever met. He's a natural salesman too, but whereas a lot of salesmen only project an image of themselves, with Sonny you know it's genuine. He's talented as well, and all the trouble he's been through has made him tougher. You've no need to worry about Sonny.'

'What word would you use to describe him?' James was eager to know.

Finnegan grinned. 'The word would be *James*. When I met him I nearly gave the game away, he's so like you. I know brothers are supposed to look alike but the resemblance is uncanny. He could be your twin. Anyway I got away with it, but more to the point, it's not merely the physical similarity. Sonny moves like you, thinks like you and has all the same mannerisms.'

James pondered this. 'Perhaps we owe more to my father than I realized. Now, what of Simon Jones?'

'A real revelation. I know we've had good reports about him, but they only scratch the surface. In some ways Simon is even more like you than

Sonny. As an accountant he's as good as you'll get, but that's just the starting point. What makes Simon special is his vision. He's capable of anticipating events rather than merely reacting to them. I asked him about the general strike that was looming when we arrived. He predicted the government would break the strike easily and the miners would be left high and dry, exactly what did happen. So then I asked him if he was worried about the growth of left-wing political power,' Finnegan paused and looked at James. 'Guess what his reply was?'

Fisher pushed his chair away from the desk, crossed his legs, and cupped his chin in his hand. Finnegan grinned broadly.

'What's so funny? James asked.

'Oh, it's just that Sonny does exactly that when he's thinking.'

James smiled ruefully. 'Going back to the question you asked, my guess would be, if Jones is all you say, that the true danger would come from the extreme right rather than the left.'

'Spot on. I know you've warned us about the danger of fascists like Mussolini and Herr Hitler, but Simon Jones is the only other man I've heard voicing those fears. That's why the word I'd use to describe him would be *visionary*.'

If James and Alice were pleased with the business report from England, they were even happier when Patrick and Louise told them of matters at Byland Crescent. They spent a long time studying the photographs sent by Hannah. The first of these, a recent shot of Sonny, emphasized Finnegan's remarks about the likeness between James and his younger brother. There was a group photograph of all those at the house, family and staff alike. Apart from Hannah and Sonny the rest were strangers to James and Alice, although a couple of the faces looked vaguely familiar. Patrick Finnegan identified them as George, the butler and Sarah.

'I remember them,' Alice said. 'George was general factotum, not the butler, when I lived there. And Sarah was a chambermaid like me, we were friends.'

Finnegan pointed to the little girl standing alongside James's nephew Mark. 'That's Jenny, the cook's daughter,' he told them. 'She and Mark are sweethearts.'

'Crikey, he's starting even younger than I did,' James exclaimed, only to endure a pummelling from a cushion wielded by Alice.

In early summer Louise Finnegan gave birth to a son, Elliot. His proud father cabled Sonny in England. 'Elliot doing fine. Plan to continue the family line.'

Within days he received a reply. 'Congratulations. If you're going to compete, suggest you start looking for bigger car soon.'

Charlotte and Jessica Tunnicliffe's return to England following their lengthy sojourn was in strikingly different weather conditions to those experienced by Patrick and Louise Finnegan. The sun shone brightly on the morning frost as they approached Southampton, reflecting gleams of sparkling light from the wake created by their mighty liner.

On reaching London they stayed for three days in the capital before catching the train north to Yorkshire. Their heavier luggage had been cared for by the porters assigned to the train, but both mother and daughter were still well laden with Christmas shopping, their personal belongings having been supplemented by the product of two days intensive shopping in and around Oxford Street.

The train was crowded even for those travelling first class and Charlotte and Jessica were obliged to share a compartment with only one occupant, a man in his late thirties or early forties to judge by his appearance. Charlotte opened the door and stepped inside. The man cast aside the newspaper he had been reading and leapt to his feet. He took the heaviest parcels from Charlotte and Jessica and stowed them safely in the overhead racks. When the process was complete Charlotte thanked the stranger. He gave a slight bow of acknowledgement and returned to his reading.

Train journeys can be fast and fun, or they can be slow and boring. Theirs fell into the latter category. Although Charlotte and Jessica had stocked up with books and magazines to while away the travelling time, the train's slow progress, punctuated it seemed, by stops at every signal and station, made concentration difficult. The ticket collector's announcement, delivered in a morose monotone, that the buffet and dining car would be unavailable did little to ease the tedium.

It was not Quentin Ivanhoe Durant's fault that his father was an aficionado of the writings of Sir Walter Scott, but Quentin Ivanhoe – he kept quiet about McGregor, his other Christian name – had to suffer the consequences of his parent's eccentricity. His nickname, from the day he started school had been 'Quid' but Quentin Ivanhoe now introduced himself as Ivo.

Ivo, having read everything of interest in the newspaper, set it aside. Glancing around the compartment his eyes met those of Charlotte. He smiled in acknowledgement to a fellow sufferer. 'An awful drag, this interminable train ride,' he said. 'Do you have far to go?'

'All the way to Yorkshire, I'm afraid,' Charlotte replied. 'How about you?'

'I am also bound for Yorkshire, so we're companions in misfortune. I'm Ivo Durant by the way.' He smiled again, a different, more intimate smile and held out his hand.

'I'm Charlotte Tunnicliffe, and this is my daughter Jessica,' Charlotte replied as she shook the extended hand.

He maintained his grip longer than might have been strictly necessary and there was marginally more pressure in the handshake than normal. Charlotte felt an old, familiar sensation.

As the train continued its stately progress north, Charlotte and Ivo exchanged biographical details. Or, to be more correct they swapped fictional accounts of their lives, these close enough to the truth to withstand all but the closest scrutiny. In Ivo's case this involved a dashing career as an officer in a county regiment (true), several decorations for gallantry (also true), and a career in insurance (almost true). He followed these with an account of a family fortune awaiting him on his father's death (untrue), added to his own wealth inherited from various other family members (definitely untrue). He also told Charlotte he was single and unattached (both slightly untrue) and that his family owned property in Yorkshire, Leicestershire, and London (most definitely untrue).

Had he told the truth, Ivo would have said that his job in insurance was a low paid clerical one and that his father would leave him only a collection of unpaid bills and a near derelict mansion in the Yorkshire Dales, secured by a crippling mortgage. Ivo could have continued by confessing that the inherited wealth had all gone to swell the bank accounts of various bookmakers, to pay for a string of mistresses and to maintain two wives, one of whom was ever so slightly bigamous. He could have added that the Leicestershire and London properties had been sold long ago to pay for his father's equally profligate lifestyle and concluded by confessing that his admittedly courageous military career had ended in a less than distinguished manner following the unsolved mystery of disappearing mess funds. All these confessions however would have necessitated Ivo telling the truth, but Ivo had long since ceased to recognize the difference between fact and fiction.

Whether Charlotte Tunnicliffe believed all that Ivo told her is open to question, but if she did recognize a lack of veracity in the tale she was clearly not about to be outdone. She embarked on the 'war hero's fiancée' story with gusto, giving it the full sympathy treatment. Ivo, as good a listener as he was a storyteller, soaked up every vestige of pathos that Charlotte could wring from the tale. Thus, in mutually agreeable conversation, they conducted a dialogue that Jessica listened to with all the amused cynicism a worldly-wise twelve-year-old could muster.

The train may not have speeded up during the latter stages of the journey, but the pair was so engrossed in conversation that it came as something of a shock when the ticket collector announced that they would shortly be arriving at Leeds City Station. Even Jessica, a mere spectator was mildly surprised by the news of their imminent arrival. As the three occupants of the compartment bustled about collecting their belongings Ivo seized the chance for a quiet aside to Charlotte. 'May I call you when you've got settled in? I've so enjoyed our conversation and I'd like to see you again.'

Once again Charlotte felt that momentary weakness, an exciting shiver. 'That would be very pleasant.'

True to his word, Ivo Durant called Charlotte a week after she and Jessica returned to Bradford. 'I'm coming to town tomorrow. Will it be in order for me to call?'

'Why not come for tea?' Charlotte replied.

The successful tea party was followed by another the next week, then a candlelit dinner. Whether maturity had bred patience or whether Ivo was biding his time, it was not until their fourth encounter that he made his move. It was late one morning and he had called on the off-chance that Charlotte would be at home. Jessica had returned to school and they had the house to themselves. Charlotte had spent most of the morning wondering what to do with the rest of the day. She was bored and restless, until Ivo turned up. She brewed a pot of tea and they sat in the sun parlour to the rear of the house. Suddenly Ivo placed his cup carefully on the saucer and stood up. Charlotte was dismayed.

'You're not going already?' she asked. 'You've only just arrived.'

'Oh no, I'm not going, or at least I hope not. I just don't want to wait any longer.'

'Wait, wait for what?' she asked innocently,

hoping Ivo hadn't noticed her voice had turned into a croak.

'Wait to take you to bed and make love to you,' Ivo told her bluntly.

He crossed the room to the sofa, pulled her to her feet, then kissed her passionately. His hand undid the button at the waistband of her skirt and the garment slipped, unnoticed to the floor.

Charlotte giggled as they walked upstairs. 'What's so funny?' Ivo asked.

'I was thinking, it's a good thing the rear of the house is private. If the neighbours had seen what we were doing in the sun porch they would probably have had heart attacks.'

Ivo smiled at the thought. 'Perhaps we should go round and check on them, make sure they're all right?'

'Oh no,' Charlotte told him emphatically. 'I've got far better plans for the afternoon.'

CHAPTER ELEVEN

In Byland Crescent, 1927 marked the beginning of a new regime for young Mark Cowgill. The illness that had imperilled his life had left long-term weaknesses. These, chiefly respiratory by nature, were identified by Doctor Culleton. Rachael talked the matter over with Sonny. 'The priority is to increase Mark's strength. He needs it to fight off infection. The only way to achieve that is through diet and exercise. I can see to the diet part, but with Billy and Frances to look after as well, I will have little time to superintend a rigorous exercise programme.'

'We could employ a nursemaid, if that would help. I have suggested it before,' Sonny offered.

Rachael cast him a withering look and ignoring his remark continued, 'The best exercise is swimming. The more Mark does, the stronger his lungs will become, and running will also be good for him.'

'It's lucky Mark is athletically inclined,' Sonny replied. 'I'll take charge of the fitness programme. If I join in it will make it more fun. It'll do me good as well.'

‘Can you afford the time?’ Rachael asked.

‘I’ll have to make time. Mark’s health is more important than work. If we get up early we can go running before breakfast then swim in the evening.’

As Sonny so accurately predicted, Mark took readily to the exercise programme. What neither of them had anticipated was the reaction of Jennifer, Mark’s friend and playmate. On the first morning, when they reached the hall before setting out on their run, Jennifer joined them. ‘Why are you up so early, Jennifer?’ a surprised Sonny asked.

‘I’d like to go too if you don’t mind, Mr Cowgill.’

Sonny eyed her slight frame. ‘Are you sure you’re up to it?’

‘Yes. If Mark can do it, so can I.’

‘Go on, Dad, let her, she’ll soon tire of it.’

After that remark, it became a matter of pride for Jennifer. She joined in every run, attended every session at the swimming baths and later, when summer came, in the outdoor pool or the sea. What is more, she did not merely join in, she competed, pushing Mark to the limit. During the school holidays, deprived of the classes Mark enjoyed at school, Jenny devised her own. She took over a series of household tasks, improvising exercises from a variety of chores such as carpet beating.

Eighteen months into the regime, neither of the young athletes showed any dimming of their enthusiasm. Even the coldest, most unpleasant weather failed to deter them. Occasionally, they even had to wake Sonny to ensure they did not miss their morning run. After one such occurrence Rachael complained wryly to Hannah, 'It's more like an athletic club than a household.'

Whatever her comments, Rachael was secretly delighted with Mark's progress. When Sonny commented, 'I don't know about the others but I'm feeling fitter than I have for years,' Rachael smiled and replied, 'I know and it shows, not only on you, but in Mark and Jennifer. Mark has grown three inches in the last year and gained over a stone in weight. That is all muscle. I tried one of the vests on him that was too big a year ago and I couldn't get it over his shoulders. So I measured him. His arms are broader than his legs were last year and his legs are very powerful. Last week I discovered him running up and down stairs. He did it ten times and at the end he was barely out of breath. He told me it was a new exercise he and Jenny had devised.'

'Don't tell me Jenny did it as well?'

'Yes and completed it,' Rachael replied. 'I admit she was panting and red-faced when she'd finished, but she was determined that if Mark could do it, so could she.'

'What's going to happen with those two?' Sonny wondered.

'Oh, they'll fall in love when the time is right. I've no doubt about that.'

'What makes you so certain?'

Rachael smiled. 'For one thing, Jenny adores Mark. Think of the way she reacted when he was ill, insisting on helping. Then there's this fitness campaign. She joined in from the start and I'm certain her motive was to encourage him. What's more she hasn't quit even now, when the regime is so much tougher. With such determination, I don't think Mark will stand a chance once she realizes what she wants.'

'But they're only ten years old,' Sonny protested.

'Yes, and they've been together since before either of them could walk. During all that time, although they may have squabbled a few times they've remained friends. Very few brothers and sisters could claim that.'

'What does Mark think about Jenny?'

Rachael grinned. 'He's never said anything but he keeps a photograph of her in his bedside drawer, where he thinks it's safe from prying eyes.'

'Would you mind, I mean the fact that Jenny is our cook's daughter?'

Rachael's smile widened. 'I think it would be the finest thing for the pair of them. What's more, so does Joyce.'

Sonny laughed aloud. 'If you two mothers have made your minds up, I don't see Mark and Jenny have any chance.'

It was a time of deep contentment in Byland Crescent. 1928 had started well, with the birth of Sonny and Rachael's second daughter who they named Elizabeth Hannah. Mark's return to health and gaining strength was further cause for rejoicing. His continuing close friendship with Jenny provided scope for much amused speculation amongst the adults, family, and staff alike. Fortunately none of the gossip reached the ears of the youngsters.

Sonny was equally pleased with the way things were progressing at work. Fisher Springs was more than holding its place as market leader, the management skills of Michael Haigh, Simon Jones, and Sonny proving pivotal to this success. They were aided in this by the performance of the chemicals subsidiary, Springs Chemical. After the merger, the company had taken the name Outlane Chemicals as it was originally part of HAC, where Charlie and Robert Binks had worked before a major row with Clarence Barker. Following which, Charlie had approached Michael Haigh, and Springs Chemicals was formed. Now Charlie ran Outlane, concentrating on the dyes produced for the textile industry, while his son Robert, head chemist, was responsible for research and development of an ever-widening range of non-textile chemicals. It was in this latter area that growth was most impressive. Simon Jones, as part of the merger exercise, had analyzed the figures and the directors studied the results with interest.

'There may come a time, when little of Outlane's

production is connected with the textile industry. Non-textile production is already a quarter of the overall total,' Sonny suggested.

'I agree,' Michael said, 'you only have to look at the forecasts produced by Charlie and Robert. Even at the most conservative estimate, we're looking for more than half of the capacity being devoted to other products within the next five years.'

'Yes, and that's now with two plants on full production, not one as in the past,' Sonny emphasized.

'So where do we see this leading?' Simon wanted to know.

Michael answered him. 'As I see it, your figures give us the opportunity to set ground rules for Outlane that will move it to another dimension. It may well be that in ten, twenty years' time, Fisher Springs will be a chemicals giant with a textile subsidiary.'

Sonny agreed. 'I can see little wrong with that. After all, if we earn a hundred pounds it doesn't matter whether it comes from chemicals or cloth. I say let's give Robert full research, development and production facilities, plus the finance to make it work. The worst thing would be to agree the expansion and have it hamstrung by lack of capital.'

'I'm rather hoping it earns more than a hundred,' Michael said gravely, 'but I take your point. What we have to decide at the outset is exactly what they need. Simon, I believe you have some more details for us.'

Simon nodded. 'Based on those figures' – he gestured to the papers in front of the directors – 'I analyzed their production needs and the research and development costs. Even taking the conservative estimates, two things became evident very quickly. One is that Outlane will have outgrown its production capability within five years. That will mean providing more premises. The other is that even with the modest forecasts Outlane will be self-financing well within the first five years, even to the extent of funding a new plant.'

'Why wait for them to get cramped?' Sonny asked. 'If we build the plant now, there should never come a time when they have to turn business away through lack of capacity.'

The decision was unanimous, the only drawback being, as Charlie Binks pointed out to Sonny, was that Robert's mother might not see her son for weeks on end. 'He already spends every hour there that he can, and more into the bargain. If I didn't work in the same building, I'm not sure I'd see much of him either. Some days he only arrives home in time to fall into bed then he's out again at the crack of dawn. Some days he doesn't come home at all.'

CHAPTER TWELVE

1928 started well for James Fisher, he had supervised the diversification of Fisher Springs into two new enterprises. He had long wanted to invest in the fledgling air travel market and alongside this he gave the go-ahead for their newspaper division to open two radio stations, the first step by Fisher Springs into the expanding communications industry. As the year progressed and the time for their annual review approached however, James became more and more concerned about the overall economic picture.

When the review was conducted, Patrick Finnegan was suffering from influenza and absent from the process for the first time in several years. When he returned to work, his first task was to read the review report James had dictated for him. It was far from being a cheerful document.

'In the short-term, there are mixed indicators from the world's economies. Although many industries have enjoyed a boom during the last few years, there are unmistakeable signs that this is slowing. Borrowing is at higher levels than ever and in many countries cost inflation is soaring. Unemployment statistics make

sombre reading and poverty is a growing threat, even to developed societies. There is an increasing level of speculation in stock markets, investment that seems out of proportion with company performances.'

If that paragraph was gloomy enough, what followed made Finnegan regret he had returned to work.

'Nor is the medium and long-term outlook any brighter. Many of the problems identified in the previous paragraph will, unless matters change radically and quickly, have serious and long-lasting effects. If, as can be judged from the indicators, the speculation bubble bursts, company failures and unemployment will surge to epidemic proportions. These in turn will lead to a period of deep recession and wholesale stagnation, the severity and duration of which are frightening to consider. Adding price inflation into the equation only serves to underline the potential for disaster awaiting the world economy.

'Turning to the political situation, the foregoing economic factors provide a backdrop for an unfolding drama that, at its worst, could be cataclysmic. Increasing unemployment and poverty will fuel discontent, giving impetus to the growing Communist movement. The unemployed feel cheated by the system that has betrayed them. Where are they to turn but to an alternative that offers security and a share in the prosperity previously enjoyed by a privileged few?

'Set against this is the increasing number of extreme right-wing governments and political parties proliferating Europe. As more of the managerial and

business classes feel threatened by Communism, it is likely that movements such as fascism will appear more appealing. That gives the potential for a violent clash between such conflicting ideologies.'

There followed over a dozen pages of statistical information used by James Fisher to arrive at these conclusions. Finnegan waded through them without finding anything that caused him to disagree with James's findings. Eventually, he turned to the conclusion.

'Fisher Springs is in an enviable position, for we are cash positive. With carefully thought out policies and rigid adherence to the guidelines we set down, we should be able to weather any difficult trading times that lie ahead. The measures outlined may seem harsh, but they are essential to the continued welfare of the group.

'The first is a policy I will refer to as the eighty-twenty rule. All sector heads are to be informed that eighty per cent of outstanding debts at any one time must be represented by no less than twenty per cent of all debtors. Alongside this will be a rigorous credit control policy. Henceforth, no new customers are to be added to the books of any Fisher Springs company without prior approval from head office. This can only be given following a stringent vetting procedure.

'Existing customers will be similarly monitored. A discount of five per cent will be available to any customer settling their account in full within thirty days. If the account remains unpaid after sixty days a surcharge of five per cent will be applied, this to increase to ten per cent if the account is still outstanding

at ninety days. At that point the customer will be sent a letter threatening legal action. At one hundred and twenty days, legal proceedings for recovery of the debt will be instigated. No deviation from the above will be allowed.

'By taking these precautions we may lose some customers and we may lose some money, but we will not lose as much money as our competitors and, in the long term, we will probably not lose as many customers. Those that remain will be the stronger more reliable ones.'

Finnegan had just finished reading the final paragraph of the report when James Fisher entered his office. He glanced at the document on Finnegan's desk. 'What do you think, Patrick?'

'Tough, very tough, but fair enough I'd say. Those that don't like it can do the other thing.'

Fisher smiled briefly. 'Well, now you've read it, let me tell you of one exception. It isn't mentioned in the report as we hadn't decided what to do about it when I dictated that. In the banking sector I want us to reduce new lending against property by half. Instead of investing in new advances I want that money to be set aside to create a reserve fund. We will use that to protect ourselves and our customers. Think of it as an insurance policy. If there should be large-scale, long-term unemployment I want our customers to be grateful they bank with us. I'd rather have them remember us in their prayers than throw bricks through our windows. I'm willing to bet a fair percentage of our home loan customers are ex-soldiers, men who fought for their country. I'm not prepared to have them face the prospect of losing their home because they can't find a job. It would be bad publicity for us and a poor reward for their sacrifice. Very few men become unemployed through choice, so let Fisher Springs be a ray of hope rather than a source of stress.'

If Patrick Finnegan required further proof of Simon Jones's talent, he would have found it had he been present at a board meeting in the UK. Following the merger, the former HAC premises at Manor Row had been converted to the group head office. All merchant operations were now conducted from WPF&D's old site.

All three directors were concerned about trading prospects. The textile industry had languished during the last decade, a situation made worse by the presence of competition from emerging cloth producers on the continent and further afield. The brightest prospects in the group's immediate future lay with the chemicals division. When the regular business of the meeting had been concluded Michael Haigh invited opinions from Sonny and Simon regarding the future direction of each sector.

'I've been examining the books of the manufacturing companies and I have to say we don't appear to be achieving the headway we hoped for. I talked to our sales people, they told me there's nothing wrong with our products or prices, but buyers are reluctant to place orders of any substance. They appear to be doing little more than replenishing stock as it is sold. Everyone's marking time, waiting for some indication of which way the market's going. The low-level of activity is reflected in raw material sales as well,' Simon told them.

'So what do we do about it?' Michael asked.

'As I see it, we must adopt a tough stance,' Simon suggested. 'I think we should adopt a similar buying policy to that of our customers.'

'I don't think we're overstocked,' Michael interjected.

'Maybe not, but there's still room for improvement. If we examine our stock turnover in detail I think we'll find certain slow-moving lines. If we are entering a recession, it makes sense to avoid having money tied up. It may be some time before the market recovers and we could finish up with wool in our warehouses that we can't shift and whose price is unrealistically high. A recession would be accompanied by a glut of wool and a drop in values and we want to be able to take full advantage of the lower prices. Then as the market picks up we'll be better placed than the opposition.'

'We've done that before,' Michael Haigh admitted.

'Another point is to do with credit control. I think we ought to weed out the slow payers, the ones we consider a dubious credit risk and reduce our liability to any one client. In a recession, liquidations and receiverships will increase dramatically. It's inevitable, but if we can avoid being on any lists of unsecured creditors, so much the better.'

'That makes sense. Perhaps we should start examining both our stock and our order book, then formulate a clear policy at next month's meeting,' Michael concluded.

In the event a letter from Patrick Finnegan received in the interim made any such discussion unnecessary. It contained precise instructions on credit control, set out in terms of stark, almost brutal reality.

On both sides of the world, Fisher Springs could only implement the new policies and see what the future would bring.

CHAPTER THIRTEEN

If 1928 started in joyful celebration for Charlotte Tunnicliffe, for her daughter Jessica, almost fourteen years old, it heralded the beginning of vague, unidentifiable discontent. Charlotte had long since given up the pretence of living apart from Ivo and he had moved into the Manningham house with the same ease that he had moved into Charlotte's bed. He was as attentive to Charlotte when they were out and about as he was industrious between the sheets. He had recently introduced her to a stockbroker friend, on whose advice Charlotte had invested an extremely large amount in an Australian gold mining company's shares. Ivo had received a large commission for the introduction, but Charlotte was unaware of the fact.

It was a momentary carelessness during the long summer holiday of 1929 that was to spark off a chain of events that was to change the lives of Charlotte, her lover Ivo, and her daughter Jessica.

To reach the stairs from her own room Jessica had to pass the door to her mother's bedroom. In their haste Charlotte and Ivo had failed to notice that the door was not closed, but had sprung slightly ajar. The sounds alerted Jessica first, not words as such, just a noise. Curiosity got the better of her and she peered through the gap between the door and its frame.

Perhaps she should have been disgusted, offended even. But Jessica was not only Charlotte's daughter – she was Jesse Barker's too. Now the fusion of their passionate natures within her was about to erupt. As she gazed into the room she could see Ivo lying on his back, his legs moving rhythmically. Charlotte sat astride him, her back to Jessica. As the young girl watched, the couple's interlinked movement increased in tempo, the sounds, in volume. There was one final violent thrusting motion, a flurry of arms and legs then Charlotte toppled to lie, gasping, alongside her lover. Jessica stared, transfixed as Ivo's naked body was revealed for the first time. As she gazed on the only too obvious manifestation of his manhood, Jessica felt a curious trembling sensation. She turned and fled down the stairs.

Had Ivo and Charlotte not consumed the better part of two bottles of wine with their meal the previous night the incident might never have occurred. Charlotte was due to visit her bank manager to review her investments and discuss any changes. The couple awoke late and in the rush to get to her appointment, Charlotte left her investment folder behind. Ivo, still in his dressing gown, remained in a corner of the kitchen reading the morning paper.

Jessica, hearing the front door slam, wandered downstairs. Assuming the house to be empty she was wearing nothing but a skimpy negligee. Sleepily, she went to the larder to pour herself a glass of milk, unaware of Ivo, seated behind the kitchen door.

Ivo was still a little drunk from the night before, drunk enough for his inhibitions to be loosened, if he possessed any inhibitions that is. He looked up from his paper. 'By God,' he thought, 'she's ready for it.' He stood up, excitement coursing through his veins at the sight of the young girl's figure outlined against the semi-transparent cotton garment. 'Jessica,' he said softly. He moved forward and as Jessica turned, his dressing gown parted slightly. Jessica's eyes widened and she felt once more that strange trembling sensation.

Charlotte had reached Queens Road when she realized she had left her folder. Going back for it would make her late, but without it the meeting was pointless. She swung her car into a side street and turned round. Reaching home, she dashed from the car into the house and straight to the kitchen. One horrified look at the scene before her told Charlotte all she needed to know and more. Without conscious thought she reached out to the draining board and picked up the carving knife used to slice the previous evening's meat.

She stepped forward, raising the knife at the same time. Over Durant's rhythmically heaving, naked shoulder, she saw the ecstasy in Jessica's eyes turn to shock and horror. Using strength she was unaware she possessed, Charlotte plunged the knife deep into her lover's back. It was the morning of Tuesday 1 October 1929, just days after Jessica's fifteenth birthday.

By late morning Charlotte was a little calmer. In the first flush of her rage, she had stabbed Ivo Durant again and again, until his lifeless form slumped to the kitchen floor, blood gushing from a dozen or more wounds. Then she had dragged Jessica, weeping and terrified for her own life, from the kitchen that had become a charnel house. Jessica had been thrust unceremoniously into her bedroom, the door locked behind her.

Charlotte had, for one demented moment wanted to kill her daughter, she was unsure what had stayed her hand. Gradually a modicum of reason returned to her disordered senses and with it came fear. Fear for the consequences of her rash act. She knew she would pay the ultimate price if her crime was discovered, knew also, that any attempt to plead provocation would result in the most unsavoury publicity. Her life would be ended and Jessica's ruined. Murder is murder, whatever the extenuating circumstances. Charlotte's only thought was how to dispose of the hideous evidence of her crime. Ivo still lay on the beautiful art deco tiled kitchen floor, as cold and lifeless as the surface beneath him.

Charlotte knew she had to be rid of the body but realized she could not achieve this on her own. She would have no option but to enlist the help of the daughter she loved and hated simultaneously. Slowly, in an almost trance-like state she climbed the stairs and unlocked Jessica's bedroom door. Jessica raised herself defensively from the bed, her tear-stained face registering renewed terror.

'It's all right,' Charlotte said coldly. 'I'm not going to hurt you, much as I want to. I need your help.'

'I'm sorry, Mother,' Jessica muttered, her voice barely above a whisper.

'Sorry isn't good enough,' Charlotte's response was flat and expressionless.

'It was him, I couldn't stop him,' Jessica snivelled.

'You didn't seem to be trying, in fact you looked to be enjoying it,' Charlotte accused her.

Jessica made no reply.

'You're going to help me. We have to get rid of him.'

Jessica's eyes widened. 'How?'

'Get dressed and I'll show you,' Charlotte ordered her.

Charlotte had been raised in Baildon and knew of a disused stone quarry high on Baildon Moors, a lonely, isolated spot, safe from prying eyes.

Charlotte described this location. Jessica listened, her attention caught despite her torment of jumbled emotions. In the end it was ridiculously easy. They rolled the corpse in his dressing gown and a sheet from the bedroom, and half carried, half dragged it to the back garden, hidden from view by the mature trees. Charlotte drove her car round the block and parked close to the gate. Together mother and daughter heaved the body into the boot, panting from a mixture of their exertions and fear of discovery.

They climbed into the car and drove the ten miles to Baildon in complete silence, made their way through the village and out onto the moors. Reaching the quarry via a bumpy ride down a long disused cart track, Charlotte stopped alongside the pit. They unloaded their cargo and took the sodden gown from around it, then rolled the corpse over the cliff edge. A second or so later they heard a thump as the body landed on the quarry floor. Jessica shivered. 'Come on,' Charlotte said. 'Let's get out of here.'

Autumn is the time of year for burning garden rubbish, so one more bonfire went unnoticed. With the aid of a jerry can filled with petrol, Charlotte destroyed every scrap of evidence of Quentin Ivanhoe McGregor Durant's presence at the house. Onto the same pyre she threw Durant's dressing gown and the bundle of cloths she had used to wash the bloodstains from the kitchen floor.

* * *

The atmosphere in the Tunnicliffe household was a curious mixture of long silences punctuated by short, mostly stilted conversations. Both Charlotte and Jessica were consumed by a variety of emotions, mostly of guilt and fear, although the terror was mixed in with a combination of love and mutual distrust. Remorse and hatred represented the extreme mood swings, resentment formed the middle ground. Charlotte doubted whether she would ever be able to enjoy a normal relationship with her daughter again. Curiously, she felt no remorse over the killing of Durant than she would have had she trodden on some loathsome insect. He had betrayed her in the most brutal and evil way possible, betrayed Jessica into the bargain, when the young girl's emotional development was at its most vulnerable.

It was in one of their less strained moments that Charlotte and Jessica held the nearest they came to a normal conversation during that time.

'The trouble is,' Charlotte said, 'you're too much like me. And your father's nature was equally passionate. With all that hot blood running through your veins it was only a matter of time before it erupted. I suppose I should have seen it coming, but no doubt that bastard recognized the signs and took his chance. Well, much good it did him.'

'I'm sorry, Mother, I couldn't stop myself, even though I knew what I was doing was wrong,' Jessica apologized for what seemed the umpteenth time.

'That is exactly what I mean. Describe what it felt like.'

'When we were doing it?' Jessica was shocked.

Charlotte nodded. Jessica gulped and said, 'Well, it was exciting, like I've never been excited before, and at the same time I felt dirty and ashamed of myself . . .' Her explanation petered out.

'Just what I thought.'

'You mean it's always like that?'

'Pretty much.'

'Then I want no more to do with it,' Jessica declared firmly.

'Oh, I'm afraid you will,' her mother said with equal certainty, 'you won't be able to help yourself.'

News of the discovery of Ivo Durant's body made headlines in the Yorkshire Post. Not that the article headed 'Naked Body Found In Quarry' conveyed much information. There was no clue as to the identity or sex of the victim, no explanation as to how they had died, or how the body came to be in the location.

Late in the afternoon of 23 October, Charlotte answered the front door of the Manningham house. The two men standing in the porch identified themselves as police officers.

'What can I do for you?' Charlotte asked, with a calmness that was wholly exterior.

'We'd like to ask you a few questions,' the elder

of the two said. 'May we come inside for a few moments?'

Charlotte let them into the hall and closed the door. She gestured for them to go through to the sitting room. They sat for a moment or two in an uncomfortable silence and then the senior officer said, 'We're making some enquiries into the disappearance of one Quentin Ivanhoe McGregor Durant. We believe you were acquainted with the man. Could you give us any clue as to his whereabouts?'

Charlotte sensed an air of unreality about the situation. The younger policeman seemed detached to the point of disinterest, leaving the questions to his colleague. The senior officer was asking questions about a disappearance, when he actually meant a murder, wanted clues as to Durant's whereabouts when all the time he knew exactly where Durant was. Nor was it only the policemen who were acting. Charlotte was equally disingenuous, pretending to a lack of knowledge about Ivo.

'Quentin Ivanhoe McGregor Durant?' she repeated, with a puzzled expression. 'Oh, you mean Ivo.' She smiled. 'I'm afraid I haven't seen him for some time.'

'I was led to believe he lived here?' the policeman asserted.

Charlotte was the picture of maidenly virtue. 'I don't know who gave you that idea. I'll admit' – she coughed, indicating a reserve regarding a delicate subject – 'that Ivo and I did have a little fling and on one or two occasions he did stay here overnight, but that was all over some time ago.'

'Could you tell us the last time you saw Mr Durant?' the officer persisted.

'I'm not sure, early summer, May or June I think.' Charlotte again smiled sweetly at the two men. 'I'm sorry to be so vague,' she apologized.

After she had closed the door behind the officers, Charlotte leaned against it for a few moments to recover her composure. Her hands were clammy, her heartbeat fast and erratic, and she was panting as if she had run a marathon. Nor would her equilibrium have been restored had she heard the conversation between the policemen as they returned to their car.

'What do you think, sir?' the junior asked.

'I think Mrs Tunnicliffe is a very intelligent woman. She is highly sexed and would remember her love life in detail for a lot longer than a few months. That vagueness was just an act. I also think she's ruthless and probably responsible for Durant's murder.'

'What makes you think that?'

The senior officer smiled. 'Use your brain,' he told his colleague. 'At the beginning of the interview I told Mrs Tunnicliffe I wanted to ask a few questions.'

'Well?' The junior officer was puzzled.

'Well,' his mentor said patiently, 'Mrs Tunnicliffe

didn't ask me what it was about – because she already knew. The problem I have is, I don't know how, when, or where she killed Durant.'

'Surely the post-mortem will tell us something?'

'I'm afraid not. When you take your family on Baildon Moor next time you have a day off, you might think you're in a lonely place, but that wild, desolate bit of countryside has more inhabitants than the average town, it's just that you can't see them. I'm talking foxes, badgers, stoats, weasels, ferrets, rats, mice and a host of other creatures, almost all of them carnivores. According to the pathologist there must have been a queue waiting to feed off Durant longer than at the Co-op when a dividend is due. He reckons if Durant hadn't been found for another week he would have been unidentifiable.'

CHAPTER FOURTEEN

Louise Finnegan was rocking the cradle in which lay her newborn son, Finlay. The doctor entered the room with Patrick and smiled as he said, 'Chickenpox, I'm afraid young Elliot will not be very comfortable, or happy, for some time; definitely chickenpox.'

Louise sighed with relief. 'We thought so, but we wanted to be absolutely sure. With a new baby in the house, I was a little worried.'

'Natural enough,' the doctor agreed, 'nevertheless, chickenpox is pretty unpleasant and highly contagious. I don't suppose Isabella has had it?'

'No,' Louise told him, 'and it's going to be next to impossible to stop her getting it within the same house. But what about the baby, will he be safe?'

'Ideally, had the baby been older, you could have shipped them both out to someone else until the infection has passed, but Finlay is far too young for that besides which, you can keep him well clear of Elliot. The only alternative is to move Isabella away. I don't suppose you know anyone who would look after her, preferably someone who's had chickenpox themselves, or who doesn't have kids?'

'Isabella's godparents have had it, their whole family got it a couple of years back,' Patrick chimed in.

'Who's that?'

'James and Alice Fisher,' Finnegan told him.

'Yes, I remember treating them. They'd be ideal if they're prepared to do it.'

Hours later it had been arranged. Neither James nor Alice hesitated for a second. 'Bring her over as soon as you like,' James told Patrick. 'Alice is already upstairs making a bed up for her.'

Thursday 24 October 1929 was just another working day. On reaching the office, Finnegan was relieved to be told by James Fisher that his daughter Isabella was well and being fussed over by all the family. 'Of course you'll have a hell of a job when you get her back. She's become accustomed to being waited on hand and foot. Dottie can't do enough for her, reading to her and calling her Bella.'

'Bella?' Finnegan asked, amused.

'Apparently, if Dorothy can be shortened to Dottie then Isabella is fine as Bella. So I have been informed.'

In England it was also a normal working day. As Michael Haigh and his co-directors supervised the running of Fisher Springs (UK), his ex-wife Charlotte Tunnicliffe and her daughter

Jessica spent the day in a state of barely controlled fear.

In America, Thursday 24 October 1929 was far from a normal working day. It began with nervousness on the part of some shareholders about the high price of stocks they believed to be overvalued. Their decision to sell spread the anxiety, and soon nervousness turned to panic as investors tried to rid themselves of shares in ever increasing numbers. As the wave of selling gathered pace, brokers were marking shares down, the more they did so the faster they plummeted. As one broker grimly observed, 'the only thing going up here is the price of chalk.'

The Wall Street Crash had begun.

By the following Tuesday, sales had reached such a level that the teleprinters jammed, unable to cope with the pace of transactions, prices sinking all the time. The panic had spread to stock markets worldwide. Fortunes were wiped out overnight, vanishing as if they had never existed.

By Wednesday 30 October, Charlotte Tunnicliffe knew she was bankrupt. Every share she owned was worthless. Even the Australian gold mining shares recommended by Durant's stockbroker friend were totally wiped out. The financial news carried by the *Yorkshire Post* that morning was bad, the headline below it infinitely worse. 'Quarry Murder: Arrest Likely Soon.'

Charlotte left her house shortly before noon and drove into Bradford. She was unable to get inside her bank for the crowd inside, spilling out onto the pavement, a mass of bewildered and desperate people. Instead Charlotte made her way up Darley Street to her solicitor's office. She spent an hour inside then returned home. She went into the sitting room and wrote three letters, sealed them inside envelopes and addressed these. When she had finished she crossed the room to the cocktail cabinet and took a glass from the shelf. It was much earlier in the day than she would normally have had a glass of whisky, but she felt the occasion warranted it.

Jessica arrived home at around six o'clock that evening, having been detained by an additional science lesson, a subject she enjoyed. Her mother's car was parked on the drive but the house was in darkness. She tried the front door and found it locked. She groped in her satchel, found her purse, removed her front door key, stepped into the hallway, and switched the light on. She looked up, her attention caught by a moving shadow. Jessica screamed, then fainted. Above the young girl's prostrate form, her mother's body hung from the banister rail, her once beautiful features distorted. The sheet she had used to hang herself wrapped around her like a shroud.

Charlotte Tunnicliffe's death, although in itself a shocking and well reported affair, was by no means as sensational as a murder trial would have proved to be.

The detective in charge of the Durant case, having heard the facts from Jessica reported them to the Public Prosecutor's Office. Charlotte's letter to the police confirmed Jessica's evidence so it was decided no further action was necessary. The inquest was held in camera, an unusual course that provoked a little speculation amongst reporters, although none of this reached the printed page.

Although Michael Haigh had not spoken to his ex-wife for nearly thirty years he soon found that her death had placed him in an awkward position. Before committing suicide, Charlotte had left letters to the police, her daughter, and her former husband. In view of the circumstances surrounding her death and the investigation into Durant's murder, these were first examined by detectives, so it was December before Michael's letter reached him. He read the content, his astonishment at the carefully phrased wording turning to dismay tinged with no little sadness.

Dear Michael,

By the time you receive this letter I shall be dead. I'm sure there must have been many times when we were married that you wished this to be so and I don't blame you for that. The point of this letter is to enlist your help. Please believe me when I say I wish I did not have to beg for it but I have no choice in the matter. If I had anyone else to turn to I would do so, but the fact is there is no one I trust as I trust you. By the way, in all I write I am including Connie for perhaps it is her help I need as much, if not more than yours.

It is not for myself you understand, for, as you will already know I have gone beyond all human help. I recognize I have been wicked and that I have committed an evil deed, so now I am paying the ultimate price for my sinfulness. It is for my daughter, Jessica, that I need your help. I will tell you why I did what I had to do, so perhaps you will not judge me too harshly and it will help you to understand Jessica.

I will not speak about Jessica's father, he disappeared from my life many years ago, and I believe he is long dead. More recently I met a man I thought I could trust but he betrayed me, in more ways than one. When I found out the full extent of his depravity I lost my head, as anyone might in such circumstances, and in the heat of my rage I killed him.

Perhaps I thought I could escape the consequences of my action, possibly I believed my wealth could protect me and buy me safety. However that too is gone, blown away by events on Black Thursday. It is ironic that part of my lover's legacy to me was a block of shares that proved totally valueless. Swift revenge indeed.

So now to the crux of the matter. Jessica has never known a father, no male to guard and guide her against other men. I'm afraid Jessica has inherited my wild, impulsive, and passionate nature and just when I hoped she would have a man she could look up to, he betrayed her as he betrayed me. Will you, Michael and Connie, take care of my poor, orphaned Jessica? It is a grave burden to lay on you, for she has seen too much, experienced things a child should not be exposed to, for her not to be damaged in more than one way.

I truly believe that if Jessica can enjoy the warmth, love, and comfort of a normal family life her own warm-hearted and generous nature will reward your generosity.

Your contrite, broken, finished,
Charlotte.

Michael Haigh passed the letter to Connie without comment. She read it and looked up, to see Michael watching her, his expression troubled. It was the look of concern that decided her.

'You'd better find out where Jessica is and we'll go for her.'

For want of guidance, the police took charge of Jessica Tunnicliffe in the first instance. She spent two days housed in a police station. Once they had taken her statement they shelved this responsibility by passing her on to an orphanage. She was, after all an orphan.

Jessica disliked being in police custody, she hated being at the orphanage even more. It should have caused her to celebrate when she was told that a guardian had been appointed for her and that she would be leaving. However Jessica was still prey to mixed emotions. Her seduction, if it could be called that, by Durant, her mother's violent reaction and Durant's murder, the disposal of the corpse, her mother's loss of fortune followed by her suicide, all combined to leave the young girl angry, hurt, bewildered, and guilty.

Two days after she had been told of her impending move, when Michael and Connie came to collect her, they found Jessica morose and silent in the bleak converted Victorian terrace house.

As they entered the building Connie's nose wrinkled in distaste. Most of the children housed there were less than ten years old, many of them with traumatic histories of violence, abuse, neglect, and various physical or mental disorders. The combined smells of stale cabbage and other cooking odours mingled with vomit, urine and worse gave both Connie and Michael a feeling of nausea they were unable to shake off until long after their departure.

They were shown into what was a grotesque misrepresentation of a parlour. Sagging chairs, their covering threadbare, were scattered in jumbled disarray. The wallpaper, stained with a myriad of irregular blotches of unidentifiable origin, hung in places from walls displaying distinct signs of damp. The curtains, if possible even more threadbare than the chairs, bore stains that could almost have been mistaken for an attempt to pattern match the wallpaper. On the floor, what remained of the carpet, more hole than carpet, had long given up the struggle to retain both colour and pattern. On two small, cheap and chipped wooden tables were overflowing ashtrays, empty beer bottles and unwashed glasses that gave a none too subtle hint as to the hobbies of the home's proprietors.

'Jessica,' Michael began gently, addressing the rigidly straight back of the girl who remained motionless, staring out of the dust-streaked window. 'Jessica,' he repeated, 'has anyone told you about us? Do you know what arrangements have been made for you?'

Jessica turned slowly and looked at them. Her very attitude conveyed hostility, suspicion, and fear. She looked, straight-faced at Michael, then, her expression unaltered, at Connie. She remained silent.

'We . . . er . . . that is, I have been appointed as your guardian,' Michael told her. 'We've come to take you away from this.' He indicated their surroundings with a gesture expressive of distaste.

Jessica transferred her gaze back to Haigh. She spoke for the first time since they had entered the room. 'Why?' she asked, her voice a dull, flat monotone.

'Because,' Michael answered slowly, careful not to use Charlotte's name, 'your mother asked me to, she wrote a letter to me before,' he hesitated momentarily, 'before she died.'

'Why?' Jessica asked again, her voice as lifeless as previously.

'Well,' Michael told her, a little more confidently, 'your mother and I were married a long time ago, but it didn't work out. She wrote to ask me, or rather us, if we would make a home for you, somewhere you would be safe and happy, and cared for.'

'Would you like to come home with us?' Connie asked.

Jessica shrugged her shoulders and turned to stare out of the grimy window once more. Michael and Connie exchanged despairing glances. On an impulse Connie crossed the room and put her arm around the young girl's shoulder. She felt Jessica stiffen for a second, then her resistance crumbled and she turned, her face ravaged with tears as she clung to Connie.

'Don't worry,' Connie whispered, 'it will be all right.'

Although Jessica was made very welcome in Baildon and was soon included in everything, and she felt, for the first time in her life, almost part of a family, there were clouds in her outlook on life that refused to go away.

The blackest of these surrounded her mother's suicide and Jessica's guilt over her part in the cause of it. Another problem she faced was at first no more than an idle thought, easily dismissed. Nevertheless as time passed the feeling recurred, that restless urge she had experienced once before. There was little doubt as to the cause of it, although even Jessica failed to realize this for a considerable time.

Michael and Connie's daughter, Marguerite, was now married and living in a cottage at the far end of the village and had offered to try and befriend Jessica if her parents thought this would help in any way. Edward, the eldest son, was twenty, three years older than his brother George, when Jessica came to live with the family. Neither of the boys had shown the slightest desire to follow their father into the textile business. Edward was an engineering apprentice and George was planning to go to university. His ambition was to join the RAF, but in time of cutbacks and talk of disarmament, this was likely to be a vain hope. The brothers, more like twins in attitude and appearance, spent much of their leisure time and a considerable part of their allowance chasing girls. The advent of a highly attractive teenage girl, one moreover rendered glamorous by her circumstances was like bringing petrol into close proximity of a naked flame. There was bound to be an explosion, it was merely a matter of time.

During the early days of his guardianship of Jessica, Michael Haigh had examined Jessica's financial situation, a depressing exercise. The Manningham house had to be sold, this going only part way to settle Charlotte Tunnicliffe's debts. In his efforts to salvage something for Jessica from the mess, Michael took Charlotte's share portfolio to a stockbroker friend. The news he received was depressing, as the broker told him that almost all the shares were utterly worthless and would always be so. Some of the companies in which Charlotte had invested, Michael was told, had already gone into liquidation, for many of the others it was merely a matter of time.

'What about those Australian gold mining shares?' Michael asked.

The broker snorted derisively. 'I reckon the best thing you could do is take the share certificates and use them as fire-lighters. It's the only way you'll get any value from them.'

Instead of taking such an extreme step, Michael had a better idea. He cabled Patrick Finnegan, requesting his advice.

Six months later Haigh received a call from the

stockbroker. The man was panting as if he'd been running. 'Did you dispose of those gold shares?' the broker asked.

'No, why?' Haigh replied.

'Thank God for that. The ticker tapes have gone wild this morning. Gold has been found on the land, lots of it. The shares were on offer yesterday at three pence with no takers, they've just gone over six pounds. How many did you say you have?'

'Well, my ward had half a million when I spoke to you but I didn't take your advice because I was told by my contact in Australia there might be a good chance of gold round there. So I bought a few more for myself,' Michael told him nonchalantly.

'In that case she's a very wealthy young woman,' the broker said. 'How many did you buy for yourself, out of interest?'

Haigh grinned into the receiver. 'Oh, another half-million,' he told the astonished expert.

The broker's professional demeanour slipped for a moment. 'Wow,' he said. Recovering slightly, he then added, 'Well, don't think of selling yet, they're bound to go much higher.'

PART TWO

1930-1934

'Behold, there come seven years of great plenty
  throughout the land of Egypt
And there shall arise after them seven years of famine
And all the plenty shall be forgotten in the land of
  Egypt
And the famine shall consume the land
And the plenty shall not be known in the land
By reason of that famine following
For it shall be very grievous.'

Genesis. Chapter 41: verses 29–31

CHAPTER FIFTEEN

Three years earlier Patrick and Louise Finnegan had built a house overlooking the river less than half a mile away from James and Alice Fisher's more palatial property. Patrick, an extremely light sleeper, was awakened shortly before 2.15 a.m. by the distant clanging of a bell. He got up and went to the window. Parting the curtains he saw a dull orange glow in the sky. He was instantly wide awake. It could only mean a fire. Then he realized where it was. 'Louise, wake up,' he screamed. 'The Fisher place is on fire.'

The mansion James and Alice Fisher had designed was built in the shape of a letter L, the purpose being to maximize the use of sunlight, a commodity in plentiful supply. There is no doubt that had the house been of a more conventional construction, the disaster would have been even more tragic. In truth it was grim enough.

The main wing, the vertical arm of the letter L, created the second storey and was occupied by James and Alice, their daughters Mary and Dottie and at that time Isabella Finnegan. In the other ground floor wing were Ellen Fisher, and her brothers Philip and Luke.

Luke Fisher was thirteen years old. He awoke a little after 2 a.m. with a feeling of unease. He smelt smoke and knew something was terribly wrong. In an instant he was out of bed, pulling on a shirt, trousers, and shoes. He stepped from his room into the corridor, the smoke was much thicker. He was coughing before he reached the next room. As soon as he shook Ellen's shoulder, she woke up. 'Get dressed,' Luke told her. 'Get out of the house. I'm going to wake Phil.'

Luke ran to his brother's room, the smoke now much thicker. He tried to rouse Phil, but to no avail. He dashed back down the corridor just as Ellen came out of her room. Together they hauled Phil with his bedding to the floor, dragged him along the corridor and out of the front door. They laid him on the lawn a safe distance from the house. Only then, when they turned to look at the building, did the full horror of the situation dawn on them. The main wing of the house was blazing fiercely. In the far distance they could hear the bell of a fire engine. Luke made his mind up instantly. 'Stay here and look after Phil,' he told Ellen, his tone one of command. 'Tell the firemen the situation, I'm going back in.'

'No,' Ellen wailed, 'you'll be killed, it's no use,' but Luke had already started running.

'I'll be OK,' he shouted over his shoulder.

For a second Ellen thought he had taken leave

of his senses as her brother had grabbed the sheet from beneath Phil and dashed, not towards the house but away from it. A few swift strides brought him to the riverbank. He dived in, immersing himself and the sheet, to emerge a second later dripping wet. Then Ellen understood.

He had barely entered the building when the fire engine arrived. As they began to deploy their equipment Ellen explained the position. At the same time Patrick Finnegan arrived, out of breath from his dash down the road.

'Isabella?' he panted. Ellen's glance towards the blazing house was enough.

Finnegan swung away to go towards the house and at that moment there came an almighty roaring sound, accompanied by the crash of falling timbers. A jagged sheet of flame leapt high into the night sky as the roof of the blazing building collapsed, imploding onto the main wing beneath. Finnegan sank to his knees in despair as his wife came running across the lawn. Shower upon shower of sparks flickered and spat menacingly around them. Louise clung to her husband, horror and grief etched in every line of her tear-stained features.

Even the movements of the firemen seemed lethargic, as if they realized the futility of their efforts. Then there was a shout from one of the officers; Ellen, Patrick, and Louise looked towards the house in disbelief.

Luke Fisher, his clothing smouldering and

ruined, presented an incongruous sight. He stood backlit by the inferno, the wet sheet draped over him, beneath which his unconscious sister Dottie was slung over his shoulder. Under his other arm, unconscious but most definitely alive, he carried Isabella Finnegan.

Patrick Finnegan spent many hours and countless sheets of paper attempting to write the letter to James's mother, but the outcome, despite his efforts seemed as brutal as his first draft.

He talked the problem over with Louise when they were alone. Their extended family now included Philip Fisher, his brother Luke and sisters Ellen and Dorothy. Fortunately, the house was large enough to cope with the influx but Patrick and Louise's private moments together were a rare and precious commodity. 'I don't know how to break the news to Hannah. 'I've put a stop on information leaking out via the company but I can't find the words to soften the blow. How do you tell a woman her son, daughter-in-law and granddaughter have been killed in that horrible fashion?'

'There's no easy way,' Louise agreed. They sat and thought it over a while, then Louise stirred. 'Why not send her the press cuttings?'

A few days after the fire one of the more enterprising journalists had interviewed a fireman who had attended the blaze. He had obtained sketchy details about Luke Fisher's rescue of his sisters, his brother, and Isabella Finnegan. The reporter talked to the townsfolk and anyone who knew the family, then visited the head office of Fisher Springs, gleaning more information with each interview. The article broke two days before the triple funeral and was repeated in every national and local paper, the headlines telling most of the facts. 'Thirteen-Year-Old Fire Hero', 'Kid of Thirteen Saves Four From Fire Hell', 'They Owe Their Lives to a Thirteen-Year-Old', and 'He Went Back into the Inferno – A Boy's Courage Saves Four', were just some of them.

'If Hannah read about Luke from us, along with what was in the papers, her grandson's bravery might help cushion the shock. We ought to tell her how much we owe Luke as well.'

'I guess you're right,' Patrick agreed thoughtfully. 'You know I'm going to have to rely on you for all sorts of advice from now on. I never realized how much James and Alice did at work. They made the business run so smoothly you never noticed the effort that went into it. I keep looking round to ask a question and there's no one there to give me answers. Now I know how lonely it is running something this big. Not only that, but the whole business world is in chaos at the moment after what happened on Wall Street.'

'You'll cope, that's why James put you in charge,' Louise told him confidently.

'I hope you're right, but it's going to take some doing. Even the way James planned for such an eventuality as this is awesome. How can I get close to that?'

'Just do your best,' Louise comforted him.

The funeral was to have been quiet, but publicity and the prominence of Fisher Springs put paid to that. The presence at the graveside of the survivors, shocked and bearing the fading yet unmistakeable evidence of their ordeal was far too newsworthy for the press to overlook. The only journalist not to cover the story was Cissie Fisher's husband; he was too close to the tragedy.

As the victims were laid to rest, Cissie, standing next to her brother Philip, held her sister Ellen's hand. On Philip's other side was Dottie. As they supported each other, brother and sisters alike weeping copiously, their brother Luke Fisher stood, alone and apart, grim-faced and dry-eyed.

Luke Fisher seemed to have undergone an instant transformation, one moment a boy, the next a young man. This attitude reflected in his demeanour at the funeral. As Louise Finnegan said to her husband, 'He knew that all eyes would be on him and he was determined not to betray the slightest emotion, anything the press could seize on. It was an amazing act of self-control, especially in one so young.'

'Would it not have been better if he had cried and got it out of his system? He must be in danger of breaking under all this pressure and publicity.'

'He did, but not in public. You were too busy after the funeral, so you didn't see Luke until much later. I noticed him slip away. He went to his room, so I left him a while, then I followed to make sure he was all right. He had been crying a little, I think, but even then he didn't let go properly, so I talked to him for a while and suddenly it was like a dam bursting. He cried and cried, which was pretty bad, but do you know the worst part?' Finnegan shook his head. 'He said he actually felt guilty he hadn't been able to rescue Mary or his mom and dad. Can you imagine that?'

'What did you say?'

'I wasn't sure at first, then I told him, from what I saw and what the firemen told us, they were probably dead before Luke woke up.'

'Well, that was true enough,' Finnegan agreed. 'The fire brigade chief said that those closest to the blaze had probably suffocated from smoke inhalation in their sleep. Did that satisfy Luke?'

'It seemed to. He cried himself to sleep and I think that did him a lot of good.'

There was a core of steel in Hannah Cowgill few would have suspected from her gentle demeanour. Even so her resolute nature was tested to the extreme by Patrick Finnegan's news. Hannah was alone in Byland Crescent when the letter, sent via Ralph French, arrived – fortunately so, as her reaction would have given away the secret she guarded so jealously.

Hannah read the letter first in the sitting room, then, to avoid the chance of discovery retired to the privacy of her own bedroom. Once behind the security of her locked door she examined Patrick's account of the tragic events more carefully. Pain invested her features as she read of the death of her son James, her daughter-in-law Alice, and her granddaughter Mary, but this eased as she read the latter part of Finnegan's narrative.

'Hannah, you must believe that even in the desperate sadness of this tragedy there is a beacon of hope. It rests fairly and squarely on the shoulders of your thirteen-year-old grandson Luke.'

Finnegan went on to describe Luke's rescue of his brother and sisters, then added: *'Louise and I owe Luke a debt of gratitude we can never repay, for his heroism resulted in the safe deliverance of not only his own brother and sisters, but also our own dear daughter Isabella.'*

Hannah's eyes, already blurred, ran freely with tears as she read Patrick's final paragraph.

'Luke is a hero throughout the length and breadth of this huge country, as you will see from the enclosed newspaper cuttings. He is held up everywhere as an example of all that is finest in Australian youth, but even the public adulation pales into insignificance compared to the feelings his family, by which I include Louise and I, hold for him.

'In his will, James entrusted the guardianship of the children to me. I would have performed this duty gladly for the sake of our friendship and the esteem I had for

James and Alice, but now I regard it as a sacred trust. Although you will grieve, as we are grieving across the world from you, you should also feel a comforting glow of pride in the courage of Luke, which is helping Cissie, Ellen, Philip, Dottie, and the rest of us to come to terms with this tragedy.

'Ralph French is writing to Connie and Michael to inform them of the tragedy, maintaining the secrecy as I am sure James would have wished.'

Although Hannah wept long for the loss, as Patrick's wife Louise had predicted, the consolation provided by Luke's heroism helped assuage this feeling. Several days later, when Hannah had recovered sufficiently to compose a letter to Patrick and Louise, she collected all the papers and photographs she had received over the years from Australia. She went to the attic and placed the bundle at the back of the parcel containing the household accounts for 1897, knowing they would be safer there than anywhere in the house. For a long time she considered destroying them, but something inside her rebelled at an act of such finality.

Under the terms of James Fisher's will, shares left in Fisher Springs and all its subsidiaries would eventually give control of the group to Philip and Luke Fisher. Their combined shareholding, eighty per cent of the issued share capital of the group would be held in trust for them until each of them turned twenty-one. The remaining twenty per cent was bequeathed to Patrick Finnegan.

In similar vein, the chief executive of each of the Australian subsidiaries received twenty per cent of their subsidiary company's shareholding for the tenure of his office only. Should any of those executives leave, retire or die, their shares would revert to the three shareholders in the parent company in ratio to their existing holdings.

This seemingly generous gesture was designed to protect the stability and continuity of the whole group. If their senior managers were given a strong enough incentive they would be less inclined to leave and with the impetus of a generous dividend, would be unstinting in their efforts to maximize profits.

As well as the trust set up for the boys, James had established similar trust funds to care for Cissie, Ellen, and Dottie. They received large sums of money, investment of which would ensure they were able to live in luxury even before they reached the age of thirty-five, when they would be handed control of the capital.

In the will James stipulated that the mansion should be kept as a family home and provision had been made for the long-term upkeep of the building. This posed a problem for the trustees, as little remained of the house but a charred, blackened shell and as there was some doubt as to whether any of the family would want to live there the trustees decided to do nothing for the time being beyond ordering the clearing of the ruin and the maintenance of the grounds.

James had appointed three trustees. Patrick Finnegan was the natural choice for one of these, James's school friend the London based solicitor Ralph French, another. Given the distance and Ralph's unfamiliarity with Australian law, his work was channelled via a local solicitor, Ralph merely holding a watching brief.

The third trustee, an equally unremarkable choice, was Louise Finnegan's uncle, Randolph Charles. Charles was the head of Fisher Springs Publications. This group subsidiary had started out as a newspaper chain, developing over the years to publication of magazines and more recently, operation of radio stations. Along with the will and trust deeds, James had left letters for each of the trustees outlining the guidelines he wished them to follow. In each of these he had stressed the need for caution, even at the expense of lower returns.

'I am firmly of the opinion that the short- and medium-term stability of the world's economies is on a knife-edge. Many institutions, including banks are at risk. Therefore, I deem it prudent to go for solid investments, well spread, in concerns and institutions you are confident can weather even the most severe trading conditions. One way of ensuring this is by investing in companies within our group. This would also increase the group's capital base. The trust deed allows for investment to bring companies within group control, via acquisition. The purpose of this is to ensure Fisher Springs can contemplate even the most

ambitious purchases without the need to resort to outside capital.'

The trustees, reading their letters of instruction, were impressed once more by James Fisher's foresight and vision. His words had been written in the middle of 1929, by winter the accuracy of his forecasts was already being dramatically underlined.

CHAPTER SIXTEEN

The headmaster looked at Simon and Naomi Jones with approval. As Joshua's parents, not only had they bred the most able pupil the school had seen, but they had willingly agreed every plan thus far put forward for their son's advancement. This, however, was going to be the biggest test of their trust in his own, slightly unorthodox approach to Joshua's education.

'Thank you for sparing the time to come to see me. I feel it is important we consider the next stage in Joshua's development carefully.' The headmaster paused and looked over his glasses at the couple, then continued, 'Joshua's fifteenth birthday is only a month away, by the time the school year ends I'm confident he will be ready for a change. He is a better than competent student in mathematics and science, in history, geography and scripture. He is also a more than adequate games player. All of these pale by comparison to his linguistic skills. So much so that I am tempted' – he smiled at Simon and Naomi – 'with your permission of course, to put Joshua forward for further education.'

'What do you have in mind?' Simon asked.

'Well, I appreciate that he is much younger than most candidates, but I believe Joshua is ready for university, to study modern and especially European languages. To be frank there is no more that his tutors can teach him in these subjects. His command of French, German, Spanish, and Italian is stunning. He is without doubt the best Latin and Greek scholar we have ever had, and both his Spanish and Italian tutors actually admitted they were now learning from Joshua. He also seems to have picked up a better than working knowledge of Serbo-Croatian, although exactly how proficient he is in that language I cannot say.' The headmaster cleared his throat in embarrassment. 'That is because we have no one competent enough to judge,' he confessed.

Naomi, who had coloured slightly at the headmaster's mention of Serbo-Croatian, burst in, 'He's far too young to go to university.'

'Yes, I agree, although Joshua is a very level-headed boy. What I wondered was, would there be any chance of Joshua being able to spend some time on the continent during the summer holidays. He needs practice to familiarize himself with the colloquial use of the languages he has only experienced in their more formal version, and he would also be able to develop a more precise accent. His German pronunciation is excellent but he needs more practice in the romance languages. If a trip could be arranged it would do Joshua the world of good. In the meantime, I could make enquiries of various contacts I have in the universities with a view to enrolling him. I appreciate that he's still young, but he's wasting time here, for we can do little more for him.'

'Are you sure they would admit Joshua at his age?' Simon persisted.

The headmaster smiled. 'With his ability I think they will enrol Joshua whenever he wants. Even on Christmas Day if necessary,' he added with a smile.

After a little further discussion Simon and Naomi left, promising the headmaster their decision when they had given the matter serious thought.

The suggestion for Josh to travel created an enormous problem for his parents. When Naomi sought refuge in Britain during 1914, following the assassination of the Archduke Franz Ferdinand, it had been as a Serb. Now Hildegard Cabrinova-Schwarz had long ceased to exist, even in Naomi's mind. Time had dulled the images of her former existence and it was only now, years later when she was considering her son's future, that the suggestion made by his headmaster brought home to Simon and Naomi an unpalatable truth.

No matter how authentic the papers Simon had obtained for Naomi seemed, they both knew these would not stand the rigorous examination associated with a passport application. Naomi would be unable to accompany Joshua on a visit to the continent. Britain, a safe haven in Naomi's hour of need, had become her prison.

It was Simon who came up with a solution of sorts. 'We dare not risk trying to get you a passport, that's obvious. Neither can we let Josh go alone, he's far too young. So, we're faced with two choices. Either I take Josh, or he doesn't go at all.'

'I know,' Naomi almost wailed, 'and I feel awful. I've let you down and I've let Josh down too.'

'Don't talk daft,' Simon consoled her. They had put the younger children to bed and Josh was in his room using his Christmas present, a radio set.

'Can you afford the time off?' Naomi asked. 'You've so much to do nowadays, with the merger and everything.'

Simon grinned. 'The merger and all that goes with it is the reason I can get time off, if Michael and Sonny agree. I didn't take any holiday last year or the year before, so now the dust has settled I can claim an extended break.'

'What about your work?' Naomi persisted.

'If we go during July and August, when trade is quietest, I don't think they'll miss me for six weeks or so. Remember, that's when wakes weeks fall.'

'What are they?' Naomi had heard the expression but didn't know its meaning.

'It's when all the mills close down. As the workers are on holiday and their families too, whole towns shut down. Each town has its own annual wakes week, during July and August.'

'Why then?'

'Well, if you asked the mill owners, they'd probably say it was so their workers could be on holiday during the best weather, but it's more probably because the heat at that time of year dries the air, to such an extent that yarn snaps too easily during spinning and weaving.'

Three days later Simon was able to tell Naomi the problem had been resolved. Sonny and Michael had raised no objections. Neither, when Finnegan had cabled from Australia, had he been any less cooperative. Simon showed the telegram to Naomi. It contained just four letters. 'H.A.G.T.,' she read, with an enquiring glance at her husband.

'Have a good time,' Simon laughed.

Setting out on a European holiday was a complex business requiring a high degree of organization and planning. Simon Jones was an exceptionally good organizer. He was also fortunate enough to have the resources of Fisher Springs at his disposal. When he and Joshua set out during the third week of July, amongst the tickets, travel documents, passports and currency, Simon had a list of Fisher Springs's agents in each of the countries they were to visit.

Despite assurances from Sonny and Michael, Simon experienced considerable misgivings at the length of time he would be away. 'I'll be phoning

Naomi every week,' he told them, 'if anything happens, be sure to let her know and I'll come straight back.'

'Listen to him, thinks he's indispensable,' Michael told Sonny.

'Everything will probably run a lot smoother without him,' Sonny agreed.

'Won't even notice he's gone,' Michael suggested.

'Oh, we will,' Sonny contradicted. 'We'll be able to get through a day's work uninterrupted.'

'OK, OK, I get the point,' Simon laughed, 'but if there is a crisis, my place is here.'

'Yes, well, if all the mills burn down and the chemical plant blows up and wool prices plummet to zero, we'll think about phoning Naomi,' Michael told him. 'Otherwise you're to do as Patrick Finnegan said and have a good time.'

Simon and Joshua's departure was a tearfully emotional one. Although the travellers had the excitement of the journey ahead to support them during the separation, for Naomi it was a daunting prospect. Although the parting didn't reawaken her earlier fear, it was the first time since their marriage that she had been separated from Simon, the first time in his life she had been away from Joshua. It was fortunate that Naomi would have little opportunity to mope during their absence. Looking after the house and caring for Joshua's younger siblings was more than a full-time occupation.

When the travellers returned, six weeks later, it was with a fund of memories, most of them good, a few sinister. As Joshua was immersing himself in his first paid employment, a temporary stint as office junior, at the other extreme of the chain of command, Simon was enlightening his fellow directors as to the countries they had visited.

'Spain is a mess, both politically and economically. The country's torn between fascism and communism and now there's no monarch to give guidance it's turning into a free-for-all to grab power. France is in a strange mood. I was struck by the difference between France and Germany. If I didn't know better, I'd have said that Germany had won the war and France lost it. In Germany everyone has an air of confidence amounting almost to arrogance. I know the Reichstag is a coalition but everyone knows who's running the show, even though they banned the leader from being chancellor because he's Austrian.'

'What do you think of him?' Sonny asked.

'Hitler? He's a funny little man with a Charlie Chaplain moustache and a love of the sound of his own voice. We were in Berlin when he was holding a rally, so we went along out of curiosity. Josh was able to translate some small part of it for me while we were there.'

'What was it like?' Michael prompted him.

'At first you didn't think much of it,' Simon replied. 'It was only later, thinking about what you'd seen and heard that it seemed almost frightening. There were hundreds of people, all absolutely silent until Hitler appeared flanked by his henchmen. It was all carefully stage managed, but as soon as he started to speak, everyone listened. It was a long, rambling diatribe, hectoring the audience and telling them of his ambitions to rid Germany of undesirables. As far as I remember he went on about Jews, blaming them for everything that was bad in Germany, losing the war, unemployment, inflation the lot. Then he said he wanted to cleanse the nation and build a new Germany that would last for a thousand years.'

'How was it received?' Sonny wanted to know.

'That's when it got really terrifying. The crowd went wild, cheering, giving these stiff arm salutes and chanting slogans. I admit I was scared, glad to get away.'

'Is there a lot of support for them?' Michael asked.

'To be honest, I think many Germans are ready to listen to anyone prepared to offer them a better deal. They've had the shame of defeat, a string of corrupt or ineffectual governments, dreadful poverty, massive unemployment, inflation, devaluation, and they're sick of it. This lot come along promising full employment, an end to poverty and restoration of German pride, so they're picking up support all the time. What the average German doesn't see, perhaps doesn't want to see, is the dark side.'

‘What do you mean?’ Sonny was listening carefully.

‘Well, most of it is whispered, but if you look carefully you can see the signs. Once or twice I heard gossip about what happened to anyone who tried to stand up to them. The favourite expression was accident prone, which I think is a euphemism for getting beaten-up, or worse. They have a load of party activists, thugs and gangsters by the look of them. One glance at them and you know there’s very little they’re not capable of. Even in public, if there are two or three of them walking towards you, you step well aside. Either that or risk a beating for your trouble.’

‘Sound’s delightful,’ Sonny commented. ‘I’m glad I’m not going to Germany on holiday.’

‘Don’t book for Italy then,’ Simon told him.

‘Is it as bad there?’ Michael was shocked.

‘Pretty much,’ Simon confirmed. ‘In fact it’s worse if anything. The Italian fascists have been in full control for a while, so there’s no check on Mussolini’s bully boys,’ he grinned at the others. ‘The consolation is the wine and the weather is much better in Italy,’ he paused, ‘and the food.’

‘Speaking of jaunts,’ Sonny turned to Haigh, ‘now that the wanderer has returned, are you OK for the annual picnic next Sunday?’

‘I see no reason why not,’ Michael smiled. ‘We might even let our nomadic friend come along.’

Sonny had introduced the picnic several years

earlier. The venue was always the same, on the top of Sutton Bank, where, if the weather was clear enough, they could see across the Vale of York and across the dales towards the distant Pennines. Before settling down to the huge variety of food supplied by the ladies, they paid their annual visit to the nearby ruins of Byland Abbey. For Sonny it was almost a pilgrimage, and he would often recount the story of how painting the abbey from his fractured memory had brought him back to England, brought him back from the dreadful confusion of the shellshock he had suffered towards the end of the Great War.

By spring of 1934 many of the fears expressed by Simon Jones, and previously by James Fisher, were beginning to become grim realities. In economic terms, America displayed the worst symptoms of a worldwide malaise. Over six thousand banks in the United States alone had closed their doors, never to re-open. Unemployment had leapt from less than four million to a staggering sixteen million. Car sales, the new barometer of the nation's prosperity had dropped to below one fifth of their level before the Wall Street Crash of 1929. On the New York Stock Exchange the Dow Jones Industrial Average had plummeted to a record low of 41.22 points and sullenly refused to climb much above that. With the National Debt rising to over twenty-two million dollars the American government had been forced to follow Britain by abandoning the Gold Standard.

Even the newly elected President Roosevelt's 'New Deal' was as yet making little impact. Beset by their domestic problems, Americans became more isolationist, an ominously dangerous policy as political strife worsened across the globe.

In the four years leading up to 1934, one king in Yugoslavia, and four presidents, two in Japan and one in both France and Peru, had been assassinated. Austrian Nazis had murdered Chancellor Dollfuss. Fascists had gained or seized power in Austria, Brazil, Bulgaria, El Salvador, Germany, and Portugal. While in Russia the communist dictator Josef Stalin had begun a 'cleansing' operation within the Communist Party and beyond that would cost millions of lives.

Yet more sinister events were being conducted under a cloak of secrecy. As the Nazis swept to power in Germany one of their first acts was the construction of a camp, the very name of which was to symbolise evil. The building of Dachau, had it become common knowledge, might have awakened some to the true, bestial nature of this new tyranny. Germany, although expressly forbidden by the Treaty of Versailles, had already begun a surreptitious programme of rearmament while at the same time many young Germans took up the recent and ever more popular weekend pastime of flying. This became possible owing to the establishment of a large number of flying clubs, a by-product of which was to give Germany a large number of highly trained and skilful pilots.

In England meanwhile, the National Coalition government, putting its faith in the near moribund League of Nations, preached disarmament to an ever-decreasing number of international listeners. Disarmament, they argued, was the noble ideal each nation should strive towards. It failed to recognize, despite dire warnings from Churchill and others, that elsewhere potential enemies were rearming faster than Britain was reducing its support and funding for its armed services. Even the sinister withdrawal of Germany and Japan from the League of Nations failed to ring alarm bells.

CHAPTER SEVENTEEN

In the Baildon home of Michael and Connie Haigh, a confrontation between Connie, her two sons, and Jessica Tunnicliffe took the form of several encounters, painful for each of the participants.

The trouble was sparked during the summer of 1933 and the aftershocks rumbled on throughout the following winter. It began one Friday in early August. Connie had set off for Ilkley to do some shopping. The shopping was pretty much an excuse to use the car Michael had given her as a birthday present. Connie lost very few opportunities to show off her new toy, although she was as yet far from experienced in handling the machine. She told George and Jessica she would be gone all afternoon. She turned away as she spoke, so failed to notice the glance they exchanged.

So intent was Connie on her expedition that she forgot the cautionary words Michael had uttered when he handed her the car keys. It was only when she had travelled a couple of miles and after the car spluttered to a halt in a deserted part of Baildon Moor, refusing sullenly to restart, that his words came back to her, 'Always check your gauges before you set off'. Like most novice drivers at one time or another, Connie had run out of petrol.

Worse was to follow, for, as Connie rummaged unsuccessfully in the boot, she remembered that Edward had used the petrol can to fill the tank on his motor bike. In doing so he had failed to replace it. Connie had no alternative but to return home on foot. At least when she got home she could send George with a can to retrieve the car.

It was an extremely warm, humid afternoon. By the time Connie reached home, she was both hot and cross. Most of her anger was directed at herself, but she reserved some of it for Edward's thoughtlessness. There was no sign of life on the ground floor so Connie dashed upstairs, assuming, quite correctly, that George was in his bedroom. He was, but, as Connie saw only too plainly when she opened his door, not alone.

There was absolutely no mistaking what the couple were doing. There was equally no doubt that they had both entered the transaction willingly, eagerly even, and were determined to extract every ounce of pleasure from it. Connie had spent a frustrating couple of hours. Her planned jaunt to Ilkley was in ruins, she was hot, tired, and grubby. In an instant she was also furious.

She took one swift stride into the room and shoved her son with enough force to dislodge him from the lodger. As he stumbled naked from the bed Connie dealt him two resounding slaps across the cheeks of his face, although his other pair would have made an easier target in the circumstances.

'Get dressed and come downstairs,' Connie screamed at him. Before marching from the room, she rounded on Jessica. 'As for you, you trollop, I'll deal with you later.'

'The problem,' as Michael told Connie when she phoned him, 'is that neither of them is a child anymore. George is twenty-one, an adult, and Jessica is over the age of consent.'

'Does that mean I can kick them out of this house?' Connie demanded.

'Yes,' Michael replied calmly, 'but you're not going to.'

'Why not?' Connie was still furious.

'Because, whatever he's done, George is our son. And whatever she's done, we promised to protect and care for Jessica when I became her guardian.'

'So that means I can't kick Edward out either?' If Connie's rage had diminished it was not noticeable.

'Whatever for?'

'Because when I was giving George a piece of my mind he won't forget for many a day, he turned sulky on me and muttered something about Edward getting away with it. I asked him what he meant and he said Edward had been there first.

Just like that, calmly, as if they were in some sort of competition,' Connie wailed.

'So what did you say to him?' Michael asked calmly.

'That's the worst part. I was all prepared to blame Jessica, after all Charlotte as good as warned us something like this might happen, but when I told George it was lucky neither he nor Edward had got Jessica in trouble, do you know what he said?'

'Tell me,' Michael prompted.

'He told me they'd taken precautions. He said the pair of them always carry something, in case they get lucky. Michael, what sort of monsters have we bred?'

It was fortunate the conversation was by telephone, as Connie was unable to see the grin on her husband's face. 'Not monsters, dear,' he soothed her, 'just normal, healthy young men, acting as young men always have and always will.'

'We never used to behave like that.' Connie had descended from the summit of her rage and was more inclined to tearfulness.

'Only because we didn't get chance,' Michael pointed out.

'Michael!' Connie protested, outraged.

'Oh, come off it, Connie, don't pretend we wouldn't have – given the opportunity,' Michael suggested.

'But we were in love,' Connie maintained.

'Love, lust, sometimes it's difficult to draw the line between them,' Michael consoled her.

A few minutes later, after promising Connie he would read the riot act to all three miscreants and to warn them about their future conduct, Michael put the phone down. 'The lucky young dogs,' he muttered, forgetting he was not alone in the office.

'Problem?' Sonny asked.

Michael explained. It was possibly fortunate that no word of their subsequent conversation ever reached Connie – or Rachael, for that matter.

When the dust settled there remained an atmosphere of tension in the house. Jessica suggested it would be better if she left and with a little reluctance, Michael and Connie agreed. In the long run it was decided they should help Jessica find a flat of her own. A suitable apartment was found near Manningham, into which Jessica moved in early 1934. Connie in particular was relieved when Jessica left. No doubt she thought the removal of temptation would cause her sons to forget her. Michael tactfully refrained from pointing out that the flat was within easy reach of Baildon, should either Edward or George have the inclination to make the journey.

If Michael and Connie Haigh had hoped that separation from their sons would lead to a quietening in Jessica Tunnicliffe's conduct, this was not to be the case. Admittedly, for the first time in her life Jessica had to fend for herself, but Charlotte had taught her daughter the rudiments of house-keeping and Jessica soon learned to cope. Her wealth helped, for what she was unable or unwilling to do for herself, she was quite able to pay others to perform.

It may have been from loneliness, or the wayward streak in her character, but Jessica soon became involved with others of a similarly wild nature. She indulged those urges with several passionate but short-lived liaisons. If she craved affection from these affairs it was not apparent, as she was prepared to cast lovers aside with the same eager enthusiasm that she had shown in taking them to her bed. All that was to change however, when Jessica Tunnicliffe fell in love for the first time. She was twenty years old.

It was a few months earlier, in the spring of 1934, that Mark Cowgill and Jenny Holgate realized what every other member of the Byland Crescent household had known for years. Perhaps they themselves had been aware of it but neither had been prepared to recognize it. If the discovery of their true feelings for one another did not come by accident, then it was certainly casual enough in origin. Since the age of thirteen, both had been much taken with the latest craze for moving and talking pictures. Their age had prevented them from attending picture houses alone, but there was never a shortage of adults in Byland Crescent to accompany them. If neither Sonny or Rachael nor Jenny's mother Joyce were available, Hannah was usually willing to deputise. Together the youngsters thrilled to films such as, *Hells Angels, Little Caesar, Anna Christie,* and *The Big Trail.* Later, once the distribution network managed to get them to Scarborough, they laughed at the antics of the Marx Brothers and Charlie Chaplain. Although they were strictly forbidden by their age from some of the gorier productions, the owners of various picture houses in Scarborough were more interested in their takings than adherence to the dictates of the British Board of Film Censors. Thus the youngsters sat in the plush seats of the cinema on Aberdeen Walk, or more correctly on the edge of them, terrorised along with the rest of the audience. This would have provoked a parental ban had either Mark or Jenny been careless enough to own up to their subsequent nightmares.

During one such film Jenny had clutched at Mark's hand for comfort. He held it tight, possibly needing the reassurance as much as his young friend. When the climactic scene ended, Mark allowed Jenny to continue holding his hand, for who knew when the next shocking scene would erupt onto the large screen. After a while, somewhat to his surprise, Mark realized he quite enjoyed the contact. In one of the film's few quiet moments he stole a glance at his companion. Jenny, conscious of his gaze, turned and smiled at him. He squeezed her hand gently, feeling the instant response.

Their adult companion Joyce, oblivious of her daughter's conduct, stared transfixed at the screen.

Now they had long been allowed to go to the cinema on their own. On this particular evening they had been to see Bette Davis in *Of Human Bondage*. If it was not exactly Mark's style of film, he had gone along dutifully, much as Jenny had accompanied him to watch Robert Donat's portrayal of *The Count of Monte Cristo*.

As always, once the lights dimmed and the projectionist set the first reel spinning, the young couple held hands. For some reason, that night the sensation felt a little different, or so Mark thought. Not uncomfortable or awkward, just different. They maintained this contact even after they left the picture house, for the streets of Scarborough at that time of night were only sparsely populated and far from being well lit, except for small oases of sound and light that marked the location of a public house.

As they walked up Falsgrave Road they discussed the film they had just seen, then Mark mentioned a subject they both knew of, but had avoided broaching. 'You know my parents are thinking of sending me to university next year?' he asked.

'Yes, I do,' Jenny replied a little sadly.

'I feel very strange about it. Part of me wants to go, but part of me doesn't.'

'You don't want to leave Byland Crescent?' Jenny asked, her voice flat and expressionless.

They had turned off Falsgrave Road, away from the main road there was even less illumination from the gas lamps. Mark stopped and turned to face Jenny, still holding her hand. 'No, Jenny,' he told the girl gently, 'it's you I don't want to leave, not Byland Crescent.'

'Me?' Jenny said in surprise.

'You,' Mark reiterated firmly. 'I didn't realize until now, but the part of me that was reluctant to go away, that was making me feel miserable, was because I'd be separated from you. Jenny, if I do go to university, will you wait for me?'

Jenny felt a great surge of happiness. 'Yes, Mark. Of course I'll wait for you.'

It was only then, awkwardly at first but with increasing confidence, that he kissed her.

He held her gently in his arms and explained that now that they had admitted their true feelings, they had no reason to hide them from others.

'I'm not sure that's wise,' Jenny said doubtfully.

'I don't care if it's wise or not. I want everyone to know.'

'Yes, Mark,' Jenny replied submissively, yet secretly pleased.

As they did every morning, the couple met in the hall prior to leaving Byland Crescent for their respective schools. Unaware that Mark's mother was coming downstairs Mark kissed Jenny on the cheek and then the pair left, hand in hand.

Rachael stared after the youngsters. Then, with

a broad smile on her face she negotiated the remaining steps and hurried towards the kitchen to impart the exciting news to Jenny's mother.

That evening, Mark strode off, again hand in hand with Jenny, now his official girlfriend, to walk along the foreshore. Sonny watched the young couple with an indulgent smile. 'That shows no sign of abating,' he remarked to Rachael.

'Nor do I expect it to,' she told him.

'Why are you so certain?'

'Oh, the fact that they've known each other all their lives, been together constantly, never had a row, barely an argument. A lot of marriages these days don't last as long as their friendship has. They've been in love most of their lives, the only thing is they've only just realized it. There's no chance they'll find out the person they're with is different to their expectations, for they know all there is to know about one another.'

'Do you think they're . . .?' Sonny didn't quite know how to phrase the question.

'Not yet,' Rachael interpreted it. 'I'll know the minute they do, but they've both been well brought up so perhaps they'll wait. It's just a matter of whether they can keep a lid on their feelings or not.'

'Would you mind? Would Joyce mind?' Sonny was concerned for Jenny's mother.

'Not really, despite what we might say to them, because there's precious little we can do about it. We approve of them being together, so why grumble if they become lovers. Things are so different nowadays. I don't think they'll go that far and their biggest test is to come next year, when Mark goes to university and Jenny to teacher training college. That is the one thing they've never experienced, separation. If they come through that as strong as ever, then they'll be together for a lifetime.'

CHAPTER EIGHTEEN

Even in the more competitive environment of a great university, Joshua Jones's outstanding ability gave him celebrity status. Once he was granted the facilities for more advanced study under learned tutors, his progress was remarkable. Within twelve months he had been marked down as the most gifted language student within a generation. As one of his tutors commented to the Dean, 'Once in a lifetime one gets the privilege of being able to teach a pupil whose talents are akin to genius. It's a little like operating a clockwork train. All you do is wind it up, put it on the right track then sit back and watch.'

The Dean's interest in Josh's progress was motivated by more than a normal desire to see his students perform well. Head-hunters have always trawled university campuses to avail themselves of the brightest talents. Many of the best scientists have been recruited by their future employers while still undergraduates. Very little of the process takes place in the broad light of day, some of it is cloaked in the utmost secrecy. Certain organizations, government departments principally, have a vested interest in keeping their activities well away from the curious eyes of onlookers. It was to the head of one such department that the Dean wrote on the subject of Joshua.

Edrith Pointon was in his mid-thirties. He was well known in London society, although few of his contemporaries could, if asked, have told an enquirer much about him, other than that he worked for the civil service. The term civil service in itself conveys little information, being a generic term covering a vast range of activities. To most, it conjures up a vision of dull, boring, office jobs, carried out as a necessary adjunct to government. In general, this may be true, but certain parts contain departments whose employees' daily routine is far from dull or boring. Edrith belonged to one such, in fact he headed it. Such was the nature of British politics at the time that it was a very small, badly funded department.

Having studied the dean's letter, Pointon summoned one of his assistants, a man who had been in the department since it was founded over twenty years earlier. 'I want you to find out all you can about this young man.' He passed the dean's letter to the assistant. 'The usual thing, background, political affiliations if any, parentage, and all you can discover about his parents' past history.'

'Is it a rush job?' the assistant enquired, 'because that would be difficult, the way things are for staff.'

'Hardly,' Pointon replied dryly. 'We've got over eighteen months before he leaves university, so even with our limited resources there should be time enough for a thorough check to be carried out.'

It was as well there was no need for haste for it was over six months before the assistant was able to give a preliminary report. 'Sir, you remember asking me to find out about the language student, Joshua Jones?'

'Gosh, that was a while back, I'd almost forgotten about it,' Pointon replied. 'Well, what's the news?'

'To be honest I'm not really sure. I've come up against a real mystery.'

The unexpected response caught Edrith's attention. 'What sort of a mystery?'

'Well, it all seemed straightforward enough to begin with. The boy comes from Bradford, in Yorkshire, as does his father. The father, Simon Jones, is a director of a major textile group. I've a copy of his parents' marriage certificate here.' He passed the document to Pointon. 'The mother, Naomi Jones, nee Fleming was married previously and widowed during the war.'

'So what's the problem?'

'When they give details for a second marriage, the party who has been married previously has to give those earlier details. So Naomi Fleming said that her maiden name was Naomi Crawley, her first husband Harold Fleming, her father

Richard Crawley a lithographic printer, her mother Suzanne Crawley, nee Batty.'

'Well, that seems straightforward enough surely?' Pointon was puzzled.

'It would be, sir, except for one little detail.'

'What detail is that?' Edrith was too curious to be patient.

'The fact that none of these people exist. In fact they never existed.'

'What?' Pointon was incredulous.

'Neither Naomi Fleming, nee Crawley, her so called husband Harold Fleming, her father Richard Crawley of her mother Suzanne Crawley nee Batty ever existed. They were neither born, married or died. Not only that, but there's cne other thing.'

Pointon was still staring at the page before him, trying to make sense of what he had heard. 'Go on,' he grunted.

'There's also no birth certificate registering the birth of Joshua Jones, or Joshua Fleming either.'

'So who the hell are they?' Pointon asked.

'I've no idea, sir.'

'Well, we have to find out. There's a puzzle here must be solved before we dare think of an approach to young Jones. I think you'd better go to Bradford and do some on the spot investigating. I'd give it to Special Branch but they're worse off than us for man-power, besides which I don't want the local plods getting wind of our interest.'

Pointon's assistant was away for over a month.

On his return, instead of reporting immediately to Edrith, the man spent several days searching through old, dusty files in the storeroom of their offices. When he eventually confronted his superior, he had a great deal of additional information to impart.

'I traced Naomi Fleming back as far as 1914,' he began. 'Before that there was absolutely no sign of her. She appeared as if from nowhere and rented a tiny cottage, a hovel in a back street near the centre of Bradford. She was very poor, took in sewing to earn a few coppers. After the boy was born early in 1915, she went to work in a textile mill nearby, farming the baby out to neighbours. Getting the information wasn't the difficult part as everyone I talked to wanted to gossip, the problem was getting them to stick to the subject. I talked to neighbours, workers at the mill, the overlooker, that's a sort of foreman, and the mill manager and finally to the owner of the dress shop where she worked before her marriage. One or two of them reckoned she wasn't English, despite her name. Her story was that she'd been brought up in Australia but the shopkeeper reckoned her accent was more European in origin. Nobody was too curious at the time as they were desperate for labour, with the war and all. It was when I was talking to one of the women at the mill that I got really lucky. She told me there had been a visit to the mill from some local dignitary, encouraging the war effort. She had been photographed along with Naomi shaking hands with the visitor. The photo had been taken for publicity and what's more she had a copy of it.' He took a sheet of paper from the file and passed it across the desk to Pointon. 'That,' he added, pointing at one of the figures in the photo, 'was Naomi Fleming in 1916.'

Edrith stared at the photograph for a long time. 'When was it in 1914,' he murmured, 'that Naomi Fleming appeared in Bradford?'

His assistant grinned. 'I got lucky again,' he told Pointon, 'I got talking to her next-door neighbour, a real gossipy old soul. She told me Naomi took possession of the cottage on 25 August.'

Edrith looked up in surprise. 'How the hell does she know that?'

'Because it's the date of the old dear's son's birthday. She also told me Naomi was already pregnant when she arrived, also that she was terrified of something. The neighbour went round a couple of days after Naomi moved in. She knocked on the door, but there was no reply, even though she knew Naomi was inside. She was walking back to her own house when she spotted Naomi through the window, cowering in the corner of the downstairs room. The old dear said Naomi was white-faced and shivering with fear.'

'So,' Pointon summed up, 'we have a mystery woman, possibly European, turning up in 1914, just as war is starting, out of the blue, pregnant and terrified. Terrified of what, I wonder?'

His assistant grinned. 'I think I can tell you,' he stated confidently.

'You know what she was frightened of?' Edrith said incredulously. 'How on earth do you know that?'

'Not only do I know what she was frightened of, I know who the mysterious Naomi Fleming really is.' The assistant was clearly enjoying himself.

'OK, explain.' Pointon was becoming impatient.

'Well, a lot of it is down to pure luck or coincidence, if you prefer it. I started in the department in 1913, when we were becoming very concerned about events in Europe, rightly so as things turned out. We had an exceedingly good network in all the European capitals, men placed in our embassies with instructions to report anything and everything that might be useful. I was responsible for collating the reports. Our man in Vienna was particularly diligent and this' – the assistant delved into his file once more and extracted another sheet of paper – 'is a report I dug out of the archives, one that he wrote at the end of July 1914, just before we declared war.'

Pointon read the document with interest. It contained details of suspected members of the Black Hand, the terrorist group responsible for the murder of the Archduke Franz Ferdinand. Edrith's assistant directed his attention to one of the names on the list, the only female. 'Hildegard Cabrinova-Schwarz, approximately five-feet six inches tall, blonde hair, blue eyes, exceptionally good-looking. Believed to be responsible for obtaining the munitions used in the archduke's assassination. Speaks most European languages well, fluent in French, German, Serbo-Croatian and English.'

'That's still not conclusive,' Pointon suggested.

'Turn over the page,' his assistant directed.

'Austrian secret police,' Pointon read, 'arrested and detained a printer connected to the Black Hand. Their search of his workshop yielded draft copies of false identity papers he had prepared for members of the gang.'

Towards the bottom of the list one name leapt off the page at Pointon. 'Mrs Naomi Fleming,' he read. 'Got you,' Edrith breathed. 'No wonder you were terrified.'

CHAPTER NINETEEN

The prosperity enjoyed by Simon Jones and his family enabled them to indulge themselves in the matter of holidays. Each summer the family spent the long break between school terms at the seaside. Although they had travelled west to Morecambe on a couple of occasions, by far the most popular venue was Scarborough. Every year the family travelled across during the middle of July, staying in the comfort of the guest house at the opposite end of Byland Crescent to the Cowgill's home. When Simon settled their bill at the beginning of September, he made a reservation for the same weeks the following year.

In those seemingly endless hot and sunny summer weeks, the family sampled the many delights the resort had to offer. By far the most enjoyable of these were the days spent on the beach. Augmented by Rachael Cowgill and her children, many happy hours were spent on the wide, flat expanse of sand in the South Bay.

Billy Cowgill was already developing into a fine cricketer. A naturally talented batsman, he threatened to outachieve both his bother Mark and their father, whose run scoring achievements of previous times were still legendary in the area. Billy had an extra talent to the other members of his family. As he grew in stature and his fingers, long and slender, were able to grip the seam of a cricket ball easily, he showed a burgeoning talent as a spin bowler.

The family were often challenged by visiting groups from amongst those categorized by Scarborough landladies as ‘comforters’. This nickname was kept for visitors from the West Riding of Yorkshire, who, when asked how long they intended to stay, would often reply, ‘We’ve come for t’ week.’

Other family outings, to quieter resorts such as Whitby, Robin Hood’s Bay, Sandsend, and Runswick Bay, were reserved for the weekend, when Simon would be on hand to accompany them. During the week, he, in company with his cousin and co-director Sonny, travelled daily to and from Bradford on the residents’ train, nicknamed ‘the resi’.

In the summer of 1934 the family contingent was depleted by one, Josh having elected to remain in Bradford. He had completed his finals year at university but was considering the option of returning for a post-graduate course. A doctorate in modern languages, his tutors told him, was all but there for the taking.

‘I want time to think it over,’ Josh told Simon

and Naomi, 'besides which I think I'm past the age of building sandcastles.'

'What you really mean,' Simon teased him, 'is that you don't want to spend all summer bowling on south beach only to be hit all over the place by your cousins.'

Josh grinned. 'There is that,' he acknowledged. 'They're far too good. Mark is an excellent cricketer, but Billy is even better. He's a natural. The way he's developing he'll finish up playing for Yorkshire, even England.'

'Did you know Sonny was offered the chance to play county cricket before the war?' Simon asked him.

'Really? Now I know where the boys get their talent from. Did Uncle Sonny tell you that?'

'No, he's far too modest. It was Aunt Hannah who told me.'

'Ah, maternal pride,' Josh said with a wicked glance at his own mother, 'a terrible thing, maternal pride. No, the real reason is, if I do decide to go back to university I want to go into the course fully prepared. Even the prospect of providing cannon fodder for two big-hitting batsmen can't tempt me away from that.'

'Oh, but you won't spend all summer working, will you?' Naomi pleaded.

'No fear, Mum,' Josh grinned. 'There are one or two rather splendid parties I've got lined up to let my hair down. Johnny Cartwright, who was in my college, is having one that goes on for two days. He's having a marquee erected and his parents have even hired a jazz band for the occasion.'

'I don't know how you can listen to that tuneless racket?' Simon objected.

'We weren't all brought up on Gilbert and Sullivan and Franz Lehar, you know,' Josh told him dismissively. 'The world's moved on since *Come into the Garden, Maud* was all the rage.'

The entertainment at Johnny Cartwright's party kept the guests enthralled. It was the era of big bands and songs from shows and the newly popular film musicals. The entertainers played a selection of the most popular numbers from Duke Ellington's *Solitude* to Cole Porter's *Anything Goes*. Slightly less classical were *The Beer Barrel Polka* and *Carry Me Back to the Lone Prairie,* but still fun to listen and dance to, as was the unforgettably titled Cab Calloway song *Minnie the Moocher*. Despite the variety of music and the undoubted talent of the band, one of Cartwright's guests failed to extract full enjoyment from their repertoire, Jessica Tunnicliffe was restless and bored. She craved the thrill and excitement of a new romance but having surveyed most of the male guests could find none to whom she felt the slightest attraction, save one or two who were, to all appearances, securely attached to other girls.

None, that is until, as the band was playing

Cole Porter's unforgettable classic *Night And Day*. As the crowd on the dance floor separated for a moment, Jessica saw a young man of about her own age in the distance. As she was admiring his athletic build, he turned to look across the dance floor and she saw he had the sort of dashing good looks she thought only existed between the covers of romantic novels. As she stared at him, she felt a familiar sensation and knew she had got to meet him. If love at first sight doesn't exist, then in Jessica's case, infatuation certainly did. Jessica sought out her host to demand his assistance.

If the engineered meeting was swiftly arranged, what followed took place at lightning speed. They danced together all night, ate Johnny Cartwright's post-party breakfast together. On the following Tuesday they had dinner together at Jessica's flat. That same night they became lovers. For three weeks they were inseparable. Jessica, no stranger to passion, had for the first time fallen completely and hopelessly in love.

They spent every night together, their need for one another all consuming. Then, on a Saturday in mid-August, they decided to take a walk through Manningham Park. Rain began to fall, heavy rain that presages a thunderstorm.

'Let's go back to the flat,' Jessica said as the first few drops began to splatter about them.

'No,' he contradicted her, 'let's go to my folk's place. It's nearer.'

Once there, they spent little time admiring the fixtures and fittings. The heat and violence of the storm raging outside was matched by the frenzy of their passion for one another. Hours later, in the soft early evening light, Jessica watched her lover sleeping. She felt a warm glow of tenderness as she remembered her own tormented past and contrasted it with the calmer waters she felt she was now entering. She switched on the bedside lamp to look around his room, the room she had failed to notice in their hasty hunger for one another. It was then that she saw the photograph on top of the chest of drawers. She stared at it in disbelief then sat up in bed, the sheet falling from her naked shoulders as she peered closely at the image. Jessica shook her lover to wake him. As he sat up, heavy eyed with sleep she demanded, 'Who is that man in the photograph?'

He followed her pointing finger, still struggling to focus. 'Oh, that,' he told her calmly, 'is my father.'

Jessica felt a rising tide of nausea surge from the pit of her stomach, the hot bile burning her throat. 'But I thought Simon Jones was your father?'

'No. Although I call him Dad, Simon adopted me when I was six, seven years old. I never knew my actual father, Jesse.'

Hampered by the unfamiliar surroundings, Jessica only just reached the bathroom before she was violently sick.

The confrontation had been a short-lived, one-sided transaction. Jessica, white-faced and trembling throughout, had refused to answer any of Josh's questions, turned a deaf ear to all his pleadings and cajoling. As soon as she had dressed she turned from him and walked, almost ran from the building. Over the next three weeks, despite a bombardment of letters and phone calls plus many fruitless visits to her flat, Josh had not succeeded in contacting her. Aware of what would happen, Jessica had avoided such an encounter by leaving Bradford to bury herself in the solitary splendour of a large London hotel, secure in the knowledge that Josh would be unable to trace her.

CHAPTER TWENTY

In early September, recognizing the futility of the exercise, Josh, distraught and baffled, joined his parents and the rest of the family in Scarborough for the last few days of the holiday. He told them nothing of what had happened in Bradford, merely announcing that he had decided against returning to university. Naomi accepted this statement at face value. It was Simon who discovered as much of the truth as Josh was able or willing to tell him.

'So, if you're determined not to return to university, what do you intend to do?' Simon asked.

'I don't know yet. I thought for a start I'd visit Europe, get some more language practice.'

Jones stared at his stepson for a while. 'It'll be a girl, I suppose?'

'What do you mean, Dad?' Josh was alarmed, defensive.

'I mean it'll be a girl at the bottom of this sudden change of heart, either she's upset you, or you've upset her,' Simon asserted.

'Is this personal experience, or have you started

writing for women's magazines?' Josh stopped short of a sneer, but only just.

'No I haven't, and it's not personal experience either. I was too busy dodging bullets, so I never had a girlfriend until I met your mother. I know you too well though. When we left Bradford, you were bright and cheerful, intent on going back to do a post-graduate course. Now, all of a sudden you've changed your mind. You're grumpy. You snap at anyone who asks you a question and have no time for your sisters. You spend a lot of time staring into space and if Mum or I ask you an even remotely personal question you fly off the handle. In fact you're behaving like a complete pain, Josh, and that's not like you. Something's obviously happened. So if it isn't a girl, what the devil is it?'

Josh was instantly contrite. 'I'm sorry, Dad. I didn't mean to behave that way. It's just that it was so good, we felt so right together, or so I thought. I really believed I'd found something like you and Mum have, then she ended it, without warning or explanation, just walked out. It's over and I don't know why. She won't answer my letters, never answers the phone, and won't come to the door when I go round. Just ended, like that, as if it meant nothing. I promise I'll mend my ways but please, don't be angry with me, I couldn't take that as well.'

Simon hugged him and Josh began to cry. 'I know what you need. A skinful of beer, or taking another woman to bed and letting her sort you out.'

'Dad,' Josh protested, shocked and laughing at the same time, despite his troubles.

'Well, they say the best cure is a hair of the dog that bit you.'

By the time Josh returned to Bradford, Jessica was beginning to feel uneasy. She was aware that something due towards the end of August hadn't happened. In love for the first time, Jessica's normal caution had deserted her. A month later she realized luck had deserted her too. Jessica was pregnant by her half-brother. Reluctantly, her mind and emotions in a whirl, Jessica too returned to Yorkshire. London was the ideal place to be if you wanted to remain hidden, but Jessica knew no one there. Once she reached Bradford she ensconced herself in her flat. She sorted through the correspondence that had accumulated during her absence.

She read with distress the increasingly bitter communications from Josh. He was hurt, she knew, but she also knew that she could never explain the reason for her actions. Strangely, it was the last, a curt note written only a few days earlier that caused her most pain.

> I recognize now that it is over between us, even though I still don't know in what way I offended. I just know that you no longer wish

to see me. Very well, I shall not pester you further. You will not hear from me again.
Joshua.

Her own troubles momentarily forgotten, Jessica began to cry. 'Oh, Josh, my poor, poor darling Josh,' she wept.

It took Jessica four phone calls before she got the information she needed. None of the girls she talked to believed Jessica's tale that she was asking on behalf of a friend. The fourth, while giving her the details and address she sought, told her, 'You'll be all right, she'll look after you. She took care of a friend of mine a couple of years ago, so you'll be fine.'

Jessica, remembering the girl's fling with a much older, married man at that time, didn't believe the story of a 'friend' either.

Close to Leeds city centre were row upon row of side streets populated with low, ugly, and for the most part, dilapidated terrace houses. Built in the previous century as low-cost housing for the rising population of workers in the heavy industries close by, they were, although by no means old, already ripe for slum clearance.

The house Jessica sought was one of these. As nondescript and unprepossessing as the rest, it reminded her of the squalid orphanage she had entered unwillingly just a few years earlier. As she waited in the hallway it was only by an exercise of rigid self-control that prevented her from turning tail and fleeing from the depressing and sordid scene.

The woman was in her mid-fifties, her dress and appearance matching her surroundings perfectly. She wore carpet slippers, the upper of one of which bore a hole through which the big toe protruded. Above these her stockings were wrinkled and laddered. A shapeless tweed skirt and a grubby blouse that could possibly once have been white were covered by a much stained wrap-around apron. The woman's hair was barely visible through a headscarf, the wearing of which seemed to be a uniform in the area. She smiled mirthlessly at her visitor, displaying uneven nicotine-stained teeth. No mean feat the smile, for a cigarette hung precariously from one side of her lower lip, the inch or so of ash threatening to join countless others on the worn matting covering the hall floor.

'You'll be here for the nine o'clock?' she enquired obscurely, her voice a harsh, cracked falsetto.

'Yes, I'm—'

'No names, love,' the woman interrupted. 'I don't want to know yours and I'm not telling you mine. Got the money?'

'Yes, it's here, just as you asked.' Jessica fumbled in her handbag and produced an envelope.

The woman snatched it from her and tore it open to remove the bundle of large white five-pound notes. She counted these slowly, her head bobbing up and down with each one. Still the ash clung on desperately. She folded the notes and with a far from erotic gesture hitched up her skirt to tuck the bundle inside her stocking top. 'All right, come on, love, let's get it over with.'

The woman turned and waddled stiffly down the hall. The turn was the last straw and the ash gave up the will to live and spiralled to the floor in a grey trail, like a burnt-out comet.

Slowly, her footsteps leaden, Jessica followed her to the appointment she knew she must keep.

Four days later, while walking to the shop at the end of her road, Jessica collapsed on the pavement. She was rushed to hospital, unconscious and haemorrhaging badly. So severe was the damage caused by the botched abortion that for a long time it was touch and go whether she survived.

Four weeks later she was allowed to leave hospital. Before her departure she had an uncomfortable meeting with the gynaecologist who had treated her. 'Well, young lady,' he told her bluntly, 'you've been very fortunate. By rights you should be dead. You're also lucky the matter hasn't been reported to the police. I suppose you thought you had a good enough reason for such a desperate act.' He held up a restraining hand. 'Don't tell me, I don't want to know. I'm afraid in one respect your luck has deserted you. The butcher who "helped" you,' his tone was scathing, 'has caused so much internal damage I think it's extremely unlikely you'll ever be able to bear a child. I suppose I should demand the name and address of whoever carried out this criminal act, but then again I guess you wouldn't tell me, so I suggest you leave and in future take more care of the body the Good Lord gave you.' He gave an abrupt nod to signify the end of the interview.

Jessica, chastened and hurt by the surgeon's comments, slowly turned and left the consulting room.

For over two months after leaving hospital, Jessica remained holed up in her flat. She neither received any visitors, nor did she venture out, save for essentials such as food. For days on end, she didn't even bother to dress, remaining in bed for much of the time. She was prey to violent mood swings, which confused her, for she didn't comprehend that in part her body still believed her to be pregnant. As her health slowly improved Jessica pondered her future. She puzzled over her new attitude. It seemed to her that the wild, spoilt, rich, and careless young girl had been exorcised along with everything else. She knew she needed a new direction, a purpose in life beyond pleasure seeking. The only restlessness within her now was the need for change, the only urge a desire for new horizons.

As 1935 dawned, Jessica started to implement her plans. Her flat was placed on the market and Jessica began looking for suitable property in London. She soon found one and made preparations to finalize the break. Before leaving Bradford she told no one apart from her former guardian

Michael Haigh of her decision. Despite the rift with Connie, Jessica still felt grateful to the couple for providing shelter and a home after her mother's death.

Michael, who had always liked Jessica, approved her plan, with one or two reservations. 'What do you intend to do once you reach London? You're a very wealthy young woman and I'd hate to see you waste your life and fritter your money away.'

To Michael's surprise, Jessica replied, 'I'm going back to school. I've enrolled in a commercial school. When I've completed the course I intend to get myself a job.' Jokingly she added, 'You never know I might finish up as your secretary yet!'

Michael grinned. 'Jessica, you can sit on my lap anytime you like.'

They both laughed and Jessica was still smiling when she left the Manor Row offices en route for the station.

CHAPTER TWENTY-ONE

After the Jones family returned to Bradford, their everyday life resumed its normal pattern. Simon went to work, the children went to school, Josh went off to Scotland on a hiking holiday with a couple of college friends, and Naomi went into the laundry room to tackle the mountain of washing and ironing resulting from the extended holiday. She was deeply engrossed in her task when the doorbell rang. The man standing in the open doorway was about Naomi's age, tall and distinguished-looking.

'Mrs Jones?' he enquired.

Naomi nodded agreement.

'How do you do, Mrs Jones? My name's Edrith Pointon, I'm with His Majesty's Government. I'm here because I believe you can help us.'

Naomi felt a twinge of disquiet. 'I don't see how I can help you.'

'I'd rather not discuss it on the doorstep. It is rather a confidential matter. Actually it's not so much you, but that extremely talented son of yours I think can help us.'

'Josh!' Naomi was baffled. 'How can Josh help you?'

Pointon gestured indoors and Naomi admitted him, her disquiet now turning to alarm.

She preceded him into the sitting room and invited him to sit down before she repeated her question. 'How can Josh help you?'

'My department,' Edrith told her, choosing his words carefully, 'is responsible for collecting and collating information from abroad, in particular from Europe. We are always on the lookout for good information gatherers, people who can blend in with the indigenous population without being noticed. I'm afraid the English are remarkably poor when it comes to other languages, so someone with the linguistic skills of young Joshua is a valuable asset. In short, Mrs Jones, I rather hope you will find it in your way to use your good offices to persuade Joshua to come and work for us in several little tasks that might crop up in Europe.'

Naomi's unease had deepened into a cold chill of fear. Endeavouring to keep her voice calm, she asked, 'What makes you think I'd use my "good offices" as you call them? Josh makes up his own mind in such matters.'

'Yes, but I'm sure you, as his mother, could exert a considerable amount of influence if you wished.' Pointon's silky tones masked a core of steel.

'Suppose I could. But why should I?' Naomi was defiant.

'Let's say I believe it to be in all our interests.' Pointon's voice was bland, the words harmless, the threat implicit in every syllable. 'My department would gain the services of a talented and highly intelligent young man. Josh would get an interesting and well-rewarded position, with the opportunity for travel and chance to hone his already considerable skills. All that a young man with few ties could desire and you . . .' Pointon paused slightly.

'Yes,' Naomi encouraged him, 'what would I get from this transaction?'

Pointon smiled, much as Naomi imagined a shark might smile. The silk was discarded, the naked steel appeared.

'You would get freedom from the fear that has been hanging over you for the last twenty years, Mrs Jones – or should I call you Hildegard?' Pointon leaned forward in his chair to add emphasis to his words. 'Let me make it clear, I'm not making any threats. That's not the way I work for one thing, for another, I'm not too sure what I could threaten you with. As far as I can see all you've done wrong in this country is a little minor deception over your identity. You've committed no crime worth talking about, merely a few forged papers. OK, if there were to be revelations, the publicity would not be very nice, but there are going to be no such revelations. Only two people know your true identity, my assistant and me, and we're not going to tell anyone.' Pointon grinned.

'Our department's job is trying to keep secrets, not give them away.'

Simon, who had rushed home in response to his wife's near hysterical phone call, asked Pointon, 'Does that mean you're a spy?'

An expression of distaste crossed Pointon's face. 'I prefer to use the term intelligence gathering, to describe our activities. We collect information and analyze it to guide governmental policy. We do not act in the manner some of the more lurid newspaper stories and works of fiction might lead you to believe. Our agents do not break the laws of the countries in which they operate. Neither do they bribe, blackmail or suborn officials of those states. In fact, for the most part the work is dull, boring, statistical routine.'

Simon and Naomi, who had both been prepared to fear and loathe Pointon, found themselves actually liking him. His easy charm and reassurances put them at their ease, they began to trust and believe him. This proved what a fine actor and accomplished liar Pointon was.

'All I want from you,' Pointon continued, 'is your help and support to persuade Joshua that a career with us would be right for him. As I said earlier, it is reasonably well-paid work, certainly much better than working in industry. He'll get the opportunity to travel, a chance most young men of his age would give their eye teeth for, what's more his travel and expenses will all be met by the department. What do you think?'

Naomi's reluctance showed in her expression.

It was not by chance that Edrith Pointon was at the top of his profession. 'It must be hard for you to let go of Joshua, particularly after all the years of struggle, when there were just the two of you and the fact that you've barely ever been separated.'

Naomi warmed to Pointon's understanding of her misgivings. It was as if he'd put her thoughts into words. She nodded her agreement.

'I assure you that Joshua will be much better off than most young men abroad, for he will have diplomatic status, which means that in the unlikely event of there being any trouble, he would have the full protection of the British Government.'

'Why are you so keen to get Josh to work for you?' Simon asked.

'Good question,' Pointon acknowledged. 'The problem with our line of work is that we can't advertise for staff, like, shall we say, more commonplace trades or professions. Officially speaking my department does not exist. You will not find it listed in any governmental statistics and' – he smiled ironically – 'we are certainly not in the phone book. As we are unable to recruit by more regular methods, we have to rely on personal recommendations to obtain staff.'

'Whose personal recommendation caused you to seek out Josh?' Simon persisted.

'Oh, the dean of his college, his tutors, people like that.'

‘So what makes Josh so special?’ Naomi interjected. ‘After all there must be hundreds of competent linguists around.’

‘Very few with Josh’s exceptional talents, believe me,’ Pointon told her, adopting the more familiar version of their son’s name. ‘But that isn’t all, by any means. There are other qualities required apart from the ability to speak a few languages. When we send someone abroad we expect them to report more than the bald facts. We want comment and opinion, reflections on local attitudes, political trends and much more. For the government to react to events abroad it helps to have prior intimation that they are about to happen. All we have been told about Josh tells us that he has a keen analytical brain, is capable of summing up situations quickly and accurately and stringing together pieces of evidence to reach a logical conclusion. Believe me, Josh is a rare and gifted young man, ideally suited to our kind of work.’

Simon had made his mind up by then. ‘I think it would be good for Josh,’ he told Naomi. ‘I know he was considering visiting Europe in any case and he needs some new purpose, a different challenge after his recent disappointment’ – he saw the quizzical look on Pointon’s face. ‘A girl let him down,’ Simon explained. ‘I’d rather he went away with a mission in life than merely meandering from place to place.’

CHAPTER TWENTY-TWO

Finlay Finnegan was just four years old. He was alone, alone and frightened. Not merely frightened, but terrified in a way his young brain could barely understand. He did not know if it was day or night. He could not move, could not speak. He could not move because his wrists and ankles were tightly bound with rope, so tight they hurt. He could not speak because something was covering his mouth. It too was tight, so tight it cut into his cheeks. It had been placed there after he woke up. He had been sick, and then he had started screaming. That was when they had gagged him. He still felt sick, the feeling of nausea not helped by the smell of his own vomit and worse. He could not see because a blindfold of some kind had been placed over his head. Occasionally the gag would be removed and he would be offered a drink of water, tepid and brackish tasting. Once, he had been offered food. Before the gag was removed there had been the threat, 'If you scream, I'll kill you.' Finlay did not scream.

He knew there were men there, knew they were

strangers, and knew in some strange way they were looking at him. They talked about him, rarely to him, except to offer water or threaten to kill him. Although they offered food and water they had no thought to Finlay's other bodily needs. The fear did not help and eventually he was unable to contain himself any longer. Sick, uncomfortable, soiled and in pain, Finlay Finnegan was a very distressed and frightened little boy.

Troubled times breed desperate men. They had been planning it for over a year. The partnership had been formed in prison where they shared a cell. One had been serving five years for burglary, the other a similar term for assault. Their main topic of conversation was money, the lack of it, and how to get some. As thieves they were, it must be said, fairly incompetent. When the Lindbergh kidnapping made international headlines they were interested, then fascinated, then determined on a copy-cat crime. That the Lindbergh abduction had ended disastrously for both the family and the perpetrator did not worry them, they thought they could do better.

Once they had been released, with the tender words of the guard, 'I've no doubt I'll be seeing you boys pretty soon,' ringing in their ears, they began selecting a victim. The criteria they used were straightforward. It had to be a child, for both men were cowards, and it had to be a child from a rich family. Casting about for a suitable match, the obvious selection was the family that owned and controlled Fisher Springs, which they had been told was the richest company in Australia.

They set about planning the kidnap, watching the family, observing their movements and the comings and goings at the house. Any of the children would have served their purpose, although they preferred one of the smaller ones. They scraped together enough money, or more precisely they stole it, to rent a house on the outskirts of town, where they would not be overlooked, paying the rent in advance.

Although they were incompetent criminals, they were skilled enough to get through locked doors at the Finnegan home. They entered the silent house in the early hours through the kitchen. Their observation had given them an idea where the children slept. It was pure chance that the first bedroom they came to was Finlay's. They had acquired a bottle of chloroform. A rag soaked in this substance was placed over Finlay's mouth, transforming him from sleep to unconsciousness. It was the chloroform that was to cause him to vomit.

Before leaving the bedroom they placed a note on his pillow, wrapped his inert form in a blanket from the bed and made their way back down the stairs and left the house, its remaining occupants still sleeping. They had been inside no more than ten minutes.

The crude, handwritten note was brutally to the point. It read, 'We got the kid. If you talk to police, we kill the kid. We want £100,000. Wait for orders.'

Shock, alarm, and distress amounting to grief followed Patrick and Louise Finnegan's discovery that their youngest son was missing. Finlay was usually the first in the household to wake up, whereupon he would wander into his parents' bedroom, sometime before 7 a.m. When he hadn't appeared by 7.45, Louise sent Patrick through to check that he wasn't poorly. It was then that he found the note.

Their first instinct, once the feeling of panic had abated slightly, was to obey the kidnappers' instructions implicitly. Patrick and Louise were unable to keep Finlay's disappearance from the other children, if for no other reason than to share their fear and anxiety. An informal family conference was convened, at which it emerged that no one had heard the slightest sound during the night. Luke Fisher reported finding the kitchen door open. It had been forced, he told the gathering.

Luke, now almost eighteen, and Dottie, fifteen, were the only Fisher children present. Their brother Philip was away on business, and Ellen visiting Cissie. When Finnegan impressed the need for secrecy on them all, it was Luke who raised the only objection. 'I don't think that's wise, Uncle Patrick.'

In anyone else this would have provoked an angry reaction, but Finnegan had too much respect for Luke Fisher. Not only for his past actions, but the clear signs of a developing intellect to match or even surpass that of his late father. 'Why not?' Finnegan asked.

'For one thing I don't think you will be able to keep it secret for long. Sooner or later it's bound to get out, however hard you try to stop it. The main reason though is that note from the kidnappers. They said "don't tell the police" because that's the last thing they want to happen. If you do what they want, it gives them a better chance of getting away with it.'

'They've threatened to kill Finlay,' Louise protested.

'I know, Aunt Louise.' Luke's face was clouded with distress. 'I hate saying this but whether we tell the police or not, the chances of getting Finlay back safely are slim, but if we fail to tell the police I reckon we reduce them even further.'

It was well past lunchtime when the decision was made, although none of the family felt in the least like eating. Patrick and Luke set off for the police station, while Louise remained at home in case they received a phone call from the kidnappers.

Sergeant Broadwith was an extremely competent detective. At that moment, probably as a consequence of his ability, he was bored. There was little in the way of unsolved crime to get his teeth into, merely a little petty larceny that was hardly likely to exercise his agile mind. He was beginning to wonder how he could spend the rest of his shift meaningfully when there was a knock on his office door.

'There are two men outside who want to speak to someone urgently,' the constable told him. 'They won't say what it's about and refused to give their names but said they wouldn't go away, said it's both urgent and serious.'

Serious, urgent and mysterious, Broadwith thought, any one of the statements would have intrigued him. The combination of all three was irresistible. He examined the two as they entered his room. He saw a tall, distinguished-looking man in his early fifties, well dressed, accompanied by a youngster of eighteen or thereabouts, he guessed. The younger of the two looked vaguely familiar, but Broadwith couldn't think why. As the older man was speaking, the sergeant noted with some amusement that his younger companion was assessing Broadwith in much the same way as he had inspected his visitors.

'I'm sorry for the secrecy, sergeant,' Patrick began, 'but the fewer people who know about this, the better.' He paused, seemingly uncertain how to continue.

The younger man took up the story. 'Please forgive my uncle, but he's very distressed. We are here because his son's been kidnapped. He's only four years old.'

Slowly, hesitantly, and with a considerable amount of prompting, Finnegan explained how they had discovered Finlay's absence. At the end of the tale he turned to Luke. 'Give the note to the sergeant, Luke.'

'Luke Fisher!' the sergeant exclaimed. 'I thought your face looked familiar.'

Luke gave a shy grin and pulled a small brown paper bag from his pocket. 'I put the note in here using Aunt Louise's tweezers,' he told Broadwith, 'only Uncle Patrick's handled it apart from the kidnappers, so I thought there might be some fingerprints on it. I also told the family to stay clear of the kitchen door for the same reason.'

The sergeant eyed the young man with respect as he shook the note free from its protective wrapping and turned it over using a pencil from the desk. He went to the door and summoned the constable. 'Take that and have it dusted for fingerprints. Use that paper bag to hold it with, then come back and take Mr Finnegan's prints. We know they will be on the note.'

When the constable had departed, Broadwith said to his visitors, 'We'll give them time to find out if there are any other prints apart from yours on the note, then we need to think of a way of getting to your place without being seen, just in case there is someone watching.'

'I've got an idea about that,' Luke told him.

Broadwith smiled encouragement. 'Go on.'

'At the back of the house, where we park the cars, there's a high wall. We can't be overlooked there because the house is on top of a hill, so here's my idea.'

An hour and a half later Patrick and Luke returned to the Finnegan house. If the journey from town was uncomfortable for the sergeant, lying spread-eagled across the backseat, it was doubly so for the constable, curled up inside the boot.

Broadwith and the constable spent several hours at the Finnegan house. Each member of the family was fingerprinted then the kitchen door and Finlay's room were dusted. Several excellent prints were revealed, so after the operation was complete the officers met with the family, when Broadwith outlined his tactics.

'The way I see it, we have to move in utmost secrecy. I don't even want to contemplate what might happen if the kidnappers get wind of our involvement. From your point of view that means you continue to sit and wait for the phone call with the ransom details. That means having the money ready for when they call,' he looked enquiringly at Finnegan.

'I can organize that within a couple of hours.'

'Good, and in the meantime I'm leaving my constable here with you. It's important we have a presence in the house and you'll all feel safer with him around.' There was no objection to this so Broadwith continued, 'When I get back to town I'm going to try to identify the owners of the prints we have from here and on the note. At the same time I've got an idea how to track down where they're holding Finlay. Has anyone got any other ideas?'

Luke Fisher looked across at Finnegan. 'Yes,' Patrick said, more confident now he knew the police were moving into action. 'Luke's going to drive you back to town. We've been talking things over and we think it would be a good idea for him to stay with you.'

'Why's that?' Broadwith asked.

'Well, if you do find Finlay and can rescue him, don't you think it would be better if there's someone with you he knows and trusts, someone who can comfort him until we arrive.'

Broadwith thought it over for a few moments. 'It's highly irregular.'

'The whole situation's highly irregular,' Luke interjected. 'How many kidnappings have you had to deal with before?'

'I guess you're right,' the sergeant replied reluctantly. 'OK, but you have to promise to do just as I tell you.'

CHAPTER TWENTY-THREE

The journey back to town was uneventful, but no less uncomfortable for the sergeant. Instead of driving straight to the police station, Luke headed for the Fisher Springs building. 'I have something to collect from my father's office,' he told Broadwith. 'I'll only be a couple of minutes.'

He was as good as his word. Reaching the office he extracted a small box from his father's desk, opened it, and placed the contents in his pocket before returning to the car. Broadwith had alerted his colleagues that they would be arriving and the station was on full alert. Luke Fisher was an interested spectator as the sergeant set the investigation in motion. He noted with approval the decisive way Broadwith tackled the job and his fellow officers' response.

'First thing in the morning,' the sergeant told them, 'I want you to find out what property has been let over the past three months. Ideally we're looking for somewhere accessible but not overlooked. Let me stress, no word of this must get out. A child's life is at stake, he's being held by men who won't hesitate to kill him if they feel threatened.'

The night dragged slowly by as they awaited developments. Luke was dozing uncomfortably in one of Broadwith's chairs when the phone rang. Patrick Finnegan had been contacted by the kidnappers. He gave the details of the conversation. The drop-off was to take place at 6 p.m. the following evening. A bag containing the money was to be left outside the rear entrance of, to everyone's surprise, the Fisher Springs headquarters.

As Broadwith replaced the handset, Luke asked him, 'Why wait until the early hours to ring?'

'Your uncle said they used a public phone, so perhaps they thought there was less chance of them being seen, or the conversation overheard at this time of the morning.'

It was over four hours later that the first breakthrough occurred. The police station's records officer, who had worked all night alongside the state fingerprint specialist, brought two folders into Broadwith's office and placed them triumphantly on his desk, stating, 'Fortunately we have files on anyone convicted within the state. The top one is the man whose prints are on the ransom note. The other was from the set you lifted from the kitchen door frame at the house.' He smiled at Broadwith, winked encouragingly at Luke and was gone.

The sergeant read both files thoroughly, his

face impassive throughout. Luke waited in a fever of impatience for him to finish. Eventually, Broadwith closed the second folder. 'Well, I don't think either of these is a master criminal. In fact I'm surprised they managed to dream up this idea. That worries me, for it might mean there's more than two involved.'

'Unless they got the notion from the Lindbergh case,' Luke suggested.

Broadwith was about to reply when there was a knock at the door. 'Sarge,' one of the constables said, his tone excited, 'we've got someone out here might be able to help.' Broadwith excused himself and followed the constable out of the room.

The door had barely settled in its frame before Luke was across the room, behind the desk, studying the files on the two men. He soon realized how right Broadwith had been, as he scanned the first folder. He finished reading it and turned to the second. It too contained a catalogue of similarly bungled crimes, most of them petty, some accompanied by violence.

He had barely returned to his chair when the sergeant entered. 'One of my men has found a woman who rented out a house on the edge of town two months ago.' Broadwith picked up the files. 'I'm just going to see if she recognizes either of these photos. We might have got lucky.'

When Sergeant Broadwith re-entered his office there was an air of excitement and determined bustle about him. He brandished the files triumphantly. 'We're making progress,' he told Luke confidently. 'The woman I've been talking to identified one of the men as the person who rented a house from her. The house belongs to her son and daughter-in-law, but they moved to Sydney just under a year ago. Our suspects took it on a three-month lease, telling her they were working in the area. That was six weeks ago.

'The house is right at the edge of town, surrounded by trees and quite thick undergrowth too, the woman says. That's ideal for their purpose in that there's little chance of anyone accidentally seeing anything suspicious.' Broadwith paused. 'But it's also very handy for us because it means we can get people close to the house, near enough to watch what's going on inside without them being seen.'

'So what's your plan?'

The sergeant looked at the clock on his office wall. 'It's ten o'clock now. I've assembled a team to go out there. Four of us to watch the house, four others further back and another four in reserve to cover breaks. We'll change the watchers over every three hours. Longer than that and they'll bake in this heat, what's more they'd lose concentration. If we get the first team into position by eleven, change them at two and again at five then wait for someone to leave the house to go for the ransom. Hopefully by that time we might have a better idea of how many we're dealing with.'

'Will you be able to see the whole house from the woods?'

'Not quite, but enough to get a fair idea of the numbers. My guess is there's just the two of them. The good thing is the woman reckons we'll be able to see both exits.'

'When do we start?' Luke was eager for action.

'Wait a minute, who said anything about you going along?'

'That was part of the deal, remember?'

'No, the deal was you would be on hand to help with Finlay.'

'Yes, but I can't help if I'm not there can I?'

'OK, OK, but you must stay back with the reserve party all the time,' the sergeant relented.

'Of course, if you say so,' Luke agreed.

Before they left the police station Broadwith had allowed Luke to phone Patrick Finnegan and tell him their plans. The news was greeted with what Luke assessed to be excitement over-laden with caution.

'Be careful, Luke,' Finnegan had warned him, 'these are highly-dangerous customers. It's not just for Finlay I'm worried, I'd never forgive myself if anything happened to you.'

'Don't worry, Uncle Patrick, I'll take care of myself, I've brought Betsy along with me.'

'I somehow thought you might. But don't take any unnecessary risks.'

'I won't. And you be careful when you drop the money off.'

The police made their base camp at the end of a quiet suburban road, well away from the prying eyes and curiosity of the occupants of the small row of neat houses. It was a fairly typical middle-class area. The dwellings had all been constructed within the last ten years but with demand for property exceedingly low, building work had ceased halfway along the road leaving a gap of over half a mile to the place they were parked. The builders, Luke noticed with some amusement, whose advertising board he could read from his vantage point, were part of the Fisher Springs Group of companies.

'Here's the plan,' Broadwith said. 'I'm going to take two of my men and position them in the woods at the back of the house then I'll come back and get the other two for the front. You stay here,' he said to Luke.

Broadwith returned, the first shift of watchers having been positioned to his satisfaction. 'The vantage points are better than I could have dreamed of, so much so, that I reckon you can get a share of the action after all. When we make the five o'clock changeover you and I will take the back.' He eyed the younger man. 'That way I can keep an eye on you as well as the house.'

Luke affected an air of innocence that did not fool Broadwith. 'What were you able to see?' he asked.

'Well, that's the good news. I'd just got the men at the back of the house in place and I stayed with them for a few minutes, familiarizing myself with the building lay-out, when somebody looked out of one of the ground floor windows. There's no doubt about the identification that woman made this morning, it was one of the suspects. The position our men are in is good because they're on a slope down towards the building, so the foliage in front of them screens them, even if those inside use field glasses. At the same time they have a clear view of the house and almost every window.'

'Have your men got field glasses, they'd be a great help?' Luke asked him.

'They would, but I daren't use them,' Broadwith said a little ruefully. 'I daren't chance the sun reflecting off them. It would give the game away.'

'Nevertheless, it was obliging of one of them to come to the window.'

'Yes, but no more than I expected. As the time for the ransom payment gets closer they're sure to get more excited and more nervous too.'

The good news helped those waiting at a safe distance from the house pass the first watch period without too much difficulty. Boredom from inaction and tension regarding the ultimate outcome made time appear to drag by. Eventually, just before Luke was about to ask, for the tenth or perhaps the eleventh time, if the first changeover was due, Broadwith stood up. He signalled to two of his men to do likewise and the pair followed him over the rise. Luke watched them disappear and settled back to wait. After what seemed an age Broadwith returned with the two officers who had been stood down. The sergeant wasted no time questioning them, merely signalling two more of his men to accompany him. Nor were the relieved men more forthcoming with news, despite Luke's wheedling.

When the second pair returned from their watch, what they had seen proved to be disappointingly little. The man identified earlier had been spotted looking out of one or other of the ground floor windows to the back of the house and once from the front. This raised speculation that he might be the only occupant of the building.

'Suppose,' Luke suggested, horrified by his own idea, 'this is a decoy building and the rest of the gang are hiding Finlay elsewhere?'

Broadwith dismissed the notion. 'You might be clever enough to think up an idea like that, Luke, but the pair we've identified are nowhere near that bright.'

Luke didn't ask whether this was clever psychology or just plain wishful thinking.

CHAPTER TWENTY-FOUR

The afternoon wore on with painful slowness before Sergeant Broadwith got stiffly to his feet. 'I'm going to swap the pair at the front over first then get the two from the back, hear what all four have to report before we go in. It'll mean the back of the house is unobserved for a few minutes but we'll have to chance that.'

'Why not take me with you when you go for the men at the back, that way the house is watched without a break?' he suggested.

Broadwith pondered the idea. 'OK, but you must promise me, no matter what happens inside the house or out, you'll take no action until I return.'

'Scouts honour,' Luke agreed solemnly.

Luke spent his first few minutes in concealment familiarizing himself with the terrain and the house. Curtains had been pulled across all of the first-floor windows, while those on the ground floor remained un-drawn. Was this, Luke speculated, to enable the kidnappers to look out and at the same time present an appearance of normality, while those on the upper storey concealed the place they were holding Finlay?

Broadwith returned. 'Nothing new to report, just more sightings of the same man. Have you seen anything?'

'Not a thing,' Luke replied. The conversation was conducted in a low whisper. 'I'm wondering if someone is guarding Finlay upstairs.' He pointed to the curtained first-floor windows.

'Makes sense,' Broadwith agreed, 'but it's a bloody nuisance. I'd like to be sure how many of them there are of them before I think about going in. Without knowing that, we'll just have to chance it.'

'You said earlier, they'll be getting twitchy by now. You're definitely going in then?' Luke asked.

'Can't afford not to,' the sergeant replied. 'Once they've got their hands on the ransom money, Finlay may be in more danger than he already is.'

Unless he's already dead, Luke thought. He remembered the lurid newspaper accounts of the Lindbergh kidnapping. Although that ransom had been paid, the boy had been murdered. There had been considerable speculation that he was already dead before the money was collected. Luke resolutely blocked such a depressing line of thought from his mind.

'If the man whose job it is to collect the money is inside the house he'll have to leave in about ten minutes,' Broadwith whispered. 'He'll need at least a quarter of an hour to get from here to the Fisher

Springs building and they dare not risk somebody else picking the parcel up. If and when that happens, I'll go get the rest of my men and spread them out so they're covering every side of the building. They have instructions to close in once I'm inside.'

'You're not going in alone, are you?' Luke was horrified.

'Better that way, less chance of making a noise and disturbing the occupants.'

No bloody way are you going in alone, Luke thought, but wisely refrained from saying it. If time had appeared to be going slowly during their long afternoon of boredom, it now seemed to have stopped altogether. Eventually however, the watchers spotted a face at the ground floor window closest to the back door, a development that signalled the beginning of a flurry of activity. 'That's the one I saw earlier,' Broadwith whispered.

Seconds later they heard the sound of the bolts on the back door being slid back, the sound travelling clearly through the silent stillness of the early evening air. The door opened and a man stepped out, looking about him cautiously, furtively almost. Luke and the sergeant remained frozen into immobility as the man's gaze swept over the wooded hillside. When he was satisfied that he was unobserved, the man closed the door and walked towards the corner of the building. They watched as he turned down the side of the house towards the front. They waited in silence long after the man had disappeared from view, watching and listening. No other face appeared at any of the windows, there was no sound of the bolts on the door being closed.

'Perhaps he is alone, after all,' Luke whispered.

They waited for a further five minutes, until they were certain the man was not going to return, then Broadwith said, 'You stay here, keep on watching and listening. I'll go get the rest of my men and space them out round the house. When they see me at the backdoor, that's when they move. You stay here throughout, do I make myself clear?'

'Crystal clear, sergeant,' Luke replied.

Minutes later, Luke saw Broadwith cover the ground between the edge of the wood and the back of the house in a low, crouching run. At the back door he paused for a moment, panting slightly, as much from the tension as the exertion. He reached for the door handle, turned it slowly, gently, silently. He pushed at the door. It resisted his pressure. The door was locked. He slowly released the handle, still careful to avoid making the slightest sound. He stood for a moment, contemplating his next course of action. He whirled as he was tapped on the shoulder. 'What are you doing here?' he hissed in a furious whisper.

'Getting you out of a fix and into the house,' Luke whispered in reply. He pointed to the ground floor window on the extreme right corner of the rear wall. It was open, no more than an inch or so, sufficient to let some air in, insignificant enough to avoid detection during their earlier scrutiny from the woods. 'That's our way in,' Luke whispered again.

Broadwith, powerless to prevent Luke short of handcuffing him, capitulated. 'OK, but stay behind me and be very, very careful not to make the slightest sound.'

'I'm going for the money,' the first one had said, 'you keep a good lookout while I'm away.'

'What about the kid?' the second one asked.

'We'll dispose of the kid when we've got the money, not before. We can't bargain if the kid's dead. We could ask for more, but £100,000 will do for starters. Then when we've got all we can, we'll finish the brat off.'

It had been a giant step for them moving up to kidnapping. Murder was, by comparison a short stride.

Now his companion was safely out of the house, the second man made his way upstairs. He wasn't going to spend all his time peering out of the windows as the other one did. They were safe enough. Nobody knew they were here. He wasn't waiting to kill the brat either. He was sick of playing nursemaid and who would know if he was already dead? By the time his partner got back with the ransom money it would be too late.

He entered the bedroom. The boy was laid on

the double bed, wrists and ankles securely tied, still wearing the blindfold they had put on him in the Finnegan house.

The kidnapper had never killed anyone before but it couldn't be that difficult, he thought. He held the gun in his hand wondering if there was anyone near enough to hear the shot.

His excitement mounted, the blood pounding in his ears sounded extra loud, then he realized there had been a sound behind him. He moved quickly for a big man, turning and pointing the gun in one movement.

He saw two men in the open doorway. His first shot hit the mark and he saw blood spurt from the police officer's tunic, high up, below the collar bone. He swung the gun onto the second man, lined it up to take the shot, aiming for the gut, but curiously found himself unable to pull the trigger. His brain willed his finger, but the finger seemed unable to exert enough pressure. Was it, he wondered, connected to the sudden pain in his chest? The last thing he saw, before slumping to the floor, unconscious and dying was the smoke curling from the barrel of Luke Fisher's gun and the pair of merciless blue eyes of the man who had killed him.

Sometimes, in more sombre moments, Luke Fisher thought that although the sound of gunshots had long since died away, their echoes would reverberate forever. At first he was preoccupied with removing the terrified little boy from the scene and comforting him, while the others attended to Broadwith's wound until the sergeant could be taken to hospital. Then, after answering interminable police questions, there had been little time to reflect on what had occurred.

The second kidnapper, returning from collecting the ransom, had been scared off by the all too evident signs of police activity. He bolted and was arrested two days later in a hotel up country. All but a few hundred pounds of the ransom money were recovered. Finlay, still frightened and traumatized by his ordeal, was back with his family.

Once more Luke Fisher was the hero of the hour. With Finlay's safe return and the kidnap threat over, the need for secrecy was gone. Hearing the news, reporters gathered at the Finnegan home like a pack of hungry dingoes. Even though the family, on Patrick Finnegan's strict instructions, refused to be interviewed, the inquest on the dead kidnapper and the trial of the survivor provided more than enough to write about. With Luke and Sergeant Broadwith required to give evidence at both hearings, there was much for the newspaper readers to savour.

To the combined Finnegan and Fisher families Luke was more than a celebrity, no ordinary hero, he was becoming a legend. Such idolatry might have gone to many a young man's head, but Luke, far from revelling in it, was uncomfortable. He had killed a man in extremely unpleasant and dangerous circumstances. Everyone seemed to want to talk about the matter, to revel in it. All he wanted to do was to get on with the rest of his life and be left alone.

A fortnight after the shooting, as the household was returning to something approaching normality, he broached the question of starting work at Fisher Springs with Finnegan. It was early evening and they were seated on the veranda overlooking the river. 'Plenty of time for that,' Patrick told him, 'come back and ask me again when you're eighteen.'

Luke coloured slightly but said nothing. He got up and walked inside the house. Louise looked at her husband. He shrugged his shoulders.

'What date is it today?' Louise asked him.

He told her.

'Oh God!' she exclaimed in horror. 'It's Luke's eighteenth birthday and everybody's forgotten it. We've been so wrapped up with Finlay and our own troubles we've not even wished him happy birthday. Some gratitude when we owe him so much.' Filled with remorse they hurried indoors to make amends.

The following Monday, Luke started work at Fisher Springs headquarters, learning the business and what made it tick. Four days later his brother Philip returned from his business trip. The first newspaper he saw put an end to his ignorance of the traumas back home, in no uncertain fashion, largely due to his brother's face staring out from the front page. The wave of publicity surrounding Luke's rescue of Finlay Finnegan had a curious effect on Philip. He knew he should feel proud of his younger brother, instead he felt resentful. Worse, for many of the reports harked back to the fire, and Philip, knowing he owed his own life to Luke, felt guilty for harbouring such envy. When he reached home and found Luke installed at Fisher Springs, the twin emotions of resentment and guilt intensified.

Their looks apart, the brothers were dissimilar in almost every aspect. Philip was studious, quiet, and cautious almost to the point of timidity, a planner and plodder by nature. Luke, by contrast was an extrovert, bold and decisive, quick to laugh, slow to anger, with a core of steel. Given their extremes of character, Luke's boldness, his courage and desire for action grated on Philip resulting in a series of clashes between the brothers. It might have been expected that Luke, six years the junior, would have deferred to Philip, but that was not Luke's nature.

As Patrick Finnegan remarked to Louise, 'Sometimes I feel like a bloody referee in a boxing match trying to keep the pair of them apart. It's not easy, many of Luke's ideas are sound, but Philip just won't see that. He will not accept anything with Luke's name on. The trouble is I can't go backing Luke all the time, if I do, Phil thinks I'm doing it out of gratitude and gets the huff.'

‘I’m sure it’ll sort itself out given time,’ Louise replied placidly.

Normally, Louise Finnegan’s assessment of human behaviour was extremely accurate. On this occasion though, she had got it completely wrong.

PART THREE

1935–1937

'Look at that white gallant,
Look at his wasted flesh,
It's the moon that's dancing
In the Courtyard of the Dead

Look at his wasted flesh
Black with twilight and wolves
Mother: The moon dances
In the Courtyard of the Dead'

Federico Garcia Lorca (1898–1936)
Excerpt from *Dance of the Santiago Moon*

CHAPTER TWENTY-FIVE

Joshua Jones required neither coaxing nor cajoling to join Edrith Pointon's small band of emissaries. Deeply unhappy and unwilling to return to university, Josh leapt at the chance of a fresh challenge. He was ready for adventure, restless and discontented. Pointon needed to exercise only a modicum of his charm and persuasive manner to convince Josh that working in Europe for His Majesty's Government would provide the outlet for his vague, unfulfilled ambitions.

Earlier, Edrith had allayed Simon and Naomi's remaining fears over possible repercussions from her past. 'When Josh comes to work for us,' he told the couple, 'the protection accorded him will also be extended to his family. Whatever Hildegard Cabrinova-Schwarz did all those years ago will be entombed in our archives. Even if some researcher was resourceful or lucky enough to discover all or part of the truth they would find themselves up against the provisions of the Official Secrets Act, the most powerful instrument at our disposal. In other words,' he smiled at Naomi, 'you are now as well protected as His Majesty the

King, the Prime Minister or any member of the government.'

In early 1935, Josh travelled to London. He attended the small offices occupied by Pointon's department for completion of, in Pointon's words, 'a few boring but necessary formalities'.

Josh's first view of the building left him singularly unimpressed. If his imagination had pictured a large, smart, modern edifice, the two-storey Victorian building in an unfashionable suburb was somewhat of a let-down. It was rundown to the extent of neglect, this careworn appearance being carried through to the interior. An unprepossessing rabbit warren of anonymous offices, some little bigger than cubby holes, did little to fire the imagination of the department's newest recruit. Pointon, who watched the slightly crestfallen expression on Josh's face with quiet amusement, explained, and in so doing gave the younger man his first lesson in the art of espionage.

'I see by the look on your face you're beginning to wonder what you've let yourself in for. Possibly you were expecting something a little more imposing.' He could see he had interpreted Josh's thoughts correctly and continued, 'The object of our work is to remain undetected. It is of little use attempting to operate in secret if everyone knows the location of our premises. That's why we picked this place. It's far enough from the centre of London to be free from association with governmental activity. If you were searching for this department, would you give this building a second glance?'

'Absolutely not,' Josh replied, his tone emphatic.

'No. And our hope is that others would think the same. So whatever pre-conceived notions you might have about our operation, dismiss them from your mind completely and permanently. The objective of espionage is to remain undiscovered by friend and foe alike.'

For the better part of his first day with the department Josh was left alone with a photographer in an attic office that had been converted into a studio. It was an unusual room, in that all the windows had been bricked up, the sole sources of light being from skylights supplemented by two banks of spotlights of the type used in the theatrical profession. The photographer, who had been introduced as Mr Smith, explained the curious construction in one concise sentence, 'If we can't see out, others can't see in.' Josh's second lesson in espionage.

For the next few hours Josh sat, stood, and leaned in a variety of poses directed by Smith. He was pictured hatless, wearing a homburg, a trilby, a cloth cap, and a bewildering succession of costumes. These ranged from sports jackets, casual coats and suits, to overcoats, sweaters, and open-necked shirts. For some photographs he wore a tie, for others a cravat, sometimes a neckerchief and in others without collar and tie altogether. He changed between suit trousers, casual slacks, plus fours and riding breeches with matching boots, and in two shots was attired successively in morning suit with top hat and evening dress.

All Josh's changes of clothing came from a large wardrobe stretching the full length of the studio's back wall. Although each shirt, jacket, or pair of trousers looked absolutely normal from the front, the rear view told a different story. Each had been cut vertically through their full length and was secured by a series of tapes that Smith tied together before posing his subject. 'Saves having to keep a lot of different sizes in stock,' he explained. 'Just as well passports don't require a rear view. Never judge anything by its appearance.'

Lesson number three, Josh thought.

The photographer flitted between a bank of three cameras positioned between the spotlights taking image upon image of Josh. Eventually, he signalled that the session was over by telling Josh to put his own clothes back on. He eyed the pile of discarded clothing and murmured, 'If you can find it under that lot.'

While Josh was dressing, Edrith appeared at the door. 'You must be famished. We'll get something to eat then I've a few more little chores for you before we go.'

'Go? Go where?' Josh asked in surprise.

'I'll tell you later.'

In a similarly bewildering fashion to the morning session, Josh spent much of the afternoon writing.

He signed his own and countless other names in a variety of coloured inks with a wide selection of pens, all with different nibs. Gradually, as the significance of what he was doing dawned on him, he realized that although Joshua Jones had not ceased to exist, he had, in the space of a few hours, been given many other personalities, the majority of which, he was intrigued to notice, were far from English.

Eventually Pointon produced a final, imposing legal document. 'This time you must sign your own name. By signing this you are bound by the Official Secrets Act never to divulge any of the activities of this department or His Majesty's Government. Even the clip holding the pages of the document together is now a state secret. It is more binding by far than even a marriage vow.'

By the time they climbed into Pointon's car the autumn afternoon was ending and dusk was falling. They drove for more than an hour, past neat rows of suburban housing into the countryside beyond. Their route seemed to have been chosen to avoid contact with towns or other identifying landmarks.

They pulled into a country lane, at the end of which was a gravelled driveway leading to a large, stone-built house of Regency or early Victorian design, a manor house Josh guessed.

'This,' Pointon told him as they alighted, 'will be your home for the next two months.' As they removed Josh's suitcase from the boot of the car, the front door of the house opened.

'Good evening, gentlemen.'

'Ah, good evening, Mr Smith,' Pointon replied. He turned and indicated Josh. 'This is Mr Jones. Jones, Mr Smith will be your tutor for the first part of your training.'

It was as well that Josh was able to absorb and retain information quickly and efficiently, for over the two months of his course, Mr Smith and three other tutors taught Josh with such rapidity and detail his brain reeled at times. When the second tutor was introduced as Mr Smith, Josh began to suspect more than coincidence.

'Is everyone in the department called Smith?' he asked.

Smith grinned. 'Everyone but you, Mr Jones. If you don't know our real names, you can't reveal them.'

'I see that,' Josh replied. 'But is anyone actually called Smith?'

'I don't think so,' Smith replied with a laugh.

The last three weeks of Josh's course were as physically arduous as the previous ones had been mentally taxing. Josh was wakened at 5 a.m. by the banging of a large gong immediately outside his bedroom. He staggered to the door, his sleep-dazed brain convinced the house was on fire. A large, muscular figure stood silhouetted in the doorway.

'I'm Smith,' he told Josh and thrust a bundle of

clothing into his arms. 'Get dressed. Cross country run in ten minutes. I'll be waiting in the hall.'

The bundle consisted of an old pair of battledress trousers, tunic, and gym shoes. Josh, who had always been a good athlete, now found himself stretched to the limit and beyond. That first morning he set off in the wake of Mr Smith at what seemed a breakneck pace. Surely, Josh thought, they couldn't keep that speed up for long. They did. As they ran, Smith, who appeared to have limitless stamina and lung capacity, questioned Josh. The answers were terse, mostly gasped. From these, Smith learned that Josh could swim, had boxed and played rugby and cricket.

When they returned to the house two hours later, Josh was exhausted. He was handed a second bundle of clothing. The accompanying commands were equally brusquely delivered. 'Shower and shave, change into these, breakfast in fifteen minutes. Half an hour rest after breakfast, then UCT all morning.' Smith turned and disappeared through a door at the rear of the hall.

'And just what the hell is UCT?' Josh wondered aloud.

UCT, as he found out, was unarmed combat training. Any lingering doubt Josh had about the nature of the world he had entered disappeared as he learned several different ways to kill a man swiftly and silently with his bare hands, and how to avoid a similar fate.

During the whole of his course, without Josh's

knowledge, his tutors had been assessing his progress. Although his mother would have been impressed by much of the report they sent to Pointon, the summary of which was that Josh was ready for field action, she would barely have recognized her son in the final paragraph. This, written by the last Mr Smith, stated that in his judgement, 'Jones is now highly proficient in all areas of combat, both armed and unarmed, and is a natural killer.'

Pointon collected Josh from the manor house and drove him back to London. On the journey he listened to Josh's description of his experiences over the preceding weeks. As he listened Edrith reflected, not for the first time, that he had driven a boy down to the manor house then returned to collect a man. In view of what he had planned for Jones, that was perhaps as well.

When they reached the office, Pointon handed Josh a bundle of papers. 'These papers contain everything you need to know about your new identity. Study them carefully, commit every detail to memory, then return them to me in the morning. Clear your room completely before you do.'

'Where exactly is my destination?'

'You'll learn that tomorrow. I suggest you phone your parents tonight, let them know you're going away. You understand once you leave here you will be unable to contact them again until your assignment is complete. All you will be able to do is send a message in the diplomatic bag through your contact at our embassy.'

Josh grinned. 'Mr Smith told me that,' he said, 'in fact three Mr Smiths told me it.' He tapped the bundle of papers. 'Is a new identity strictly necessary?'

Pointon smiled, more or less without humour. 'If someone, shall we say of unfriendly disposition, were to discover your true identity, they, or their agents could pose a threat to your family as a way to put pressure on you. It's extremely unlikely, but I believe in being over cautious.'

Studying the documents in the privacy of his room, the dark significance of Pointon's words came to Josh. For the first time he felt alone, alone and a little afraid. The following morning, he handed Edrith the bundle of papers and placed his suitcase on the floor.

'That's the lot,' he said. 'Underwear, socks, shoes, everything.'

Pointon indicated a chair and began to question him about the information contained in the paperwork. When he professed himself satisfied, he crossed to the safe and exchanged the paperwork for another, smaller packet. 'This contains your passport, bankbook, and some currency, sufficient for your immediate needs. You can draw more from the bank as and when required. You sail later today. All that remains is for me to give you details of your destination and assignment.'

Pointon indicated a suitcase placed alongside the

desk. 'There are four sets of clothing inside, along with all you will require. I want you to change into one of them now and leave your own clothes here.'

CHAPTER TWENTY-SIX

The trouble that had been brewing between Phil and Luke Fisher finally erupted when Luke had been at Fisher Springs a little over a year. With the brothers now established in the family business, Patrick Finnegan had declared his intention of taking life slightly easier and spending more time with his family. He and Louise were particularly keen to devote as much attention to Finlay as possible. Their youngest son, although completely recovered from the physical effects of his kidnapping ordeal, still demonstrated unmistakeable signs that the trauma was continuing to cause emotional aftershocks. In tending Finlay's needs, Patrick and Louise were conscious of the attention needed by their other children.

When Patrick awarded himself a month's holiday with Louise and the children, the first lines of the script for a confrontation between the Fisher brothers were already being written. The brothers had equal numbers of shares, so they should by rights have equal power, the balance being held by Patrick Finnegan. Philip however, older and more experienced, regarded the company as his to run with everyone deferring to him. Luke was far from deferential by nature. For the first two weeks of Patrick Finnegan's holiday Philip would also be away attending a newspaper publishing convention in America, now accessible by aeroplane in a convoluted series of interlinked journeys.

The conference had been a great success. On the last day, the head of an Australian publishing company, who had seized on the excuse provided by the convention for a cruising holiday with his wife, approached Philip and engaged him in conversation. His opening remarks puzzled Fisher. The rest of the discussion moved him from perplexity, to annoyance, and thence to fury.

'I'm glad to see the deal went through OK,' the magnate began.

'Sorry, what deal?' Philip asked.

'Your purchase of those three radio stations.'

Philip blinked. 'You say we've bought three radio stations from you?'

'Yes, part of my plan to scale down. I'm not getting any younger you know. I got the cable confirming the deal this morning. Your brother Luke signed it yesterday. Didn't you know about it?'

'Oh, er, yes. I just didn't know it had been finalized,' he replied lamely.

The interchange had taken place in front of a group of delegates to the convention, whose scepticism of Fisher's denial of ignorance showed clearly in their expressions.

On his journey home, there was a delay at the airport where a vital two hours was lost, causing Philip to miss two connecting flights. This added a day and a half to his travelling time. When the taxi finally dropped him outside the Finnegan house it was at four in the morning. The trials and tribulations of the journey added to the burning sense of anger at Luke's usurping of his authority. Tiredness eroded the normal inhibitions in his behaviour.

It was Dottie Fisher, the only other occupant of the house at the time, who gave her account of what followed to Patrick and Louise Finnegan. She had summoned them by phone and when they were able to make sense of her words through the hysterical sobbing, they returned home as fast as possible via a network of trains and road.

Two days later, on the veranda, Dottie was in one of the swing chairs alongside Bella Finnegan. The younger boys had been banished inside with instructions to avoid the minstrel gallery. Dottie began her tale.

'I was woken up by a dreadful shouting. At first I thought we had burglars, but then I recognized Phil's voice. He was screaming at Luke, accusing him of all sorts of awful things.'

'What did Luke say?' Louise asked.

'He never spoke a word from beginning to end. I came out of my room to see what it was all about. Phil had dragged Luke out of bed and got him onto the minstrel gallery. He'd got his hands round his throat, pinned up against the banister rail. I thought he was going to strangle him, he looked really mad. He might have done as well but the rail gave way and they both fell through into the hall. I had to call the hospital to get them help. Luke wasn't too badly hurt, apart from some bruises and a broken arm but Phil was unconscious and had broken a rib and his left leg. The hospital set Luke's arm and when they were sure he wasn't concussed, they released him.'

'Where's Luke now?' Finnegan asked.

'He's gone,' Dottie blurted out, close to tears.

'Gone? Gone where?' Patrick and Louise asked in unison.

'I don't know,' Dottie wailed. 'But I think he's gone for good.'

'I don't understand. What do you mean, gone for good?' Louise was agitated.

'When he came back from the hospital he went straight to his room, took his suitcase from under the bed, then, because he was struggling with one arm broken, he asked me to pack it for him.' Dottie turned to Louise, tears streaming down her face. 'He got me to pack everything, clothes, money, bankbooks the lot,' she cried. 'That's why I think he's gone forever.'

'But where will he go? What will he do?' Louise, too, was crying.

'He didn't say anything, give you any reason?' Patrick asked.

'No, he just said it was better this way. Oh, and he left a note for you.'

Finnegan ripped open the envelope and took out the single sheet of paper. He read the note out loud.

Dear Uncle Patrick and Aunt Louise,

Dottie will have told you what happened by now. It is clear I can neither work with nor live close to my brother any longer, so I have decided to leave. It is not for his sake but for the good of the whole family. I shall continue to hold my shares in the company and will keep a close watch on its progress. The annual report and accounts along with my dividend cheques should be sent to the Sydney branch of our bank from where I will collect them. If my brother raises any objection remind him of the penalties for assault and grievous bodily harm.

Thanks for all you have done for me. I'm sorry it had to end this way. I don't expect I shall see any of you again.

Luke.

The abrupt tone of the final sentence was the last straw, for Louise, for Dottie and for Patrick

Finnegan as well. There were tears from all of them, everyone apart from Bella Finnegan. She picked up the note and read it once more, her pretty face suffused with rage. At that moment as the phrase 'I don't expect I'll see any of you again' struck home, a cold, implacable hatred for Philip Fisher was born in her.

When Philip Fisher left hospital, his leg still in plaster, he naturally returned to the Finnegan house, the only home he knew. His stay in hospital had been a strange experience for him, as of time suspended, for he received neither visitors nor letters. Philip, although he was unaware of the fact, had been ostracised.

The changed situation became apparent when he reached the house. No welcoming party came from the door to greet him. Louise had taken the children out for the day, so it was Patrick Finnegan alone who saw the taxi arrive and opened the house door. He watched as Philip struggled to manage the unfamiliar crutches prior to paying the driver.

'Don't bother,' Finnegan called to him, 'you're going to need that driver. You're not stopping here.'

Philip looked round in alarm and astonishment.

'You'll have to find somewhere else to live,' Finnegan said, approaching the taxi. 'Louise won't allow you in the house. You're not welcome.' He indicated a pile of boxes and suitcases stacked on the veranda. 'I suggest you get the driver to help you with those.'

Finnegan turned to walk back into the house. 'And don't rush back to work either. The staff know what happened to Luke. You're as popular there as a cockroach in a salad.'

Although Philip did return to Fisher Springs the strained relations with Finnegan and the hostile attitude of the rest of the employees made life difficult for a long time. He knew his actions were disapproved of, deep down he was ashamed of them. He wished he could meet up with Luke and apologize. But Luke was long gone. Philip learned rapidly how high a regard people had for his brother, how low their opinion of him was. He became used to issuing instructions only to get the stinging reply, 'Luke wouldn't have done that,' or, 'what was wrong with the way Luke did this?'

Although Patrick had to work with Philip, conversation between the two men was strictly limited to business matters, even that was often stilted. Philip would dearly have loved to exert the power of his greater shareholding but dared not put himself into opposition with Finnegan. He was aware that if Patrick obtained Luke's shareholder vote he could use it to kick him out of the company. The attitude between them was one of armed neutrality. Philip, cut off from all family contact, was unaware that none of them, not even Finnegan, had any more idea as to Luke's whereabouts than Philip himself did.

CHAPTER TWENTY-SEVEN

One of many who had immigrated to Australia in the early part of the century was an Italian, Gianni Rocca. He hailed from Montespertoli in Tuscany, where his family had been involved in winemaking for centuries. Gianni was the youngest of five brothers and the family business could not support all of them. So he had arrived in Australia with only a small amount of money left from the savings he had used to pay for his fare.

Although life in the new land was hard at first, Gianni tried his hand at several jobs in the early days. Eventually, he found a job that paid well enough for him to afford to send for his fiancée Angelina. Gianni had one advantage over most of his peers. He was from a good family, had been well educated, and could speak, read and write English fluently. He was also proficient in French and German. It was this facility with languages that landed him the prize job. An enterprising newspaper editor, aware of the influx of large numbers of immigrants from Europe, had decided to run a regular supplement in several languages.

This, he felt, would help keep the newcomers au fait with developments in their adopted country to everyone's advantage. It would also boost the newspaper's circulation, an equally important consideration. The newspaper needed people proficient in European languages. Gianni was one of these. The editor was Randolph Charles, the newspaper part of the Fisher Springs Group.

It was there that Gianni met Luke Fisher, who on first joining the family business was to learn the workings of the newspaper industry. The two were from widely different backgrounds, one a young representative of a bold new industrial aristocracy, the other from an older, gentler culture. Despite this, or perhaps because of it, the two got on famously.

Gianni was content for most of the time, his job was secure, his home life agreeable, but winemaking was in his blood, he day-dreamed of establishing a vineyard. The Australian climate and soil were right, Gianni was sure. In more practical moments he realized these were mere fantasies. Creating a vineyard is a long, laborious, and expensive business. It takes many years of hard work and a substantial capital investment before the owner receives any reward for his time and effort. Although Gianni was comfortably placed there was no way he could afford such a gamble.

One evening, as they were relaxing after work in a bar close to the newspaper offices, Gianni had told Luke of his dream.

‘That’s interesting,’ Luke said. ‘I remember when I was small, my parents went to France. When they came back my dad said he reckoned we could make wine here just as good as the French – or the Italians for that matter,’ he added.

Gianni had all but forgotten the conversation when one evening there was a knock on his house door as he was sitting with Angelina and the children. He was surprised to find Luke Fisher standing there. ‘Luke. What are you doing here? Is something wrong?’

‘No, Gianni, nothing’s wrong. I’m here to offer you the chance to make your dream come true.’

Gianni’s wife, Angelina, might have had doubts about the wisdom of the gamble her husband was about to embark on but these were laid to rest with the terms of the contract Luke insisted both she and Gianni inspect before all three of them signed it.

‘I want Angelina to be named as a partner in this enterprise,’ he told Gianni, ‘because it will be you and she who are responsible for finding the site for the vineyard, clearing the land, planting the vines and nurturing them until we get our first crop. I will not be on hand much of the time but I will ensure there are always more than adequate funds available for the development, even providing for unforeseen circumstances. This’ – he produced a long, complicated looking legal document – ‘is the contract I have had drawn up. It makes provision for you and your family to ensure you will not suffer financially even if the venture proves unsuccessful. I want you to take it to an independent lawyer, have him check it over and when he is satisfied with it, sign it and send the bill for his fees to me.'

'You say you will not be about, what do you intend to do?' Angelina asked.

Luke had told them of the events surrounding his departure, some of which, exaggerated and distorted were already being rumoured widely within the group. He grinned at Angelina's question and replied, 'I'm going to travel for a while, enjoy myself a bit while I can, then in a few years' time I'll find something useful to occupy myself.'

'You'll have enough money to get by on?' Gianni asked, but it was more of a statement than a question.

'I think so.' Luke grinned. 'Even the cost of the vineyard doesn't scratch the surface. If I wanted to, I could live off what I have for the rest of my life. Since my parents died, the dividends have been piling up at the bank despite the recession. Now things are beginning to improve so they should get even better. Patrick Finnegan and my brother are quite capable of running the business without me so I might as well sit back and take the money.' If his smile was a little forced, only Angelina noticed it. 'I get the best of the deal, the dividends still come to me, and I don't have to work for them.'

After Luke left, Gianni and Angelina spent a long time discussing the exciting new direction their lives would take, eventually however, their talk turned to their recent visitor.

'He seems very content with his lot, as he says he's got the best of both worlds,' Gianni stated.

Angelina regarded him fondly. 'Sometimes, Gianni Rocca, I think you have all the wisdom in the world, at other times, like now for instance, I believe you know absolutely nothing.'

'What do you mean?'

'Could you not see the truth behind those brave words? Could you not tell the anguish in that young man's soul? You should have watched his eyes, they spoke volumes. He is angry, hurt, and bitter. You remember his words, "I'll find something useful to occupy myself with, in a few years' time". What sort of statement is that for a young man to make? Or, "I'll sit back and let the dividends come to me", that's the sort of thing a man of seventy would say. No, mark my words, Gianni, Luke is deeply distressed, and who can blame him? He has cast himself adrift from everything he loves, his home, his family, the business. No wonder there is such sadness in his eyes, such emptiness, and loneliness in his voice. The future he spoke so bravely about must seem very bleak to him now.'

Gianni thought over what Angelina had said. 'Do you think that's why he is doing this?' He indicated the document on the table.

'Of course I do, although I doubt whether Luke recognizes it as such. I think he is trying to replace part of what he has been forced to abandon.'

'It is a good deal for us though, isn't it?' Gianni sought reassurance.

'Very much so,' Angelina was positive. 'If I had any remaining doubts, his offer to pay the legal fees would have convinced me. I didn't have doubts though. I knew as soon as I met him that what you told me about Luke Fisher, what everyone else says of him, is accurate. He is a very fine young man, with strong principles. He has a lot of strength and he will need it in the next few years.'

'I wonder where he will go, what he will do?' Gianni mused.

'I think he should travel abroad, visit America, Europe, and Asia perhaps, but of one thing I am sure, he will return to Australia eventually. Although he may have cut himself adrift, his home is here. He won't be able to keep away.'

New Year's Day 1936 in Byland Crescent had been a special occasion. The celebrations at Christmas were extended, as always, to include the wider circle of family and friends. Along with Michael, Connie and Edward Haigh were Simon and Naomi Jones with their family. The Jones brigade, along with Marguerite Haigh and her husband were staying at the guest house at the opposite end of the Crescent, to avoid the house bursting at the seams. Despite the absence of George Haigh, now a junior officer in the Royal Navy, and Joshua Jones who was said to be travelling through Europe, the occasion was a special one.

The previous night Mark and Jenny had been out for dinner and dancing at one of Scarborough's many fine hotels. As the band played Jimmy McHugh and Dorothy Fields' composition *I'm in the Mood for Love*, Jenny gently sang in Mark's ear.

'I'm glad about that,' Mark whispered as she repeated the words of the title.

'Why?' Jenny demanded suspiciously, leaning back slightly in his arms to look at him.

'Because, these months apart at university with only letters to keep us in touch made me realize how much I miss you, how empty each day is without you to share it. Jenny, will you marry me?'

'Mark,' Jenny protested, half laughing, half embarrassed, 'we're in the middle of the dance floor.'

'Yes and we're staying here until you give me an answer,' he said as he pulled her close.

'Oh no, I'll give you my answer when we get back to the table.'

'OK.' Mark took her hand and pulled her from the floor. He saw her seated then asked, 'Well?'

'You haven't even got a ring,' she protested.

A waiter appeared at her shoulder. He proffered Jenny a silver salver on which was a single rose and a small blue velvet box. As if in a daze Jenny murmured a word of thanks to him and looked up to see Mark watching her anxiously. She opened the box and gasped with delight. The diamonds of the engagement ring twinkled and glistened in the half-light of the ballroom. Jenny slid the ring from the box and placed it on the tablecloth. 'You do it,' she commanded.

Mark picked up the ring and slipped it onto the third finger of her left hand.

'That's it, then,' Jenny said a little obscurely.

'Does that mean you will marry me?' Mark asked hopefully.

'My dear, silly, wonderful, Mark Cowgill, of course I'll marry you. I've been in love with you ever since I can remember and I've been waiting and hoping you'd ask me for the last three years. These months apart have intensified all I've felt for you for so long.'

The following morning, Rachael Cowgill, who had been consulted about Mark's plan, was like a cat on hot bricks. As the morning wore on, her impatience mounted, despite Sonny's calming pleas. Eventually, she could contain herself no longer and announced, 'I'm going to ask him.'

She marched upstairs and knocked vigorously on her son's bedroom door. After a moment a sleepy voice called, 'Come in.'

Rachael opened the door. Mark was sitting up, the bedclothes tucked under his chin. As he surveyed his mother drowsily, she demanded, 'Well, did Jenny say yes?'

From by Mark's side a hand appeared above the bedclothes. The diamonds shone brighter still in the morning light.

'Oh, congratulations, darling,' Rachael said loudly. 'I'll be sure and congratulate Jenny too when I see her.' With that she beat a hasty retreat.

Sonny was prowling about in the hall when Rachael returned downstairs. 'Well, dear, did Jenny say yes?'

Rachael smiled enigmatically. 'I think so, darling. In fact, I think Jenny said yes to a lot of things.'

Later that day, Rachael took Mark to one side. 'Mark, I know that to you this is one of the happiest days of your life and that the happiness you feel has no comparison. However, may I remind you that this is your grandmother's house and she is unaware of the circumstances in which I found you and Jenny this morning? Please, respect that.'

'Sorry, mother, it won't happen again.' Mark said sheepishly.

Rachael leaned forward and kissed her son on the cheek. 'Oh, I'm sure it will – but not here.'

For the most part, the conversation during dinner that evening centred on Mark and Jenny's engagement. The family was delighted by the announcement, none more so than Hannah. Mark, the most cherished of her grandchildren, had arrived with his mother in Byland Crescent soon after her husband Albert had died, when she believed Sonny was also dead. It had been Mark and Jenny's childhood antics that had lifted Hannah from the abyss of depression. Now, years later, Hannah felt uplifted once more, renewed by the couple's happiness.

As with so many dinner parties at that time, talk turned to the political unrest spreading throughout Europe and beyond. Simon Jones and Sonny, who agreed with Michael Haigh that there was a threat from communism, both held that the greater danger came from those fascist dictators now flexing their muscles. The supine attitude of the League of Nations to Mussolini's invasion of Ethiopia was cited, as was the worsening crisis in Spain where right- and left-wing confrontations were worsening rapidly. Mark and Jenny, who might have been expected to identify with the apparently more charismatic leaders of the right, were passionate in their disavowal of fascism, particularly its overtly racist policies.

'How can you persecute a man for being a Jew, or a Romany, or Slav by birth?' Mark asked. 'They didn't ask to be born that way, they didn't have any choice. You might just as well punish a man for being born with red hair or blue eyes, or for being left-handed.'

'We had trouble with Germany once this century,' Hannah agreed. 'It will happen again in exactly the same way. They will seek an excuse to attack the smaller countries around them and before we know it we will all be dragged into the fight.'

Naomi gripped her lips firmly together at the latter comment. Simon squeezed her hand comfortingly under the table.

Sonny lightened the moment by remarking, 'If Mr Chamberlain leaves us anything to fight with, that is. All the reports tell of Germany rearming and he goes on about reducing our armed forces. The man's a disgrace.'

'Fascism is evil,' Simon remarked. 'I saw a little of what it is capable of when Josh and I visited Germany and they'd only got a toe-hold on power then. Heaven knows what they'll be up to now. It's not just Germany though. Austria, Italy, and Bulgaria are also run by fascists, as is Portugal. With outright civil war in Spain, if they were to fall to the nationalists that would mean the whole of the Iberian Peninsula will be run by right-wing extremists. France would be virtually surrounded and her politics is in such a mess she could easily fall to a fascist puppet regime. Then they'd be only twenty-two miles from the Kent coast. We've already had evidence of their methods, from Mosley's Black-shirt thugs on our own streets. Does anybody want to live under a regime controlled by those animals?'

CHAPTER TWENTY-EIGHT

On the morning of 21 January 1936 England was in mourning. King George V had died late the previous evening. His son Edward was now sovereign. In Byland Crescent the family and staff gathered round the radio a week later to listen as the funeral service was broadcast to the nation. In London, Jessica Tunnicliffe stood with the crowds lining the streets to pay her respects.

Whatever Jessica imagined would be the outcome of her move to London, it was not the series of boring, dead-end jobs that followed her graduation from business school. She stuck these out with a grim determination. One or two she left quickly as a result of her unwillingness to comply with employers whose concept of her job description was radically different to Jessica's. She had left the latest of these, her parting shot to her employer being, 'explain that when you get home' in reference to a series of scratches inflicted by her fingernails down both cheeks of the amorous employer's face. Her only satisfaction was the thought of the man's wife's reaction to the unmistakeable scars.

Then Jessica met Antonia Harcourt, middle-aged, slim and still attractive, a dedicated career woman. She worked for the employment agency with whom Jessica was registered, but thus far they had not met. Antonia specialized in finding and placing applicants for more responsible posts. When Jessica's file had landed on her desk, Antonia enquired why she had not seen it before.

'She's young and fairly inexperienced, only recently qualified,' the partner replied.

'Yes, but she seems ideal for one post I'm seeking to fill. I think I'd like to meet her.'

Jessica liked Antonia. She spoke her mind, did not make empty promises, and was perceptive enough to work out the true reason for Jessica's speedy departure from one or two jobs. For Antonia's part, she listened and watched the young woman at the other side of her desk, her impression growing more favourable as the interview progressed. She terminated it with the words, 'I have a position in mind for you but I need to check with the employer first. It is a slightly unusual job, quite different from what you have been used to, and in the first instance you might be bored by it, but I promise you when you've been there a while you will really enjoy it. Do you want me to put your name forward?'

Jessica agreed and after she had left, Antonia picked up the phone and dialled a number. The phone was answered, a voice saying simply, 'Yes.'

'Would you please ask Mr Smith to ring Antonia Harcourt?'

'There is no Mr Smith here.'

'Of course not, thank you very much.' She put the phone down and waited.

Fifteen minutes later her phone rang. The receptionist informed her that a Mr Smith was holding. When the call was put through Antonia spoke first, 'Mr Smith, thank you for calling back. You asked me to look for a suitable young woman. I believe I have a candidate for you.'

'Do you have a file?'

'Yes, I can have it sent if you wish.'

'That will be in order.'

On Friday morning a courier arrived. 'You have a file to collect for Mr Smith.'

Antonia handed him a large envelope. Later that afternoon she received a further phone call.

'Please inform the young woman that I shall contact her with a view to meeting her. If she interviews well, she can have the job.'

Antonia rang Jessica. 'It might all sound a little mysterious, but I can assure you it is nothing to worry about, it is perfectly above board.'

When the interview was over, Jessica returned to her flat, still somewhat mystified as to why she had agreed to take the job. It is one thing to take up a position without knowing the precise details of one's duties, another to know absolutely nothing about what that job entails. Similarly, it is not uncommon to begin working for an employer without knowing everything about them and their operation, different again to know absolutely nothing about who they are or what they do.

As Jessica was puzzling over why she had agreed, Antonia Harcourt received another phone call from Mr Smith. 'The interview was satisfactory and the young lady accepted the position. We will send your fee in the usual way.'

'Thank you, Mr Smith. I hope she will prove satisfactory.'

'I'm sure she will,' Edrith Pointon said.

It was several months after starting her new job that Jessica became aware of the nature of the organization for which she worked. She might, had she known more about the workings of the civil service, have realized at the beginning. Very few junior clerical assistants are required to sign their acceptance of the more rigorous ramifications of the Official Secrets Act, but Jessica was not to know that.

She spent her days typing reports from various parts of the world, many of them new to her, without realizing the significance of their content or the process of their acquisition by this tiny government department. Gradually however, as she began to absorb more and more of the information she was transcribing, Jessica began to wonder how this small organization got hold of such obscure facts. Even then the full significance of it all would probably not have dawned on her but for a conversation with her section leader.

In the anonymous building where she worked, there was nothing grander than a rest room containing two armchairs that had seen better days, a cabinet containing crockery and cutlery, a sink and a gas ring for boiling the battered kettle. Jessica, who had spent all morning wrestling with a report on the political situation in Bulgaria, was more than ready for her lunch break. Mrs Crane, Jessica's section leader, was seated in one of the rest room's dilapidated armchairs reading a magazine. She looked up when Jessica entered and smiled. 'You look tired dear, that report getting the better of you?'

'Those damned place names are bad enough,' Jessica responded, 'but the surnames are impossible. Even when I've managed to decipher them from the appalling handwriting my typewriter ties itself in knots attempting to put letters next to one another that clearly don't belong there. I'm just glad nobody wants me to pronounce them. Why can't we have reports from somewhere pronounceable, like Godalming or,' she stuttered, 'or Nottingham or Leeds?'

'I don't think we'd need spies to report on events in Godalming, dear,' Mrs Crane stated calmly, 'or Nottingham or even Leeds for that matter.'

‘Spies,’ Jessica echoed numbly, ‘spies, does that mean what I think it means? All those reports I type are from spies?’

‘Of course, dear,’ Mrs Crane was as calm as ever. ‘How on earth do you think we get such detailed and confidential information?’

Jessica thought for a moment. ‘Is that why they’re all headed by the name “Smith” and a number?’

‘That’s right. It’s to protect the identity of our people in case documents fall into the wrong hands.’

‘Are any of them actually called Smith, I wonder?’ Jessica mused.

Mrs Crane laughed. ‘I very much doubt it. I once asked the boss that question. He’s always referred to as Smith too, you know, but all he would say was, “My dear, Mrs Crane, do I look like a Smith?”’

From then on the reports took on an extra significance for Jessica.

Almost half a century earlier, the foresight shown by Albert Cowgill, Sonny’s father, in persuading his fellow directors to invest in the fledgling chemicals industry was demonstrated time and again throughout the years of the depression in the figures of Fisher Springs UK. In previous times it had been Hannah’s nephew, Charlie Binks, whose brilliant and innovative chemical dyes had boosted group profits, latterly these had benefited from a wide range of chemicals produced by Charlie's son Robert.

Although Charlie still headed Outlane Chemicals, he concentrated more on sales and administration, leaving the technical side of the business to his son. Charlie recognized that, although he was a talented chemist, he could not match Robert's brilliance.

Robert's contemporaries also shared this view. His name always came into the reckoning when major concerns in the industry were head-hunting. Many offers were forthcoming but Robert was not to be lured away. He was content in the work he did, uninterested in the offers, flattering though they might be. His ambition did not stretch to money or acclaim – it was centred on his work.

Knowing this, and his son's devotion to the family business, Charlie would have been considerably surprised had he been party to a meeting Robert had during the autumn of 1937. It had been arranged by telephone, the content of the call mysterious enough to arouse Robert's curiosity. The caller stated that he represented certain eminent figures whose concern was that British technology and scientific expertise were suffering by comparison with other nations. These persons had empowered him to approach scientists of the highest repute to ensure the country could respond and arrest the neglect should the need arise.

It all sounded rather tenuous, the meeting itself contained little more in the way of substance.

'My principals,' the visitor began, 'are of the opinion that if events take a certain course this country will be in urgent need of its best scientific brains. They have asked me to interview outstanding candidates who would be prepared to place their talents at the disposal of the nation, should that prove necessary, as we are fairly sure will be the case. One of the first names mentioned was yours, Mr Binks.'

Robert looked at his visitor, intrigued, mildly bewildered, and vaguely alarmed by his words. 'Let's get this straight,' he demanded, 'are we talking about war?'

'We would always hope and pray that war can be avoided. However, we are concerned that if war becomes inevitable we do not begin hostilities unprepared. To be frank, Mr Binks, while other nations have taken more than adequate steps to strengthen their position and kept up with the latest scientific developments, we have seen our own position steadily weakened through neglect and lack of investment in areas vital to a potential conflict. At the moment, to put it bluntly, we are so unprepared it would be like doing battle with a tank, armed only with a bow and arrow.'

Robert thought about it for a while, then asked, 'You have mentioned your principals once or twice, do I take it you mean the government?'

The man smiled thinly. 'Shall we say various semi-official, but influential and interested parties?'

In the end Robert agreed to give the matter due

consideration and consented to the request for confidentiality. The caller left his visiting card on departure, requesting Robert call him when he had reached a decision.

After he had gone Robert pondered their discussion for a while. He needed an opinion from someone more au fait with the political situation than he was. He reached for the telephone and rang Simon Jones. 'Simon, I need your advice, you know how it is, stuck in the laboratory, I don't get much of a view of the outside world. I'd like you to fill me in with political developments in Europe.'

Robert's unease at the visitor's scenario of the future was heightened by Simon Jones's opinion. Two days later he dialled the number on the visiting card and waited to be put through. 'Hello, it's Robert Binks here. I've thought things over. You can count me in. Should the need arise, I'll be at your disposal, Mr Smith.'

CHAPTER TWENTY-NINE

Mark and Jenny had been impressed with Simon Jones's chilling predictions over the New Year dinner table. They resolved to watch developments in Europe with greater concern. They were young, fired by the idealism of the young. They were not communists, nor even socialists, but had that highly developed sense of justice and fairness perhaps only the very young or the very old possess. When they read early reports of fighting and worse, they, as many throughout Europe and beyond were doing, were determined to try to help.

For Mark's parents, Sonny and Rachael, and for Jenny's mother Joyce, their children's decision was a painful one, but one they could not, in all conscience, contest. While protesting the madness and danger of the proposed expedition they fell short of forbidding it. As Rachael put it, 'Perhaps if enough young people across the nations demonstrate their feelings strongly enough, politicians will be forced to rethink their policies and abandon such dangerous lunacy.'

So in the spring, Mark and Jenny set sail, bound

for the northern Spanish port of Santander. When they arrived, Spain was in confusion. So contrary were the reports that it was difficult to establish which side, if either, was in the ascendancy. The ideal that had inspired them to travel to Spain, threatened to drown, swamped by the rising tide of obstacles in the path of their desire to contribute in some undefined useful way. They were stuck in Santander for over five weeks with no clear idea where to go next. Eventually, they made contact with an agent of the International Brigades, a fierce-eyed, moustachioed Basque whose command of English was at best fractured. He introduced them to a small band of equally enthusiastic, hopelessly amateurish fellow volunteers culled from several European countries. He directed the group to head for Madrid, or if they found their route to the capital blocked by nationalist forces, to make instead for Valencia.

A small handful, including Mark and Jenny, opted to try to reach the republican stronghold of Valencia. They had a plan, albeit a vague and basic one. They would head east and south, roughly following the course of the River Ebro, heading for Lograno, then on to Zaragoza, eventually hoping to reach the east coast south of Tarragona. From there, if they were successful in getting that far, they could follow the coast southwards towards Castellon de la Plana and thence to Valencia. There was one major stumbling block, in that they did not know and had no way of finding out which towns and villages in their path were in republican hands and which were held by nationalist supporters.

They had only been on the road a few days when they ran into trouble. Just east of Lograno, their sights set on their next destination, they were fired on from long range by a small band of nationalist supporters. The party scattered in disarray. Mark and Jenny made their escape to the south into the beautiful wooded valleys and countryside of La Rioja. Their information about the route they should take, gleaned from a couple of elderly and inaccurate maps they had been shown in Santander, was sketchy to say the least. They were unaware that every stride was taking them into the Sierra de Cebollera, devoid of all but a few marks of human habitation in the form of a handful of tiny hamlets. They were, not to put too fine a point on it, completely and hopelessly lost.

The ambush, if ambush was the right expression, was simply enough achieved. Mark and Jenny, exhausted, afraid, and running out of supplies, had fallen asleep. One minute they had been resting in the shade of an olive grove, the next they were awakened by the unmistakeable sound of the cocking of a rifle bolt. They sat up to find themselves surrounded by a group of eight men, all armed, all hostile in appearance.

Their stay in the country had afforded them

little time to assimilate much of the Spanish language, certainly not enough to talk themselves out of this crisis. Mark closed his eyes and uttered the two words that would establish their credentials and earn them either a cheer or a bullet. 'No Pasarán!' he voiced the rallying cry of the republican movement as confidently as he could muster, while gripping Jenny's hand tightly. 'No Pasarán!' he repeated.

He heard the response from their captors. 'Viva La Pasionaria!'

It was all right. They were in the hands of republican guerrillas. From the high plateau of these noble utterances, what followed descended abruptly into something more resembling farce. The problem was the language barrier. After several highly unsuccessful attempts at communication in Spanish and English, Jenny asked if any of the men spoke French. One of the guerrillas shuffled forward. '*Un petit peu, Mam'selle,*' he offered shyly.

From that point, but still with considerable difficulty, Mark and Jenny managed to tell the guerrillas all that had befallen them since their arrival in Spain. Through the severely limited medium of their new interpreter, they managed to convey the fact that they were English, information that seemed to astonish and amuse their captors much more than Mark and Jenny considered proportionate. It certainly seemed to spur the guerrilla leader to activity. He motioned to the couple to get up and the whole party moved off down the hillside.

'Where are they taking us, do you know?' Jenny whispered.

'I've no idea,' Mark replied, 'I thought he said something that sounded like Carmen, but I can't be sure.'

Several hours later, tired, dirty, hungry, and thirsty, as dusk was beginning to bring welcome relief from the hot afternoon sun, they reached a small hamlet. The leader turned and spoke to Mark, his arms flailing with gestures as if this would aid his understanding.

Mark nodded and turned to Jenny. 'I think he said this place is no problem.'

They did not stop in the village but continued into the woodland beyond. Another hour's walking brought them to a clearing containing two cabins and several makeshift tents.

The leader knocked on the door of one of the cabins. A woman who looked to be in her late twenties opened the door and strode out. She was strikingly beautiful, her long raven black hair framing a face whose high cheekbones and olive complexion gave her a look of vivid beauty.

Mark and Jenny were close enough to hear the conversation between the leader and the woman. Although the words meant nothing it was clear from his deference that the woman was in charge. She dismissed him with a nod and turned to the couple standing before her. What she saw evidently amused her for she smiled and gestured to the departing leader. Her English faultless, but slightly accented she said, 'He tells me you have come to support our cause, but you ran into trouble. It would be ungracious to refuse help given at so much risk to yourselves. Why not come inside and tell me about it, you must be hungry. We can talk as we eat.' The invitation was more of a command. It was reinforced by the revolver stuck into the waistband of the woman's skirt.

The cabin she showed them into was surprisingly spacious. Although sparsely furnished, it was clean, the smell of pine lending a sweet, wholesome fragrance to the atmosphere. 'Sit down,' their hostess invited, a command Mark and Jenny were happy to obey, for the danger of their situation, added to the long march, had tired them.

'I am Carmen, or at least that's what I'm known as. It isn't my real name – we don't use them for our mutual protection. That way, if the nationalist pigs were to capture any of our group and torture them all they would get is a lot of nicknames, not the true identity of our comrades.'

In normal speech her voice was low, slightly husky, but clear and sweet in intonation. Carmen continued, 'You' – she pointed at Mark – 'I will refer to as El Ingles, while you, my dear' – she turned to Jenny – 'will be La Chica. The man leading you here we call El Gitano because his mother was of gypsy blood. Mostly we choose our own nicknames but I have picked yours for you as you don't speak our language.' She smiled at the couple.

Encouraged by this, Mark, remembering his grandmother's love of opera, asked her 'Are you called Carmen because you love toreadors or because you work in a cigarette factory?'

Carmen laughed, a rich and joyous contralto sound. 'I worked in a cigarette factory a long time ago, before I was married.'

'You're married?' Jenny asked in surprise, it seemed strange to find a married woman living as an outlaw.

'I was.' A cloud passed over Carmen's face. 'My husband was killed.'

Mark hastened to change the subject from something obviously causing distress. 'What exactly is this place?'

'This is one of several camps we have in the region, bases we use to operate from and to hide in when the need arises. We found out a long time ago that our best way of attacking the fascists was not in strict battle, for they are much stronger in numbers and far better equipped than we are. They have German and Italian armour and planes to bomb us before we can engage them on the ground. So we banded together in this wilderness and adopted the tactics used by your General Lord Wellington over a century ago.'

'What are those?' Jenny asked.

'He used small bands of Spanish and Portuguese

guerrillas, the word means partisan, to ambush and harass Napoleon's forces, weakening them with surprise attacks until he was ready to engage them in battle. The terrain here is ideal for that kind of warfare. We break into their magazines, steal their munitions and explosives, then use them to attack their owners,' Carmen told them with a chuckle.

'Are there many of you?' Mark asked.

'Never enough,' Carmen told them frankly. 'I suppose almost a thousand in total. Not all based here. When we banded together the man we elected as leader suggested we operate this way and it has worked very well so far. There are five bases around the region. When the rest of the men return there will be two hundred here. The men who brought you here were just a security patrol on the lookout for enemy activity in the area to make sure we are not taken unawares.' Carmen grinned. 'We prefer to reserve such surprises for the fascists.'

'How long have you been living this way?' Jenny asked.

Once more they saw the cloud of sadness in Carmen's face. 'Over a year now, since I met the leader of our group.'

'Who is he?' Mark asked again to get away from the obviously painful topic.

'We call him La Trompetista. He is a great man. He has been a great friend to Spain and to our cause.'

'He's not Spanish then?' Mark persisted.

Carmen looked at him with some surprise then smiled. 'No, he is not Spanish. You will meet him in time, all being well, but he is away at present. Now, you must be hungry.'

As they ate, Mark and Jenny's thoughts were on Carmen, her obviously tragic past and the feeling she had shown when speaking of the mysterious guerrilla leader, La Trompetista. Carmen's reverence when speaking of this shadowy figure was apparent. Jenny, with the insight of her own love for Mark, suspected that Carmen loved La Trompetista.

For the next weeks, Mark and Jenny were taught the rudiments of field-craft and guerrilla warfare by Carmen and other members of the group. They learned to move silently through the woods, leaving little or no trace of their passing. They were taught how to recognize signs of enemy movement, looking for wheeled tracks or footprints, disturbed wildlife and other indications that intruders might be in their vicinity. They learned how to load, cock and aim a variety of weapons, from automatic rifles to a wide variety of pistols. They were taught the basic tricks of hand-to-hand fighting, the use of the dagger and certain unarmed combat methods involving parts of the body they would not have expected could be turned into weaponry. Although the gunsmith showed them how to use the various arms at their disposal, they were forbidden to practice with them.

Carmen explained, 'Sound travels a long way in this wilderness, we cannot afford to give our position away and shooting is a sure signal of our presence. Besides which' – she added with a grin – 'ammunition is scarce and the only target worth shooting at is a fascist.'

Carmen herself instructed them in the use of explosives, how to set a detonator, where to place the charges to best effect, how much fuse to allocate, sufficient to give them chance to retire to a safe distance and several other techniques she admitted she had learned from their leader. During all the time they were being given this training they saw only those who had been in camp when they arrived. As the weeks slipped by it became clear that Carmen was growing increasingly anxious for news of the rest of the group. Then, late one night as Mark and Jenny lay together in their cot of roughly hewn pine, they heard the sound of a horse being ridden into the encampment. It was clear this posed no threat, for they heard no cries of alarm, merely murmured conversation followed by silence.

The following morning they were awakened by the sound of hoof-beats echoing in the distance. When they emerged from the cabin, Carmen was standing outside, a half empty cup of coffee in her hand, gazing towards the edge of the forest. She turned towards them and gave them a slow, lazy smile.

'Buenos Dias, amigos,' she said softly. There was

an air of dreamy contentment about her, in sharp contrast to the worried frowns of the previous days. 'You retired too soon, you missed our leader. He arrived late last night and is gone already. The men are ordered to high alert as there is much enemy activity reported in the area. He has planned several attacks to make sure they get a hot reception. So everyone must play their part, including you and me. We will take the remaining men and commence patrolling the area close to this camp, through the forest to the east and northward.'

'What of the south and west?' Mark asked.

Carmen pointed towards the mountains. 'If they get across, I'll be very surprised.' Adding with a grin, 'I hope they try it, with a bit of luck the wolves will feast well!'

CHAPTER THIRTY

Jesse Barker, or Jack Barlow as he now styled himself, had prospered in the United States during Prohibition. The Italian immigrants he had befriended onboard ship had proved invaluable contacts. They and their 'families' were always on the lookout for frontmen to lend a respectable façade to their illegal operations. Jesse was ideal for their purposes. His easy charm and honest seeming manner were sufficient to allay the suspicions of the most diligent enquirer. The fact that most of the police who might have made life difficult were receiving substantial payoffs undoubtedly helped.

Not that the operation was totally without troubles. Concealing the illegal distilleries and brewing plants, cloaking the transport of illicit liquor by disguising each shipment within more innocuous produce, provided constant logistics problems for the 'families'. In those areas too Jesse was to prove more than useful, his agile and inventive mind enabling them to stay one step ahead of the authorities.

Their biggest headache however was provided

by the competition. Prohibition had generated the market in which the rival organizations could flourish. They had not yet learned that cooperation was far more profitable than confrontation. Greed had driven the various faction leaders to criminal activities in the first place. The golden years of the Prohibition Era gave them money and power. Greed drove them to want more of both. Greed ensured that even when they got more it was insufficient. With the ready availability of a whole range of highly efficient and deadly tools for the disposal of unwanted competitors many bloody encounters resulted. Some, unlike the St Valentine's Day massacre in 1929, were conducted behind locked doors, others, as the gangs grew in power and influence, were carried out more openly.

By the time Prohibition was ended by the passing of the 21st Amendment to the Constitution in 1933, a considerable share of the alcohol production, distribution, and selling markets was in the hands of organizations whose other activities were still highly illegal. Gambling, protection, prostitution, organized labour and drug trafficking, were all part of their portfolio, all criminal, all lucrative.

As their legitimate counterparts spread and grew via acquisitions, so the criminal element diversified via liquidation. It was one such event that was to mark a turning point in Jesse's fortunes. It was time for one of the periodic inspections of their retail liquor premises, now able to display and advertise their services only. These visits were conducted by the head of the 'family' and his two most senior henchmen, accompanied by a large phalanx of bodyguards. Jesse, now promoted to controlling their chain of bars, formed part of the escort. As the group was about to enter one of their bars in a small side street, a window on the first floor of the building opposite was flung open and a machine gun belched forth round after round of bullets from within. The fusillade of shots lasted no more than a minute, the perpetrators making their escape via a backdoor to avoid detection or reprisals.

Of the latter there was little chance. All three 'family' heads, the killers' prime targets, were dead, as were four of their bodyguards. The curtain of fire hurled across the narrow street had killed two innocent bystanders as well and injured a dozen more. Three of the injured were later to die of their wounds. Among the injured was Jesse Barker, having been struck by bullets in the shoulder, chest, and thigh.

His recovery was a slow and painful affair. Although the bullet wound in his thigh was only superficial, the one that had entered his shoulder had smashed his collar bone as well as the clavicle itself. The bullet in his chest had caused the most serious damage of all three, breaking three ribs before coming to rest in the lower part of his right lung. Nor were these injuries Jesse's only problems. The incident was of such a grave nature as to bring the full glare of publicity to bear on both perpetrators and victims alike. Jesse's past and his association with the criminal fraternity came under scrutiny from both police and immigration officials. It was soon discovered that Jack Barlow was a fraudulent identity.

As Jesse signed his discharge papers and paid his hospital bill, he became aware of someone standing alongside him.

'Jack Barlow?' the man asked politely.

'Yes?'

'You're under arrest,' the policeman stated calmly. As he spoke Jesse felt cold on his left wrist. As he turned to investigate the cause, the second policeman completed the closure of the handcuffs. 'Let's go,' he was ordered.

The ensuing trial was a foregone conclusion. Charged, found guilty and sentenced under the name of Jack Barlow, Jesse found himself sentenced to a three-year term for running a brothel. During the trial, the District Attorney's office had paraded a succession of prostitutes who told the court that they worked from the rooms above a bar managed by Jesse. It was Jesse who controlled them and to the despair of his defence attorney, they each confessed that it was to Jesse they paid twenty per cent of their earnings by way of rent. In an interesting sideline, one that delighted the press contingent covering the trial, the prosecuting attorney asked one of the girls what happened if they were unable to pay the rent.

'Aw gee,' the girl replied, 'Jack pays it for us. Jack's so kind to us, a real gent. If we catch a dose he pays the doctor's bills until we can work again, so none of the girls minds if he wants a freebie.'

Once the conviction was secured and Jesse had been led away to start his sentence, immigration officials wrote to their counterparts in England, enclosing copies of Jack Barlow's fingerprints in an effort to discover his true identity.

Back in 1912 a fight had broken out in a pub in the East End of London. One of the participants, an Armenian well known amongst the more unsavoury elements of local society, had been taken to hospital, his jaw and three of his ribs broken in the assault. His assailant, whose argument with the Armenian centred on the non-payment for goods supplied, was taken to the local police station, where he was charged with causing an affray. This charge was upheld at the subsequent court hearing, the more serious matter of causing grievous bodily harm floundering for lack of supporting evidence. The pub's regulars proved remarkably short-sighted when called upon to testify for the prosecution.

As part of the due process of law, in line with newly available technology, the convicted man's fingerprints were taken and his file was sent to Scotland Yard. A note was placed in the file two years later, following which it laid gathering dust in the Criminal Records office. Twenty-one years later, following receipt of a set of matching prints, the file was extracted. The officer who had called for the file read the contents with surprised interest. He reached for the phone and asked the switchboard operator to connect him to Special Branch.

'I think you'd better come over and have a look at something,' he told his opposite number. 'A file has just become active again after more than twenty years and in it there's a note of your interest in the man.

'No,' he continued, in response to the other officer's question, 'it doesn't say why you were interested in him. His only conviction is for a pub brawl, but your departmental note says, "believed to be dead". Well, he wasn't, he isn't, and now he's surfaced in America of all places.'

In the summer of 1936 Jack Barlow became eligible for parole. Unusually, for one with known gangland connections the state offered no opposition to his early release, so he left prison in early September. As the heavy steel door clanged shut behind him, he adjusted the brim of his hat and prepared to set off to walk to the nearest highway where he hoped to hitch a lift to the local town. He looked round and saw two men approaching.

'Jack Barlow?' the smaller of the two asked him.

'That's me,' he agreed with a twinge of foreboding.

'Jesse Barker, alias Jack Barlow, you're under

arrest for violation of immigration laws,' he was told. The only consolation Jesse had was that he had been spared the long walk to the highway, for the two immigration officials bundled him into their car and drove him straight to Chicago.

Little about the ensuing deportation worried him, for he realized that the death of several leading members of the gang had weakened his position. At best his future was uncertain, at worst he was highly vulnerable. His major concern was the knowledge that the American authorities were aware of his true identity. They could only have learned this from information received from Britain. Some months later as he was put on board the ship that would take him back to England, Jesse experienced serious misgivings about the extent of the British authorities' knowledge of his past.

Danny Malloy's determination to acquire wealth stemmed from the poverty of his family's early days in Australia. The easiest way he could think of was to marry it.

He was good-looking, no doubt of that. His pedigree, part Italian part Irish, ensured both his looks and the abundance of accompanying charm. Few girls could resist the combination, nor did Danny assist them to. He was more than prepared to satisfy their eagerness to explore all his physical attributes, but he was unprepared to commit to a serious relationship. Danny wanted a girl with more than just good looks, more than a willing partner in the oldest indoor game. He wanted a girl with an extra asset – money.

Danny worked on a sheep station close to town, so every Saturday night would find him in the local dance hall. It was there, in the summer of 1937, that he first set eyes on Dottie Fisher. She was tall, fair haired and attractive. She had a superb figure too, but that was only part of it. When Danny learned her identity, his thoughts immediately turned to another figure – that of a bank balance. The name Fisher was synonymous in the area with wealth, extreme wealth. Danny determined to cut himself in on a share. He contrived first to meet, then to woo her.

To Dottie, barely nineteen and from a sheltered background, Danny seemed everything a girl could wish for. He was good-looking, more than that he was handsome in a way rarely seen off the screens at the local picture house. His fine features framed dark passionate eyes. His ready smile displayed his abundant charm, his muscular figure rippled with youth and vigour. It did not take long for Dottie to fall in love with Danny, or rather the myth of Danny.

Others were less sure, Patrick Finnegan for one, his wife Louise, for another. At first they thought Dottie was merely infatuated in a way that would quickly blow over. They failed to notice the warning signs that might have enabled them to take preventative action. By the time the situation became clear it was too late, for them and for Dottie.

From their first meeting neither Patrick nor Louise liked nor trusted Danny. The charm that had ensnared Dottie grated on them, they felt it to be no more than a veneer. Nor were they enamoured by his inability to befriend their own children. Louise was quick to point out that Malloy, his eyes firmly set on the main chance, seemed to ignore anything he thought irrelevant or of little use to him, a fact, Patrick conceded, that he had also noted.

It was with great reluctance and in response to continuous long-term pleading from Dottie that Finnegan, in his role as guardian, agreed to allow Dottie's marriage to Danny Malloy. The wedding, he told the couple, could take place the following spring. Dottie dearly wished she could invite her brother Luke. However, none of the family had the faintest idea where Luke had gone.

CHAPTER THIRTY-ONE

Before setting out on their first patrol, Mark and Jenny were equipped with arms and ammunition for the first time. The pistol Mark received, he was surprised to discover, was of Italian manufacture, while Jenny's rifle was a British one, both captured from the enemy.

The patrol was scheduled to last over two weeks and had been meticulously prepared for. Each member of the patrol was issued with a rucksack containing essential supplies. For the most part they trekked through thick forests of Scots pine giving way in places to beech woods of stupefying beauty. Had it not been for the grim reality of their situation, they would have found it to be a highly enjoyable hiking expedition.

For days on end they traversed the region, the only signs of life being the occasional flocks of speckled starlings or less gregarious curlews and on two occasions a lone falcon, hovering before swooping in a deadly curving dive on some luckless small rodent.

On their sixth day out, Carmen led the patrol through a dense patch of beech forest. They were struggling with a particularly tangled patch when she held up a warning hand. They halted and crouched, listening to the silence of the forest. In the distance they could hear the sound of movement in the undergrowth. They waited, their breathing controlled to avoid the slightest escape of sound. The distant noise grew louder. Whatever or whoever was moving through the woods was coming towards them.

Still they waited, every member of the patrol holding their gun at the ready, index finger curled round the trigger. Louder and louder the sound grew nearer. Whatever was approaching was close by now. Nerves as taut as piano wire, the small group waited, rigid as statues.

Suddenly, startling the waiting guerrillas, the intruders burst through the last clump of undergrowth and paused. They looked round but failed to notice the waiting group. Then the leader, massive and magnificently built, lifted his noble head and caught wind of them. With a quickly uttered sotto-voce comment to his companions, the red stag moved rapidly away to be lost immediately in the dense briar. As his harem of hinds moved obediently after him, the guerrillas relaxed, breathing it seemed for the first time in minutes. All except one, who lifted his gun. Carmen pushed the barrel firmly down again. 'No,' she commanded. She emphasized the ban on shooting by placing her finger to her lips.

The day had proved particularly tiring for Mark.

The heavy going through difficult terrain was only part of it. He had been on guard all the previous night, so when they finally made camp that evening, exhaustion threatened to overcome him before he finished his evening meal. This was, of necessity an uncooked one, for if a shot fired at deer would have betrayed their position during the day, a campfire at night would have been like a beacon to their enemies. One of the guerrillas had made a batch of his native speciality, gazpacho, the chilled soup made with tomatoes, onions and garlic. This was accompanied by chunks of bread, slightly stale by this time, some chorizo sausages, a handful of olives, a piece of cheese and some fruit. Washed down with some red wine, this acted as a sleeping draught to the weary Mark.

Jenny and Carmen exchanged amused glances as he fought to stay awake until the end of the meal. They watched him sleeping for a few moments then began to talk, their voices low, for several more of the group were also asleep.

'What was it made you want to come here?' Carmen asked.

'It all seems rather pointless and silly now we're here but we both hate fascism fiercely. It's not as if we're communists, or socialists even, but I don't think you have to belong to either faction to detest something as evil as fascism. We'd wanted to help for long enough. Then when we read some of the reports of what the nationalists had done we couldn't stay away. We haven't done any good though. Perhaps we should have stayed at home. Sometimes I think we're just a liability.'

'Never think that,' Carmen's voice was sharp in its reproof. 'That is the worst thing you could have done. Far too many governments and politicians are preaching non-intervention. That policy is slowly strangling our struggle. You and people such as you, volunteers from all over Europe and beyond, do an immense amount for our cause. You don't have to throw a grenade or fire a shot. The effect of your presence, your demonstration of support and solidarity do an immense amount for our morale. That in itself is sufficient justification.'

'What turned you into guerrilla?' It was a question Jenny and Mark had long wanted to ask, only now did Jenny find the courage.

Carmen's face grew bleak. She remained silent so long that Jenny feared she had upset her, that she would not reply. When at last Carmen spoke, her voice was low, her tone hard.

'I married young, which is often the case here. I was only sixteen. My husband came from the same village, a pretty little place near the Portuguese border, close to the town of Badajoz. Our daughter was born the following year. My husband was a socialist, not prominent, but active. I was just a housewife and mother. When Badajoz was attacked my husband fought the nationalists, we all did, but it was of little use. They overran the city. Once they had gained control, the atrocities began. God knows how many they killed by the time they'd finished. Anyone suspected of republican sympathies was a prime target. We were high on their list. They killed my husband and daughter. She was just eight years old. They would have killed me too, sometimes I wish they had, but I escaped.' Carmen's words seemed to hang for a lifetime in the stillness of the cool evening air.

'How did you escape?' Jenny was drawn to ask the question as if by a magnet, while fearing to stir up further bleak memories.

'I suppose you could say I was lucky. They saved me until last, which was their misfortune, for their work was interrupted. A stranger came into the house, a man I'd never met. There were four of the nationalist pigs, but he disposed of them and carried me away, out of the house, out of the town, away to safety. I remember little of what happened. I was only half-conscious, as much from shock and grief as anything. It was days later before I took any notice of what was happening.'

'He must be quite a man,' Jenny suggested.

'He is.' There was enthusiasm in Carmen's voice, the first since their conversation had started. 'He is strong and clever. He worked out that the nationalists would be searching the approaches to the Portuguese border, knew also that Salazar had ordered his troops to seal the border against republicans seeking to escape the aftermath of Badajoz. So, instead of heading west he took me eastward until we were clear of danger. Eventually, we found our way here, to La Rioja. We'd gathered a few companions en route and as we got here we met up with a band of men who had all fled their homes in much the same way. We formed a group under one of their leaders, there were more than a hundred of us by then. The leader, El Herrero, it means blacksmith, was killed in fighting close to Zaragoza last November. That's when we elected La Trompetista to replace him.'

'Was it he who rescued you?' Jenny asked.

Once more she heard the warmth in Carmen's voice. 'Yes, it was. He rescued me and taught me to look forward, not back. When we elected him as our leader, it was the best move we could have made. Since that time, we have only lost three men and that was because they were betrayed.'

'Why do you call him La Trompetista?' Jenny asked.

'Ah, that is not my secret to tell you. Perhaps he will reveal it when you meet him.'

Two days later, the patrol ran into trouble. It was no fault of their security, pure misfortune that they were in the wrong place at the wrong time. As they emerged from the neck of one side of a wooded valley they were surprised by a band of nationalist irregulars, who had the advantage of having come from the opposite hillside a few seconds earlier.

Carmen's group were outnumbered three to one. Before they were even aware of the presence of the opposing force a salvo of shots rang out. The first of these cut down the leading guerrilla. As he was carrying their only automatic weapon his death increased the odds against them dramatically, the wounding of two more guerrillas lengthened the odds even further.

The rest dived for whatever cover they could reach, with the exception of Mark Cowgill. Luck was with him in that the opposition did not expect such a seemingly rash act. Swiftly, he covered the fifteen yards or so to the dead man, knelt by the lifeless body and grabbed the weapon from his slackened grip. Using the corpse as makeshift cover, Mark loosed off a long burst from the Sten gun he had acquired. The hail of bullets sprayed the nationalist position like a lethal hose. So confident had they been of their superiority, that they had not deemed it necessary to adopt defensive positions. For six of them, cut down in that first lethal swathe, it was a fatal error.

Four more of the attackers perished in the next few seconds. Over the next half hour there was only sporadic gunfire, the only significant injuries being inflicted by Carmen, who dispatched two more of the nationalist force with unerringly accurate shooting from the high-powered sporting rifle she carried.

The odds were now even. As the afternoon sun got lower in the sky the fascists found it more and more difficult to spot movement from the guerrilla group. Carmen passed the message to her comrades to begin an encircling movement. She ordered Jenny forward to join up with Mark.

'He will form the centre of our advance. You will take position on his left, while I go to his right. The others will fan out on either side of us, about twenty metres apart. We must keep in a shallow semi-circle to avoid shooting at one another. When we are all in position I will give the signal to the outside men to move off.'

The engagement that followed was short, brutally bloody, and one-sided. Although the guerrillas lost one more man, the result of momentary carelessness and a lucky shot, when it was over, the lack of response from the nationalists signalled an effective end to the response. It was only then that Mark looked to his left. His heart lurched sickeningly. Jenny lay motionless in the wispy grass, her face a mask of blood. Frantic, heedless of any remaining danger, Mark dashed across and knelt beside her.

The bullet intended to kill her had barely grazed her temple, the force from its passage sufficient to stun her temporarily. As Mark bathed her wound from his water canister she stirred and opened her eyes. She shut them immediately, the glare of the setting sun sending a pounding through her brain.

All but two of the nationalists were dead. One was unconscious, close to death. The other, one of their leaders, was also dying from a bullet wound to the chest. He was still conscious and although he knew he was mortally wounded, remained determined to take some of the hated republicans with him. He crawled from his place of cover towards the advancing guerrillas. He could see a gap in their line and headed towards it. He slipped past the oncoming enemy and crawled on hands and knees, resting from time to time as the pain in his chest worsened.

His vision was blurred with pain now, but he could see figures in front of him, one kneeling, tending a fallen comrade. He could hear their voices too, dimly, as if at a great distance although they were only a few yards away. He knew he must act now or it would be too late, consciousness was beginning to slip away.

Slowly, he removed a long-bladed knife from a scabbard at his belt. He crept nearer. The eyes of the recumbent figure were closed, the kneeling man had his back to him. Easy, he thought, raising the knife high above his head, willing his failing body to one final effort.

Jenny opened her eyes again. She blinked, convinced she had double vision. Mark was crouched solicitously over her, but he seemed to have two heads, one above the other. There was a loud bang. The last thing Jenny remembered was one of Mark's heads exploding.

CHAPTER THIRTY-TWO

Carmen congratulated herself at the accuracy of her long-range shot. She grinned with pleasure. None of her men could have achieved that, she thought with pride. In the tangle of arms and legs on the ground it was difficult at first to tell one from another. She rolled the headless body to one side and grinned once more at Mark.

'Carmen. What happened?'

'One of those pigs was about to knife you in the back, so I blew his head off. He fell on you and winded you then you both fell on poor Chica. How is she?'

'She was coming round slowly until this happened.'

Carmen stretched her hand down to pull him to his feet. 'Come on, my little hero,' she teased him. To Mark's astonished embarrassment no sooner was he upright than Carmen kissed him, a long and passionate kiss. 'Don't go getting ideas,' she told him when she released him, 'that was just to say thank you for saving all our lives.'

'Oy,' a weak but clear voice from the ground protested. 'Leave him alone, he's mine.'

They looked down, Jenny was awake once more.

Carmen laughed. 'I'll let you explain,' she told Mark. 'The rest of us have work to do. You stay here and take care of Chica. We'll need to go soon but I know the others will want to thank you before we set off.'

She moved to walk away, but Mark detained her. 'Carmen,' he said, his voice nervous, hesitant. She looked back. 'They won't all want to kiss me, will they?' The clearing seemed filled with the rich, echoing sound of Carmen's laughter.

Mark finished dressing Jenny's wound and went to the mountain stream to refill both water bottles. He returned to find her wide awake and sitting up. She smiled and asked him to help her to her feet.

'What's been happening while I've been at the stream?' Mark asked.

'From what I could see I think they moved all the bodies to one place. Then they kept bringing armfuls of wood and stacking them near the corpses. While they were doing that Carmen was doing something to the bodies but I couldn't tell what.'

'I do hope she wasn't robbing the dead,' Mark suggested, horrified.

'I don't think Carmen would do that.' Jenny's voice was gently reproving. 'Perhaps she's going to light a funeral pyre for them.'

In the event both guesses were wide of the mark. When Carmen returned with the rest of the guerrillas, the men crowded round Mark, patting him on the back, shaking him by the hand, muttering, 'Gracias, Ingles,' and calling him a hero. Mark was relieved to see that was the extent of their gratitude.

Carmen told Jenny what they had been doing. 'We've gathered all the corpses into one place, our men as well as the fascists. While the rest of the men were collecting wood for a fire I set about laying charges amongst the corpses, all linked together and connected to trip wires. If anyone tries to move even one of the bodies all the explosives will detonate and with a bit of luck we'll be able to kill a few more fascists.'

'What's the idea of the fire?' Jenny asked.

'Ah, that serves two purposes. First, it will burn all night. I've arranged for one of our men to stay and keep putting logs on until dawn. That will keep wolves and other scavengers away and also denote our position to the fascists in case any are close enough to see the light. In the morning he will make the fire up again with the remaining logs and top it off with green wood and foliage so it sends up a big smoke signal. If the fascists don't see tonight's fire they'll be sure to see tomorrow's smoke.'

'Carmen,' Jenny said fervently, 'I hope I never offend you, but if I do will you give me chance to leave Spain before you take reprisals?'

Carmen laughed and hugged her. 'Chica, you could not offend me if you tried. You are not only my comrade, you and Ingles have become as a brother and sister to me.'

It was dark by the time the depleted guerrilla force started out on the first leg of their long journey back to the camp. Walking in the forest at night was a slow, difficult and dangerous business, but Carmen was determined they should reach the head of the valley before stopping for the night. It was almost ten o'clock before they achieved their objective. It was only after they stopped that they realized they were hungry. They ate their simple meal quietly, their conversation muted. Far below they could see a red glow in the distance.

'Alfonso is keeping the fire going well,' Carmen commented.

'I though you used nicknames, but Alfonso sounds more like a Christian name,' Mark suggested.

'Oh, his name is not Alfonso. We only call him that because he resembles the old king.'

Dawn was breaking when Carmen woke. Nobody else was stirring. She stretched and stood up, a little stiffly at first. She folded her blanket and threaded it through the straps of her rucksack. As she moved, Carmen felt a sudden, momentary lurch of nausea, seconds later she was sick, a natural reaction to the events of the previous day. She walked towards a rock on the edge of the steep valley side, from where she had a commanding view down the gorge. A distant plume of smoke rising high into the clear morning air told Carmen that Alfonso was still hard at work. Time to wake everyone.

The guerrillas' advantage over their fascist enemies owed little to chance. One of their group, nicknamed El Bosquero had worked in the area all his adult life. He had lived in a small village to the north of the region until the day he returned home, to find no home. A pilot of the fascist forces had developed engine trouble and jettisoned his bombs on what, from the air appeared barren, uninhabited land. The plane crashed despite the pilot's attempt to lighten his load. The forester, with his home, his wife and family wiped out, had no difficulty identifying the culprit. From that moment he became an implacable enemy of the fascists. Dispossessed of his home and all that he loved he joined the guerrilla band, hungry for vengeance.

Carmen's patrol had just one more day's travelling, when Alfonso, accompanied by El Bosquero, caught up with them. Everyone listened to the news the forester had brought. Everywhere, it seemed, the war was going badly. He reserved the worst news until last. The guerrillas had been betrayed. They had been told of a big nationalist convoy on the move near Zaragoza, a prime target. Their leader had decided it was worth committing a large force to attack the convoy. The news was false, the convoy a decoy. When the ambush was sprung, so great was the carnage that only twenty-five of their force of six hundred escaped. The rest were dead or wounded, some captured. The only good news was that La Trompetista had escaped. He had gone to Madrid on some secret business following the debacle. 'He told us to return to the other camp across the hills. Before we did that, five of us went to the homes of the two traitors. They will not betray anyone else,' the forester told them grimly. He proffered a piece of paper to Carmen. 'La Trompetista sent you this note.'

Carmen read it, her face bleak. 'We are to remain in the high mountain camp throughout the winter. It will be safer there,' she told them. 'When he wrote this he must have assumed we would be back at our own camp. He wants all but a handful to go and join the main group. The rest will maintain the camp as a last refuge. We must collect our things en route.'

'I have sent four men to take mules loaded with supplies direct to the camp,' the forester told her, 'I was heading there myself until I saw Alfonso's bonfire. There will be ample food and provisions to see you through, but I must warn you it will be a very harsh winter. That will be no bad thing for you. If you can remain hidden from the enemy until the end of October you will then be safe until spring.'

'How is that?' Carmen asked.

'You will be much higher in the mountains. The

snows will block the valleys and make the terrain impassable.'

'How can you be so sure?'

'Because I know these woods, I know their moods and the signs they put out of the changes taking place. I look at the trees and the shrubs. I watch the deer and the rest of the wildlife. They know, much better than we humans, what is happening, and what is going to happen. I learn from them. The forest and its inhabitants are already preparing for winter. It is unusual for that to happen so early. The deer are rutting a month earlier than normal, small rodents are moving towards the shelter of the valleys.'

When they reached the camp, El Bosquero taught Mark the rudiments of survival in the wild, Carmen acting as interpreter. Mark had the advantage of being a reasonably competent fisherman, the result of numerous expeditions with his father in childhood.

'Don't be tempted by wild boar and deer,' the forester told him. 'They can only be killed with a rifle and the sound will attract other creatures.'

Mark grinned at the oblique reference to their fascist enemies.

'Of course, once you are snowed in you could take a deer or a boar safely, but only at severest need. Fish will be easy to catch, for they are unused to the ways of anglers hereabouts. Now I can show you how to trap pheasants. When the mules arrive with the supplies I shall cut some hair from their tails for you. Thread some raisins onto the hair and leave it where the pheasants feed. Some hours later you will be able to go and pick up the dead pheasants.'

'How come?' Mark asked.

'Pheasants love raisins. They will eat them in preference to any other food. The hair gets stuck in their gullet and they choke.'

'You're an old villain,' Carmen told him.

The forester grinned. He showed Mark how to set traps for rabbits, how to stupefy roosting birds by burning sulphur under the trees they were in, and a host of other tricks. 'You must beware of competition for your food. Always remember that what you eat is attractive to others also. The main predators are wolves, foxes, and mink.'

'What fish are there here?' Mark asked, hastily changing the subject.

'Trout, bass, carp and pike mainly.'

When the supplies had at last arrived and been offloaded. Carmen selected the three men to remain with her, Mark, and Jenny. She chose the older, less agile guerrillas. They watched the rest of their comrades disappear into the forest. Suddenly the camp seemed empty and lonely. At first Jenny put this change down as the cause for Carmen's demeanour. She seemed listless, at times irritable, and prone to sudden attacks of nausea. One morning, a week after they had been parted from the rest of the group, Jenny and Mark were concerned that Carmen had not emerged from her room in the cabin by nine o'clock. Jenny knocked on Carmen's door. Receiving no reply she opened it and went in. The room was in darkness, the rough pine shutters unopened.

'Carmen,' Jenny said softly, 'are you all right?'

There was no reply, but Jenny could hear a gentle sobbing from the bed. She groped her way across the room and sat beside her friend.

'What's wrong, Carmen?' Jenny asked, although by this time she had already guessed.

'I think you know,' Carmen said through her tears. 'I am going to have a baby.'

CHAPTER THIRTY-THREE

In London, Jessica Tunnicliffe's probationary report was a glowing one. Several months after her appointment had been ratified, Edrith Pointon summoned Jessica's section head, Mrs Crane, to his office.

'The department is taking on new responsibilities, Mrs Crane,' Pointon told her. 'That means I'm going to need people I can rely on to fill some new roles that I will be creating. Some of that will involve bringing outsiders in to take on specialist tasks but there are some managerial and administrative positions I would rather fill from within our own ranks. The first of these is a co-ordinating job, with a good deal of secretarial work and needs someone with the ability to handle people. Who do we have capable of filling such a role, if anyone?'

Mrs Crane thought it over for a while before replying, 'Well, I suppose I could do it if needed,' she told him.

Pointon was definite. 'No, Mrs Crane. I'm going to need you here more than ever. You will have more than enough on your plate.'

'In that case,' – Mrs Crane had been given time to think – 'the best candidate would be Jessica Tunnicliffe. She's quick, neat, and accurate in her work, gets on with everybody, can use her own initiative and can be left to get on with things. To be honest her talents are a little wasted in my section. The only factors against her are her youth and relative lack of experience.'

'Right, bring me her file and some samples of her work and I'll think about it. Now on to other matters. I have an urgent message to send.' He waited while Mrs Crane took out her notebook and pencil then continued, 'Mark this "urgent, repeat urgent". Send: "Immediately you receive this, proceed to London for further posting. Highest priority".' He paused. 'Send that to Smith 12, in the first available diplomatic bag. I want a flash on the envelope, "Embassy staff to ensure urgent delivery without fail". That's all, Mrs Crane, and make sure you get that off within the hour.'

After Mrs Crane had left, Pointon took a sheet of blank paper from his desk. On it he wrote, 'J is safe and well, E.P.', placed the note in an envelope and sealed it. He opened a file and glanced at it before addressing the envelope to Mr & Mrs S. Jones, at an address in Bradford.

Three days later Jessica was ordered to report to Pointon's office. She had no prior indication of the reason and was left wondering what she had done wrong. Edrith's words soon eased her fears.

'Miss Tunnicliffe, I've had good reports on your work for us and have inspected some examples of it. The department is expanding, taking on new and different responsibilities. We will soon be handling work of a scientific nature produced here in Britain. I need someone to work with a small team of scientists, preparing and delivering reports on their work, managing them and taking all extraneous duties from them to allow them to concentrate on their work. You must know that all scientists are mad' – he smiled gently – 'or at the very least eccentric. I'm offering you the job. Do you think you can cope with a bunch of crazy characters?'

Jessica smiled back. 'I'm sure I can, Mr Smith. I've lived amongst eccentrics all my life.'

'Good enough. I'll brief you on the exact nature of the job then give you the files on the men you'll be working with. If studying them doesn't put you off, nothing will.'

In the mountains the first snows of the winter had dusted the Scots pines overnight, but the day was crisp and clear with a keen frost underfoot. A week had passed since Carmen had told them she was pregnant, a week where time in the camp had seemed suspended. 'I'm going fishing,' Mark announced that morning, 'anybody want to come along?'

Jenny would have loved to go with him, but Carmen was feeling unwell and begged Jenny to stay with her. They watched Mark disappear into the forest. The chill in the air made both women shiver. The camp was situated on a plateau, that and the density of the surrounding forest made detection, even from relatively close quarters, a remote possibility. Over time the guerrillas had come to realize it was even safe to light a fire in the grates of the cabins without fear of discovery. The other men were busy hauling timber into the camp and sawing logs to dry out and provide adequate fuel for the harsh weather the forester had predicted. Carmen and Jenny seized an armful apiece and retired to their cabin. Carmen brewed some coffee while Jenny banked up the fire. Then they settled down to talk.

'What did you feel when you realized you were having a baby?' Jenny asked. 'I mean, with you being on your own. I thought Spain was very strict about such things?'

'Hah,' Carmen snorted contemptuously, 'you wouldn't believe me if I told you. The number of children born out of wedlock in Spain is greater than probably any country in Europe. Of course the authorities conceal the facts, but it is so, I can tell you. At first I was horrified, the thought of bringing a child into the world at such a dreadful time, without a father's protection. Then I began to consider other things, my own past for one. Perhaps it was as if I had been given another chance, to make up for the loss of my daughter.'

'I don't know if I should ask this,' Jenny said

hesitantly, ‘don’t answer me if you don’t want to. But who is the father?’

Carmen smiled. ‘I don’t mind you knowing, it is not something I am ashamed of. The father is our leader, La Trompetista.’

‘I wondered if he might be, when I saw you after he had been here you were so different, so happy.’

‘That was when the child was conceived. Perhaps I guessed then what was going to be the outcome.’

‘Do you love him? Will you marry him?’ Jenny asked.

‘Love, that’s a difficult one, perhaps not the way you and El Ingles love each other, but I respect and admire him. When I’m with him I feel young again, so perhaps in a way I do love him. As for marriage, no I don’t think we will ever marry. Our ways will separate, soon I think, for he has much to do that I cannot be part of and besides that we come from different worlds, different cultures.’

‘What of your future, where will you go, what will you do?’

Carmen patted her belly. ‘This is my future, inside here, where I will go, who knows. If I am spared, perhaps to Ibiza.’

‘Ibiza. Why Ibiza?’

‘My grandmother lives on La Isla Blanca, as we call it. It means the white island, because all the houses there are painted white. My mother’s mother lives near a little village called San Juan Bautista,' she lifted an eyebrow at Jenny.

'St John the Baptist?' Jenny guessed.

'Clever girl,' Carmen mocked her. 'The island is sparsely populated, mostly farms and fishing villages. I think it will be a safe place to bring up my child, if I can get there.'

'How did you come to be lovers, after all you had endured I'm surprised you could bear to go near a man?'

Carmen smiled again, this time at the memory she was about to share. 'We had been travelling over a month, away from the hell that was Badajoz. Much of that time I'd spent mourning my loss, unable to conceive a future bereft of my husband and daughter. Then one night, when we had both drunk too much wine I felt the need of a man. Do you know that feeling?'

Jenny blushed but remained silent, so Carmen continued, 'Not, you understand, to make love, just to put his arms round me, comfort me with his strength. So I crept over to where he was sleeping and got beneath the blanket with him. Of course he got aroused and I was flattered. The more he got aroused the more did I and that was that, once we'd started we couldn't stop, didn't want to stop, and couldn't get enough of each other. It might sound strange and it may shock you but it was much better than with my husband.'

Jenny giggled.

'What are you laughing at?' Carmen demanded.

'Perhaps it was doing it outside,' Jenny suggested.

'You'd know,' Carmen retorted with a sly grin, 'and if you and El Ingles continue behaving as you are doing you'll finish up like me.' She patted her belly again.

'Whatever do you mean?' Jenny asked, her eyes wide with exaggerated innocence.

'Sometimes I wake very early. So do you and El Ingles.'

Jenny was scarlet with embarrassment. 'Did anyone else see us?' she begged.

Carmen smiled. 'No, I waited a while before waking the rest of the men, to give you time together.'

'I'll make another cup of coffee,' Jenny was desperate to change the subject.

'Good idea,' Carmen agreed, the wicked grin reappearing as she added, 'then we can talk some more.'

The warmth of the cabin and the heavy fragrance of the burning logs were soporific and the girls were dozing as twilight softened the afternoon air when they were startled to instant wakefulness by the sound of someone whistling outside. Jenny recognized the strains of Richard Rodgers' *Blue Moon* and relaxed. 'That's El Ingles.'

Seconds later the door opened and Mark stood there, a triumphant grin on his face. 'Dinner has arrived,' he announced smugly, holding up a short piece of line, from which half a dozen large brown trout dangled.

'Well done!' the girls cried in unison.

'And for tomorrow's menu,' like a conjurer Mark held up his other hand, displaying several large carp.

In Australia Philip Fisher had taken a long-term lease on a small flat in one of the more affluent suburbs of town. There, despite one or two dramatic early setbacks, he became a better than average cook. He spent his leisure time reading, listening to music and interesting himself in every facet of the business empire he now considered his. Philip had always been of a solitary disposition, to him being alone did not equate to loneliness. He adopted the pleasant custom of buying an occasional bottle of wine, a luxury he was well able to afford. He gave no thought as he drank it of the process of winemaking, for Philip's imagination did not work that way.

It was some time before the full after-effects of the quarrel between Philip and Luke Fisher became apparent. As Patrick Finnegan remarked to his wife, 'This will either be the making or breaking of Phil, I'm not certain which.'

'I'm not sure I really care much one way or the other,' Louise replied. 'I know that sounds hard, but after the rotten way he behaved I've no sympathy for Philip, all I care about is what has happened to Luke.'

'I take your point,' Patrick agreed. 'But bear in mind, I've to work alongside Phil. It doesn't stop me worrying about Luke, but if I want to retire I need to know Fisher Springs is in good hands. I owe that much to James and Alice.'

In the event Patrick Finnegan's fears proved groundless. In some curious way it seemed as if the crisis had altered Philip completely. Staff at Fisher Springs found him more approachable, less dictatorial. Although still not as bold as Luke, he seemed to have shed a good deal of his former caution in decision making.

As a way of combating his solitary lifestyle, Philip joined a local tennis club. He soon progressed from novice status, to competence. From there he gradually became a very good player. He was in great demand as a doubles partner, much less so as a singles opponent, his ferocious serve and volley game scaring off many fellow members. It was in the 1936 mixed doubles tournament that Philip found himself drawn to partner Amelia Baxendale.

Although at twenty-seven no older than Philip, Amelia was already divorced. Her own family wealth was added to by a generous divorce settlement from her husband, whose preference for the bottle rather than the marital couch had done much to contribute to the failure of the marriage. Amelia did not miss her husband, but she did miss the pleasures of the marital couch.

The on-court success of the doubles pairing was soon matched off-court. Phil and Amelia began to be seen together at many social functions. They were gossiped about, but not excessively, for both were free agents, their obvious pleasure in each other's company a cause for comment rather than scandal.

It was a mutually fulfilling relationship. Amelia, freed from the shackles of an unhappy marriage, was far from ready to rush back to the altar. However, she did need the companionship of a man. Philip, for the first time apart from a few minor infatuations in his teens, discovered the pleasure of walking into a room with a beautiful woman on his arm. More exciting still was his introduction to the delight of a beautiful woman sharing his bed. He, like Amelia, was unprepared for the commitment of marriage, but equally, neither of them wanted the relationship to end. They were content, confident in each other's company, happy with the fulfilment they derived from one another.

CHAPTER THIRTY-FOUR

October in the high mountains was marked by clear bright days. Although the sun shone for most of the hours of daylight it conveyed little heat at those altitudes and the occupants of the guerrilla camp woke each morning to a glittering landscape rimed with frost. The highest peaks of the *sierra* were already capped with snow and it seemed only a matter of time before the forester's predictions were borne out and their camp became cut off. Mark Cowgill's outstanding memory of that month was of blistered hands and a continuously aching back, brought about by the sawing of countless trees and branches. Along with the strongest of the guerrillas, Mark spent every day cutting timber into manageable lengths for transportation back to the camp, where all four men reduced them to logs of the right size to burn in the stoves of the three inhabited cabins. They were fortunate that the abandoned lumber camp had enough saws and woodworking tools to make the job easy, though arduous.

Of the three cabins in occupation two were used

as dormitories, the third as a combined social area, where the group would foregather for meals and recreation. Carmen, on realizing they would be spending the winter there, had sought the advice of El Bosquero, the forester, who had told her, 'These cabins were only built for summer use. The loggers would abandon them at the end of September, returning the following April. Look to make them waterproof and keep the wind out, for they will otherwise be cold, too cold for you to survive. Ensure also you have sufficient fuel and in the coldest weather keep the stoves burning night and day.'

Fortunately there were two amongst the party whose skills were invaluable during the winter. The first was a small, insignificant looking man with sad mournful eyes that reminded Mark of a chastised spaniel. It was good that the guerrillas had been sent copious supplies of flour and other foodstuff to aid their survival, equally important was the presence of a baker to convert them into loaves, cakes, and pastries.

The second talent of immense value was possessed by a former carpenter. His skill was soon demonstrated when the firewood was being sawn, his rate of production being four times that of his less experienced colleagues.

Once the logs had been stacked under cover, Carmen directed the carpenter to turn his abilities to the problem of weatherproofing the cabins. The three men occupied one of the dormitories,

Carmen, Jenny and Mark the other. As the carpenter began work on the latter building he found a useful ally in Mark Cowgill, who had spent many happy childhood hours watching and occasionally helping his father in the workshop at the rear of Byland Crescent. That experience now came in more than useful. By the end of October all three cabins had been made snug, warm, and as weatherproof as many more permanent buildings. The isolated party was able to look forward to the coming winter with a degree of confidence.

The wisdom of these precautions was demonstrated as early as the last day of October. Whereas virtually every preceding day had seen cloudless skies and bright sunshine, the end of the month brought a complete change. The sun was hidden behind a pall of dark grey cloud from the moment they woke, by early afternoon snow was beginning to fall, lightly at first, then as the short autumn afternoon wore on, with increasing vigour. By dusk a blizzard was raging and the hillside was shrouded in a blanket of white.

The following morning brought no respite and by the time it stopped snowing, in the early afternoon their camp was sealed off from the outside world by over a foot of snow. The guerrillas were safe from enemy attack. They were also, effectively prisoners. One factor that had received little consideration during their preparations to withstand the winter in isolation had been how to pass the time. The novelty of staring at the snow field outside their cabin soon wore off and Carmen, realizing there was a problem to be addressed, convened a meeting.

Jenny suggested they pool their talents to instruct the others in some specialist skills. 'The carpenter can give us woodworking lessons, and the baker can teach us the arts of cookery. You and I,' Jenny told Carmen, 'can supplement his knowledge with our own. El Ingles and I would like to improve our Spanish you can all help teach us that, in return we can help you learn English. Carmen can act as translator,' Jenny told them.

'I could give guitar lessons,' Segovia announced. His nickname derived from his skill with the instrument, which, although not matching the levels of the maestro, was considerable.

'Yes and some recitals too, we'd all enjoy that,' Carmen added. 'The evenings might prove long and boring, but with music and song we can pass them well, but what of El Ingles, has he nothing to contribute?'

'I have an idea, Carmen,' Mark explained. 'It's great that we should keep our minds active through the winter, but we must also think of our bodies. When spring comes and we want to leave we may have been six or seven months virtually without exercise. It will be doubly difficult terrain for muscles weakened by lack of use. I think it would be good to have daily exercises to keep fit otherwise we will be in poor shape when we need to use them. For the rest of my time I shall try to keep us supplied with fresh meat and fish as the weather allows. If some of El Bosquero's methods pay off, we should have a steady supply to balance our diet, which in itself, will help our fitness.'

'Good enough,' Carmen agreed. 'I suggest we make out a rota and plan each day.' She paused as an idea came to her then added, 'El Ingles, how confident are you of being able to get adequate supplies of meat and fish?'

'Fairly sure.'

'In that case we can have some fun. We can organize a special meal, once a week, say on Saturday night, and each of us can prepare and cook it in turn using skills we've learned in cookery class.'

'Bravo!' Jenny cried enthusiastically.

Carmen grinned. 'Your Spanish is improving already.'

The novelty of the new regime helped pass the days and weeks faster than any of the small group could have hoped. It seemed that they had barely become isolated, before November was passed and December was upon them. Although November had been virtually free from further significant falls of snow, when they sat down to their first weekly dinner of December, the skies were threatening. As they were finishing the delicious stew of rabbit cooked in herbs prepared by Carmen, it began snowing and continued uninterrupted for almost forty-eight hours. When the snow eventually stopped, parts of the camp were under more than six feet of snow where the driving northerly wind had caused drifting.

A week later, Mark sought out Carmen. 'I've been watching the movement of deer in the forest. They do not wander far in this weather. If you will allow it I think we can advertise venison on the restaurant's Christmas menu. All I need is to borrow that hunting rifle of yours and take Chica and Segovia with me. The camp's safe enough in any case and the sound of gunfire will be muffled by the snow.'

Carmen agreed, so the following day Segovia's guitar lesson was forfeit as he accompanied Mark and Jenny into the woods, heading towards the lake. Instead of a fishing rod, the trio carried a long pole, ropes, and Carmen's rifle. After half an hour's walk, easier in the forest as the snow lay less thickly there, they reached a small spinney of beech trees, one of which bore a small but distinctive groove scored into the bark at head height. Mark stopped them there.

'This is the place I was aiming for,' he told them in a whisper. 'See where I cut the bark with my knife? The deer will be over there' – he gestured to the east – 'no more than a mile away. Here's what I want you to do.'

Jenny and Segovia listened intently as Mark outlined his plan. 'I want you to go to the left,' he told the Spaniard, 'walk for ten minutes, and then turn right. Walk another ten minutes then stop.

This tree' – Mark patted the ancient beech – 'is taller than the rest. Head straight back towards it, you will have completed,' Mark paused and looked at Jenny, 'What's Spanish for 'triangle'?

'*Triangulo*,' Jenny said gently.

'*Si, un Triangulo*,' Mark told Segovia. He turned to Jenny. 'I want you to go to the right and do the same. The wind will be behind you when you start to walk towards the deer, so they should soon scent you. They'll hear you as well.'

'But won't we be in the line of fire?' Jenny protested.

'Don't worry about that. I shall hide here. Being downwind of the deer they won't know I'm here so I'll wait until they have passed me before shooting.'

He watched them disappear into the forest and settled down to wait.

Christmas was as festive as they could make it. The menu for the meal devised and supervised by Carmen, the baker and Jenny, was in rich contrast to their bleak surroundings. The diners sat down to a table decorated with fir cones and holly, gathered by Mark in the surrounding woods. Candlelight added to the festive spirit and the meal itself was a delight. They started with venison liver pâté, enriched with onions, garlic and chorizo sausage and served with warm rolls straight from the oven. The main course, although lacking in vegetable accompaniments, was a delicious venison casserole, the sauce for which, a stock made from the bones, was flavoured with juniper berries and red wine. For dessert Jenny had utilised the dried fruit sent by their comrades to make a passable imitation of a Christmas pudding. Between courses, the guerrillas were serenaded by Segovia on his guitar, accompanied by the carpenter, who, they discovered had a fine baritone voice. The quality of the meal, washed down with several bottles of fine Rioja wine, enabled them to forget for a while the difficulties and danger of their situation. Even the snowstorm raging outside seemed only seasonal.

The warmth of the cabin, the excellent food, and the fine wine they had drunk combined to loosen Mark and Jenny's inhibitions. As soon as the party broke up, they retired to their bedroom in the adjacent cabin. Once inside their room their habitual caution deserted them, the small but unmistakeable sound of their lovemaking carrying further than normal in the stillness of the night air. Still seated at the deserted dining table, a glass of Rioja her only consolation, Carmen began to weep, silent tears trickling down her beautiful cheeks. She wept for her young friends, seemingly so confident and secure in their happiness, oblivious to their plight. She wept for the loss of her husband and daughter, destroyed by the butchers she hated so fiercely, and she wept for her country, torn apart by strife. Most of all she wept for her lover, who she doubted she would ever see again, the father of her unborn child. She wept for herself in her desolate loneliness and for the uncertain future of the child she was carrying. A child she knew would never know a father's love, for his future and Carmen's were different roads and neither could tread the other's.

She thought of the English couple, El Ingles, so like her lover in many ways and La Chica, who had become as a sister to her. They had come into her life when she was at her lowest ebb, their bright optimistic youth had buoyed and lifted her spirits, and now they were the fastest of friends. Carmen knew that all they had been through – were still going through – together, was forming an unbreakable bond, a friendship that would last as long as they all survived. The sound from the cabin grew a little more urgent, demanding. Carmen grinned and raised her glass in a silent toast to the couple within.

CHAPTER THIRTY-FIVE

In Byland Crescent, had it not been for the children, Rachael Cowgill would have cancelled the festivities. It was now nine months since Mark and Jenny had left for Spain. During that time their anxious relatives had heard no word from or about the young couple. As the Spanish war rumbled on, with increasing signs that the nationalists led by General Franco were gaining the upper hand, the fate of republican supporters grew increasingly uncertain.

Sonny and Rachael, Hannah and Jenny's mother, Joyce, spent many fraught hours trying to work out a way to obtain news of their children. The great difficulty they faced was that whereas most of the foreign volunteers going to Spain travelled under the aegis of various political organizations, Mark and Jenny had gone independently. That left no channel for communication back to their loved ones at home.

All the waiting family could do was hope and pray, contain their impatience and try to distract themselves as best they could. During the summer following the pair's departure Sonny had contrived to organize many outings from Byland Crescent, using Mark's younger brother Billy as the diversion he needed. Billy's blossoming talent as a cricketer made him much in demand, even at the age of fourteen. So precocious was his ability that not only could he command a regular place in the school team, amongst boys four and five years older, but when the school season finished, local club cricket beckoned, albeit amongst the lower teams. Family outings had accompanied Billy's every appearance on a cricket field that summer. Other diversions filled the gaps, anything Sonny could devise to turn everyone's attention, his own included, away from events on the Iberian Peninsula. As a measure, it had only been partially successful. For a few brief hours they might have been able to turn their thoughts away from Mark and Jenny, but as soon as they returned to the environs of Byland Crescent the reminders of the young couple were too many and varied to be ignored. When summer and the cricket season ended, even those diversionary tactics failed.

By Christmas the worried relatives had to admit they were despondent about Mark and Jenny's chances. As they sat down to their Christmas dinner, few, if any of their family held out much hope of seeing Mark and Jenny again in the near future, if at all.

If the months preceding Christmas had seemed to fly past, the early part of the New Year, 1937, dragged interminably for the small group incarcerated in the hills. Although they had devised much to while away the hours of their captivity to the weather, there were still long periods where boredom could have crept in. The diversity of background of the members of the group enabled them to entertain one another with stories of their own region. Thus the Spanish contingent learned more about Yorkshire from Mark and Jenny than most of their compatriots knew of the whole country of England. They heard of the rich variety of the county, from coast to countryside, mill towns to ancient and splendid cities, from high moors and fells to rich and fertile plains. The climate too, as Mark told the intrigued Spaniards, so diverse it was possible to experience all four seasons in a single day. In return, Mark and Jenny were told of life in the west of Spain, Carmen's home for many years, and of her formative years on the island of Ibiza, where her grandmother still lived. The baker told them of life in the capital, Madrid. The carpenter described the diverse beauties of the Basque region, while Segovia dwelt longingly on his native Granada, that ancient and beautiful city dominated by the splendour of the improbably pink Moorish palace of the Alhambra.

As February drew to a close Mark detected the first signs that the severe winter was beginning to ease with the start of a slow, painfully gradual thaw. The prospect of being able to leave the camp, by now more of a prison than a refuge, brought with it fresh problems for the small band of captives. Carmen was now more than six months pregnant. How, they wondered, would she be able to cope with the difficult and sometimes dangerous terrain they would encounter before reaching the lower slopes? Jenny and Mark discussed the dilemma as they lay in bed one night. A gale was raging outside, but this time it was a softer, westerly wind, enhancing the thaw.

'What we should do, in normal circumstances, is insist that Carmen remains here until the baby is born,' Jenny suggested.

'For all we know that might be a choice we don't have,' Mark told her. 'It may be starting to thaw now, but there's no guarantee that in a couple of weeks the snow won't return and we'll be trapped again. Nor would I fancy the journey to the lowlands in the immediate future. If we got caught in a blizzard it would be hard enough for us to survive, much worse for a pregnant woman.'

'That's all true, but there are other considerations to take into account. If the baby's born here, what do we do if there are complications? I have no experience in such matters, nor do I suspect do any of the men. Another thing, babies need to be kept warm and as far as I know there isn't a stitch of clothing we could put on a newly born infant.'

'So you think we ought to try to get Carmen, despite her condition, to undertake the journey before the baby comes? When is it due?'

'The end of April I think.'

'Ok, but I still think we should make provision for the baby to be born here,' Mark suggested.

'Now that thought really terrifies me. I'll speak to Carmen.'

'I've been worrying about it too,' Carmen confessed. 'Back in October it all seemed so far off and less important than our own survival, now I dread to think of the journey down the mountain as I am. Given the choice I'd rather remain here until after the baby comes.'

'What if there are complications?' Jenny voiced her fear.

'Don't worry about that. I've been through it all before, remember, so I know what to expect. They say the first time is the worst, but I had no problems then, so I'd be far happier here than risking the baby and myself on a hazardous trip down the mountain.'

Mark's first contribution to the conversation was a telling one. 'What we have to consider in that case is the baby's needs. I don't know much about them but I guess they have to be kept well fed, clean and warm like any other young animal.'

'That's pretty much it. I can look after the feeding side without problem, but as to the clothing, that's a big worry.'

'There are plenty of towels we could use as nappies,' Jenny suggested.

'True enough and I have a couple of blouses we could unpick and sew into baby garments,' Carmen agreed. 'They will be fine for going next to the baby's skin, however what we could do with is some warm woollen clothes to protect it from the weather.'

'From what I remember, my mother and grandmother spent most of their time knitting before my brother and sisters were born,' Mark said.

'We can't knit anything, we have no wool,' Carmen told him. 'Even if we did have, we've no needles to knit with.'

Carmen and Jenny spent a few minutes looking through their assorted clothing, finding several cotton garments they could adapt for the baby. Throughout this time Mark had been pensively silent. Eventually he asked, 'Could you use old woollen garments, unravel them to make new ones.'

Jenny gave him an exasperated look. 'You're not paying attention,' she told him severely. 'If you'd been listening, you'd have heard Carmen say we don't have any needles. Even when they're unravelled they will be of no use until they can be knitted again.'

'Of course,' Mark agreed. 'Well, I'll leave you to get on with it.'

Carmen watched him leave then turned to Jenny. 'You haven't upset him have you?' she asked anxiously.

'Not him. He's had an idea, but wants to keep it to himself and surprise us with it. He loves surprising people.'

'What sort of an idea?' Carmen persisted.

'Who knows, but I'll tell you one thing, if it works we'll never hear the end of it.'

For the next two days neither of them saw Mark except at mealtimes. No matter how hard they tried to wheedle information from him as to what he was up to it was without success. Nor were the other men of any help, for they had obviously been co-opted into the plot and remained equally silent. The third day was the group's weekly dinner, prepared that week by the baker. It was already on the table when Carmen noticed two of the group were absent. Before she could comment on this, the door opened and Mark, accompanied by the carpenter entered the cabin. Both men were grinning broadly.

Mark walked up to Carmen and from behind his back produced several irregularly shaped balls of wool in a variety of colours, obviously culled from a number of garments belonging to the men. Before the women could protest that these were of no use, Mark ushered the carpenter forward. The craftsman gave them both a shy smile and presented each with two pieces of wood, cylindrical in shape, thin and pointed at one end, about a foot in length. On the butt end he had glued a round piece of cork cut from a wine bottle stopper. Mark and the carpenter had made each of them a pair of knitting needles.

The women stared at them, then both began to laugh. 'So that's what you've been doing,' Jenny said, 'clever old you.'

For the next few weeks both women were busy from dawn to dusk and beyond, knitting furiously, cutting and sewing cotton garments. Jenny found, to her astonishment, that she had a talent for knitting bootees, and a multi-coloured blanket was produced, while Carmen concentrated on small cardigans and dresses. Mark and the carpenter continued their activities, presenting Carmen first with a collection of small wooden buttons they had patiently made then sanded to a smooth finish, later a rocking cradle for the baby to sleep in. The time seemed to fly past as quickly as the movement of the needles and before they realized it March was drawing to a close. The camp was virtually free of snow, the rivers swollen by the melting snow on the hills. Once they subsided from their current levels, the route to their mountain hideaway would be open once more, and danger would threaten again.

Although the days were bright and warm there were still sharp frosts at night. These, combined with the remnants of snow, brought about a more immediate danger. Carmen, already beginning to show signs that the baby's arrival would not be too long delayed, slipped on a patch of ice and fell heavily. Although she experienced considerable pain for the following few hours, to her relief labour did not result. It was not only Carmen who was relieved. Jenny, deputised as midwife, was beginning to experience misgivings about her new role.

* * *

It did not take long for Dottie Fisher, now Dottie Malloy, to realize that married life and marital bliss are not necessarily synonymous. The knowledge came with awful certainty less than a week after their short honeymoon. Danny seemed permanently angry, why and with whom, Dottie was unsure. But she soon found out that when Danny was angry he vented his feelings on the nearest target. Unfortunately this usually meant Dottie.

Very soon the tiny bungalow on the sheep station became more of a prison than a home. Although the station was a large one, the owners didn't live there. They journeyed to the station only once a year, preferring the more agreeable social life in Melbourne. Danny was left to manage the station and the large flock of sheep alone, except when the shearers descended for the annual clip. Dottie's prison, the bungalow, was little better than a solitary confinement cell.

Sometimes she was not even allowed to accompany Danny on his weekly trips into town. She learned to dread these days, for Danny would invariably come home drunk, the smell of stale alcohol on his breath mingling with perfume and other less pleasant odours that suggested he had enjoyed some female's company intimately. Occasionally, he would force his attentions on Dottie, the embrace she had once yearned for turned into a grotesque parody by his perfunctory and brutally basic technique. Dottie knew she was merely a receptacle for his feelings. Any woman would have served the purpose; her only attraction, in his eyes, her availability.

It became the exception rather than the rule for Dottie to awake on a Sunday morning without fresh bruises to testify to Danny's enjoyment of his Saturday outing. She did not have to work hard to earn these, a word out of place – sometimes a look in her eyes was enough. On one of her increasingly rare visits to town, Dottie's bruises were spotted by Louise Finnegan. On being questioned about them, Dottie made the mistake of telling the truth. Louise told her husband, who, with Dottie's best interests at heart, took Danny to task over the matter.

The root cause of Malloy's anger was his sense of feeling tricked and trapped by the marriage. He had entered into it expecting the union to provide him with a short journey to Easy Street. He was unaware of the terms of Dottie's father's will. He had been too excited by his proximity to so much wealth to ask. It was only after their marriage that he found out.

He visited Patrick Finnegan to request money to fund a few of life's necessities, principal among these, alcohol. Patrick delivered the unpalatable truth, his dislike and mistrust of Malloy turning the chore into a pleasure. Louise's report on Dottie's bruises gave him free rein to indulge in a little plain speaking. 'You're not getting a penny out of me,' he told Malloy. 'As Dottie's guardian I have complete control over her affairs. If you think I'm going to turn money over for a drunken wastrel like you to piss against the wall and fornicate with, you can think again.'

'How long have you got control for?' Malloy asked through the red haze of his anger.

'Forever. There's a clause in Dottie's father's will that stipulates that if I, or her trustees wish, we can withhold even the interest on her money ad infinitum.' Patrick stared at Malloy in disgust, and with distaste in his tone added, 'That, to save you looking it up, means every time you ask.'

It was following that conversation and Finnegan's comments about the bruising that matters got even worse. The outcome was not precisely what Patrick or Louise Finnegan had in mind, for thereafter the beatings increased in both regularity and severity, while her trips to town diminished in proportion.

Dottie did not even have the distraction of a baby on whom to lavish her frustrated affection, or to help pass the weary, dragging, lonely hours and days. The prospect of a family was now one Dottie dreaded, given Malloy's temper. Not that there was much chance of such an event, happy or otherwise, for Malloy seldom went near her except with his fists. Well, to be fair to Danny that wasn't strictly true, sometimes he used his boots or his belt as well.

There was no pleasing him, try as she might. And Dottie did try. She tried harder than she had ever tried in her life, but to no avail. Nothing she said, or did, pleased him. If she tried to make the bungalow pleasant he would sneer that she was aping her former luxury, if she tried to cook for him it was either underdone, or burnt, or tasteless, or not what he had wanted. If she rebelled and refused to cook, he beat her, telling her it was her just desserts for being an idle slut.

CHAPTER THIRTY-SIX

Angelina Rocca's prediction about Luke Fisher's immediate future had proved highly accurate. He had made his way to Sydney, where he enjoyed the social life to the full. Young, handsome, rich and charming, there was no shortage of female companionship to enhance his enjoyment of the city.

By the New Year, he was in Paris. He soon discovered that a single, young and wealthy Australian loose on the continent of Europe was a magnet for available females, some respectable, others less so. He enjoyed the company of both, the less respectable slightly less so.

He was introduced to a Brazilian girl, no more than three years his elder. Ramona had been married at sixteen to a forty-seven-year-old multi-millionaire. Surprisingly, the marriage had been successful, possibly a little too successful, if rumour was to be believed. The widowed Ramona neither confirmed nor denied the gossip that suggested her husband's fatal heart attack had been caused by Ramona's excessive physical demands.

After his death Ramona went into deep mourning. Once the required twelve months was over, she decided to travel. When she was introduced to Luke Fisher, Ramona had been celibate for more than two years. Luke was young, handsome, and virile, with a dancing imp of mischief in his vivid blue eyes. Ramona looked into those blue eyes and decided two years was long enough.

Luke had drunk a little too much champagne during the evening. Curiously, when he awoke next morning his head did not ache, but his shoulder did. He opened his eyes to discover the cause of this phenomenon. He saw it was Ramona, her head resting on his shoulder, her long, dark, lustrous hair spread out on the pillow like a fan. He smiled, remembering, and lifted the sheet that covered them. He looked down at her slightly tanned body, the full, firm breasts, and slender waist, and was instantly aroused. He took her hand and gently guided it towards him. Ramona smiled a drowsy sensual smile as she felt the touch on the palm of her hand.

'Again?' she asked, her English heavily accented, her voice husky with passion.

'Again,' Luke confirmed, his tone decisive, 'and again and again.'

They were together almost six months, travelling throughout Europe. But the affair was beginning to burn out. Both had fresh fields to conquer. Luke wanted to see more of the world while Ramona wanted to sample more of the world's men.

Nevertheless, there was real regret at their parting. Ramona stood on the platform of Athens railway station, weeping as she embraced Luke.

'Take care, my little kangaroo,' she used his pet name for the last time. 'Go out and do great things. I was never enough to satisfy the restless urge in you. Someday, somewhere you will find a woman who does, then you will settle down, but for the meantime this is your chance, don't waste it.'

'Goodbye, Ramona.' Luke was close to tears himself. 'I'll never forget you or our time together. Don't forget to look me up if you ever get to Australia.'

Ramona gave that throaty chuckle that preceded a mischievous remark. 'You'd better not forget, but don't go issuing rash invitations. What would your wife and three children say if I turn up on your doorstep?'

Luke entered the fantasy with a grin. 'If the children are boys, they'll probably whistle and say, "Lucky old Dad".'

They parted in laughter and although Luke was sad throughout the train journey across Europe he found adequate consolation once he boarded the liner bound for the United States. He found it in the bed of a fellow passenger, an American divorcee with the face of an angel and the soul of a nymphomaniac. The voyage was long enough for them to derive complete satisfaction from one another's company, not long enough to weary of it, so there was no regret when they disembarked and went their separate ways.

Luke lost himself in the vast continent, once or twice, literally. He visited as much of North America as he could, even taking in Canada. It was only when he sat down once more to a solitary meal in a luxury New York hotel that Luke felt the first pangs of homesickness. Two days later, Luke knew he was ready to return home. He had travelled far enough, seen parts of the world he had never expected to visit but knew he was ready to quit the itinerant lifestyle and settle down. To what, he was unsure, but one thing he knew, once he reached Australia he was certain he would never leave again. Perhaps it was as well Luke could not see into the future, or had not heard the saying, 'If you want to hear God laugh, tell him your plans.'

From the moment Luke disembarked he was at a loose end. It was all very well returning to Australia through homesickness, but none of the conditions that had led to his self-imposed exile had changed. He took a taxi from the docks to Fisher Springs' banking subsidiary, where he drew out a large sum of money and collected the small pile of correspondence that had been accumulating during his absence. Luke ordered the waiting taxi driver to take him to the nearest decent hotel.

Once inside his hotel room he began opening the mail. The first two envelopes contained copies of Fisher Springs' annual reports covering the two financial years since his departure. The profits revealed in these and the figures on the attached dividend statements made him smile with surprise and pleasure. He laid aside the enclosed letters from Patrick and Louise Finnegan to read later.

The next envelope's contents pleased Luke as much as the earlier ones. It was a progress report from Gianni and Angelina Rocca. They had located and purchased a parcel of land suitable for a vineyard. Part of this had been cleared and planted using imported vines. These appeared to be flourishing, but Gianni would not order the clearance and planting of the remaining land until he was completely satisfied that a viable crop would result. Gianni, it seemed, as well as having a talent for viniculture, had inherited his family's business acumen.

Luke's next letter was dated a year earlier. It was from his brother Philip, full of contrition for his actions, begging Luke to return home. Luke tossed it into the waste bin. The letters from Patrick and Louise caused him much thought. He decided he would reply to these in due course. There remained one envelope unopened, a bulky one. The contents left Luke in a state of total confusion, so much so that it took him many days to sort out his emotions at the news it conveyed. He didn't recognize the handwriting and turned to the last page, whistled with surprise before beginning to read.

Dearest Luke,

Mom and Dad wanted to write to you with the dreadful news I have to impart, but I insisted I should be the one to do it. I'm sorry to tell you that Cissie and her husband Bob drowned last year in a boating accident. You remember they moved to New Zealand? Well they took to sailing but were capsized in a sudden squall. The attached newspaper cutting will tell you the facts. I'm so sorry, Luke. We buried them in the family plot, alongside your mom and dad and Mary. I know how distressing this will be, I just wish I could be with you to help share your grief.

He put the letter down, his heart heavy with sadness, guilt and a desolate loneliness. It was a long time before he could bring himself to pick it up and read on.

I wish you were here with us. We all miss you so, Mom, Dad, the kids and Dottie. Dottie is married now, but she is very unhappy because her husband is a brute. The strange thing is I thought it the first time I met him, when he was trying to be charming, but Dottie couldn't see it. Mom found some bruises on Dottie once. I think he beats her regularly. I worry about what will happen, he seems to be getting worse. There are lots of stories about him in town, getting drunk and going with other girls.

We don't see anything of your brother at the house since Mom made Dad kick him out for what he did to you. I've hated him from that day to this, sometimes it hurts me, the hate, and missing you. I met him in town one day, he tried to say hello, but I told him to get lost. I hate him because he was wicked to you, because he drove you away from your home, from your family, everything you love. It was a noble thing you did, Luke, but sometimes I cry because you're not here. That's why I hate Philip more than anything, because he took you away from me. I don't know any other way, I can only be as I am, blunt, outspoken, sometimes to the point of rudeness, Mom says. You see Luke, I love you, and I have done for years, even when you didn't notice me. I owe my life to you, I've known that a long time, but that's got nothing to do with how I feel for you. I have no shame in writing this, no shame where you're concerned. I know you'll think of this as some adolescent fantasy but I don't care. It isn't, I know that, so I'll tell you the right of it then you'll come to see it's true.

When you left, I was just another scrawny kid you teased and played cricket and tennis with. Well, I've changed a bit since then, so I sneaked off to town last week and had some photos taken. They're in the other envelope. I don't think I'm the ugliest duckling in the flock but I'll let you be the judge of that. You see what I mean about having no shame where you're concerned?

I'll say it again, I love you, Luke Fisher, I always have, and I guess I always will.

Yours, Bella.

Luke breathed heavily as if he'd been running. At first amused, then shocked and astonished by the latter part of Bella's confession, he ended in considerable confusion. Idly, he opened the attached envelope and slid the photos out. In his mind's eye he saw Bella as she had been when he left, a gawky, skinny kid, all arms and long bean-pole legs, with tousled fair hair and a talent for outrageous language. The hair was still blonde, as blonde as that of her mother, the legs even longer, but no longer skinny. The girl looking out from the photo was a child no longer. She had filled out to a radiantly lovely specimen of womanhood. None of his erstwhile lovers, not even the duskily stunning Ramona, could hold a candle to Bella Finnegan for looks. Despite this, Luke's attention was held longest by her steadfast blue eyes, eyes that seemed to be willing him to believe all she had written, eyes that defied being taken lightly. He had already decided he would return home to pay his respects to Cissie and her husband Bob. Now he knew there were other compelling reasons for his return.

CHAPTER THIRTY-SEVEN

Danny Malloy slept late on Sunday mornings, recuperating from Saturday night's excesses. On arrival home the previous night he had vented his frustrations and the imagined ills in his life on Dottie, in what had become an established ritual. The beating he had given her left him with a sense of satisfaction on which to retire to bed and lapse into an alcoholic stupor. It had left Dottie weeping and forlorn, with a black eye, a cut lip, and a mass of bruises to her upper body and to her arms where she had tried to defend herself.

Danny woke shortly before noon the following day. He woke up because something had disturbed him. He sat up in bed, his head aching. It was the sound of a motor car, an unfamiliar noise on the lonely sheep station. He staggered from the bed. He was still dressed from the previous night. His mouth felt brackish, bitter. He tripped over his discarded boots and sprawled headfirst against the bedroom dresser. He banged his temple on the sharp corner. His headache worsened. He was morose and irritable. Who the hell had come to disturb him on a Sunday?

Danny put on the offending boots and went into the adjacent living room. He gazed out of the window, squinting painfully as the dazzlingly bright sunlight hit his long-suffering eyeballs. As he managed to focus he saw a large, expensive-looking motor car parked close to the fence surrounding the bungalow's small patch of garden. Standing at the front of the car was a man Danny had never seen before.

To Danny's shock and mounting anger, the stranger was embracing Dottie, who seemed to be enjoying the experience. Danny could barely believe the evidence of his eyes. His temper flared. His headache began pounding harder. Dottie had a lover, and they were embracing in full view of his own home. Danny flung open the front door. He stormed down the path, the very model of an outraged husband.

'You dirty slut. What the hell do you think you're doing?' he shouted.

Before Dottie or the stranger had chance to reply, Danny opened the gate and seized Dottie by one arm. He wrenched her to one side, accompanying the move with a vicious backhanded swipe that left a red weal across her cheek.

'Stop that,' the stranger commanded, his voice as hard as steel.

Danny was in no mood to be told what to do

by anyone, let alone the man he suspected was Dottie's lover. 'Like hell I will,' he shouted. He prepared to deliver a punch that would teach the bastard not to mess around with other men's wives. 'You take yourself off my land before I give you a hiding you'll remember the rest of your life,' he roared.

By way of a reply the stranger smashed a savage right hook into Danny's face. The punch landed square on his nose, the force dumped him on his backside. His head hit the garden fence with a sickening thud. He sat against the fence, his broken nose bleeding copiously. The stranger hauled Danny to his feet and propped him against the fence. Any thought Danny had that might have been from concern for his welfare soon vanished as the stranger, ignoring pleas from Dottie, gave Danny a more severe beating than any he had administered to his wife. Eventually the man relented and Danny slid to the ground, a whimpering heap of agony and fear. Both his eyes were blackened, his lips split and swollen, his ribs so bruised it would be weeks before he could breathe without pain.

The stranger looked at Danny with disgust and stirred him with the toe of his boot.

'I'm Luke Fisher – Dottie's big brother,' he added by way of explanation. 'I'm taking her away from you,' he told the half-conscious, barely comprehending Malloy. 'And that' – he nudged him again with his boot – 'is just a taste of what you'll get if you try to go near Dottie again. So, if you value your skin, don't even think about it.'

Luke's voice was calm and gentle once more as he turned to Dottie. 'Go get your things.'

Dottie began to weep.

'Don't cry over him, love. He's not worth it. Now run along and pack.'

Dottie smiled, a watery smile. 'You called me love, Dad always used to call us love.'

Luke smiled. 'Run along and get ready,' he ordered.

'What about Danny?' Dottie was still worried.

Luke eyed the near comatose figure at his feet. 'Bugger Danny,' he said cheerfully.

Patrick and Louise Finnegan were sitting on the veranda. Patrick had fallen asleep, the newspaper he had been reading lying ignored on his lap. Louise too was barely able to concentrate on the book in her hand, Margaret Mitchell's classic *Gone with the Wind*. Her attention strayed from the doings of Rhett Butler and Scarlett O'Hara as she heard the sound of an approaching vehicle. Her interest sharpened as the motor car swung into the drive and stopped next to Patrick's. She blinked in surprise as Dottie climbed out of the passenger seat and waited for the driver. Louise adjusted her glasses to get a better view. The next minute her book went flying as she leapt to her feet, screaming, 'Patrick, wake up! Luke's back!' By which time she was down the steps and haring across the lawn.

'What?' Patrick answered groggily. He struggled to his feet and gazed after his wife. He made to follow her but before he had taken two strides, the house door flew open and his daughter whizzed past going like an express train. Her father blinked in bemusement, shook his head to clear the last vestige of sleep and after a wary glance at the house door in case any more of his family came hurtling out, followed his wife and daughter to discover why they had suddenly gone mad.

Fatted calf was not on the afternoon tea menu, but the meal and the welcome were still all a returning prodigal could have wished for. There was almost a family row over the seating arrangements. Louise settled the dispute.

'Bella, you sit next to Luke, Dottie you sit on his other side, the rest of you take your usual places.' Dottie smiled, the younger children sulked, and Bella gloated.

Any lingering doubts Louise had over whether her eldest daughter was carrying a torch for Luke had long since vanished. Bella had shown little interest in boys, which was one indication. Her insistence on writing to tell him about Cissie's death, had converted Louise's suspicions into certainty. Whether it was an infatuation that would pass, Louise was not sure. If so, Louise trusted Luke enough to know Bella would come to no harm by it. If it was more long-lasting than a mere girlish crush, Louise could think of no better outcome. Bella was brash in her outward demeanour, outspoken and forthright, but Louise knew she was also steadfast and immovable once her heart was set on something.

Luke Fisher found himself in a curious position. He had returned home with three objectives in mind. To visit Cissie's grave, to sort out Dottie's problems and to put a dampener on Bella's infatuation. The photographs she'd sent him had unsettled him a little. His noble intention was wavering since he saw her outside the house. He realized the photos did her less than justice. Nobility vanished in a flash. To cover his confusion Luke talked, almost non-stop throughout the meal. He told the family of the places he had visited, the sights he had seen, and the people he had met. In deference to Bella's feelings, he omitted any mention of any of his racier exploits.

He announced his intention to visit the cemetery the following day, but he would only be staying for a few days. His plan was to take Dottie with him to Melbourne where he intended to buy a place and Dottie would keep house for him.

After the meal he told them he wanted to take a walk over to the Fisher mansion. He would go alone, he decided.

In deference to his feelings, Louise commanded the rest of the family to stay and help with the washing-up and other chores.

It was a lovely evening, one of those he had kept in his memory all the time he had been away. Luke lay face down on the cool grass of the lawn.

He heard the swish of footsteps and smiled. Without removing his gaze from the blackened shell of the building he said, 'Hello, Miss Isabella Finnegan.'

'Hello, Luke Fisher,' she replied and lay down alongside him. 'How clever of you to guess I'd be along.'

'I came back because of Cissie, because of Dottie,' he paused and turned to look at her, 'and because of you. I came with the intention of telling you to forget this silly infatuation for me, to go out and find someone else.'

Bella felt suddenly cold, her hand trembled. Luke placed his hand on hers and smiled, that so familiar, so longed for smile.

'The trouble is I'm not sure I want you to forget me, I don't want you to find someone else. I'm being selfish and inconsiderate and I should be old enough to know better, but there it is.'

'Luke, I'm nearly fifteen, you're only twenty-one. A few years more won't alter anything, not for me. I know that sounds like big brave talk, but you see I'm not a bit like other girls. I see things different. I've always known what I want in life, so you'd better get used to the fact.'

Luke suddenly saw his way clear. 'How about this for a plan? Tomorrow I'll talk to your mom and ask her permission for us to write to one another while I'm away. How does that sound?'

'Apart from the bit about being away, fine. But promise me one thing.'

'What's that?'

'Promise you'll tell me everything in your letters, not just the highlights as you did at tea, then, if I find you've been with another woman, I'll cut your balls off.'

'Bella!' Luke protested, shocked.

'That's me, Luke,' she said cheerfully. 'Not some namby-pamby little girl. I say and do what I think and if people don't like it, to hell with them.'

'I believe you,' Luke said in wonder. 'What other surprises have you for me, Bella?'

'Only this. When you get me, you get a full partner in life. As far as you're concerned that means just what you think. I just hope you haven't worn yourself out before you found me.'

Luke laughed, only half believing what he was hearing. 'I think I might be able to manage,' he murmured. 'Anything else?'

'Yes,' she ordered him. 'Kiss me.'

Their first kiss, her first kiss was much as expected, sweet, with only the vaguest hint of passion. When he released her, she looked at him for a moment.

'Very nice,' she said dryly. 'Now would you mind kissing me as if you meant it?'

Luke seized her, crushed her against him, and kissed her savagely, only to be met with an echoing ferocity. He felt the fire within her, the answering inferno in him. When he eventually released her, Bella looked at him, her face a study in contentment. 'Much better,' she told him.

'Yes, Bella.' Luke Fisher, bold and decisive in business, twice the hero of all Australia, the man who had defended his sister against her brutish husband, realized he had met his match.

Before Luke and Dottie set out for Melbourne, Louise was party to a conversation on the subject of romance. 'I've come to ask you a great favour,' Luke told her, 'but first of all I'd better tell you what it's about.'

'I'd guess it has something to do with that impulsive, headstrong daughter of mine,' Louise replied quietly.

Luke blushed, but agreed. 'Yes, it's about Bella, or rather,' he corrected himself, 'about Bella and me. What I'm here for is to ask your permission to write to her after I leave here and for her to write to me.'

'I see no reason for you not to write to each other. After all you have been like brother and sister.' Much as Louise liked him, she could not resist a little gentle teasing, besides which she wanted to know exactly how the situation stood.

'Well, that may have been the case once,' Luke declared boldly, 'but not now. I didn't realize how I felt about her until recently, but the thing is, I love Bella, and not as a sister. As a girl, a girl I hope will continue to feel the same way about me as she does at present. I know you're going to tell me how young she is, that's part of the reason I'm leaving. I'm frightened I'd do something I'd regret, something that would upset you and Patrick. Besides which, I want Bella to have a fair chance to change her mind.'

Louise relented. 'Luke, I've known for a long time how she felt about you. Going away is a lot more than many young men in your situation would do. I don't think you need worry about Bella changing her mind about you though, she's not made that way.'

'I certainly hope she doesn't,' Luke declared fervently.

Louise smiled at him. 'That tells me a lot and I'm pleased for you. If I wanted to choose the ideal man for Bella, you'd do. She may be headstrong, she may be impulsive and outspoken to the point of rudeness, but she's also very loving and extremely loyal.'

'We're not talking commitment, or at least I'm not,' Luke assured her, 'although Bella seems determined. So I take it that you've no objection to us writing to one another?'

'Absolutely not.' Louise crossed the room and hugged him. 'You've become like a son to Patrick and me, and I hope you become a son-in-law as well.'

Bella's reaction to the consent was overwhelmingly ecstatic. Before he and Dottie departed for Melbourne, Bella seized the opportunity for a quiet word with his sister.

'I want you to look after Luke,' she told Dottie. 'I don't want him getting into any bother, so if you wouldn't mind scaring off any girls that would be great.'

Dottie's eyes opened wide, she whistled gently in surprise. 'So that's the way of it,' she said. 'I did wonder why you and he kept sneaking off on your own.'

'Absolutely,' Bella confirmed. 'He's mine now and off-limits to anyone else. I don't want any Melbourne girls trying to get their claws into him.'

'Don't worry,' Dottie reassured her. 'I'll play the dragon for you, but I think you're worrying over nothing. I doubt any Melbourne girl could hold a candle to you.'

CHAPTER THIRTY-EIGHT

By the first week of April, Carmen knew the baby was becoming as impatient about being held prisoner as the rest of them and would soon demand early parole. One afternoon, as the light was beginning to fade, they heard the sound of approaching hooves. It was El Bosquero, travelling by donkey. The news he brought was urgent and grave. As he told the rest of the party all that had happened, Carmen read the letter he had handed her from their erstwhile leader, La Trompetista.

> Querida (my darling),
>
> The news I have to tell is all bad. Throughout Spain the nationalists are gaining the ascendancy. They have the armour, the tanks, and planes and they have the backing of German and Italian troops and supplies. Of our group less than seventy-five remain. The rest are all dead, wounded or have deserted. I judged it time to disband. Our great adventure that we began with such high hopes has perished on

the cold steel of the enemy's mighty engines of war.

I have sent our men away, told them to return to their families, their homes, if they are still there. Find their farms, their cottages and try to come to terms with the new order. For those with you in the mountains I urge the same. I regret I never met our British comrades, from what the men told me they are of the highest order of courage. Would that their bravery had been better rewarded.

Now I come to the part I can hardly bring myself to write. For you and I, it is also a time of parting. From all I have learned, what has happened here is merely the prologue. Sinister and deadly moves are taking place, the outcome of which is too awful to contemplate. That means I am needed elsewhere. It is so cruel that we should be torn apart when we have been able to spend so little time together in our beautiful mountain idyll. As I write this I can picture you there, your beauty complementing the natural splendour. I see you laughing and tender, serious and gentle, ever caring, always passionate. I long to hold you in my arms once more, to feel your body against mine, to know once more the sublime and supreme honour you bestow on me when you share yourself with me. But that can no longer be and my heart breaks to think of it. Perhaps what was between us was too beautiful to last, like a flower that enriches all around it with its beautiful blossom, the fragrance of its perfume, only to be cut down all too soon by the murderous cruelty of the frost. So this is farewell, Querida, I can write no more of us, think no more of us, except for the sadness of parting, the glory of our fleeting moment together.

The messenger who carries this letter has instructions to take you with our English friends, by ways only he knows, to the coast. Valencia is safe, for the moment. Once there, they will be able to get a boat to France and will be able to return to England. I have also been able, with a stroke of fortune, to arrange for a fishing boat to take you to Eivissa, to your grandmother's home. There, in the quiet of the island, you should be safe.

Vaya Con Dios, Mi Querida.

Carmen looked up from the letter. Tears, bright but unshed glistened in her eyes. 'When was this written?' she asked, numbly.

'One month past,' the forester replied quietly.

'He is gone then?' Carmen asked the question, already knowing the answer.

'Yes, he is gone.' He indicated the only too visible

evidence of Carmen's condition. 'He knew nothing of this?'

'No, he did not know and it is better that it should be so, for as things have happened he would have been torn between duty to me and duty to his country. It would have destroyed him and he is too fine a man for that.'

At two o'clock the following morning Mark and Jenny were woken by a pounding on their bedroom door.

'What is it?' Mark cried, fumbling in the dark for the gun he kept at the bedside.

'La Chica. I need La Chica, I need her now.'

Despite the urgency of this request it was breakfast time before the baby arrived. Mark was the first to inspect the new arrival. 'Allow me to introduce you,' the proud mother told him. 'This young lady is Senorita Consuela. Consuela is Spanish for consolation. I think it is fitting, for she is consolation to me for all I have lost.'

Three weeks later, when they judged it safe for Carmen and Consuela to travel, the party left the camp for the last time.

'Many things have come to an end, many others will end soon, perhaps this is just one more,' Carmen said wistfully as they gazed on the mountain retreat that had been their home for so long.

Their safe descent from the mountains owed much to the skill of El Bosquero. As they prepared to descend the last ridge, Mark and Jenny, who were leading the party, looked back towards the mountains. Carmen, mounted on El Bosquero's donkey, was silhouetted against the setting sun. It provided the English couple with the most enduring memory of their friend, poignant and symbolic, of a woman alone, child strapped to her breast, rifle raised, the butt resting on her thigh.

Once they reached the fertile plains of La Rioja, they bade farewell to the men. The forester guided Carmen, Mark and Jenny on the long trek eastwards and south, following the course of the mighty River Ebro towards the sea. By mid-May they had reached Valencia. There Mark and Jenny, aided by El Bosquero, succeeded in buying passage on a ship bound for Marseilles.

The four of them stood on the quayside, their tears of farewell unashamed. Now that it was safe to do so they swapped details of their true identities.

Carmen smiled and looked at the baby in her arms. 'Now I have decided she will have a second name. She will be called Consuela Genoveva, in honour of our friendship. Genoveva is the equivalent of Jennifer, my midwife, comrade, friend – the sister I never had.'

Jenny's eyes brimmed with tears.

Much to Mark and Jenny's surprise they also discovered Carmen's nickname to be a double bluff.

'You mean your name actually is Carmen?' Jenny asked.

'Of course, that was the best part of the joke.'

'What of Consuela's father?' Jenny wanted to know.

Carmen looked at her tiny daughter, peeping out with wide eyes at the strange world she had entered. Carmen shook her head. 'All that is past. At one time I believed your tiny island could produce nothing finer, but that was before I met you two.'

'You mean Consuela's father is an Englishman?' Mark asked in surprise.

'I do indeed.' Carmen winked at him. 'So you'd better look after Mark, Jenny, now you know how I am about Englishmen.'

'I think I'll be able to cope.' Jenny leaned forward and hugged Carmen, the two women embracing in an unspoken farewell.

As they stood on the deck watching the port recede into the distance, Jenny gave one final wave to the two tiny, indistinct figures on the quayside and smiled. 'When will we reach England?'

'That should be the beginning of July, with any luck,' Mark said. He paused for a moment then said, 'Good Lord, I've just remembered something. I've had an idea.'

'What is it this time?' Jenny had learned to be suspicious of his ideas. Mark told her. For once, he was surprised to find there was no objection. 'Darling, that's a wonderful plan.'

'I wonder what we'll find when we return?' Mark speculated.

Jenny laughed. 'I don't suppose much will have changed, it never does.'

In that she was more than a little inaccurate. During their absence Britain had witnessed the abdication of Edward VIII and the reluctant accession to the throne of George VI. The nation was looking forward, hoping, and praying, for a period of peace and stability, which proves that even a nation's hopes and prayers can go unanswered.

Edrith Pointon read the report on his desk with great interest. It was long, comprehensive, and detailed. Much of the commentary would have done credit to a vastly more experienced operative. There was however one major flaw. The actions of his agent throughout had more than transcended his brief, that of an observer. Such a disregard for his terms of reference would need correction before he returned to the field. The potential danger of the next assignment was far greater.

Edrith rose from his desk and summoned the agent waiting in the outer office. 'Sit down. I want to go through your report.'

The interview that followed was uncomfortable. It started badly. 'This is very exciting' – Edrith indicated the report – 'as a work of fiction it would sell very well, but I cannot recall anything in my instructions to you before you left that involved taking sides in the Spanish war, joining a band of guerrillas and becoming their leader. Of course I may be mistaken, so if my memory is at fault, please correct me.'

'No, your memory isn't at fault. I know I wasn't supposed to become involved and I'm sorry. But it became too much, to stand by and act as if I didn't care. What I witnessed in Badajoz was the last straw.'

'Oh, so it had nothing to do with you becoming romantically involved with a woman?' Pointon asked.

'No, not then, not until much later. And even if I hadn't become *involved*, as you put it, I would have acted just the same. Any man worth his salt would have.'

'Tell me.'

'Badajoz was in turmoil. The nationalists overran the city, took control, then systematically set about butchering anyone suspected of republican sympathies. What happened was pure chance. I was passing a house, heard screams, and guessed what was happening inside. I went in, I couldn't stop myself. There were four nationalist soldiers there. They'd killed her husband, slit his throat. Then one of them stood guard over her, while the others took it in turns to rape her young daughter. The little girl bit the last one so he stuck his bayonet in her belly and ripped her open. When I went in she was writhing on the floor in agony, her guts spilled out, dying in a pool of her own blood. I shot the one guarding the mother then handed the pistol to her and she killed the others. She used a lot of bullets before they were dead, making them suffer as much as she could.' He paused, his eyes moist with tears as he whispered the final horror. 'Then she shot her own daughter to put an end to her suffering. The little girl was just eight years old. Perhaps now you can understand why I found it impossible to stay neutral, detached?'

Even Pointon, hardened though he was could not help but be moved by this account. 'This was no isolated incident then?'

Grim-faced, he replied, 'By no means. It was happening all over the city, that, or something similar. We escaped, after she had set fire to the house. She was determined to burn the place down, almost as if she was trying to burn it from her memory, but of course she could never do that. We travelled east, as quickly as we could to get away from the obscene things that were happening there. It was pure chance that we became attached to the guerrillas, no plan of mine to become their leader. We did what little we could but the fascists were too well armed. They had German and Italian backing, troops, planes and supplies, while the republican side was divided by factional in-fighting, some groups supporting the communists, some socialist led, which meant there was no clear planning or strategy. The result was inevitable.'

'Did the woman escape?' Edrith asked.

'I've no idea. I do hope so. Carmen has suffered

so much. I did what I could, I sent a man who knows the terrain better than anyone to get her away. He was taking her to the coast, to Valencia, the republicans still controlled it then. The plan was for her to travel by fishing boat to Ibiza, where her grandmother lives. She had an English couple with her in the mountains, a young couple who joined the band much as I did, by accident. They had acquitted themselves well by all accounts, but whether any of them escaped or not I've no idea.'

'Who were they?' Pointon wanted to know.

'I couldn't tell you. I never got to meet them.'

Edrith tapped the report. 'I can understand your actions better now. In the circumstances I'd probably have done much the same. Especially if Carmen is as beautiful as you make out,' he added with a grin. 'I suppose it got pretty cold in the mountains,' he insinuated.

'I never noticed the cold.'

'I bet you didn't. Now we must move on. Tell me, what do you know about heavy water?'

'Heavy water? What's that?'

'I thought as much. What you don't know, you're going to have to learn. You are going back to university for a short science lesson with one of our tame professors.' Pointon indicated a pile of papers on a side table. 'There's a bit of light reading for you,' he said with a smile. 'Study it, familiarize yourself with it, and report to the boffins next week. You understand?'

'Yes, sir.'

Joshua Jones got to his feet and gathered all the reams of documents, papers and reference books which would provide background material for the task he had been given.'

'By the way, when you finish reading that lot you can visit your family. You have four days.'

'Thank you.' Josh grinned at the prospect.

The room assigned as a study was windowless, and he only noticed the passage of time when he paused to drink cups of tea brought to him at regular intervals by a pretty secretary. On a couple of occasions, the girl, taking pity on the handsome young agent, supplemented these with a plate of biscuits, which he received with a grateful smile.

Eventually, when he reckoned his brain had assimilated all it could for one day, Josh decided to quit. He glanced at his watch and was surprised to see that it was long after office hours. He got up and stretched, stiff from having remained seated for so long. He took the key Pointon had given him out of his pocket and locked the door, before heading down the corridor.

CHAPTER THIRTY-NINE

Josh noticed how quiet the building seemed, the usually busy offices empty, their normal incumbents probably already at home or heading there. He wondered briefly if he was the last to leave, apart from the porter, who remained on duty throughout the night until his replacement arrived for the day shift. At least the man would be able to report on how industrious he was, Josh thought with a smile.

He had almost reached the large general office at the end of the corridor, when the door to his right opened, and a young woman stepped out. Unable to stop, Josh collided with her, sending her reeling to one side and causing her to drop the pile of folders she was carrying. The files scattered their contents onto the threadbare carpet. Josh muttered an apology and bent to start picking them up.

He froze as the woman told him in a sharp tone, 'Don't touch those. They're none of your business.'

Josh looked up, startled not so much by the terse command, but by the woman's voice, which he recognized immediately. 'Jessica! What are you doing here?'

Her face drained of all colour. Josh saw her reach out a hand to steady herself against the wall. 'Josh!'

He repeated his question, this time in a marginally calmer voice, although he felt anything but calm.

'I work here,' Jessica told him. 'Or at least I work for the department, but not usually in this building. And you, why are you here?'

'If you work here, you'll understand when I tell you my name is Smith. To be fair, I don't usually work here either. I have just recently returned. I'll be going away again in a few days.' Josh paused, and then added, 'Perhaps now we've bumped into one another again, literally, you could give me an explanation for acting the way you did?'

Jessica knew what he was referring to, and suddenly, aware of the extreme gravity of the situation and the dangers they all faced, knew she owed him the truth. It was the least she could do for him, possibly all she could do for him.

'I will explain, Josh, but not here. Give me a hand to collect these files and then we'll go somewhere for a drink.'

He scooped up some of the folders as Jessica did the same and watched as she stuffed these into her briefcase. He noticed that after she collected her coat she took the case with her. As with so much of the department's work, Josh guessed, it didn't end when the employees left the building.

The pub she chose was all but deserted and they took their drinks to a secluded corner where there was no chance of their conversation being overheard.

'You're looking really fit and well, Josh,' Jessica said, by way of breaking the ice. 'I guess part of that might be because of the department's training, but I somehow don't think you acquired that suntan in England.'

Josh smiled. 'Hardly, I was in Spain until recently.'

'Working as Mr Smith?'

'Yes, and I expect very soon I'll be on my travels again. What about you? What role do you play for our mysterious employer?'

'I've been put in charge of a project that involves a lot of screwy scientists and inventors with crazy ideas. They call it the nuthouse. The hope is they will come up with something really useful should there be another war. It's about all we can do for the moment with the ban on rearmament.'

'I think another war is all but inevitable, sadly,' Josh's face was troubled. 'What the outcome will be, I dread to think. So, are you going to tell me why you chucked me like that? It was fairly brutal, to put it mildly.'

'I know it was, and I'm sorry for having to do it and for the way I did it.' Jessica looked miserably into her glass, and then drained her drink in one gulp. 'Come on. Let's get out of here and I'll show you why I acted as I did.'

It was only a few hundred yards to her flat. They walked in silence, each preoccupied with their own thoughts. Jessica unlocked the door and Josh followed her inside. She switched the lounge light on and stood in the middle of the room. As Josh looked round, she turned to face him.

'You remember how it ended between us?'

Josh nodded. 'How could I forget?'

'It was the night you took me back to your house. I was so happy then. You were all I wanted, all I needed. With you I could forget what I had been, what my mother had been and had done. With you I felt safe, protected, whole. I wanted nothing more than to be with you.' She hesitated. 'Then, after we made love, I saw the photograph. You remember?'

Josh nodded as she paused again. He looked at her, puzzled, until he saw her gesture towards the mantelpiece. He looked across the room and his jaw dropped in amazement as he saw the photo in the silver frame. 'I don't understand. Where did you get that from?'

'It's mine. My mother gave it to me. It's all I have to remember him by, because I never met him. She told me his name was Jesse Barker and that he was my father. When I saw the identical photograph on your bedside cabinet and you told me it was a photo of your father, it was then that I realized that the man I'd been sleeping with, the man I had just made love to, the man I was hopelessly in love with, was in fact my own brother. That, Josh dearest, is why I had to end it so abruptly, no matter how hurtful it was to you. Believe me, although you may think it was agonizing not knowing why I ditched you, it doesn't compare with the knowledge I had to carry. Nor did what followed.'

She saw Josh's baffled expression. 'You see, my dear Josh, you gave me an unexpected present. That was why I had to visit a backstreet abortionist in Leeds to get rid of the child I was carrying. Your child and mine, Josh, conceived in love and ignorance of the sin we had committed. And in doing so, I almost died. Indeed, there were times I wished I had, but those things are past now. However, in having that botched operation I ruined my chance of ever having a family.'

'Oh, Jessica. My poor, poor, Jessica.'

Josh reached out and took her into his arms. She sobbed as she clung to him.

'What a bloody awful mess,' he told her. 'I am so very sorry for bringing all this on you.'

'Don't be silly, it wasn't your fault any more than it was mine.' Jessica managed a watery smile. 'How were we to know that the attraction between us was unnatural, sinful?'

'Jessica, it wasn't unnatural. It was just unlucky. There is nothing we could have done about it. No way we could have resisted an attraction that was subconscious.'

'I didn't mean to be so cruel to you, but surely now you know the facts you can see why I had to act the way I did? I resolved that you would never learn the terrible truth of it. But when I saw you again today I realized that with the whole world going to hell, I had to let you learn the truth. Anything less would have been unfair.'

Josh looked across at the photo. 'Do you know what happened to him?'

'I neither know, nor care. The damage he's done is as much as I want to know.' Jessica shrugged. 'My mother told me she thought he was dead because he vanished at the start of the war, but nobody knows for sure. She also believed it was his brother who was hanged for murder, but to be honest everything about Jesse Barker seems to be shrouded in mystery.

'She also told me she thought my passionate nature was a result of her genes and his.' She smiled bitterly. 'I haven't exactly been a pillar of moral rectitude and now I'm paying the price for it. Perhaps, without knowing it, you've also inherited something of the same gene as well. Remembering how enthusiastic you were about the physical side of our relationship, I doubt you've been exactly celibate since we split up.'

Josh thought of Carmen and the tempestuous, passionate, nature of his affair with her before he had been forced to abandon her in Spain, but wisely refrained from commenting.

They talked for a while longer before Jessica said,

'I think you should go now, Josh. I have a lot of work to do and tomorrow I need to catch an early train for Birmingham. Added to that, I guess, knowing our leader, that you will also have a fair amount on your plate.'

Both of which were true, but they weren't the real reason, although Jessica fought against admitting it. Seeing Josh again, being close to him, having him hold her in his arms had aroused all the old feelings. Despite the forbidden nature of their relationship these wouldn't, couldn't, be subdued much longer. Far better to remove the match from close to the powder keg.

Josh wasn't taken in by Jessica's excuses, but he recognized the wisdom of her words. He walked over to the door, holding her hand for one final time. When they reached the entrance he turned her to face him. 'Goodbye, Jessica, my dear sister. Stay safe, stay well, and be happy.' He leaned forward and kissed her, a brotherly gesture, no more. Then he was gone.

Jessica locked the door and leaned against it, panting as if she had just been running. She went through to her bedroom, undressed and climbed into bed. The events of the past two hours had drained her. For a brief moment, when they were standing close together by the door, a part of her had wanted to return that kiss, wanted Josh to stay, wanted him to take her to bed and make love to her all night long as he had once done.

She knew these thoughts were wicked, but they

refused to go away, no matter how hard she tried to banish them. Her weary brain could not decide whether she was evil or only weak. She turned on her side and began to cry, sobbing uncontrollably until eventually, torn apart by her misery, sleep overcame her.

Jessica hadn't lied to Josh, she did have an early train to catch. She was away for three days. When she returned to the department's headquarters, as she walked along the corridor she half expected to see Josh striding towards her. However, by the time of her return, Josh was visiting his family before he became ensconced within the world of science.

It was Hannah Cowgill's eightieth birthday. In more normal circumstances this milestone would have been the cause for a more spectacular event, but with the family experiencing deepening fears about the fate of Mark and Jenny, a family dinner at the Grand Hotel was seen as more suitable.

Late in the afternoon of the great day, George, the butler, answered the telephone at Byland Crescent. The ensuing conversation was animated and prolonged. As it ended, Rachael, who was crossing the hall asked, 'Who was on the telephone, George?'

'It was the Grand Hotel, Madam,' George replied. 'Apparently, there was some confusion over the numbers for this evening's booking.'

The party assembled at the Grand Hotel

included all those from Byland Crescent, family and staff, Michael and Connie Haigh and their family and Simon and Naomi Jones with their younger children. As they took their seats Rachael said to George, 'I see they've still got the numbers wrong.' She indicated the two empty chairs at the end of the table.

'I think not, Madam.' George pointed towards the door.

Rachael looked towards the entrance and her heart almost stopped. Standing just inside the doorway, hand in hand as always, were two unmistakeable figures. Older, thinner and deeply suntanned, but without doubt her son and his fiancée.

Rachael leapt to her feet, staring across the room causing all heads to turn in the same direction to see what had brought such a reaction and expression to her face.

The head waiter announced, to the shocked surprise of the whole table, 'Mr and Mrs Mark Cowgill.'

Jenny whispered to Mark, 'Accompanied by Master or Miss Cowgill.'

For once Mark, master of surprises, was speechless.

PART FOUR

1938–1939

'He that outlives this day, and comes straight home,
Will stand a tip-toe when this day is nam'd,
And rouse him at the name of Crispian.
He that shall live this day, and see old age,
Will yearly on the vigil feast his neighbours,
And say 'To-morrow is Saint Crispian.'
Then will he strip his sleeve and show his scars,
And say 'These wounds I had on Crispian's day.'
Old men forget, yet all shall be forgot,
But he'll remember, with advantages,
What feats he did that day.'

William Shakespeare
Henry V. **Act IV, scene 3**

CHAPTER FORTY

Christmas of 1937 was a time of hope for some, of deepening anxiety for many. In Byland Crescent it was a mixture of both. Hope centred on Jenny Cowgill and the child she was due to produce any day now, and anxiety for the darkening political situation in Europe.

The couple had told of their experiences in Spain, enthralling the whole family with their exploits. They told of the friendships they had formed and of the lives of the people they had lived with. They also told of Mark's decision onboard ship for them to be married by the captain.

'It was so exciting,' Jenny told them. 'The captain was honoured to be asked. We were surrounded by complete strangers but we didn't care.'

The family was a little disappointed to have missed what would have been in the tradition of Byland Crescent a celebration to remember, but knew that the couple had always done the unexpected and were happy for them.

For Jenny's husband Mark, taking his parental role seriously, it was a hectic time. His job as a trainee salesman for Fisher Springs Wool Merchants was no sinecure, added to which was his whole-hearted devotion to his new hobby. Inspired by the tutelage of his Spanish comrade the carpenter, Mark spent many hours in his father's workshop to the rear of Byland Crescent. With Sonny giving instruction on the more sophisticated equipment Mark was fast becoming a skilled woodworker. Billy, anxious not to be outdone by either his father or elder brother, joined them and the trio set about producing a range of useful and decorative items for the house and its occupants.

Some of their work was conducted in secrecy, the results not revealed until Christmas morning, when an astonished and delighted Jenny was presented with a cot and a rocking cradle all beautifully carved and hand painted. Nor was it only the male members of the family who were kept busy. The baby's mother, two prospective grandmothers and great-grandmother spent many hours knitting and sewing garments and other essentials. Jenny even producing several sets of bootees on the bespoke knitting needles she had used in Spain and lovingly treasured since her return.

Mark and Jenny's account of their experiences in Spain had served to highlight a deepening unease felt by Sonny and his fellow directors over developments in Europe and elsewhere. 1938 saw Germany increase its stranglehold over its neighbours, annexing Austria and occupying the Sudetenland while at the same time intensifying its hate-driven persecution of Jews, a policy aped by Hitler's lap-dog Mussolini in Italy. As Germany was showing increasingly brutal evidence of its power, to the west another French government collapsed, exposing further frailties in a political system lacking strong or credible leadership. Further afield a triangular battle was being fought by China, Russia, and Japan in the face of Japan's imperialistic ambitions towards China and Siberia.

Worrying as such troublesome developments were in a business sense, for Michael Haigh and Simon Jones there were more immediately personal concerns. Michael and Connie, with a son serving in the Royal Navy, knew that if British interests were threatened, he would soon be involved. Even greater and more immediately threatening was the fate of Simon and Naomi's son, Joshua. Apart from occasional one-line missives from Edrith Pointon they had neither heard nor seen anything of their son for two years until an unannounced visit lasting only four days before he returned to London and on to the unknown.

Concern over the course of future events influenced several decisions that might otherwise not have been made. In Australia, Philip Fisher and Amelia Baxendale overcame their reluctance and got married. It was a simple ceremony, attended by neither the bride's family nor that of the groom, the only witnesses being mutual friends from their tennis club.

Two days after this event, the groom's brother-in-law, Danny Malloy, paid a surprise visit to the Finnegan house. His subsequent interview, icily conducted, was by way of an attempt at reparation by Danny.

'I've decided to quit the sheep station,' he told Louise. 'I'm no good at it and it's no good to me. I've quit drinking. Apart from necessary supplies this is the first time I've been into town since Dottie left me. I'm joining the army, in fact I've already enlisted. A lot of blokes reckon there's going to be a war, in which case I'll probably get sent overseas. All I'm asking is permission to write to Dottie. I don't know where she is, but if you are willing to forward the letters that would do for me. Maybe she won't read them, I wouldn't blame her if she tore them up and threw them away, but I'll feel better for having written them.'

Louise was slightly mollified by Danny's contrite attitude. 'I'm not promising anything. I'll ask Dottie if she is willing to receive them. That's as much as I'm prepared to do.'

Danny agreed to this and left shortly afterwards. As he walked slowly down the drive, Louise watched him from the doorway. He seemed a lost, dejected figure of a man, the brash, abrasive charm of former days completely absent.

* * *

Andrew Michael Cowgill was not happy. When he was unhappy, everyone within earshot was made painfully aware of it. If they disapproved of his vociferous and angry outburst, Andrew Michael was either unaware of the fact or careless of their opinion. He might have been considered inconsiderate, lacking in social graces even, for the occasion was splendid and had been organized specially, with Andrew Michael as the principal guest.

He had been attired in some extremely strange garments, not at all becoming to a young gentleman. He had been hauled from his warm, comfortable habitat to a strange, cold, draughty building. A long wait outside had done little to improve his temper. It was early March, a cold northeast wind was blowing, and he had been manhandled, prodded, and inspected by a host of complete and extremely rude strangers.

Nor did matters improve once they entered the building. First there had been some extremely odd and very loud music that echoed round the high ceiling of the strange place. This was accompanied by some very bad singing. He hoped things would get better once the wailing stopped, but not so. Before he had recovered properly he was snatched from the arms of the woman he loved by yet another stranger, one clothed in a long white dress, a gown that contrasted in a very un-manly fashion with the stranger's beard. To compound the felony this weird character showed no sign of releasing his hostage, instead he waved a flickering flame in front of Andrew Michael's eyes, gesticulated with a large book, and then proceeded to douse him with large quantities of icy cold water.

For seven-week-old Andrew Michael, enough was enough. He decided to register his unhappiness with as much force as possible. The high, vaulted ceiling of St Mary's Church in Scarborough provided excellent acoustics for the lusty bawling of the newly baptised infant.

'Nothing wrong with his lungs,' Sonny whispered to Rachael as they listened to their grandson's cries.

Andrew Michael's great-grandmother, showing few signs of having entered her eighty-first year, listened to the din with a mix of fondness and nostalgia.

Once reunited with his mother, Andrew Michael decided honour was satisfied. Having been thwarted in his attempt to gain sustenance from the food store she had cunningly concealed beneath an admittedly smart costume, he declared his boredom with the whole proceedings with a mighty yawn, expressed his contempt for the way he had been treated with a satisfyingly loud expulsion of wind and fell asleep. It had been, after all, a highly stressful day for such a young gentleman.

Luke Fisher had been in a quandary for several weeks. He told Dottie his plans one morning over breakfast. Although his sister found them difficult to accept, she was more concerned with the effect on Bella.

'I'm going to tell her in person,' Luke said. 'It's not the sort of thing you can say over the phone or trust to a letter. I hope she'll understand.' His face saddened. 'If not, I'll just have to accept the fact. I'm going to ring Aunt Louise this afternoon to arrange it.'

'I'll come with you when you go, I'd like to see the folks again.'

Two days later Luke and Bella sat on an old tree trunk in the grounds of the ruined Fisher mansion. The tree had been felled many years earlier by Luke's father and fashioned into a seat.

'OK,' Bella prompted him, 'tell me the bad news.'

'How do you know it's bad news?' Luke played for time.

'For one thing, the look on your face. And for another, the fact that you've been here over two hours and haven't kissed me properly. So come on, out with it.'

'OK. I've decided to go to England. I'm going to join the RAF – if they'll have me. It looks as if there's a war coming. I've been thinking about learning to fly for a long time. If I join the RAF, I'll get free flying lessons. If war comes, so be it. If not, I'll be a fully qualified pilot.'

'That's not all of it, you could learn to fly here in Australia just as easily,' Bella objected.

'You're right, of course.' Luke smiled. 'There is

more to it but it's difficult to explain properly. It seems there's a clear-cut choice in the world at the moment. Usually good and evil become blurred. But not now, not with what's happening in Europe. If war does come, Britain will be vulnerable. My mom and dad may have left England a long time ago, made a new life here, but they still loved the old country. I've been thinking about all this, but most of all I've been thinking about Saul.'

'Your older brother?'

Luke nodded. 'I was too young to know him. He was killed in France when I was only two years old. Mom and Dad talked about him a lot and I grew up worshipping his memory. He died defending freedom against aggression. That's being threatened again. If I didn't go, I don't think I'd ever be able to stand at Mom and Dad's graveside again.'

There was a long silence between them. Bella put her hands on his cheeks so that they were looking into one another's eyes. 'I do understand. I hate it. And I could say or do all sorts of things to keep you from going, keep you here, keep you safe. But if I did you'd finish up hating yourself and hating me. I couldn't stand that.'

He looked into her eyes, steadfast and loyal, brimming with tears and felt a surge of love for this young girl he had known all her life, but was only just beginning to understand. 'I don't deserve you, but part of the reason I'm doing this is for you, for us.'

'I know that too,' Bella acknowledged. 'And although I'll detest every minute you're gone and worry myself sick until you return, I shall be proud.'

He kissed her tenderly, a long, lingering kiss of gentle sweetness. Somewhere in their contact they awakened the passion smouldering within them, the kiss changed, became charged with the full, tempestuous fury of their mutual desire. Still locked in the fierce embrace they slid from the seat to the grass, the coolness of the earth doing nothing to chill the heat of their ardour. Eventually, panting and breathless, they disengaged. Still lying in one another's arms, they stayed until the storm abated.

'I shouldn't have done that,' Luke told her. 'I don't know how I controlled myself.'

'Me too. I wanted you to go on. I wanted to give myself to you, wanted you to make love to me.'

'We mustn't. It would be wrong and I couldn't live with myself or face your mom and dad for that matter.'

'It's too bloody cruel,' Bella burst out. 'I'll be sixteen soon then we could do what we want.'

'I'm not the sort of bloke who'd do that, not when I'm going away.'

'I know,' Bella said despondently. 'But just for a few minutes I wished you were. So you take damned good care of yourself, do you hear me? We've got a lifetime of unfinished business, you and me, and I don't want to die an old maid wondering what it would have been like if I'd been a few months older, or you'd not been such a gentleman.'

Surprisingly, Luke laughed. 'Too bloody true. I'm not missing that if I can help it. I promise to do all I can to return in one piece then the minute I get back we'll settle it once and for all.'

Bella chuckled. 'I'd love to see Mom's face if we did it the minute you get back – on her lounge carpet.'

Luke's laughter echoed from the surrounding trees. 'Perhaps it would be better if I let you know a few days before I arrive then you could come and meet me, in the flat in Melbourne.'

'Now you're talking sense. Give me chance to do some shopping. After all, you won't be allowed out of bed for a week at least.'

Before her marriage to Philip Fisher, Amelia had never wanted children, had never given them much of a thought. If she had been asked she would probably have shuddered and said she regarded them as small, noisy, dirty, and anti-social. It was something of a shock therefore when the doctor confirmed her suspicions. Amelia Fisher was pregnant. Her first thought was how Philip would react. They had never discussed having a family, never considered the possibility. Before their marriage they had taken every precaution, but once they tied the knot such measures had been relaxed. The outcome, Amelia supposed, was inevitable.

She hurried from the surgery across the town to the Fisher Springs building, determined to share the sensational news with all haste. It was lunchtime, as good a part of the working day as any to grab her husband's attention. Amelia, although by no means displeased with the tidings she had to impart was nonetheless a little anxious as she waited for the receptionist to tell Philip of her presence.

When she entered his office, Philip was leaning back in his chair, eyes closed, his feet propped on one corner of his desk.

'Is this how you spend your working day?' she asked him severely.

Philip grinned. 'I'm thinking,' he told her, without opening his eyes.

'What about?' Amelia demanded.

'I was thinking we should move, the flat will be too small for us before long.'

Amelia sank into the chair at the other side of the desk, astounded. 'What do you mean too small?'

Philip opened his eyes, swung his feet from the desk and sat upright. 'Well, I suppose we could turn the spare room into a nursery, but it would be a bit cramped. Far better to move now.'

'How did you guess?' Amelia gasped. 'I only saw the doctor an hour ago.'

Philip's smile widened. 'I've known, or rather

suspected for a couple of weeks now. When I saw the doctor's appointment on the pad by the phone it more or less convinced me. The last doubt I had was settled when the girl told me you were outside. You wouldn't have come straight here unless you had something interesting to tell me.'

Amelia was anxious to know how he felt. 'What do you think about it?'

He stood up and walked over to her, pulled her to her feet and put his arms round her. 'I could never imagine why any woman would want to go through the pain and suffering of childbirth, never thought anyone would be prepared to go through it for me. If you're happy about it, I am. In fact I'm delighted.'

Amelia smiled, but said, 'Promise me one thing though.'

'What's that?'

'Promise you won't stop loving me when I'm fat and unsightly?' she begged.

He laughed, but told her sincerely, 'Like I said, it's a miracle anyone would go through nine months of discomfort and all that goes along with bearing children. That you're willing to do that for me – for us, just makes me love you more.'

CHAPTER FORTY-ONE

Joshua Jones had finished his tutelage at university and was listening to Edrith Pointon's instructions.

'This assignment means you must be totally under cover. No question of confronting the enemy, taking sides, rescuing damsels in distress – because you won't be going to a shambles like Spain. This time you'll be up against an enemy that is ruthless, cunning, and highly efficient. You're only there to gather information and evidence of their strength, no more than that. So let me tell you what I want from you. I'll be brief, because there is much for you to do. You have a lot of documents to study, and when you have completed your preparations, you leave. The mission you are going on is without doubt the most difficult and dangerous any of our agents have ever undertaken.' Edrith paused, before adding grimly, 'And the consequences should you fail could be cataclysmic.'

Although Pointon had promised to be brief, the discourse he delivered before handing the documentation over was a lengthy one.

‘We know the Germans are attempting to develop some kind of super weapon. We cannot be certain what exactly it is, because thus far we have been unable to penetrate their security. All we have is a few rumours, but add to that the extreme measures they are taking to keep the project secret and we are beginning to fear that it is indeed something terrible. However, it isn’t all bad news’ – Pointon smiled slightly – ‘because one thing we have learned is that the project has run into very big problems.

‘They have turned for help in solving these to a man who is profiled in several of the documents in your pile. We need to find out if they are making progress and, if they are, how much. Above all, we must discover a way of stopping them – even if it means killing the man who could provide the solution for them.’ Pointon looked straight at Joshua. ‘Your task will be to find this out, and if necessary, to act on it.’

Jesse Barker’s return to England was less than triumphal. As soon as he disembarked he was arrested. He was relieved to find the questions asked were more hopeful than searching, so, without conceding that they had no grounds for prosecution, police handed Jesse over to Special Branch.

Although his interrogation was a good deal more intensive and revealed a greater knowledge of his past, it was apparent that Jesse had committed no offence on British soil, so there was no reason to hold him. After several dire warnings as to his future conduct, Jesse was freed.

He had been released from custody, but with his past exposed, his present difficult and his future uncertain. Jesse was penniless, homeless and without any means of support. England had changed radically since his departure a quarter of a century earlier. Jesse was alone in a strange land, albeit his homeland.

He managed to find lodgings, of a temporary nature, in a hostel in the East End of London, an establishment run by the Salvation Army. The long years of the depression had created a great demand for such accommodation. Many men had been placed in a similar situation to Jesse. The tenure of a bed in a bleak dormitory shared with tramps, drunks and others unable to cope with life was uncertain. From there however, Jesse managed to gain employment, a poorly paid job as a warehouseman for a company selling cheap, shoddy second-hand furniture. He also obtained a room in a seedy, rundown house divided into bed-sits. His years of internment in Greece, the privations of his early post-war existence and incarceration in an American gaol had taught Jesse to live frugally. He determined to save enough money to leave London and return to his native Bradford where he confidently expected some of his family still lived.

It proved to be a long, hard struggle, but

eventually, after almost a year, Jesse considered he had saved enough money to risk the gamble. He gave notice to the owner of the furniture company and quit the bedsitter. He had little regret over either parting. Having burned his boats and with only a small portmanteau containing his worldly possessions, Jesse purchased a third-class railway ticket and boarded a train for his journey north.

Jessica Tunnicliffe was fully occupied by her new role, organizing the boffins under her control and searching for suitable premises to house them in the event of 'the balloon going up'. Her task was but a small part of a hectic scramble to recoup lost ground. As with most of the department, Jessica devoted all her time and energy to the task, but for her, it proved a welcome distraction from the turmoil of her personal life and the terrible emotional upheaval she had suffered.

Jessica had met and interviewed all but one of the scientists who would form part of her team. The last of these involved a return to her hometown. She boarded a train for Bradford, in her case was a slim dossier bearing the name of the man she had arranged to meet, Robert Binks. Given the limited budget allocated to her, Jessica might have been expected to travel third class, but such was not her style. Her considerable wealth enabled her to upgrade to a first-class carriage. Had she chosen not to do so, she might have found she was sharing a carriage with her father.

If Jesse's return to England had proved chastening, his arrival in Bradford was bewildering to say the least. His first task was to visit his parents' old home. He arrived to find the site he remembered as a row of low-cost back-to-back houses had been bulldozed to make way for a council estate. Thwarted on this score, Jesse decided to visit the house where Charlotte Tunnicliffe had lived. Once again he retreated, baffled, for the occupants, who had been in residence less than six months knew nothing of the history of the house. All he was able to glean from them was that the property had changed hands twice in the last five years.

Doubly frustrated, Jesse ended his first day in his hometown in a small hotel close to Bradford city centre, of the type used by commercial travellers. The unappetising fare served up as an evening meal did little to lighten his depression.

Morning brought renewed optimism and a plan. If Jesse could not get news of Charlotte from the new occupants, he would perhaps have more success with the neighbours. He took a tram to Manningham. If he could find her, she might be able to put him on the right track as to the whereabouts of his family.

After several false starts and one or two abruptly closed doors, Jesse eventually got news of

Charlotte. It was not the news he was expecting. The elderly couple who lived opposite Charlotte's house had information they were happy to share even with a stranger.

Jesse pointed across the road. 'I'm trying to trace the lady who used to live there, but nobody seems to know where she's moved to. I wonder if you can help?'

The couple glanced at one another in some perplexity then the woman, a small, slender, bird-like creature, thin legged and with hands bent by arthritis to resemble talons, asked doubtfully, 'You don't mean the Tunnicliffe woman, do you?'

'That's right, Charlotte Tunnicliffe. Can you tell me where she moved to?'

'Er, not exactly,' she replied nervously. 'Are you a relative?'

'No, just a friend. I've just returned from America,' he added, by way of explanation.

'Well, the thing is, dear' – she looked at her husband for support that was not forthcoming – 'I'm afraid Mrs Tunnicliffe is dead.' Her tone lowered reverentially. Pleased by his stunned reaction she continued, 'A shocking business it was, in all the newspapers for months. I'm surprised you didn't read about the murder. Oh, but you wouldn't have if you were abroad.'

'You mean Charlotte, Mrs Tunnicliffe that is, was murdered?' Jesse could scarcely believe it.

'Oh no, dear.' The old biddy had probably not

had so much fun in years. 'She committed suicide, she did.'

'But I thought you said she was murdered?' Jesse asked, bewildered.

'No, no, she wasn't murdered, she committed the murder. Didn't she, dear?' The old woman looked to her husband for confirmation.

'That's right,' he said obediently. He probably never spoke unless asked a question, Jesse thought.

'So, who was murdered, if it wasn't Charlotte?'

The woman wore a black dress and Jesse was reminded forcibly of a crow. Even to the carrion-like way she was picking over the remains of the scandal. She took up the story again. 'The man – her fancy man, by all accounts.' Her voice sank even lower. 'They found his body in a quarry on Baildon Moor with ever so many stab wounds. And that's not all.' Her voice was by now little more than a whisper. Jesse had to lean forward to hear what she was saying, although there was no one else within a hundred yards. 'When they found him, he hadn't a stitch of clothing on, naked as the day he was born. Isn't that right, dear?'

'That's right.'

Jesse began to wonder if that was the full extent of the man's vocabulary.

'So what happened to Charlotte?'

'They found her a while later, hanging from the banisters,' the old woman told him, almost salivating with delight. 'They say she'd lost all her money and when the police were on to her for murder, she knew the game was up and did away with herself. She left a note admitting everything.'

Jesse swung away in horror and distress. The couple watched him take a few steps down their drive then the man spoke unbidden for the first time. 'There was a daughter.'

Barker froze in his tracks, shock turning to disbelief. 'What!' he exclaimed, turning to face the old couple. 'A daughter, did you say?'

Whether the husband was overcome by the effort or the pecking order had been restored was unclear, but it was the old woman who resumed control of the conversation.

'You're right, dear,' she told him, 'I'd forgotten that. Yes there was a daughter.' She looked round, as if expecting to see a gallery of eavesdroppers. Her voice lowered once more. 'There was some talk around here at the time, people saying the reason for the murder was that the man had been,' she paused, colouring slightly, 'you know, trying it on with the daughter. It was only a rumour of course and I never listen to gossip.'

Jesse was too overcome with emotion to notice either the unconscious humour of this contradiction or the outrageous lie. 'How old was the little girl?' he asked.

'Oh, she wasn't little, she was quite a young lady, very pretty too as I remember. I thought once or twice, you're going to be a heartbreaker before long, my girl. I suppose I was right too,' she reflected. 'Although I never thought it would be her mother's heart she broke.'

'I don't suppose you can remember how old she was?' Jesse's casual question masked his rising excitement.

'Now, that I can tell you. She was fifteen. The papers were full of it.'

'So that would mean she was born when, in 1915?' Jesse hazarded a guess.

'1914,' the woman corrected him, 'September or October 1914, just after war broke out.'

'Can you remember her name?' Jesse could barely contain his impatience.

'Oh now, dear me, what was she called?' The old woman racked her brains. 'Jennifer or Jacqueline, something like that.'

'No, it wasn't,' the husband interposed with the longest speech he had essayed throughout. 'Her name was Jessica, Jessica Tunnicliffe. Although I heard it said she had no right to that name, that Mr Tunnicliffe wasn't her real father.'

The last part of the husband's effort was wasted, for Jesse was beyond hearing. The elderly couple watched him blundering down their path, his gait that of a blind man.

He had a daughter. Jessica, so obviously named after her father. Tears rolled down his cheek, his every step seemed to echo the word, for he was unaware that he was repeating it, 'Jessica, Jessica, Jessica.'

It was one thing discovering you had a daughter of whose existence you had been unaware for almost twenty-five years, but quite another to trace her. The trail had gone so cold he had no idea where to look for her, or who to ask.

After much deliberation Jesse realized he had no alternative but to overcome his natural reluctance and go to the police. They would have records concerning the murder and Charlotte's suicide. Those records might give some clue as to where to begin looking.

Taking the bull by the horns, Jesse approached the police station. He found the procedure far more complicated than he had imagined. He had no idea of the murder victim's name, merely a vague idea of where and when the crime had taken place. That was just the start of the problems he had to overcome. The desk sergeant illustrated the difficulties.

'In the first place, we would have to dig about in our archives to find the files. That would hardly be a priority as it was a long time ago and the files are closed, by all accounts. Even then there's no guarantee they'll contain the information you're looking for. Above all, there are strict regulations about disclosure of confidential material. The officer handling any such request would need strong evidence that you have a valid reason. Are you sure you can provide such a reason?'

Jesse assured the man that he could.

'Very well then,' the officer told him, 'I'll pass

your request along but I'm making no promises. The best I can suggest is you call again in a couple of weeks' time.'

The money Jesse had so carefully scrimped and saved was beginning to dwindle at an alarming rate. To counteract this and to help pass the time Jesse sought both cheaper lodgings and employment. He obtained the lodgings first, a bed-sit in a terraced house off Bowling Back Lane. The rent was not in keeping with its tawdry condition but was much more in line with Jesse's constrained budget, especially after he managed to secure a position as a warehouseman in a local woollen mill.

The job, as Jesse was told with some relish by a fellow worker on his first day, had come his way thanks to an unfortunate and tragic accident. A delivery of wool had arrived, this needed unloading from the railway wagon and transferring to the top storey of the mill. Jesse's predecessor had been responsible for operating the crane that hoisted the bales one by one up the four storeys then bringing them inside with the assistance of a baling hook. Attempting to secure one of the bales the man had mistimed his grab with the hook, overbalanced and toppled from the open delivery door.

'One minute he was there, the next, gone,' the informant told him with a certain macabre glee. 'He fell four storeys onto the cobbles. Splattered he was. His head was crushed like an eggshell, blood and brains all over the place,' he added with relish.

It was three months before Jesse made any headway with his enquiries. He was ushered into an interview room at the police station. The room's sole occupant, a plain clothes officer, looked up as Jesse entered but did not stand, nor issue any greeting other than to wave in a cursory manner towards the only other chair. It was a sparsely furnished chamber, plain to the point of bleakness, the only items of furniture the two chairs either side of a cheap wooden table vaguely reminiscent of Jesse's time in the furniture warehouse. There were however two bulky files on the battered surface of the table, the sight of which gave Jesse grounds for cautious optimism.

The policeman pulled a blank piece of paper from within one of the files and commenced writing laboriously on it. Even reading upside down Jesse was easily able to distinguish the rounded, clumsy block capitals. 'Request for confidential file information' the heading ran. The officer spoke for the first time, 'Name and address?'

'Jesse Barker, Flat 2, 43 Bowling Back Terrace, Bradford.'

The policeman's pen hovered over the name, Barker, for a moment and the officer gave him a swift glance before recommencing his laboured scrawl. The gesture left Jesse with a vague feeling of unease.

'Right,' the man said when he had finished noting

down the details. 'What do you want to know, and why?'

'I'm trying to trace Charlotte Tunnicliffe's daughter, Jessica. Charlotte and I were lovers just before the war started, but I lost touch with her. I've been overseas and since I returned, only recently found out that Jessica had been born. I believe Jessica is my daughter.'

'Can you prove it?'

'Not precisely,' Jesse replied, 'but the dates are right and the name similarity is too much to be mere coincidence.'

The officer did not reply but began a slow perusal of the documents in one of the files. It seemed to take an age as he scanned each one with deliberate thoroughness. Eventually, he came across one which, by the shape and colour, Jesse recognized to be a birth certificate. The man read it with agonizing slowness while Jesse waited in a fever of impatience. After what seemed an age, the policeman replaced the certificate in the file and looked up.

'It would seem your supposition is correct, Mr Barker, the birth certificate for Jessica Tunnicliffe names you as her father. As such, I can authorize release of whatever information the file holds regarding the whereabouts of Miss Tunnicliffe, but of course I must tell you this information is more than nine years out of date.'

He delved into the file once more and after a short while came up with a closely typed sheet of foolscap paper that Jesse could see was headed 'Internal memorandum'. The officer scanned this a little more swiftly than the birth certificate.

After a preliminary clearing of his throat, he said, 'It would appear that following your, er, that is Mrs Tunnicliffe's death, Miss Tunnicliffe was placed in a foster home for a short while. When her mother's will was produced, being a minor, she was placed under the guardianship of a' – he glanced down at the memo – 'Mr Michael Haigh of' – he glanced down once more – 'Cecil Avenue, Baildon. We have no record of her movements following that.'

'Michael Haigh, I remember him, vaguely,' Jesse said. 'He was Charlotte's first husband, I believe.'

'Well, that's all the information I have Mr, er, Barker.' Once more Jesse noticed the slight hesitation over his surname.

'Thank you for your assistance, you have been most helpful.' Jesse made his escape, not without an element of relief.

CHAPTER FORTY-TWO

As a nation, the English are not very good at coffee. Ask any Frenchman, Italian, Turk, or Greek and they will tell you so with great animation. They will give you their opinion of the drink served up in England as coffee. Fortunately, they are likely to lapse into their own language for the more graphic description of the brew. Despite this regrettable shortcoming there are certain liberties with the drink even an Englishman will not allow. Another particularly English trait however is a reluctance to complain. Josh had taken one sip of the liquid presented to him as coffee and decided to overcome this reluctance. Not only was the substance bitter, but the temperature of the liquid was somewhere between aired and tepid. Josh looked round the near empty restaurant but there was no sign of the waitress who had served him, a gruff matron of more than middle years.

Josh had travelled by train heading east through Germany, his mission taking him into the heart of Nazi territory into danger far more potent than he could have imagined. He had now been in

Salzburg almost a week, posing as an engineering student from Hamburg with a keen appreciation of classical music. If asked, he would say he was fleeing from the unending Wagner proliferated throughout Germany and had decided to visit Mozart's birthplace in search of respite.

In reality, he was following an industrialist from the Ruhr valley whose plant appeared to be producing some distinctly martial materials. Josh's instructions were to find out exactly what was being manufactured in such strict secrecy. He had managed to get a job at the plant, working there for five months while trying to glean what little he could. Now he had opted to follow the man, find out who he contacted, and hopefully pick up some information. If necessary, he was prepared to use some of the skills he had acquired during his training to examine the papers in the industrialist's study at his holiday home in the new Greater Germany as Austria had become following the Anschluss. Thus his arrival at the admittedly well-appointed restaurant, staring at a cup filled with a strange, unpalatable brew.

'Excuse me, sir,' a voice said politely. 'Can I help you?'

Josh came out of his reverie to find a waitress standing attentively to one side of his table. He blinked in surprise. The dour, whiskered hausfrau, dispenser of poisonous potions, had been replaced by a vision of youthful and radiant loveliness.

'I saw you looking round and wondered if you need anything further.'

Josh recovered from his shock and smiled at the waitress, no difficult task. 'Er, yes there is,' he said. 'Would you mind tasting that for me?' He indicated the cup on the table. 'I think there's something wrong with it.'

The waitress stared at him for a long moment then picked up the cup and took a sip from it. Her face wrinkled in disgust. 'I'm very sorry sir, I'll replace it immediately.'

She was as good as her word, returning only a moment later with another cup. She watched anxiously as Josh tasted it cautiously. He smiled.

'Now that is a delicious cup of coffee.'

The waitress gave him the full benefit of her lovely smile and Josh felt his heartbeat change gear momentarily. He searched desperately for some means to detain her, to engage her in conversation. 'Tell me,' he began, 'the town seems very quiet considering it is the holiday season. Why is that?'

He studied the girl as she replied. She really was delightfully pretty, her soft, naturally blonde hair falling in gentle waves to her shoulders, framing a face of outstanding beauty, her delicately pink complexion in striking contrast to her vivid blue eyes.

'I'm not sure, I think many people have stayed at home this year. Perhaps because there is so much uncertainty, they have decided against taking a holiday.'

Josh waved his hand at the near empty restaurant, only three tables of which were occupied. ‘It must be boring for you when it is quiet like this.’

‘I can always find something to occupy myself.’ Adding with a smile, ‘If all else fails I can talk to what few customers I do have.’

‘In that case I’m delighted you’re not busy.’ He noticed the pink of her complexion deepen slightly. ‘I admit that although I’m enjoying my stay here it is very lonely on one’s own.’

They chatted idly for a while. The waitress liked this young man, so different from the swaggering, arrogant young Germans she was used to serving. In a strange way, she thought, he was unlike a German altogether. Suddenly she became aware that he was asking her a question. She came out of her daydream and re-focussed her attention.

‘Could you see your way to taking pity on the stranger in your midst by showing me round your beautiful city?’

‘I make it a strict rule,’ she told him severely, ‘never to go out with anyone until I have been introduced to them.’

The young man stood up. He was tall, taller than she had guessed, and moved with the grace of an athlete. He bowed, not in the stiffly formal Teutonic manner and without clicking his heels together. It seemed a quaintly old-fashioned, courtly gesture. Extending his hand, he said, ‘My name is Jörgen Schmidt.’

She surprised herself with the ease of her response. 'Mine is Astrid Erikson.'

To Astrid's surprise, instead of shaking hands he bowed over hers, raised it to his lips and kissed it. Still holding her hand, he looked up, his eyes alive with mischief. 'As there was no one else around we had to introduce ourselves, so now that's done will you come out with me?'

Astrid was suddenly confused, flustered, her heart fluttered slightly. She knew she should refuse. He was a complete stranger and moreover he was a German. Astrid detested Germans. She looked into his eyes, their pleading look was too much for the remnants of her resolve. 'Very well,' she agreed weakly, in what she hoped was a stiff and formal manner.

It didn't seem to have worked, for Jörgen, far from being rebuffed, smiled broadly. He had a nice smile, Astrid thought, it was no polite social gesture, it stretched right to those lovely eyes of his. Stop it, behave yourself, Astrid thought.

'What time do you finish work?' he asked.

'I didn't mean today,' Astrid protested.

'I did,' he retorted. 'I don't believe in wasting time.'

'I can see that,' she remarked tartly. 'Suppose I told you I was on duty until midnight when the restaurant closes?'

'Then I'll wait for you outside at midnight.'

The sincerity in his tone made her blush slightly, she weakened. 'I'm not supposed to be here today.

I'm filling in for Helga, the lady who served you. She has a dental appointment and will be back in an hour. I'm free any time after that.' Jörgen's smile was so delightful. Astrid felt her knees weaken.

'Good, I'll wait for you outside, shall I?'

She looked into those glorious eyes and capitulated 'Why stand around outside, why don't you wait here?'

'What a wonderful idea. With luck the restaurant will remain empty then we can talk some more, get to know one another better. I'd like that a lot.'

'I'll just clear those tables,' Astrid said to cover her confusion. Her cheeks were hot, she was sure they were a riot of colour. She turned away hastily. 'I'll be as quick as I can,' she added.

Luke wrote to Bella.

> They're training us to fly, but in an odd way. We're flying planes without engines! Gliders, I mean. At first it's a terrifying sensation going up in one of them but once you're airborne, wow! It's almost completely silent. All you can hear is the noise of the wind displaced by the glider, a gentle sort of whooshing sound, not unlike running water. That, and the creak of the glider itself. It's a bit off-putting until you get used to it. The warmth of the thermal currents takes you

higher and higher in spirals then you get chance to look around you and it's an amazing sight. The countryside here is very pretty, far greener than back home, but with lots of other shades and colours as well. You can see for miles on a good day, all small farms (that's what they call stations over here) not big ones like back home. I'll bet some of them are no more than two or three-hundred acres. As well as the farms there's lots of woodland, small villages and towns. It reminds me sometimes of those jigsaw puzzles I used to help you with when we were younger. Listen to that, makes us sound like an old married couple (Wishful thinking!). I'm stationed in Yorkshire and I reckon it must be close to where Mom and Dad came from, because when I listen to some of the locals talking it sort of takes me back, a word or a phrase, even the way they pronounce things. I suppose if I had time I'd try to find out, although Fisher is a common surname. I don't have the time though, they keep us pretty busy with flying and all sorts of other drill. There are a lot of rumours around, some say we'll be on the move pretty soon when we're allocated a squadron. The blokes all reckon there's going to be war. They're a decent lot, just the odd one who has that arrogant English way of looking down their nose at you.

I've bought a car to run around in, it's a beaut. An open Bentley sports car. Boy, there were some green-eyed looks when I pulled up outside the mess with it. You should see the roads here, they're not a bit like home. All narrow twisting lanes with high hedges. You need to keep your wits about you. I reckon the bloke who designed them must have been on the bottle! So that's what I'm up to, behaving myself as I promised I would. Oh but I miss you so much though. I have three photos of you. One of them I keep on my locker by my bed, one in my wallet and one I put in the cockpit whenever I fly, so you're with me all the time, day and night. I want this business over with as soon as possible then I won't have to rely on photos.

Until that moment, when I can hold you in my arms and know I'm the luckiest bloke alive.

With all my love,
Luke.

It had taken Louise Finnegan quite some time to overcome the difficulty in persuading Dottie to agree to Danny Malloy writing to her. The memory of the beatings, the cruelty, and infidelities she had suffered at his hands was too fresh.

'I honestly believe he's changed, maybe Luke managed to knock some sense into him.'

'I think it would take more than that,' Dottie replied bitterly.

Louise had hastened to reassure her. 'Don't get me wrong, I'm not saying I condone what he did, but I've asked around and it seems he might have changed his ways. I even sent Patrick to one or two of the places Danny used to frequent and they said he hadn't been seen for months.'

'Maybe he's scared he might be separated from my money.' Dottie was still far from convinced.

'He said he had joined the army and I'm not suggesting he's a reformed character, but surely it would do no harm to read what he has to say. After all, you don't have to answer his letters.'

Dottie reluctantly agreed. With Luke's absence in England Dottie was rather lonely in Melbourne so she had suggested to Louise that Bella might like a trip to the city. When she arrived, Dottie greeted her with enthusiasm. The two had been friends since Bella could walk, almost like sisters and Dottie's dearest wish was that they would soon become sisters-in-law. Nonetheless, Dottie could not help a little gentle teasing at Bella's expense.

'I've put you in Luke's bedroom,' she told her, adding slyly, 'I thought you'd like that, and it'll get you used to the room.'

The innuendo would have had many young girls blushing but Bella was of a sterner calibre. 'It'd be a bloody sight better if Luke was here,' she told Dottie bluntly. 'But I suppose with him on the other side of the world at least I'll get some sleep.'

'Bella!' Dottie protested in feigned shock. 'Whatever do you mean?'

Bella eyed her. 'You know damned well what I mean. I should be able to check the bed out, make sure it's strong enough for when he returns. Oh, by the way' – she fumbled in her bag – 'speaking of absent lovers, I've got something for you.' She pulled an envelope out, 'It's a letter from Danny Boy, but don't go all maudlin on me when you've read it, just because you're not getting any these days.'

Dottie's mock horror increased. 'You don't care what outrageous things you say, do you?'

'Not much,' Bella agreed cheerfully. 'It's the way I'm made and if people don't like it, they can do the other. I'm not going to change, especially as your brother seems pretty keen on me the way I am.'

Dottie smiled at her affectionately. 'You'd do almost anything for Luke, wouldn't you?'

'No almost about it. He walked through fire for me and I'd do the same for him. I was below the age of consent when he left but if he'd wanted me then I'd have let him, not only that I'd have gloried in it. Sometimes,' she added wistfully, 'I wish he had.'

Dottie hugged her. 'One thing I will tell you, it

might make the waiting worthwhile. Luke told me before he went you're the most precious thing in his life. He's got everything a man could wish for, but he'd give it all away rather than lose you.'

CHAPTER FORTY-THREE

Josh's senses were on high alert, every nerve taut, as he recalled every part of his training. The house was in darkness. Outside, the moonless night was equally lacking in light, the woodland close to the house showing only as an outline of a deeper blackness. Through this dark wood Josh moved slowly and silently, hooded and clad from head to toe in black, leaving no trace of his passage. As he neared the dark bulk of the mansion his footfall grew if anything gentler, pressing silently on the previous autumn's fallen leaves. Avoiding the gravelled path, he moved noiselessly towards the large building. Surely and confidently, he approached one end of the façade of the dwelling. There was neither sound nor shadow as the stealthy approach continued. He reached the sanctuary of the front wall of the building and with a certainty born of prior knowledge went to a window left slightly open, the hot summer night breeding carelessness from the occupants within.

There was the merest hiss of sound as the window was eased carefully open then the unbidden visitor vanished from sight, slipping as silently as a ghost inside the house. Within moments a shielded lamp threw a gentle glow from one of the rooms on the ground floor, the light, such as it was, masked by the heavy velvet curtains drawn tightly across the window.

Less than half an hour later the light was extinguished and the curtains drawn back as silently as they had been pulled to. A few moments later, with equal discretion the intruder left by the same route he had entered. With total lack of haste but extreme caution Josh reached the safety of the woods and merged easily into the sanctuary of their cover, a deeper shadow in the blackness. The night scene resumed its silent tranquillity. No trace was left to suggest the intruder's presence.

Astrid turned over, her bed cold, incomplete. She thrust out an arm, for warmth and contact, or the warmth of contact but met no resistance, merely a comfortless sheet. She emerged reluctantly from the depth of sleep, from the pleasant dream she had been enjoying and raised herself on one elbow.

'Jörgen,' she called softly, 'where are you?'

'I'm here, *Liebchen*, I'm here,' the reassurance came from the other side of the room. Seconds later he slid into bed alongside her, all muscular, lean physique. He was aroused too, Astrid could tell.

‘Oh no,’ she murmured in mock reluctance, ‘and you’re frozen too, where have you been?’

‘You can warm me up,’ he told her as he wriggled ingratiatingly into her arms.

Much later, Astrid was lying watching Jörgen sleep. Less than a month earlier, when she had known Jörgen only three weeks, he had suggested a day’s walking in the countryside around Salzburg. ‘We could take a picnic,’ he’d told her, ‘find a quiet spot by a river or stream and rest there. I’d like to get to know the area better.’

He also meant he wanted to get to know Astrid better, but she had already guessed that. The day had dawned bright and cloudless, the early warmth suggesting a level of heat unusual for May. They had walked all morning, pausing occasionally to admire the picturesque scenery. Astrid smiled as she remembered their delight at finding a picnic spot almost identical to the one they had envisaged. The exercise, the food, and the heat of the day made them sleepy. After they finished the meal they were disinclined to continue walking.

‘Let’s stay here until the heat lessens,’ Jörgen had suggested.

‘What do you intend to do while we’re here?’ Astrid asked him severely.

‘Just rest,’ Jörgen told her, ‘sometimes I think I can never get enough rest. Why not tell me more about yourself,’ he’d prompted, ‘we never get chance to talk. Do your parents live in Salzburg?’

It was true, Astrid had reflected, they knew so

little about one another. Apart from his name and the fact that he was an engineering student from Hamburg, the only important fact Astrid knew about Jörgen was that she was more than halfway to being in love with him.

'No,' she told him, 'my parents lived in Vienna. My father died when I was sixteen. I was about to begin studying at university when he died. My mother re-married almost at once to a man I disliked.' Astrid had paused and looked at him, watching carefully for his reaction. 'So I came to Salzburg to be with a boy I knew, we became lovers but it did not work out. He returned to Vienna but I stayed here.'

'I'm glad about that.'

Astrid smiled as she remembered him leaning across and kissing her lightly on the lips, their first kiss. 'Very glad,' he'd repeated emphatically as he lay down. 'Now I'm going to have a little nap.'

Within seconds he was fast asleep. Astrid had watched him for a while, an indulgent smile on her face then decided to lie down alongside him. It was late afternoon when Astrid awoke. Jörgen still lay sleeping alongside her. Although the sun was much lower in the sky neither the heat nor the humidity had lessened. There were a few threatening clouds in the distance too, Astrid noticed. Reluctantly, she decided she must wake him. She leaned over, gently shaking his shoulder. Jörgen came from sleep to alert wakefulness as quickly as he had gone to sleep. He looked up at her and smiled then reached up and kissed her once more, another gentle salute.

'I dreamed about that while I was asleep,' he told her.

'It's after five o' clock,' the severity in her voice masking the secret thrill of pleasure at his words, 'and it looks as if we're in for a storm.' She pointed to the distant clouds.

'Good heavens, yes. Why on earth didn't you wake me earlier?'

'I was asleep too,' she confessed.

They hastily collected the remnants of their picnic, folded the travel rug, and set off walking back towards the distant city.

Astrid remembered the storm that accompanied the latter half of their journey back to Salzburg. It had been conducted to the accompaniment of Wagnerian flashes of lightning, crashing, tympanic rolls of thunder and relentless, hammering rain so violent its impact was as painful as hailstones. By the time they reached the outskirts of the city they were drenched from head to toe. Avoiding the inviting shelter of a clump of trees, 'Danger from lightning,' Jörgen gasped between thunderclaps, they opted instead for the limited cover provided by a shop doorway while debating their next move.

'I'll take you to your flat,' Jörgen shouted. 'Then go on to my hotel.'

'No, you won't,' Astrid screamed back defiantly. Their conversation took place in competition with the increasingly frequent and dramatic clashes of thunder. 'I'm not letting you wander the streets in this weather. It's at least two miles to your hotel. You can stay at my flat until the rain stops.'

They had completed their journey in a series of scuttling runs, like terrified animals, pausing in the safety of any makeshift shelter they could find. It was with immense relief that they entered the small building that contained her apartment. They paused in the hallway of the flat to catch their breath. Water streamed from every part of them onto the linoleum floor, forming ever-widening puddles.

'I'm going to take my outer clothes off,' Astrid said, 'then I'll fetch you some towels. You can get undressed here to save my carpets.'

Jörgen watched appreciatively as she stripped down to her underclothes. He followed her with his eyes as she walked down the hallway. Only after the inner door closed behind her did he begin unbuttoning his shirt. Seconds later the door opened again and Astrid thrust two large towels round it. When he had finished undressing, he towelled himself dry and wrapped the other decorously round himself, tucking the edge of it in at the waist to secure it. He was standing looking ruefully at the sodden heap of discarded clothing when there was a knock on the hall door. 'It's OK, I'm decent,' he called out.

Astrid had put on a dressing gown after drying

herself. Jörgen speculated briefly that she was naked beneath it, then told himself to behave. He grinned at her. 'What do you suggest we do with these,' he indicated the wet garments.

'Bring them through to the bathroom. We'll wring them out in the bath to get rid of the worst of the water then I'll hang them up to dry. There's a creel above the bath.'

The apartment, though small was neat enough to give the impression of spaciousness. The hall led into a large room that doubled as a dining area and a small lounge. Astrid preceded him to the second door which led to a bathroom that contained a large cast-iron bath. Side by side they leaned over the bath, extracting the worst of the water from their clothes. Gradually each became aware of the other's proximity. Astrid had sensed the clean, masculine scent of Jörgen. She felt a small quiver of excitement within her. She cast a covert sideways glance at him. His exposed upper body, the chest lean and tanned with a light covering of hair was just as she had imagined it. Somehow she could tell that Jörgen too was becoming aware of their nearness.

It was as he finished wringing out the last garment that he straightened. As he did so the towel, secured only by the fold at the waist, slipped. He made a despairing lunge at it but missed and the towel slid to the floor. Astrid moaned, a soft whimpering sound of pleasure as she saw the all too evident sign of his arousal.

'Astrid,' he said softly, his voice husky with passion. 'Astrid,' he repeated.

She'd moved towards him and they kissed, the fierce hunger of their desire replacing the gentler exchanges of the afternoon. Without a word she'd escorted him to the bedroom. Her dressing gown slipped to the floor unnoticed and unmissed. She turned to face him, naked before him for the first time. He gazed appreciatively at her for a long second, his eyes hot with need. Then she was in his arms, her soft skin against his, urgent as his own. Locked together they laid on the bed, impatient to be one. She arched her back slightly and sighed with pleasure as he entered her.

The memory made her smile again and she lay, drowsy and content in the darkness listening to Jörgen's breathing, such a comforting sound. Her sleep drenched thoughts turned on the marvellous way life had turned round for her. Out of the blue she had found Jörgen, or he had found her, and now each day was filled with him, every moment apart was a moment wasted. Although she still knew little about him, that would normally have worried her, but strangely with Jörgen, Astrid felt completely safe, protected, at ease. He was, she thought, kind, courteous and thoughtful, loving and tender and without a trace of German arrogance. Astrid's thoughts rambled as she walked the precipice between sleep and wakefulness.

Suddenly her attention became focussed. Jörgen,

to her amusement, had begun talking in his sleep. She listened to the quiet muttering, straining to make sense of the words. With a shock she recognized some and was jerked from the last vestiges of drowsiness by them. 'Why,' Astrid thought, 'would her lover, an engineering student from Hamburg, be talking in his sleep *in English*?'

CHAPTER FORTY-FOUR

Jesse Barker had visited the offices of HAC, assuming that was where he could make arrangements to meet Michael Haigh. This idea was thwarted when he found the premises to be occupied by a company unknown to him called Fisher Springs UK. Such were his duties at the mill that the only time Jesse could travel to Baildon was at weekends. June was sliding into July by then and he made three unsuccessful journeys to the village before he succeeded in finding anyone at home.

It was late on Saturday afternoon, the sun was streaming down on neatly clipped beech hedges, tall, sturdy trees and the stripes of a newly mown, immaculately tended lawn, when Jesse rang the doorbell and waited. He had just decided that his journey was yet another wasted one when through the stained-glass panel of the outer door he discerned movement in the hallway. Seconds later the door opened. The distinguished-looking man with a thick mane of grey hair was in his early sixties, Jesse estimated. He looked enquiringly at his visitor and Jesse, remembering his errand asked, ‘Michael Haigh?’

‘Yes?’ The single word contained a wealth of puzzlement.

‘You probably won’t remember me, certainly won’t recognize me for it must be well over thirty years since we met, but I’m Jesse Barker.’

‘Good God!’ Michael exclaimed. ‘I thought you were dead.’

Jesse grinned apologetically. ‘Not so, I’m afraid. I’ve only recently come back to England,’ he said, glossing over both the reasons for his long absence and his abrupt return. ‘I’m trying to contact any of my relatives, one in particular, and I believe you might be able to help me.’

‘I’ll do what I can, although I’m not so certain how much help I can be, but come inside and we’ll see.’ He turned and preceded Jesse down the long hallway. ‘Tell me,’ he asked looking back at his visitor, one hand resting on the lounge door handle, ‘exactly how long is it since you left England?’

‘I sailed from Dover in 1914.’

Michael froze for a long moment then looked at Jesse, sympathy mixed with curiosity. ‘Have you had absolutely no news from England during that time?’

‘None whatsoever. I was interned in Greece for six years, then after my release I worked in Italy for a while, saving up enough money for a passage to America. I stayed there for a long time but lost my job during the depression and used the last of my savings to get home. It's been a bit of a hand to mouth existence.' Jesse's brief account was close enough to the truth as to make no matter.

'Oh dear,' Michael said in dismay, 'then I'm afraid most of what I can tell you is bad news, but go on inside I'll get Connie to make us all a pot of tea.'

'Connie? Oh, that's right, I remember now, you married Uncle Albert's daughter, my cousin Constance Cowgill, didn't you?'

'Correct.'

Although Connie was inclined to be a little stiff with Jesse at first, she soon relented when it became apparent that he was in total ignorance of all that had happened following his departure from England. The years had not dealt kindly with her cousin she thought, remembering the dashingly handsome, charming young man who had been replaced by a man whose careworn expression, unhealthy pallor, and downtrodden air, spoke of someone for whom life had been a constant struggle, and a losing battle at that. The news her husband was about to impart would do little to cheer him.

'Like I said earlier, most of the news I have for you is bad, some of it shockingly so,' Michael began. 'I'll start with your parents. Your father and mother are both long dead, I'm sorry to say. Your father died of a stroke and after all that had happened I don't believe your mother thought she had anything left to live for. They might have put some fancy medical name on the death certificate but for my money she died of a broken heart.' He paused to allow the sadness of this news to sink in before continuing.

'Nothing to live for,' Jesse echoed, 'but surely not just because of me. What about Ephraim and Clarence?'

'Your twin brother Ephraim was killed in France during the war,' Michael told him gently. 'You were also presumed dead as no one had heard from you for so long. It happened a lot with the confusion of war. Your cousin Sonny was thought to be dead as well, and then he turned up four years after the war ended. As if the thought that they had lost you and Ephraim wasn't bad enough there was that ghastly business over Clarence. I think that finished them off.'

Jesse was puzzled by the turn of phrase. 'Clarence,' he repeated numbly, 'what happened to Clarence?'

'Jesse, I'm afraid there's absolutely no easy way to tell you this,' Michael paused to gather his thoughts. 'Your brother Clarence was hanged. He was convicted of two murders, one on the battlefield, and one after the war, a man who was involved in blackmailing him over the earlier crime.'

From his pre-war gunrunning activities to his involvement with gangs in America during the Prohibition era Jesse had witnessed many acts of savage violence, but the knowledge that his own brother had committed and paid the ultimate penalty for two murders shocked him immeasurably. His distress was apparent to both Michael and Connie. It was some considerable time before he recovered enough to speak. The couple exchanged glances and watched sympathetically as their visitor, a shrunken beaten parody of his virile former self, struggled to come to terms with the dreadful tidings.

At last with an almost visible effort Jesse pulled himself together sufficiently to explain the main reason for his visit. If their news had shocked him, his was enough to startle them.

He fumbled for the right words. 'Since I came back to Bradford it seems to have been one horror story following another,' he paused and looked at them. 'A few weeks ago I got some news I could scarcely credit, it was so horrible. Now all this on top is almost more than I can bear.' Jesse braced himself and the physical effort seemed to help him a little. 'Many years ago, before I left England, Charlotte Tunnicliffe and I had an affair.' He looked at Michael. 'All this happened just before the war, long after your divorce from her,' he reassured him. 'And the long and short of it is, as you know, that I've heard nothing of events in England since then. Imagine my horror finding out that Charlotte had murdered her lover and committed suicide. It was only by pure chance that I discovered

Charlotte had a daughter, a girl born in 1914, a girl called Jessica.'

'Are you saying Jessica is your daughter?' Connie interrupted.

'Exactly,' Jesse agreed. 'When I heard Charlotte had christened her daughter Jessica, I was convinced in my own mind. So I went to the police for help. They eventually agreed to look in their files and that's when I found out that Charlotte had named me as Jessica's father.' Jesse smiled bitterly. 'They looked at me a bit askance when I gave them my name. I thought that might have something to do with my own colourful past. I never dreamed it might be down to Clarence's misdeeds. Anyway they showed me the birth certifcate and that's when they told me you had become Jessica's guardian. That was a kindly act in the circumstances. So that's why I'm here really, to find my daughter.'

'You want to get in touch with her?' Connie asked.

Jesse nodded.

'You do realize she may not want to have anything to do with you?' Michael suggested.

'Yes, and I'm not sure I'd blame her,' Jesse replied honestly. 'I've hardly been a model parent. But I've only just found out that I have a daughter.'

When Jesse left he had secured Michael's promise to write to Jessica. With that he had to be content. As he remarked on parting, 'After all these years a few more weeks, or months, can't make much difference.'

The letter from Baildon arrived in mid-August. Jessica glanced at the envelope, recognized the handwriting, and put it in a safe place. It would be one of Michael's infrequent but always welcome missives, full of local gossip and solicitous enquiries regarding her health and happiness. She smiled, it was so typical of Michael Haigh's kind and caring nature. She would read it later when she had time.

Having put the letter away she forgot about it. She was very busy and her time was limited as never before. Even as the politicians talked of peace, preparations for war had been stepped up within the department. Her section categorized by Edrith Pointon as 'Jessica's mad boffins', was no exception. For several weeks Jessica had been working seven days a week, on many occasions late into the night. The need for secrecy was paramount, both to conceal their activities from an enemy and the public. Little of the 'scientific advisory group's' meetings was committed to paper, even less conveyed by phone.

The deteriorating political situation in Europe and Britain's lack of preparation underlined the need for urgency. The only time the group could gather in security and secrecy was at weekends. One weekend Jessica had arranged accommodation for the team in a quiet country hotel in the

Midlands. The agenda comprised selective gatherings of smaller groups pooling the specialized talents of individual scientists. The weekend would conclude on Sunday evening with an inclusive meeting where progress could be reported and problems aired.

However late the closing session ended, Jessica would be on duty on Monday morning to report to Pointon. She had a talent for organization and management which made the work highly satisfying. After her report to Edrith she would spend the next two days compiling internal memos on the group's activities that would go straight into the department's secret files, only to be opened in extreme need.

As she travelled to the meeting Jessica pondered the weekend ahead and the character of each of her team. Although they were not the mad boffins characterised by Pointon she had to admit they were a pretty mixed bunch. Virtually each of them had at some time displayed semblances of eccentricity. Apart from Robert Binks, that was. Jessica liked Robert, but he also puzzled her. He was, Jessica thought, like a kindly but inattentive elder brother, with all a brother's indifferent charm towards a younger sister. Jessica was unused to such treatment. She had become accustomed to men who were demonstrably attentive, some of them over-attentive, but Robert's apparent lack of interest in turn amused and piqued her. Recently though, Jessica had caught him looking at her, not admiringly, but, there was no other word for it, oddly. The forthcoming weekend, Jessica thought, promised to be interesting in more ways than one.

It was on Saturday night that matters came to a head. Jessica had organized a buffet style dinner in a private room. There the group could mingle and chat, even talk shop, without fear of eavesdroppers. After the meal, most of the party, many of whom were in their middle years at least, retired for the night. Jessica felt oddly restless and at a loose end. She decided she would like a drink, so she left the remaining scientists in a huddle and headed for the bar. She ordered a gin and tonic and was about to pay for it when she heard a voice behind her say, 'I'll pay for that, and a pint of bitter too.'

Jessica turned, to find Robert, a large white £5 note in his hand, smiling at her as he instructed the barman to make sure the beer came with a good head on it. He grinned at Jessica. 'The trouble is, they don't know how to pull a decent pint round here. I wish you'd organize some of these meetings in Yorkshire.'

'It would be a long way for some of them to travel,' she told him repressively, adding, 'you've seen how doddery a few of them are, a few breaths of good Yorkshire air would knock them over.'

'Fair enough,' Robert conceded. 'I suppose I'll just have to put up with the beer.'

They took their drinks to a secluded corner of the bar. The hotel had few guests, so they had the room virtually to themselves. They chatted about the meeting for a while then Robert asked, 'What makes an attractive girl like you hang about with a bunch of nutcases such as this lot?' He pointed towards the room they had recently left.

Jessica laughed. 'It's my job, and in a few months' time what we're doing is probably going to be of great national importance. What about you?' she turned the tables neatly. 'You're so much younger than the rest of them, yet you've reached the top of your profession otherwise you wouldn't be here. How have you done that, is it from sheer brilliance or great self-sacrifice?'

'The latter mostly. I left school and went straight to work at the chemical plant and since then I've been so busy there's been no time for a social life. I dropped into a habit of working until I'd solved a problem or got to a logical stopping point. That meant some pretty weird hours, sometimes all night. My mother used to hit the roof,' he told her with a rueful grin. 'But father told her at least I wasn't out boozing and womanizing, so in the end she accepted it.'

'You must have had some relaxation surely? I can't believe you've never had a girlfriend, you're not exactly repulsive.'

Robert lowered his voice. 'I'll tell you a secret as long as you promise not to laugh.' Jessica nodded. 'I've never even been out on a date with a girl, let alone kissed one.'

Jessica stared at him in disbelief.

'It's true, but that doesn't mean I don't find

women attractive, I just never seemed to get round to it. Now I'm beginning to realize all that I've missed, but I think you have to start doing that when you're young, so I reckon I'll finish up as an eccentric old bachelor mumbling away to myself in the corner of some weird laboratory.'

Jessica showed no sign of breaking her promise not to laugh. Far from wanting to break into laughter she looked appalled, but before she could respond Robert suggested another drink. Jessica was surprised to find her glass was empty. While Robert was away at the bar, she had chance to collect her thoughts. On his return she said, 'Listen, Robert don't be put off by not having started young, that doesn't make a scrap of difference. A lot of women would actually find that more attractive than if you were accustomed to the opposite sex. As for not knowing how to go on with women, you seem to be doing very well sitting here talking to me. We've been here half an hour and I haven't yawned once or made an excuse to leave, have I?'

They left the bar a couple of hours and two more drinks later, both slightly tipsy and content. Robert insisted on escorting Jessica to her room although it was a floor higher than his own. She put her key in the lock and turned to say goodnight. Robert was standing close behind her. They stared at one another for a long moment then they seemed to flow into each other's arms. Still locked in a tight embrace Jessica reached behind her for the door handle, to find Robert's hand there before hers. Together they turned the handle and entered the room.

Several hours later, as Jessica was drifting off to sleep, she murmured, 'How was your first kiss, then?'

'So good I can't wait for the second,' he told her, his voice tight with desire.

'Robert!' she exclaimed. 'Are you trying to make up for lost time?'

'I'm a scientist,' he told her in mock seriousness. 'Theory's all very well, but the practical is much better.' Sleep was postponed.

Jessica woke early on Sunday morning. She lay for a moment then reached across for Robert. Her hand met his as she turned to find him smiling at her.

'I lay here watching you sleep. You're so beautiful, Jessica. I can't believe my luck in being here.'

'If luck comes into it, then I'm the lucky one. A lot of women don't know what they've missed.' Her hand disengaged from his and began to caress him. 'Oh dear me, Robert,' she said, 'I've got work to do and . . .'

They arrived late for breakfast. Had the rest of the scientists been younger, more attuned to the ways of young people, they might have noticed their bedraggled appearance, Robert's failure to shave, or the fact that they were wearing the same clothing as the previous evening, but then, as Edrith had said many times, they were 'mad boffins'.

CHAPTER FORTY-FIVE

It was that rarest of events, a Sunday off. Astrid sat with Jörgen over breakfast. She wanted to ask him about the words he had muttered in his sleep but was afraid. Afraid on the one hand that he might dissemble, dismissing it as her imagination, on the other that he might confront her question with a downright lie. There could have been a perfectly rational explanation but Astrid could not envisage what it might be. After some moments deliberation she decided on surprise tactics.

'Jörgen,' she said, her voice deliberately casual, 'what were you dreaming about when you were talking in your sleep?'

Jörgen looked up, startled. He laid the serrated edged spoon with which he had been attacking his grapefruit on the plate. 'Oh Lord!' he exclaimed in dismay. 'I wasn't, was I?'

Astrid nodded, not trusting herself to speak. Her face was a mask of distress.

The question and Jörgen's answer had both been reasonable, but for one fact. Both had been delivered in English. In Astrid's case, heavily accented, and much less than perfect. In Jörgen's, the faultless, colloquial, and perfect delivery of a native.

Jörgen stared at her. 'Astrid, please believe me. I never wanted to lie to you. I came to Salzburg as part of my work. I had absolutely no plans to fall head over heels in love with a wonderful girl while I was here. However, that is what happened and I am so glad it did.' He reached across and took her hands in his. 'The deception was necessary, but now I must tell you the truth. You may despise me, may decide to turn me over to the police, but whatever your decision, what I'm about to tell you in the next few minutes will place me entirely in your power. I could have maintained the lie, dismissed the incident as imagination,' he added in an uncanny echo of her thoughts, 'but I love you far too much for that. You are too sweet, too honest, and too dear to me for me ever to lie to you again.'

Astrid made no response, merely stared at him.

He looked into her deep blue eyes for some sign of understanding.

'My name is not Jörgen Schmidt. I'm not an engineering student. And I have never been to Hamburg in my life,' he paused and then added with defiance, or possibly bravado, 'I am in fact English and I was sent to Germany to discover certain details about an industrialist, the products he manufactures and his factory. When he and his family moved to Salzburg for the summer, I followed them. I thought that while he was away from the rigid discipline of work he might relax his guard and become careless. At home and at his factory security is so tight I couldn't get near him.

'All the time I've been in Salzburg, except when I was with you, I've been watching him and his family and reconnoitring his house. Last night while you were asleep I broke into the house.' Jörgen's face grew suddenly grimmer, more forbidding. 'I discovered all I needed to know, much more than I wanted to know. The factory in the Ruhr valley is involved in a research project, the ultimate aim of which is to produce a weapon so terrible it defies description. Even though I know a lot about such things, even I can barely grasp what havoc such a weapon could wreak. Fortunately, work on the project is at such an early stage that I don't think it will be ready for some years yet, but the papers he obligingly left on his desk showed that they have achieved a breakthrough in their research that transforms it from an interesting concept into a feasible proposition. If what they are working on can be stabilised, a bomb no bigger than this table and weighing less than half as much as conventional ordnance would be capable of wiping out the population of a town the size of Salzburg in a split second. More than that, the blast waves from such a weapon would raze every building to a heap of dust and rubble and leave the ground sour for a generation or more.' He paused and looked at Astrid. Incredulity, horror, and disbelief mingled in her expression.

'So that's the truth behind Jörgen Schmidt. I am in fact an agent of the British government, my real name is Joshua Jones, and you have the power of life and death over me.'

There was a long silence, an eternity before Astrid spoke. 'I like Joshua,' she said, her tone matter of fact, 'it is a far nicer name than Jörgen.'

Josh looked at Astrid, caught between hope and disbelief. 'You mean you're not going to give me away?'

'Of course not.' Astrid's tone was as casual as if she were taking an order in the restaurant. 'I love you, Joshua Jones. I loved you even when I thought you were one of the odious master race. But I am so glad you're not. What you've told me explains a lot. I have been puzzled for weeks because you seemed far too nice to be German.' She smiled, the glorious smile that made his heart turn somersaults and added, 'But there is one strict condition I will impose on my silence.'

'What's that?' Josh asked, still a trifle nervous.

She leaned across the table and told him, her voice scarcely above a whisper.

Josh listened and smiled. 'That's absolutely no problem. I'll attend to it as soon as I get back. I must return to London. After that I'm overdue some leave, so I'll catch the first train back here. The round trip shouldn't take more than ten days. Let's see, today's 26 August, if I leave today, I should be back here by 5 September at the latest. In the meantime . . .' he paused.

Astrid leaned forward once more, allowing her dressing gown to part, revealing her beautiful figure. 'Yes?' she questioned, her voice barely above a whisper, 'in the meantime, what, my darling?' The rest of their breakfast remained uneaten.

They parted later that day, a tearful farewell at the railway station. As his train was about to pull out Josh leaned from the carriage. 'I love you, Astrid. I want to spend the rest of my life with you. I promise that the moment I return I'll fulfil your condition. We'll be married immediately.'

He arrived in London to report to Edrith Pointon on 31 August. The following day Germany invaded Poland.

Despite Josh's desperate pleading, Edrith refused point blank to authorize his return to Europe. The crisis was deepening with such terrible speed that every operative the department possessed was withdrawn from the continent. Josh even tried to phone Astrid, but on the single occasion that he managed to get a connection, the phone in her flat remained unanswered. It was no fault of Josh's, no fault of the operator that he was informed there was no reply seconds before Astrid entered her apartment and picked up the receiver, to hear only a dialling tone.

Josh had no recourse but to wait on events. His waiting was not prolonged. Only two days after his return he learned, with a sinking heart, of the ultimatum delivered by the British and French governments to Germany in support of Poland.

The morning of Sunday 3 September 1939, radio listening figures must have broken all records as people throughout Britain and further afield tuned in for news of the worsening situation. By contrast congregations at churches across the land must have been decimated as even the most devout churchgoers remained in their living rooms, crouched over their wireless sets.

In Byland Crescent, Sonny twiddled the dial until he found the Home Service. Four generations of the Cowgill family listened, although to be fair the youngest of them had no concept of the import of the broadcast.

Elsewhere, Simon and Naomi Jones heard the news in Bradford, Michael and Connie Haigh in Baildon. Across the other side of Bradford, Jesse Barker, still waiting for news of his daughter, also listened. So too did Luke Fisher at an RAF station somewhere in England that had already gone onto a war footing.

In Australia, the news was greeted with shock and dismay in the Finnegan household. Bella, her heart heavy with worry over the safety of her boyfriend Luke Fisher, for once wept instead of swearing. Dottie Malloy heard it and began, despite their differences, to be concerned for her errant husband Danny. Danny too listened, in company with a large contingent of fellow servicemen in a training camp. The news was greeted with equal dismay by Philip and Amelia Fisher, the crackling, interference ridden broadcast doing little to reduce the gravity of the content.

Back in England, Jessica Tunnicliffe had actually managed a day's leave. She was in bed in her London flat when the phone rang. Edrith Pointon had phoned to instruct her to report to department headquarters immediately after the Home Service bulletin. 'You'll understand why when you hear it. Your first job will be to round up your boffins. They must start work straight away.'

Jessica put the phone down and rolled over. 'You're working for the government now,' she told Robert. 'Full time.'

'So it's war.' Robert looked at Jessica's slender naked form alongside him. 'You'll be my liaison officer, I suppose?' Jessica nodded. He began to caress her. 'Very well, then, let's liaise.'

When Jessica left for the apartment she walked through the lounge. Unseen, unnoticed, on the mantelpiece still remained the unopened envelope, inside which was the news from Michael Haigh of her father's reappearance.

The broadcast relayed by the BBC to all corners of the globe was even heard in Salzburg, where Astrid Erikson, increasingly despondent about seeing or hearing from Josh, listened with terrible sadness to the measured, didactic and precise tones of the British Prime Minister, Neville Chamberlain.

'I am speaking to you from the Cabinet Room at 10, Downing Street. This morning the British Ambassador in Berlin handed the German government an official note stating that unless we heard from them by eleven o'clock that they were prepared at once to withdraw their troops from Poland, a state of war would exist between us. I have to tell you that no such undertaking has been received and consequently this country is at war with Germany.'

Even before Neville Chamberlain's fateful declaration, preparations for war had been given greater urgency throughout Britain. Windows everywhere were being criss-crossed with strips of sticky brown paper to reduce the hazard from flying shards of glass, giving the appearance of a nation-wide noughts and crosses competition. Gas masks had been issued to most of the population, together with instructions for them to protect themselves by means of rudimentary air raid shelters. In the event, these would prove ineffectual against the impact of a bomb dropped from high altitude, let alone its detonation, but they gave some comfort to the more concerned and nervous citizens.

It was a thin dividing line between urgency and panic. In a considerable number of instances the testing of air raid sirens proved all too realistic, despite prior notice having been given. All refugees and immigrants, classified as enemy aliens by the authorities, were rounded up and taken before inspection tribunals. These usually consisted of local dignitaries and as such, given broad terms of reference, there was little consistency in the decisions they reached. Their brief was to categorize all who appeared before them according to their perceived threat to national security. Those branded category 'A' were interned, those categorized as a 'B' risk had their freedom of movement strictly curtailed, while those in band 'C' were free to return to normal life, although there was little normality in those days.

Nor was it only foreigners whose pattern of existence became disrupted once war broke out. Even before Chamberlain confirmed the existence of hostilities, the government, fearful of the massive potential for casualties in crowded towns and cities once bombing raids began, ordered the evacuation of more than a million citizens, most of them children, to relatives or complete strangers in safer parts of the country. Some were even sent abroad. No enemy had set foot on British soil, yet somewhere in the region of 1.5 million evacuees had been created.

Thousands of special trains carried their precious human cargo on long, tiring and, for the most part, bewildering journeys to strange places with even stranger names, and equally unfamiliar new ways of life. As most of the migrants were children, the first task was to ensure they were safely housed, their fears eased, and their confusion ended. For some this was never achieved, for others the whole process was too upsetting and they drifted back to the towns regardless of the heightened danger. Yet again there were those whose evacuation, even the painful separation from loved ones, provided the basis for new, lifelong friendships. Sadly, in many cases the fear that had caused the authorities to order such drastic measures proved tragically justified. Loving parents had sent their children away for their own safety. Those parents perished in the ensuing onslaught, leaving large numbers of grieving, homeless, orphans.

In every town and city throughout Britain, outside the most vulnerable targets, public buildings, police and fire stations and the like, sandbags were filled and piled as a defence against bomb blasts. Signposts were removed from all roads. Wire was strung from poles across rural roads to prevent their being used as landing strips by enemy aircraft. The blackout was introduced, it was each householder's duty to ensure that no light could be seen from outside the house. All street lighting and signs were turned off. Britain had been plunged into darkness.

Throughout the land, with no idea of what the future might hold, people watched and waited.

THE END

AUTHOR'S NOTE

You may wonder why I have not described exploits from World War II here. This is a family saga, not a war book. The stories of some of the characters will be told elsewhere, but as an end piece to this book, I shall simply quote the following statistics, ones that I read while researching for the novel. The figures speak for themselves, loudly and far more eloquently than anything I could write.

World War II was the biggest conflict in the history of mankind. During its six years:

- 100 million people were called to arms in theatres of war across the globe.
- 55 million people were killed.
- Of the 55 million, only 15 million were members of the armed forces.
- Of the civilian casualties, 20 million were Russian. Over 6 million were Jewish and 4 million were Polish.